Praise for Death Runs in the Family

"The family that slays together stays together! A rollicking family adventure for sick and demented gorehounds!"
- **Sean Yseult**, bassist of WHITE ZOMBIE - Author of I'M IN THE BAND. *www.SeanYseult.com*

"DEATH RUNS IN THE FAMILY entertains with a combination of over-the-top absurd and hilarious situations along with a healthy dose of zombies and gore. It also touches the heart at the end."
- **Verhoskan**, creator of THE ZOMBIE MOVIE DATABASE. *www.Zmdb.org*

"This is one f-ed up book! After reading it, I needed some heavy-duty sandpaper to scrape the residue of the twisted world Jason Stryker created off of my brain. If the literary universe was made up of only disturbing road trip horror comedies, this one would still stand out as the most twisted, the most heinous, and the most perverse of the lot."
- **Patrick D'Orazio**, author of COMES THE DARK, INTO THE DARK, and BEYOND THE DARK. *www.PatrickDorazio.com*

"DEATH RUNS IN THE FAMILY is an entertaining macabre novel for readers with an penchant for black humor. A road story with quirky characters and a grisly twist that will delight horror fans."
- **Richard W. Haines**, director of CLASS OF NUKE `EM HIGH and WHAT REALLY FRIGHTENS YOU.

"DEATH RUNS IN THE FAMILY is weirdly twisted, wickedly humorous, and endlessly violent. Translated: a damn fine piece of dark fiction I recommend."
- **Jonathan MoOn**, author of HEINOUS.
http://MrMoonBlogs.blogspot.com

"DEATH RUNS IN THE FAMILY-A fun, twisted, bizarre family adventure. Imagine STAND BY ME with the undead!"
- **Todd Smith**, lead singer of POLKADOT CADAVER and DOG FASHION DISCO. *PolkadotCadaver.com*

"An utterly unique road trip. Jason Stryker's DEATH RUNS IN THE FAMILY has got guts. And gore. And above all, heart. It's darkly funny, creepy, even savage in places...but this is, beneath it all, a book about love, loss and wondering how we find our way in the world."
- **Joe McKinney**, Author of DEAD CITY and FLESH EATERS.
http://JoeMckinney.wordpress.com

"A Hilarious Multi-Generational Zombie Road Trip Full Of Love! Jason Stryker's Death Runs In The Family is full of subversive humor, casual yet aggressive gore, and the love between a boy and his grandpa. The raw, sick, and twisted imagination of this author is a delight and the book's originality is refreshing. If you like the walking dead, moustaches, taquitos, sky diving, knife fights, and enough puke to clean a street (and who wouldn't) this is the book for you. You will not be able to stop reading until you fall asleep clutching the book in your hands. I loved it."
- **Calvin A.L. Miller II**, author of *HET MADDEN, A ZOMBIE PERSPECTIVE and THE ZOMBIE'S SURVIVAL GUIDE, THRIVE IN THE ZOMBIE APOCALYPSE AFTER YOU TURN...*
http://www.CalvinalMillerii.com

"As grotesque as it is funny, this endearing tale of randomness and stomach turning events will capture even those who claim to have heard it all."
- **Matt Foran**, lead singer of CIRCUS OF DEAD SQUIRRELS.
http://www.CircusOfDeadSquirrels.net

"Why would anyone care about my opinion of this book? No one knows who I am."
- **Mike Odd**, lead singer of ROSEMARY'S BILLYGOAT.
http://www.RosemarysBillygoat.com

Death Runs in the Family

Jason Stryker

Skelty Press, LLC

Skelty.net
Created by Fuzztalkradio.com

Acknowledgments

This is my list of those people, who this book couldn't have been possible without:

Robb Petersburg
Pure Romance by Jaclyn Loose
Deb Lustig
Kiley Stoltz
Justine Friedrich
Wilder and Christine Salazar
Jason Jones
Becky Suess
Brandon Noble
Nicole Webinger
Ashley Schmidt

This book is dedicated to someone who needs to be thanked more than anyone: my wife, Tiffany Stryker. For countless years of being the most supportive person involved in my dreams. With such a high divorce rate in this country, it certainly gives her immunity until at least the year 2015...well, maybe. It all depends how big of a celebrity I become.

Secondly, to my ultimately amazing Grandma and Grandpa for their assistance with so many things, whether it was reassurance or that extra currency I needed. Audrey and Vern Smith (Cheatmuch), there, now your real names are in here. I definitely couldn't have done it without you both.

Ryan Friedrich, a recent (by recent, I mean eight years) addition to my family who has enough confidence in making things happen for me that he pledged to get every book from me for the next decade. That's some family loyalty if I've ever heard of it!

Mr. Randy Srsen, or whatever name he goes by today; The Acoustic Gangsta, Flip-Flop Dean. This was the first book that he ever read that wasn't forced on him by a school district. Even though the only feedback I got was "more blood," he went through the torture of reading the rough drafts, for that I commend him.

Sonja, Douglas, & Jenna Harris, Hmmmmm… Thank you for always promoting me; finishing a first round of editing for me; and helping give me that backbone for the various things I needed throughout life. You've truly been supporters in my odd choices for years. I couldn't ask for more.

Laura Davis, a friend from years back, someone who I have a lot of good memories with and shared my last year of trick-or-treating with at the age of eighteen. Thanks for getting me in trouble by making me stay out too late all the time, just kidding. I blame Taco Bell for that. Hopefully, these pages of weirdness make you excited to be a contributor to the beginning of my writing career.

Virginia Friedrich Clemens, my mother-in-law, no offense, but I hope you never read this. I don't want you getting grossed out or anything. Appreciation is given for your excitement in everything I do. Never did I think so many would be proud of me, and you were one of the first.

Jamie Yakeleya is somebody I don't know personally, but was one of the first people to pledge on my Kickstarter page. He gave me faith that someone outside friends and family could possess interest in such material. Thanks partly to this man, my insanity may pay off.

To everyone who attended the First Annual Owatonna Zombie Pub Crawl, I couldn't have made it this far without your contributions. Whether the motivation was supporting me or getting cheap drinks. All in all, I made some great friends there, and met some other people that didn't mind drooling blood the entire night.

Jon Wocelka, the ogre who came down with me to the bar countless nights to spread the word of the Zombie Pub Crawl, which turned into him buying me drinks and slurring out the promotion. A great friend, no matter how creepy he may be at times.

And last, but definitely not least, Sarajoy Porter of Edit Write Away for an immaculate editing job and having such a deep interest in my work. I couldn't have imagined working with someone better on this.

Table of Contents

Chapter 1: Seniors Have Weak Immune Systems

It seemed like Grandpa had been smoking since the dawn of time. In every picture I saw of him, he had a cigarette pressed in between his fingers, even when he was a child. Imagine that, a parent letting their six-year-old child develop lung cancer at such a young age. Grandpa was one of those guys who believed that smoking didn't cause cancer. It was all just an old wives' tale. I swear to God that sometimes he talked about it as if it was a choice to get cancer, like an STD or something.

He spent all day sitting in his rocking chair, which was as old as he was, living off his retirement fund, while I ate whatever I could without him noticing, sometimes even condiments. Not that I didn't care for condiments. I actually preferred them to meats and cheeses as long as they came in a bulk quantity. Whenever he caught me, he would make me stop to smoke with him, which made me pale-faced every time.

When we sat there, as we did every single day, he would tell me the story of the pack of cigarettes that he had sealed in a purple plastic case. It snapped shut with the force of a thousand winds to protect them from damage. I don't really know the story too well, because I always just half-ass acted like I was listening to him talk when really I still couldn't get over all the moles on his head. There were more moles on his forehead than city markers in the United States. It also didn't help that vomit leaked from my lips every odd day of the month when I was forced to smoke until I became sick.

Anyway, it was something about how, during the Vietnam War, Grandpa and a buddy of his from high school, named Olaf, were stationed together somewhere in another country. I'm pretty sure that it was somewhere around North Korea. They were in a bunker together, firing against their opponents, when Olaf was struck by a stray bullet that penetrated his chest. The chest wound rendered Olaf practically immobile. With the last adrenaline-fueled motion from Olaf's withering form, he handed Grandpa a pack of cigarettes, where the lucky smoke had been flipped, filter down. It came straight from the mouth of Olaf, since he'd been preparing to smoke it when he was shot. He was never able to light the last stress reliever of his life. He made Grandpa promise to save that last cigarette until his dying day. So Grandpa made an annual tradition of smoking one cigarette from the pack in Olaf's memory. They had to have been staler than a bag of chips from 1987, but still he swore it was the best cigarette of his life, every time. But, like any old man, he was delusional and a horrible driver.

One fateful day, Gramps and I were sitting around the TV, as usual, watching reruns of "Guiding Light", which I never understood because the storylines were always so mixed up. There were video-cassettes upon videocassettes in neat rows that were only episodes of the overly dramatic soap opera, in no particular order. I had no idea how he knew what VHS to pick, since the majority had their labels torn off. Everyday, he would get in the mood for a different episode that consisted of somebody smooching with a cast member that they shouldn't have been smooching with. We were in the middle of watching somebody kissing their dad when out of nowhere Grandpa said, "Code Camel", which was code for, "I'm having a heart attack! Get me the damn cigarette!" It was a situation that my personal geezer had discussed with me after a negative appointment at the doctor's office. Immediately, I jumped up, grabbing the case off of the shelf. It was more difficult to open than a jar of pickles, sealed by a bartender. I let the person needing medical attention open it for me. He shoved the last blood-spattered cigarette into his mouth without hesitation. His frigid, wrinkly hands struggled to keep it in his mouth, while I lit match after match that consistently went out, due to the drafty windows along with the stupid window shades that kept hitting me in the face.

I could see the rage in his eyes, so, with my quick wits, I grabbed the lighter for the grill. It was the one that was about as long as a bubble gum cigar, but it contained more unhealthy content. Once I got it lit, there was an immediate relief of tension. As I watched him smoking, I realized that it was Grandpa's last ciga-rette and the last time that I'd ever talk to him again. Maybe I should've told him how much he had meant to me, but, then, I thought that was just "pussy talk" as Grandpa would say. So I grabbed myself a hot dog from the fridge that I left unpackaged for such an occa-sion and continued with my daily life. I watched him as his eyes slowly closed. The cigarette butt teetered between his lips before slowly slipping out of his mouth.

Just when I was starting to relax in my brown leather recliner, that I had to talk Grandpa into freeing from the dumpster for me, he initiated the convulsing, like he had rabies, except with no foaming of the mouth. As he sat there shaking, I swear I heard every bone in his body crack; it was disgusting. I've had pop rocks that made less noise. I went into the other room to call the hospital so that they could come and body bag Gramps, but, when I got back into the living room, he had vanished.

I knew that something was wrong. I wasn't the smartest kid in class, but I definitely wasn't the dumbest. I knew he was dead; I witnessed his death. If he wasn't dead, he would've inhaled the last couple of drags himself, instead of feeding the rest to the carpet. Immediately, I got into my dark gray sweat pants that expanded four extra sizes, because I knew I was in for a journey. You never know how much will be eaten after an extended period of time. I was tying the strings that ran along the elastic band in my pants when the dog started to bark outside. That mutt could never keep his trap shut, but, due to the certain circumstances, I resolved that it might be in my best interest to check it out.

I ran to the window, rubbing away the thin layer of brown dust in a circular motion. I peered through the smudges from my oily hands, and there was Gramps, for some bizarre reason, devouring the dog, tail first. This was by no means an attractive dog either. Trash was a floppy-eared Basset Hound that was severely overweight, because I liked to feed him for the week all at once. Grandpa was always a bit of a moron, but, come on. Everyone knows that if you're going to eat a live dog, you submerge its head into your mouth first. It should've been common sense that devouring a dog bottom first was a bad idea. I scurried down the creaking stairs before stumbling out of the front door to nab Grandpa and bring him back inside. By the time I got over to Trash's violated body, his tail was all bone with a few strings of mangled flesh, dripping the blood that pulsed out just above his rear end. Grandpa's hand was in the exact same condition from the dog chomping on it the whole time. His fingers clung onto the hand by threads of skin, juices draining from the puncture wounds that invaded his arthritis.

I grasped the busted up garden hose that had drifting strands inching away from its cortex within my two hands, allowing it no way to break free. I wrapped it around Grandpa, forcing his arms to his side as I squeezed him like a bottle of mustard, and I escorted him inside. I tied him to his rocking chair, avoiding the splinters that protruded from the hose when I tightened it. As I was attempting to make a knot with it, which is more complicated than tying a cherry stem with your tongue, I heard the paramedics shifting their vehicle into park in the driveway. Before I could get to the door, they were already beating their knuckles raw on the manufactured wood.

I rushed towards the pounding, trying to think of a logical explanation to tell the medics. When I unlatched the door, they burst in without giving me a chance to use my awesome explanation that I still wasn't sure of. Their immediate response to Grandpa was obvious, since nothing on his body was moving, not even an exhale, which assured the paramedics that he was dead. One half of the paramedic team came over with his sky blue eyes and charming smile, hoping to console me at such a supposed desperate time. I told them the whole kit and caboodle of what had happened, but, of course, they ignored my story as they would any other "child with an out of control imagination".

The other sweaty, less attractive paramedic (from a woman's point of view) started performing a variety of tests, all of which verified my story, leaving less to be desired when they took me in for questioning. The unattractive paramedic turned to me with an expression of remorse. While hunched over the corpse of my Grandpa, he shifted his attention over to me, rotating his head enough to get me into focus. He told me that my legal guardian was in fact dead. He told me this right before his face went into a state of shock. As he fell, face first to the floor, I could see that Grandpa had shoved a hypodermic needle into his spine just below his skull. The attractive paramedic placed his two fingers against the ugly's neck, while Grandpa played dead – dead, like how a normal corpse is. A stunned look came across his face as he became addicted to Grandpa's appearance. He whispered to himself a ludicrous plan about how he could become rich for discovering Grandpa, but I found him first. The stud muffin mad dashed for the door, attempting to get his hands on the 2-way radio, but I tripped him with my hyper extending leg that stuck out approximately two feet, diminishing his hope for escape. I wasn't a murderer, but I couldn't let them perform experiments on my Grandpa.

I saw Gramps with that determined look in his eyes, heading straight for the paramedic that was strategically knocked to the tile. Gramps was coming at him with his lucky steak knife that still had stains of pork on it. He plunged it directly into the oxygen obtainer's stomach, while sawing upwards using the ridges on the blade to his advantage. The amount of effort Gramps put into it helped him make it partially through the paramedic's ribcage before taking more interest in what was inside the anatomy of man. He didn't hesitate to shove his whole head in between the butchered layers of skin to get to the still functional organs of our medical pal. I understood his need to feed, since he had morphed into a zombie, but I was still pissed about all those times I was told not to eat too quickly or I'd get gut rot. So what if I liked my chicken more on the rare side. My chicken was never anywhere near as rare as a ripe corpse. Also, it wasn't full of as much disease. At the rate Grandpa was scarfing his dinner down, he was going to get a hemorrhage of some sort. Blood flooded over the back of his head when he ventured deeper for the pancreas, risking being caught on a rib. In that scenario, he would be held under bodily fluids until he was drained of oxygen, if oxygen was even an issue.

Agreeing with my current thought process, I did the only thing that I thought was necessary. I took as much food as I could cup in my arms out of the cooling box. I was only wearing a short sleeve shirt, but I would worry about the frostbite later. Gramps couldn't have been a hypocrite about it, since he had more on his plate than I did. Or, should I say kitchen floor? So there was Gramps and me, side by side, he with the raw entrails of former lifesavers and me with a pound slab of lean ham (they were out of the fatty version at the store). I passed out during the excitement of trying to see if my belly could detonate. It couldn't. That was the last thing that I remembered before waking up on the floor, drenched in green puke that was coated in a pink slime. Green beans plus raw ham must've equaled a lethal combination.

There was a sharp sting that shot from the pits of my stomach to the tip of my wee wee. I could detect a major pee getting ready to decorate the interior of my pants yellow, not willing to wait for anything. I carefully walked to the bathroom, trying not to leak in my whitey tighties, while I looked around the room and noticed that the bluish hue in the paint on the walls was plastered all over with red. Grandpa was seated in his chair, fixated on "Guiding Light", as usual. On the dining room table, which was cluttered with dirty dishes, sat the dehydrator with strips of human flesh waiting next to it, ready for dehydration. I pointed my pinky finger at Grandpa, commanding him not to move until I finished using the restroom, because we needed to talk about some important issues. Grandpa had a look in his eyes that could've torched a kitten alive. It was identical to the expression on his face at his dying moment when he became frustrated with me. I slammed the bathroom door shut, pleading with the lock to hold someone's body weight for once. Wouldn't you know it? He must've gotten up out of his chair with the quickness to satisfy his urge to piss me off. He wouldn't stop belting the door with his wicked, open-palmed slap, making as much commotion as possible. What angered me the most was that he knew noise made it hard for me to drain my earthworm. I screamed at him, because it was the only thing that I could do that didn't involve my hands, which were currently occupied. With one hand, I held my wiener, while, with the other, I grabbed the metal rod that was wielding the toilet paper roll in the holder. Every few seconds, I could get a limp stream of tinkle out, but Grandpa's hand consistently reached in the smidgen of an opening that the door was ajar. I continually, furiously, smacked the intruder with the toilet paper bar. Looking at the clock on the wall, that lacked numbers, I found that it took me a minimum of ten minutes to get the necessary urine out of my body. The lousy part of the deal was that it had a spray effect that soaked into my clothes. There has never been a happy kid that, while peeing, missed letting salt-flavored nastiness moisten his pants, never.

I came out of that door with a vengeance. I don't think there's a number high enough for how many times I smacked him in the head with the aluminum toilet paper rod that I held in my hand. I had to tie him up to his chair again, so he could catch his cool. It was no problem; when you're an angry, fat kid, there is no way that someone from the crustaceous period can overpower you.

The first thing that Grandpa did when he sat down on his chair was push the power button on the TV remote. The further back his pointer finger went, when he pushed down the button, the more the skin tore from the muscle. The more the skin tore from the muscle, the more the muscle separated from the bone. Eventually, it ripped so bad that I highly doubted it would ever function again. I just laughed, taunting the remote in front of him, regardless of the consequences. He flipped out and tried to wiggle his way out of the chair, but all that did was make his skin peel off from the constant rubbing against the ropes. What a moron. I sat on the couch, turning on G & S for some early 1990's children's sports, full of padding along with an over abundant amount of spotters for safety. It was a sub-channel of Nickelodeon that always amused me. I always wanted to watch it, because they constantly aired a TV show called "Guts". It was the ultimate test of courage and strength. Really, they should've just gotten rid of the tough man contest already and replaced it with "Guts", because whoever won "Guts", against all the other top people, would really be the strongest, smartest, and most agile person alive.

Gramps had always been one of those guys that hated everything. He used to always tell me to cut my hair when it was longer than an inch, because I was "trying to be a hippie". When I told him that I wanted an earring, it was, "Only fags have earrings. Do you want to be a fag?" For being an old guy, who reeked of cheap cologne and swore that he had been laid, but lead suspicion to the opposite, he sure did know everything. I was definitely adopted, or, at least, I hoped so. Our noses don't match at all, so I'm sure that we're not even related.

Grandpa suddenly began making the loudest noises imaginable just to torque my nerves. He sounded like a hyena, getting its head sawed off with a butter knife, which was not a pretty sound. I surrendered my will, and, finally, I looked over to him, because I was trying the whole if I ignore him, maybe he will go away method. But he didn't. He was over there, rocking in his chair, but, as soon as I gazed in his direction, he quit making noise. Grandpa's middle finger stood straight up, aiming its sights at me. I served one right back at him, but I guess he could only dish it out, because that caused him to make more of an uproar. I took the time out of my day to double take his crusty middle finger. As it turned out, he wasn't flicking me off at all, but, instead, he was pointing to the medicine cabinet. I looked at the clock for a rough estimate of the time. It was time to take my ADD pills. What a bunch of crap ADD pills were; I didn't need them. I earned every D- I got in school without them, scrambling the chemical balance in my brain. I brainstormed for a bit, thinking that if Grandpa could remember my pill time, then maybe I could train him to be the same dilapidated geezer that he used to be, only cooler.

The telephone rang, so I decreased my interest in fossils and strolled over to the phone that was an original from the test models. You had to spin the dial to whatever number you wanted, only to wait for it to gradually come back, so you could dial the next number, and repeat at least six more times. Grandpa refused to replace it with some higher form of technology. I put the receiver up to my ear, learning that it was the school, wondering why I hadn't been there in the past few days. I broke out into the crying performance, playing my favorite piece. I called it, "I'm in deep grieving, because my Grandpa's dead." They bought it, like a building employed with chimpanzee secretaries.

It became the time to see how smart Gramps still could've been, or should I say narrow-minded. I broke out Grandpa's favorite game: Trivial Pursuit, Edition 1. He had the same edition since the game was released back in 1981. It didn't matter what question card it was, since he memorized every single answer in the game. If he knew all of them when he was alive, he had to remember at least one answer after becoming an unsanctified, walking corpse. I commenced taking the contents of the game out of their packaging, but, as soon as I laid the cards flat on the floor, Gramps would pick them up. He would study them for a brief moment before gnawing on them, soaking the glossy cardboard in saliva. I guess he thought that the material looked like reflective skin. I was thinking that I'd begin my teaching lesson with the alphabet. I grabbed my flash cards with the pictures of animals on them (for example, L is for lion). No wonder I still didn't understand how to spell a lot of words or the difference between X and Q; animals just weren't that appealing. The only reason I could distinguish big words was because the thesaurus was entertaining. There are so many different definitions for excrement.

I ran through all of the letters, words, or anything simple enough that I thought he could register. Nothing. I could educate a preschooler on how to set up a trust fund for their children (if I knew how to do that) before I could teach him how to brush his teeth. Oh, well. Like the guy who pushed the shopping cart down the street told me, "Hard work pays off in the end."

I pried the leg off of our coffee table with a few wiggles, smashing the stained wood against the back of Grandpa's head. It rattled his brain inside of his skull until he was rendered unconscious. I wasn't sure if it was possible, but, what the hell, anything can be possible if you put your mind and strength into it. The mind didn't matter that much when I had muscular guns attached to my torso. I pushed on his rocking chair, attempting to slide it across the room to get him into the spare room, but the entire effort ended in him tipping over into a funky position. It looked like he fell asleep while kneeling on the floor. I was at my last straw. I had to do it the hard way by waiting for Gramps to wake up. Whenever he decided to awake from his slumber, I would lead him over to the spare room, tripping him inside. I sure didn't have enough energy to drag him in there. I might've fainted at the thought of the exercise it would've taken to walk over there at that point. I waited for the zombie to arise, while I ate a bag of chips that I laid on my stomach with open side towards my face. I watched episode #465 of "Guiding Light" to keep myself occupied, since I didn't want to get up to eject the tape or to retrieve the remote that was a whole three feet away.

There was a twitch in one of Grandpa's functional fingers. I stood up, brushing the partial chips off my stomach onto the carpet with my greasy fingers. I walked over to where Grandpa was uncomfortably positioned. He introduced to me how the dead rise from their slumber, which is with no coordination or understanding of how to get to their feet. He stumbled around with this expression on his face that duplicated mine when I was hungry, but he lacked the groaning noises coming from his stomach. They came from his vocal chords instead. He lunged at me in an instant, but I stuck my foot out, so, wouldn't you know it, he took a fall, right through the doorframe. The only problem was that his shinbone hit me in the ankle, giving me that irritable feeling you get when your funny bone gets bumped. I heard another snap, hoping that I wouldn't have to replace another piece of furniture when he got better. I checked inside the room for damage, but, to my relief, the damage was only to Grandpa. The muscle behind his ankle had totally been removed from the bone. The skin around the wound was stretched out, dangling from his leg. The blood didn't pump out of the laceration, but, instead, it drained out gradually in thick, greenish ooze, leaving a film over the muscle.

Why are old people so brittle? Oh, yeah, peanut brittle. I thought I had some left over in my candy drawer. I ran upstairs with enough anticipation to make it feel like it took days. When I made it to my magical drawer of mystery, I found nothing of the brittle sort. There were only a couple of gumdrops left behind from ancient Egypt that I stole from an emperor. I had been saving them for a desperate situation. The lack of color in them worried my potbelly. I spent the next half an hour trying to nibble them down to a swallowable size. Once I consumed the pieces of history down my feeding tube, I slid down the stairs on my belly. It wasn't the smartest decision, I discovered, as I ran to the bathroom. While my stomach was emitting acids into the toilet bowl, I identified the stench of pee coming from myself. That was the least of my concern as I remembered that I didn't lock Grandpa in the room.

Gramps was crawling out of the room, dragging his left leg behind, because, of course, I also forgot to shut the door. I blanked on setting up his learning material anyway. I stepped over him, straining my thigh muscles, which was my punishment for not practicing the splits. I had never been an overachiever in gymnastics. I turned the television on, changing it to the Spanish channel with English subtitles, as I threw all my kids books onto the lint-barraged floor. I dragged Gramps back into the room by his bad leg, sticking my finger inside of the wound to get back at him for the goofy feeling he gave my leg. I left the room, and then blocked the door with the couch. The thing may have been missing tons of padding, but I was sure that it would still hold him. If the weight didn't, then the fumes from the cat piss would. I needed to abandon him within my trap for an extended period of time so that he could absorb all of the knowledge that I was teaching him.

I had to find something to keep me entertained after I finished the rest of the crumbled chips that I spilled on the floor. Those were up out of the carpet faster than a high-powered vacuum could salvage them. After I swallowed my chips, I tried to think of the best thing that I could spend my spare time doing. The most superior idea that I had in a while popped into my head: utilize the shovel at the park. I took my brand new, cobweb-decorated scooter out of the garage that was adorned by actual spiders. I rode it a couple of houses down, pushing myself along until I reached the park. It was just the thing to do after a hard day's work of loafing around, constructing myself a waterless moat around a shovel. If you fling the sand far enough, you can make mountains around the moat too. It's the ultimate protection for any man's machinery.

It was the first time that I had ever broken curfew to go to the park in the middle of the night. Living in a house with squeaky floorboards was difficult to escape from, since I couldn't sneak out through my window. It was a combination of it being high up along with my belly not being slim enough to shuffle through it. I was impressed at how menacing such any enjoyable place could be at an abnormal time. Only a few lights along the pathway were on, but they were far in the distance. They didn't have filtered bulbs either. All of them had a dim yellow tint to them. I don't see why this creeped me out; since I had a walking dead Grandpa at home, how creepy could anything be? I noticed some noises coming from out of the dark trees that aligned the path. Ultra low sounding moans and shrieks of the unknown flooded the atmosphere around me. I knew that it was only my imagination running off with me, but the fear was still there. The interior of my sweatpants became heated as I ran my scaredy-pants self all the way home. I knew that I was a little old to be pissing myself, but, then again, remember; everyone always told me that I was a wuss. So, it must've been true. It had been a long time, since I had dampened my pants outside in a non-summertime season. I had forgotten how the cold nights in spring make urine frost over on your leg.

I rushed into the bathroom with the guaranteed vacancy when I got home. I snatched up the loofa from the shower to aid me in washing off my leg along with my "you know what". After I positioned myself in a fresh pair of pants and undies, I felt like a brand new boy. Normal people might've gone the other route and taken a shower, but I avoided those at all costs. I've never been one to be nervous about how I looked everyday. I'm more worried about the internal organs in my anatomy being well nourished than the outside appearing and smelling "good".

Since I was the babysitter, I figured that I should probably check on Grandpa to see how he was doing. I strained my vocal chords from the couch waiting for a reply with a good reason of why I should let him out. If he soaked up any knowledge, he would've replied to me. I heard a mumble from the opposite side of the door, speaking something in Spanish. It was one word that sounded like "carne". I couldn't believe it. I left him in there with books along with subtitles on the Spanish channel, and he absorbed the language like a sponge. There was no proof of him learning the English language yet. He could've, at the most, tried to pick up a book. Boy, I would have allowed my anger to rip on him if I had the motivation to yell some more. I could hear Grandpa's stomach growling from the other side of the door, begging for the input of nourishment. It had been a while since he had eaten. Common sense told me that I should probably feed him something to get him to shut up. While I was at it, I figured that I should shut off that damn Spanish channel too.

The only thing I could think of for food was our dog Trash, since he wasn't looking for a frozen, ground hamburger meal. I despised that dog because of everything that it represented, which was nothing. Trash was the loudest, most annoying dog that I hadn't fed for a while either. I'm sure that he had enough meat left on his bones to satisfy Grandpa's craving. I roused up from the couch of ultimate comfort to go to the drawer to grab the duct tape. I opened a new package of it, even though there was already an open one. I walked outside carrying the leash together with the tape to aid me in bringing the dog inside. It wasn't easy getting such a resistant dog inside under those measures. Sure, I felt a little bad for practically executing our dog, but, then again, if a cow is considered a food supply, why not a dog? Trash was settled there, encircled by a puddle of his own blood. The grass around him dripped beads of blood, while he lay close to motionless because, I'm deducing, of a lack of food and water. It was a hell of a lot easier than I expected it to be. I still took no chances, and I wrapped the duct tape around Trash's mouth just so that he wouldn't rip Gramps to shreds. He already did a number to one of Grandpa's hands. I couldn't risk further damage to the geezer. I had to basically drag the dog in by his collar, flattening his windpipe. By the time I got him into the room with Grandpa, he ceased to move anymore. I chose to believe that he was sleeping, so it wasn't animal abuse.

I didn't injure helpless animals; only buff body builders being that they were at least some competition. Since the dog was presently in the room, not putting up a struggle, I thought what the hell. I changed the channel in the room to some good old-fashioned soap operas. Where else would Grandpa learn to properly pronounce words other than from his favorite thing in the whole wide world? Luckily, Gramps couldn't crawl over the couch that was blocking the door, so I didn't have to hurry, while I was in there. He was more interested in Trash anyway. Perchance, not so much, Trash compared to what internal organs were resting within the dog. I shut him in the room again until a later time, when Trash would vanish.

I went into the kitchen to cook up a box of macaroni and cheese, family size. I made it with 3 packets of cheese and a melted stick of butter. I needed a good healthy meal, full of grains, joined with dairy products to keep me going after a hard day's work. I seated myself with the big steel pot and the giant wooden spoon that I stirred it with in hand. I had a favorable conversation with myself about the important issues that I had been dealing with lately. Some may call me crazy, but, if I didn't have a conversation with myself every once in a while, then I wouldn't be talking to anyone. It's challenging not having any friends. After all the food and exciting topics, I passed out with my arm stuck in between the couch cushions.

When I awakened, all I felt was a film of butter inside my intestine lining all the way up to the roof of my mouth. For some reason, I was also wearing the pot I cooked my food in on my head. While I was trying to figure out exactly what happened, I noticed that the sun was shining brightly, attacking my eyes, which drove me to move out of its way. I must've slept for at least twelve hours, considering that the sun was beginning to go down already. Lying on the couch outside of Grandpa's only exit, I heard him inside the room, speaking full sentences. I had to be an exceptional teacher. I considered maybe going to school in the education field when I grew up. I leaned over the couch, pressing my ear against the stained wood, to eavesdrop on what he was saying. The rotten rack of meat was repeating lines from the shows like, "I can't believe it! I wouldn't have slept with you if I knew you weren't my sister!" And, "I'm not really your father. I'm a clone who has gone back in time to make love to you!" The dialogue was butchered from the show that was now spoken slow and mispronounced by Grandpa. Progress was being made, though, which was the only thing that mattered, since his memory was being sparked.

I joined Gramps in the room, because I thought that if he was learning how to talk again, he could, most likely, understand me. I explained our current situation to him. I wanted to let him know that I wanted to help him, not destroy him. He wouldn't listen to a word I was ejecting from my mouth. He continued to show me this picture of him with Olaf, standing in the trenches, posing for the camera, in the middle of battle. No wonder why the guy was a fallen soldier in the war. With an obsession that lasted that long, there had to have been a gay love affair, but Grandpa was strictly against those. In a soft tone, Grandpa consistently repeated the word "merger". I agreed with him that yes when two men make love with each other, in a way, they have merged. He seemed kind of terrified and had this expression, symbolizing disbelief, on his face. At the same time, he looked like an unusually grumpier old senior. Gramps grabbed one of my Barbie's, I mean, G.I. Joes, and began to gnaw on its head, messing up the pretty blonde hair.

I left the room to give me a while to think about the whole problematic situation. By "merger", did he mean that he wanted to have one last go at Olaf's body before he could finally rest? Merger, merger, merger... I couldn't stop replaying it in my dome. I decided that it may have been time for me to put on my thinking cap. Grandpa was currently stupid. If I replaced the G with a D, it spelled murder, I think that sounded correct. How could someone mistake a G sound for a D sound anyway? Moron. Or else, maybe he acidentally said an M sound, instead of a B sound. That could mean that he wanted a burger.

I made it simpler by asking him if he meant murder or burger. He just brought up the whole merger business again. I composed the most brilliant plan ever. I told him that #1 was murder and #2 was burger. All he had to do was lift up the number of fingers that coincided with whichever one he chose. He lifted up his right hand that previously had a few working fingers, but now they were all mutilated from God knows what. There was one still intact, but it was only holding on by a dangling tendon. The blood had discontinued draining from the wound by that point in time. I screamed at Grandpa for still being idiotic. I directed him to raise his other hand, the one that still had fingers. He had turned out to be the most tedious person that I have ever had to deal with. Even if it was the same person that I'd dealt with for the past twelve years. Handicap, undead Grandpa was way worse than cranky, senior citizen Grandpa. He lifted up his other hand, but it wasn't there anymore. I became confused at how he could lose an entire hand. When he put his arm back down, his hand appeared. It held on for dear life by a couple major veins that were strained before they snapped, sending his hand to the ground. His blood grew a darker green color that almost resembled black. The trail of blood from his arm reached the floor before the weight pulled the remainder of his hand down. Obviously, he was a high maintenance type of guy. I stood there, struggling to think up a way that I could get him to let me know which number he meant. Similar to the start of a chant in a quiet voice, he started to say #1. I was proud of him, even though it was all due to my magnificent tutoring skills. Now, if I could've only recalled which option was #1. It should've been as elementary as devouring a piece pie for me. #1 was murder, because I picked #2 for burger. I picked #2 for burger, because it was my all time favorite combo meal. If I ordered two of them, I had the greatest chance of getting full without reaching the desperate measure of getting three combo meals. I was so excited that I figured something out on my own for once.

I ran up to Gramps with haste to be positive that he meant murder. He nodded his head with rapid speed as quickly as a normal man could, except a normal man's skin wouldn't shift around as much on their skull. It looked like it was going to slide right off, splattering against the floor. So how the hell was he going to murder someone who was already buried six feet in the dirt? I felt like I was on Jeopardy. I was the host; I was the contestant; and I was receiving no type of payment. What a crappy deal that was. Well, I thought about why he wanted to find the stiff. By thinking about it, I meant sitting on the couch, shoveling down leftover chili, attempting to take my mind off of it. Then, it hit me, just after the last kidney bean entered my mouth. Why would the crusted blood on the cigarette turn Grandpa into a zombie if Olaf wasn't already one? The reason behind it became crystal clear to me. Grandpa wanted to murder him, because Olaf handed him this fate, knowing what would happen. I wrote all the information that I had gathered on my trusty, yellow notepad. I knew that I would forget it in an instant if I didn't. I brought Grandpa's attention towards me with a racket, so I could read him my note. (I read it to him, while aware that he had a reading level lower than a preschooler.)

> *Deer Grampa,*
> *do yu want to kil this guy becuz he made you*
> *ded? It was becuz he new that he wuz part of*
> *the livng ded, huh?*
> *Let me kno,*
> *Gary Helty*

I know, I know. It was a miracle that I could even spell my own name, but you get the point. Gramps did too, even though he hardly understood anything. If we outset anywhere, it should've been finding out where Olaf was "buried". I brought out the world map, but I struggled to distinguish the states in such a tiny country. Then, I realized that a map of the United States might simplify my search, compared to a world map. Land of the free, home of the brave, or so the guy said who hooked up our illegal cable. I rummaged through the house for hours, searching for a big fold out map before locating it beneath the coffee table. Alright, so were here, smack dab in the northwest side of Vermont. I injected the rear of a pen into the socket of where Grandpa's pointer finger used to be eminent, pushing down the meaty material. I directed him to point out on the map to where he thought Olaf would most likely be. Gramps pointed to the rear side of his underwear that had a tag on the back. I got up close to read it, baring the stench. The tag read, "Made in Oregon". I thought that was pretty sweet, since Oregon was only a state or two away. Then, I re-examined the map, coming across the real Oregon along the coast on the other side of the country. I was originally thinking of New Hampshire – a common mistake. What a bunch of crap that was. I inquired to myself how we were supposed to get across the country with me not at the legal driving age? Grandpa was completely useless, having two mangled hands along with an ankle that was practically shredded from wear and tear.

If a national television network made a show about us, it would probably be called "The Zombie Cripple and the Kid". I should really be first in the title, considering that I didn't smell as bad. So, on second thought, it should be called "Gary Helty and the Wheelchair Bound Un-dead Reject". I guarantee that we would receive more viewers, just for having such a kick ass title.

It seemed like quite the endeavor to cross such a vast terrain, and I guessed that it would cost a lot of money. I was uncertain as to how Grandpa was going to drive that far with non-functioning hands. Not being noticed for being a rotted corpse by everyone would be a feat as well. I could imagine how it would go. Gramps and I would be driving down the road, minding our own business, when some little kids point us out to their elders. Angered by being spotted by the adolescents, Gramps lunges out of the passenger side window (which is still rolled up) and emits shards of glass into ozone. Gravity does its job and sends the shards into my face. Grandpa lands on the hood of the attacking car, crashing through their windshield. The windows acquire a thick layer of blood impairing the right for me to view the inside. During the whole confrontation, I lose control of the vehicle, because I'm attempting to extract glass from my face. In the end, we both die a horrible death. I painstakingly needed to die with dignity, for example, like choking on a hotdog in one of those national hotdog-eating contests.

I felt a snack and rest coming on. My brain was frying like a brain on drugs (you know with the frying pan and eggs, that never fails to be a good meal either). I boiled some hotdogs in a pot filled with milk while frying some eggs and bacon. It's more ball busting than you would think to cook three different things at once on the highest temperature. After they were all prepared, I mixed them together. I called it "The Scrambled Helty Massacre". If you smear the top with Easy Cheese, it doubles the chances of having a weakness for it. After laboring for about half an hour, attempting to finish it, I finally dozed off.

When I woke up later on the next day, there was a cat that was ripped to shreds on the floor. It was ground into the carpet, too, making it nearly impossible to get out. I didn't care since I wasn't the maid. Grandpa must've had a hankering for something nummy. Some people need to recognize that it's not the quality; it's the quantity. If he expected me to clean the carpet, he had another thing coming. I would've smacked him in the face and then run away. Besides he made the mess, it was his carpet, he should shampoo it. It would be child labor if he made me do it anyway, which would be illegal. I'm a firm believer in the law. I latched onto the arm of the couch, raising myself up to my feet. The path to the bathroom was a long one, yet I managed to stumble there, missing the random ribs strewn across the floor. Something about that Scrambled Helty wrenched my stomach into knots.

When I was in the middle of unbuttoning my pants, I heard an abundance of water pounding the base of the shower. I questioned why the shower would be on. It was not like Grandpa needed to shower. I didn't leave it on the night before either. I hadn't even occupied it for a week. Then I heard the most terrifying sound that I had ever heard in my life coming from the shower. The voice echoed a noise so horrifying that the only words it could be described in are "I have a lovely bunch of coconuts". I was positive that it was Grandpa from the sheer volume of hideousness in the tune. He always sang a song off key in the shower, and now I knew what. But I wish I didn't. The shower curtain slowly peeled back, exposing the subject matter behind it. The uppermost section of Grandpa's body popped out. His age stained ribs dug out from beneath his flesh. The decay was already setting in, affecting the smoothness of his skin. He was cleansing his ribs with my pink, I mean, dark blue loofa. He was becoming fairly skinny, leading me to believe that he barely ate. Boy, did I escape out of that bathroom as quick as I could, but not because I was scared or anything. I don't get scared. The only reason I left in such a hurry was caused by that Scrambled Helty Massacre with Easy Cheese. I was making a mad dash down to the basement toilet when I tripped on the litter box at the top of the stairs. I descended down the stairs, tumbling like a drunken acrobat.

I must've nailed my head pretty good on the concrete landing, seeing that my vision was cloudy. When the double vision cleared up, Gramps was directly in my face. He was staring into my eyes, communicating to me how he hoped that I had a nice trip and couldn't wait to see me next fall. I comprehended that he wasn't joking, because old people don't joke. They're only grumpy and brittle. I became hungry for peanut brittle again before I remembered that it was gone. There was no use getting excited over nothing. I got that peanut brittle out of my thoughts when Grandpa initiated bodily harm to me. His type of malevolence was made up of him trying to grab me, which in turn was poking me in the neck with the nubs of where his fingers were prefixed. I stood up, scampering as speedily as I could up the stairs to the main floor bathroom. Again, not because I was scared or anything, but, you know, because of the Scrambled Helty. I had a moment of peace until Gramps made it upstairs. Then the banging on the door commenced, so I barricaded it shut with my leg brawn. I wasn't going to let him stop me this time; determined was what I was. I packed a collection of towels under the door that made it nearly hopeless to open.

When my wiener was thoroughly drained, I questioned myself as to why I was afraid of a guy that might as well have been an amputee. He crawled slower than a turtle that wasn't even participating in a race. Plus, he reeked of rotten squirrel mixed with cheap cologne. I marched out of that bathroom, angrier than a beaver. In return for the disturbance, I socked him right in the eye if I had the balls. Truthfully, I just walked out, giving him an explanation that he couldn't deny. I made it clear that if he wanted to find Olaf, he needed me to go into public places to get items for him. After a piddling family quarrel, involving loud words, accompanied by hard objects, we saw each other's points. After the exchange of high-pitched screams, it appeared to me that I didn't teach him anything. Over time, his brain must've gradually revived things that he had learned in life. It's approximate to when you don't use a part of your body a notable amount, like your legs, they become weak or even useless until you start using them again. Kind of like how I can walk now after overworking my legs, Grandpa can think, form words, and even pronounce them right at that time. I was certain that if I didn't help Grandpa find Olaf, he was going to make for damn sure that he got rid of me. My choices were pull my own plug by not assisting Grandpa, kill Gramps before he could off me, or slay Olaf, who I didn't know anything about. He was presumably out snacking upon tons of innocent people at that modern moment. My decision rested on Grandpa. But if I executed Gramps, the state would probably give me a new home with brainless people that would force me to go to school. So I would call this a vacation or road trip, if you prefer that term. I agreed to cooperate with him to find Olaf as long as I gained free combo meals for every meal on the way there and back. I wouldn't be happy with only one thing off the dollar menu either, like I usually got. By the smile on his face, I managed to tell with certainty that it was a deal (if it was a smile at all). The tissue on both cheeks was tainted with infection, but I preferred to call it an extended smile.

We needed to get a wooden leg or crutch for Grandpa before we did anything else. There was no way that he would be able to mutilate Olaf by crawling on the ground with broken appendages. But where was I going to find the money for something as high tech as a wooden leg. I bet that they cost and an arm and a leg. Grandpa wriggled at a sluggish speed into his bedroom. I followed, keeping tabs on him and being optimistic that he might show me something useful for once. He gathered himself in the corner, where there was a square patch of lime green carpet that was placed within the default forest green carpet. Only a fool wouldn't notice that there was a hole underneath the cushioned landscape. Gramps picked at the corner of the off-colored piece of carpet with his teeth for an abundance of time before asking me in the most polite way possible to help out. Calling me tubby little hooligan was his way of hinting that he needed a helping hand. I expressed to him how much I loved him with a kick to the kidney. After the chunk of carpet was removed, a wooden door with a steel ring appeared. I inserted my two fingers inside the ring, pulling the door open with ease. Beneath the wooden exterior was a safe that had the spinning combination pointing up. I gladly let Gramps do his damndest to try to open it, since he refused to confide in me with the code. It was amusing to watch him slide his tongue from side to side, striving to get the numbers right. He overshot them many times, but he didn't mind with all the helpful words that I dedicated to him along the way, such as "loser" and "useless piece of crap". Eventually, his ability with his tongue paid off when the lock made its last click. All I had to do was give it a tug. I yanked at the supposedly unlocked lid, but it didn't budge because... it was still locked. The one thing that I thought he could pull off didn't happen.

I had watched the other kids pick the combinations on the lockers at school back in the day, so I had a grasp on how to do it. Three clicks later, I had that thing open, not bad for a kid who could hardly spell his own name. I dislocated the lid from the safe sluggishly, so it would be more exciting when I finally viewed the contents. There was no reason to be ecstatic, for all that was inside it was another safe. I used my magnificent lock-picking skills to open the smaller version of a safe also. I swiftly unsealed the safe, expecting to find another safe buried within, but, instead, the innards glimmered with stacks of money. I didn't know how much was in there until Grandpa force-fed it to me, while I was still in awe. There was $350,000 in retirement money from years of being a janitor. The government gave the rest to him from the mental and physical anguish that he went through in the war.

Chapter 2: Preparation for an Amputee

I had absolutely no worries about money problems anymore. Getting that leg for Grandpa, getting to Oregon, tons of fast food, all would be a cinch now. I was off to the store to purchase Grandpa's brand new leg. There was only one place for a specialty product such as this, "Amputee's Heaven". The slogan was "if you've lost it, we've found it".

On my way down the mean streets of Vermont, I witnessed all sorts of frightening sights. There were people firing semi automatic guns out their SUV's windows at a house, a big giant spider jumped at me out of nowhere, and fat citizens jogged on the side of the street at a mediocre pace. Alright, so there were only fat people jogging, but it's too bad that they were wearing sweat suits. I really should've worn one of those to be polite. I'm sure nobody wanted to see my stomach hanging out, because all I had clean was my "Jesus is my homeboy" t-shirt that I got three years earlier in a size small. A lot had changed in the past couple years... a lot.

After multiple blocks of strenuous exercise, I began to wobble uncontrollably. My knees gave out from under me as I collapsed onto the concrete. I was resting in a twenty-liter sweat puddle on the ground before I regretted not thinking of better transportation than the body of a mortal. I couldn't conceive how I'd left my scooter at the park, how I longed for its company once again. As I was dreaming about the love that rolls you away, a little girl came up to me riding on this pink and white striped bike. The bike tires screeched to a halt, painting a black streak down the sidewalk. She leaned down to me, informing me about how fatness could cause heart attacks with some other added nonsense. That gave me all the more incentive to push her underweight ass off of her bike. She dropped to the ground at an angle, skinning her knee across the rough concrete. When the hemoglobin surfaced, I reminded her to wear the proper protection while riding. I had to pull her off it again by her ponytails, being that she was quicker to get up, but, as usual, in the end, I reigned supreme.

I refrained from using my energy as I coasted half a block down the hill until I reached the home of the cripple's dream. In front of the store, I gazed up at the sign, making sure that I was in the right place. The sign read "mute heaven" in bold neon letters. I was outraged until I used my observation expertise, seeing that some of the lights were just burned out. After striving to reach my objective, I had finally made it. I went through four grueling blocks of twists and turns, downhill journeys, and sweaty stomach cellulite.

I walked up the ramp for the wheelchair, doomed to the electronic door that opened at a snail's pace for me. The place was gigantic for having such a small target audience. I was in a good mood; I thought maybe I'd do something special for Gramps. A jaw replacement would be nice, in case he took too many blows to the face or else a spare eye for when I dug my thumb inside the socket in a fit of rage. It was bound to happen.

Aisle five was my first stop to shop in the convenience store for the naturally and unnaturally mangled. That aisle had all of the reserve parts for anything related to the face. I couldn't wait to check out the variety of counterfeit eyes. The glass cases were stacked one on top of the other, packed full of different colored eyes. It was complete with vampire colored eyes that had red outlined with yellow irises. There were also cloudy white eyes, made specifically to make people appear to be one of the undead, but what use would Gramps have in an eye that would make his eye look exactly the same as before? I called the sales person over so that he could unlock the heavily defended case for me. I wanted to get Gramps the vampire eye, since he would never expect something so extravagant from me. It would look wonderfully sweet. Mr. Salesman came over, asking me why I believed I needed a fake eye. I explained to him that it was for a little something I liked to call "none of your business". I apologized to him only for the sake of getting satisfactory service. I had him bring the eye up to the check lanes to hold onto it until I was ready to be checked out. He didn't trust me enough to let me keep it on me.

I took a gander down the rest of the aisle to see what else they had to offer. They had fake ears for the burn victims, hair that looked like it was plucked from a goat's chin, along with miscellaneous other things that proved useless to my needs. I added some fake ears to my basket, accompanied by the chin hair from a goat. I got the ears for entertainment purposes only. I wanted to chuck them at acne-ridden kids when they walked past me. I headed down to the aisle with the systematic lower body devices. I needed to make sure that Grandpa could stand with a fake leg. I shopped for crutches in the event that he would need assistance walking. There were all sorts of them: Wood ones, metal ones, and even some overpriced titanium ones. That was what I went with. Nothing could beat some cheap labored, expensively priced titanium. The salesman took the crutches up to the lanes for me while I searched for the last entry on my list: a prosthetic leg.

Destiny came to me while I was making my way to the fabricated legs. I caught the eye of a beautiful girl. She was about 5'4", 220 lbs with the steady arms of a husky goddess - my kind of woman. I became a witty, little Satan when I questioned what a sexy beast such as herself was doing in a crummy place like that. She was looking at replacement hands that she claimed were for her mom. Her hands were covered by rubber cleaning gloves that she attempted to hide behind her back; I smelt something fishy. I introduced myself to her as I shook her hand. Her name was Christina. It was a darling name for some-one who shook hands like a man. I had to find a way to escape the beast. She wouldn't stop displaying her pearly whites to me, and I didn't know what to do. I gave her every possible reason that I could think of to make   her   fear   being   near   me. I told her a tale of how I contracted Hepatitis C from a steak knife that I cut my big juicy pork loin with; also, how window curtains could entertain me for hours when they blew in the wind (that one wasn't a lie). But, this woman wasn't scared away by anything. She was still fixated on my gorgeous body. I couldn't blame her for that, though, but talk about a freak! I slipped a single fake ear that I swiped into her pocket when the sales person wasn't looking. When the trap was set, I bellowed out the word "SHOPLIFTER". Christina gave me a bewildered look before security made it over. They asked me what the problem was as they tried to calm me down, since I was flailing my arms about as I yelled it over and over again. I explained to them how she was stealing a fake ear for no apparent reason. She kept claiming that she had no need for a fabricated ear, further proving my point. I advised them to search Christina's coat pockets if that was even her real name. When they made their way into her left pocket, guess what they found? A fake ear, just like I had expected. Hardcore criminals like that should be locked up in prison for eternity, but I'm sure she will get off tonight with how the court system is ran now-a-days. It's a shame when a life of crime is the only option left.

Now I could, without interruption, get back to shopping for my shabby old Grandpa. The last thing that I needed to get was the leg. The choices were unimaginable. There were so many to choose from, just like everything else in the gymnasium-sized store. They varied from extravagant bendable legs to ones that looked like chunks of wood carved into leg form with the blunt end of an axe.

At the end of the aisle, there was one that screamed out Grandpa's name. It was comparable to a piece of wood shaped like a leg. It didn't bend at all and looked like it was carved out of a dresser with that natural wood finish. It was perfect, antique looking just like Grandpa. I snatched up the fancy pants bendable one too in the extremely rare case that Grandpa would hate the one that I picked out for him. I had collected all of the items that I needed on my trip, so I ventured up front to the checkout. In the checkout lane, they had the impulse buys that I had always been a sucker for. There were matching pairs of silicone hands that you could curve the fingers however you wanted by locking them into place at any point. They were a must buy; that way, Gramps could actually hold onto the crutch that I was going to buy him for a mean joke. At least I still had the goat's hair. When the cashier rang up the total cost, she raised her eyebrow in concern, expecting me not to have the money. When I whipped out the hundreds, I was afraid that her eyes were going to burst. They looked swollen to the extent that another surprise would make her heart explode along with them.

Someone must've called the cops, because they stalled me there with the offer of free candy. I knew it all along, but I'm a sucker for candy. Before I could finish my lollipop, the oinker with a badge showed up, asking me where I got all the funds. No matter how much I revealed it to them, they wouldn't believe the truth. I ended up having to call up Grandpa over the whole occurrence. He had to convince the sunglass wearing cops that he distributed the cold hard cash to me. Hours later, I was finally on my way home with the various body parts that I had purchased in a hefty plastic bag. I would've ridden my bike home, but somebody had stolen it from my safekeeping, which was, well... I had leaned it against a light post. Some people have no respect for other people's property, O.P.P.

So I was walking on an uphill slope in the dead of night, freezing my ass off in upper body wear that should've been considered a half shirt, holding onto a bag heavy enough to tear off my arm over an extended period of time. If that happened, it would've been kind of like a slip-n-slide down the hill. That was if you replaced the water with blood and the tarp with concrete, which would be one painful ride. My nipples became hard while my flabby body conjured up sweat to overtake my skin. I needed to scramble to get home, but I had trouble even pulling off the maneuver labeled the fast walk. The streetlights went out as I trotted underneath them, abandoning me inside the darkness with a pinch of light that peered out of the house windows. I took it as a sign that I was unfathomably special. I was almost home when a car pulled over to the side of the road beside me. From out of the vehicle emerged a couple of teenagers (they were the equivalent of hell for me). They chased me home on foot, calling me tubby, while shouting at me to keep running. They were lucky that I was in a pleasant mood, or else I would've let them have it. Instead, I allowed them to chase me so that they could get some amusement out of something deadly. I'm a nice guy like that.

I put extra effort into making it home at breakneck speed only to reach the end of my mission, facing the screams of my "commander" for exceeding my time limit. I advised him to shut the hell up while throwing the wooden leg at his chest. He babbled on about how the product wasn't good enough for his liking, questioning if I picked out the worst counterfeit leg in the store. I told him in a demeaning manor that I picked out the antique looking one just like him. I viciously threw him the expensive leg. At the moment of impact, he was driven into the wall behind him. He still wasn't happy with the goodies that I showered him with, so I informed him about the secret present that I bought him with his money. I pulled the hands, which were clearly visible, out of the bag, showing them to Grandpa. I think that he actually liked them with the ear-to-ear smile that he shelled out to me. I demonstrated to him how the fingers bent whichever way, latching into place at any point. I showed him slowly and bent the fingers back and forth at a pace that a child who had recently been dropped down the stairs could've comprehended. It struck me that my teaching lesson pissed him off, but it was a hate-hate relationship, like any abnormal, dysfunctional family had.

Chapter 3:
Death, Destruction, and Small Children

The prosthetics would need to be tested out to make sure that all of them were functional. I grabbed the electric saw from Grandpa's workshop to prepare his mangled limbs for complete amputation. As I slid the blade across his wrists and leg, slivers of meat clung to my arm hairs. I united the prosthetic limbs onto the dark oozing stumps. After it was completed, I decided that if we were going to test them out, we might as well take a trial run on Grandpa's ability to feed. And, if Grandpa was going to test his ability to kill, I might as well organize the victims to my benefit. There was this guy that I associated with from school that would be the perfect first victim. His name was Johnny Pal, or at least that was what everybody called him. It sounded like a really stupid name to curse your child with. This was one of those guys who thought he lived on the top of Mount Cool, so he didn't fight. Everybody else stomped the crap out of me for him. He himself was as skinny as someone who only had fourteen dollars a month for groceries. It could take little to no effort to bring him down to beg for mercy. I heaved Grandpa into the car and revealed to him that I was taking him out for dinner to get him all riled up. I was forced to drive, since Grandpa wanted me to make myself useful if he kept me alive. He always parked it by entering the garage backwards, which made no sense to me at all. Gramps thought it would take less time to leave, but he wasted more time attempting the tedious task of backing it in there. I got inside the rusted baby blue babe magnet, ready for a different kind of action. I turned the key in the ignition waiting for the uproarious racket to come from the muffler before I took off. I was ecstatic about the opportunity; I couldn't have dreamed of being able to drive at such an early age. I slammed on the gas pedal to squeal the tires as the car flew in reverse into the garage, where the car was divided in between the back wall. I stepped out of the car to dislodge all of the broken wood and nudie magazines (that I previously hid in the depths of the garage) out of the rear axle.

After cleaning the obstruction, we could finally be on our way. I cautiously pushed down the gas; this time going forward. I was racing down the street at the hypersonic speed of fifteen mph. It was the fastest that amazing piece of American crap could go; we needed a foreign car. I cruised the quicker route that led me to "Cars for Cash" downtown on Birch Street. We pulled into the gravel parking lot, where a sign read "100% cash down" along with a smaller sign below it that said "Foreign Cars for Foreigners". When we met with the salesman, I convinced him to sell us a vehicle, even though we weren't foreign, with my fist. Well, the wad of cash that was clenched in the center of it might've helped too. It's funny how a wad of wealth can buy you anything, even heaven. A glass of holy water a day keeps the devil away. We departed from the local business with a "like new" Subaru that was supposedly Paul Hogan's car before he got famous. Grandpa tore the leg off the car salesman to use it for a snack until we got to Johnny Pal's house. He was spinning it around eating away at the skin, like a rack of lamb, which made me hungry for a gyro. The exposed meat slid between his fingers dripping onto his lap, like thick custard made with an inflated amount of flour. Gramps threw the leftover leg in the backseat before he licked the blood from his hands. There were still scraps of skin remaining in between his teeth that I had to point out to him so that he could pry them out with his artificial fingernail.

With the headlights out, we stationed ourselves across the street from Johnny Pal's residence. I sent Grandpa to my enemy's doorstep, certain that he would be spotted by the neighbors. He was still becoming accustomed to walking with his new legs, adjusting to the different textures on the ground. He moved like he had a clubfoot while the other foot was broken. His left ear was dangling there, swinging in the wind, only restrained by his hearing aid that was lodged in the open wound. I swear that I could smell the stench of him even with the car windows rolled up. I might've cared if I hadn't lived with it for so long before, plus I myself reeked of body odor along with urine from all of the exercise and accidents I produced in my pants. Gramps knocked on the screen door, making minimal noise, but still this little girl must've heard him as she came to the door. He ruptured the screen with his hands as he seized the girl's cranium in the middle of them. As Gramps stepped into the residence, the innocent child tried to run backwards to escape. Grandpa pressed his knee against her stomach with so much force that it lacerated her head from the body. Blood spurted out like a sprinkler where most of the holes were clogged with grime. The decapitated loved one dropped to the floor, creating a bacteria ridden pool on the welcome mat. The door enclosed behind him, the only thing that I could do then was delay until the all-clear signal. I turned on some 1980's hair metal, rocking my socks off until I caught a glimpse of Gramps in the window flicking me off, which was the signal.

I made an effort to fast walk to the door, which ended up being more of a slow walk with a shuffle. I eventually made it without being apprehended. When I opened the door, there were blood and guts everywhere. Intestines were swinging from the ceiling fan that was circling on the highest speed. The intestinal juices were spraying against the walls along with anything else that crossed its path. Grandpa's nutcase personality must've caught up with him, because a stomach was punctured with a nail inside of a picture frame of the family. It was no longer just feeding anymore. It developed into a sick obsession of slaughtering the untainted, like any run-of-the-mill serial killer. I located Grandpa in the dining room, feasting upon the woman of the household. They were on top of the dinner table. She was on her back as Grandpa was angled over her face. Her throat was split where Gramps made the incision to extract her windpipe from her throat as he sucked the fluids out, like he was siphoning a diesel gas tank. He also spread out his discolored tongue to lick her eyeballs clean of any blood or moisturizing nonsense that was applied by the contact wearer. I could distinguish the clear eye drop liquid when it mixed in with Grandpa's rotten saliva. I climbed the steep stairs to the upper level to check who was up there, if anyone. I infiltrated Johnny Pal's room. The contents of the room were packed with cartoon related video games along with action figures of a similar type (if dolls are considered cartoon-like). It was the coolest room in the world, so I pissed in every nook and cranny of it.

A noise entered my eardrum from the room next to me. It was the echo of a big baby crying. I invaded the adjacent room and caught Johnny Pal huddled in the corner. He was in deep mourning on account of his immediate family perishing. What a loser. Mine were, too. The difference was that I still had to live with one of my family members, but you don't hear me crying about it. I snagged the back of his unworthy head and advanced his face into the highest point of the bedpost. It pierced through the back of his skull and prodded his eyeball out through the exit wound. His plasma that was dyed a shade of red speckled my face almost poking my eye out with his eyeball that sprung out at me. I inconsiderately attempted to work the post out of his head, but I wasn't strong enough. I peeled off a worn fork that was literally molded to an aged dresser next to the bed. I stabbed the fork through his neck many times, poking insignificant holes in the other side, where the uppermost section of his vertebrae was stationed. The tendons were snapping the more I plunged the fork into them. I spread the hemoglobin on my face with the back of my hand, hoping to clean it up, because it was causing what felt like a rash. Once I used my common sense, I wiped down my face with my shirt, purging it of blood. To finish the job, I had to yank on his shoulders and plant my shoe on the bedpost for leverage so that I could detach his skull from his neck bone. Murder is hell of a lot of work. I'm not totally definite on why I did it. But it was done, and there was nothing that I could do about it anymore. I hauled Johnny Pal down the stairs, banging his neck bone against every step. I wanted to keep a good portion of his body as a trophy of the thing that I hated the most.

My concentration was broken when I ran across the kitchen. I rummaged around in anything that opened, but there was no meat. I felt like a pregnant woman, since I had a craving for it that I couldn't replace with anything else I found.

In place of the meat was tofu. All of the other foods involved something healthy. Healthy sucks. But, I was starving to death. Every time my eyes fixed to the cupboards, they always seemed to stray right back to Johnny's headless corpse. I put on an apron that read "Kiss the Cook" along with a sweet chef's hat, fixing for a large meal. I located the biggest meat cleaver in the kitchen, because, if I was really going to do that, I wanted to do it correctly. I hurled Johnny Pal up onto the kitchen counter as I proceeded to dice his fingers into thin slices. I separated as many of the bones as I could out from the meat, being that there is nothing worse then being in the middle of enjoying an extravagant meal and abruptly fracturing a tooth on a bone. I cleaved some of the flesh from the body, carelessly, to store in the crock-pot for a stew later. I wrapped up those slender pieces of finger up in a tortilla. I was attempting to make miniature finger rolls, like they have at all of those parties with a bunch of women. All of my wisdom about cooking came from what I liked to call "tubby instinct". Whatever meat remained, I tossed in the oven on a cookie sheet at 375 degrees. I wasn't much for seasoning; I liked my meat plain. The crock-pot took awhile, so, by the time my "Johnny A La Gary" was prepared, Gramps was on his second meal.

It was the first time in an eternity that Gramps and I had a meal together at the table in a room without a TV. He had the limbless torso of the father lying in front of him without any silverware anywhere near him. Those rotting hands were squishing the entrails, brewing them into a curdled cottage cheese consistency with a cherry pudding look – the kind with cherry chunks in it. It bugged me when various organs got blended together, unless it was hotdogs. On my side of the table, I had my stew in a mixing bowl with potatoes, carrots, and purple jellybeans. I know. I know. Jellybeans don't go in stew, but it's exceptional. They melted into the other juices perfectly, creating a tasty film around the other ingredients. It would be the latest craze if everybody wasn't too cowardly to try it. Next to my stew, I had a sizeable plate of sliced fingers that were wrapped in tortillas with a thin layer of mayo (not miracle whip), lettuce, cheese, and fruit roll up. Yeah, most people would have probably thought that the fruit roll up was the weird part, too. I considered the lettuce to be an odd addition, since it was healthy. It was a meal fit for a cannibal king. I consumed it all. The roast beef sandwich, the pot roast, the sirloin stomach, and some liver and onions. I was bewildered at how much better human meat was compared to any other type of meat that I had ever had. I sealed some hamburger type patties (that I had assembled incase I had time in the near future to grill them) in a large, ziplock baggie.

I inspected the living room a single time more before we got our asses out of there. There were entrails strewn about everywhere. By the amount of blood and guts that were plastered to the walls, I was guessing that at least four people had been slaughtered, maybe five, if you launch a small child in the mix. The sun was beginning to rise over the dew covered grass, which made me make more of an effort to be prompt.

I didn't want to be spotted leaving the crime scene. We still had to change into their clothes, considering that there was no way that we could get out of that place unseen when we were covered in enough blood to drown the Pope. When we got upstairs, I chose this pair of jeans that had worn out holes in the knees, paired with black leather chaps to go over them. I had to wear the Dad's garments because I was too hefty to squeeze into anything else. I had to suck in my breadbasket to even fit into those. It was a relief to get out of that "Jesus is my homeboy" shirt (only to swap it with a tar-stained, plain white shirt with cut-off sleeves). The excursion down the stairs took forever because of Grandpa's walking disability that enabled us to only take one step at a time. I had to expose the inner briskness within him by prodding him in the back with a wire coat hanger. He accelerated a teeny bit. But, he tended to only when I got on his nerves, since anger fuels adrenaline. My hand was on the doorknob to the front door when I witnessed a car pulling into the driveway.

Both of us moved out of sight, one of us on each side of the entrance. Grandpa took his stance behind the door while I positioned myself in front of the door to open it when the visitors came up. Two people exited the station wagon. It was Johnny's best friend for life along with his mom. Everybody called him Mike the Murtilizer, and they called his mom the town bicycle. They arrived at the door, poking the dimly lit doorbell. I unsealed the wooden blockade, showing my face in his friend's premises. Mike was in awe that I was there. I think that he knew something was up, but what was he going to do about it? I explained to him that Johnny and I were having a play-date, so I offered for them to come in. I didn't want to be rude. The instant that they stepped foot into the house, Grandpa fractured the doorframe from using too much power when shutting the door. He took the mother into his arms, striving to devour her as Mike bolted for the back door. On his way down the hall, Mike nailed his head on a paint can that I left hanging from the doorway. Its sole purpose was to damage Gramps, but Mike had to screw it all up. He fell over onto his back, where his head continued to seesaw from side to side in a daze. I hunted under the bathroom sink for some toilet bowl cleaner, not shedding any anxiety over what brand it was. When I obtained it, I went back to Mike, where I got on top of him with a knee weighting down each of his shoulders. I plugged his nose so that he had to open his mouth for a gasp of breath. When he inhaled the crisp oxygen, I dumped the cleaner down his soon to be burning throat. He choked and disgorged, spraying the cleaner universally with every convulsion, until he eventually quit making any motion.

He wasn't so tough anymore in his clothes that were spotted with colorlessness. I find it humorous how if one wrong thing enters your mouth, your life will be snatched away from you in an instant. I had to fulfill my babysitter duties by checking up on Gramps to make sure that he was finished with chow time. He was done with his meal, so I mentioned to him that there was dessert in the hallway for him to munch on. Gramps was finally gaining some meat on those bones of his. It was like his stomach never filled anymore. He consumed raw beef, like there was no tomorrow. The walking digestive system went back to chow down on Mike the Momma's Boy. I snuck off into the kitchen to begin grilling my burgers on a grilling device that plugged into the wall. As I was pressing down the lid on the grill, I heard a disgusting noise coming from the hallway. It was to the harmony of creamed corn hitting the ground in clumps. I left my cooking arrangements to do research on what the mysterious noise was.

Gramps was knelt on the floor, puking up everything that he had ingested. Most of it was coming out in slabs that were only partially digested. If he chewed his food, then maybe it wouldn't have been so agonizing.

The cleaner in Mike's blood stream must've had a crummy repercussion on Grandpa, too. I wondered how long he was going to vomit for. It had been almost five minutes of constant puking, and he was still going. It originated as pulpy, moderately digested food, but then it evolved into stomach bile, and then murky blood. The spewage from the depths of Grandpa's innards were slowly traveling down the hall. I could barely walk on the slimy substance without slipping and breaking my neck. A couple of minutes later, his valves shut off, causing him to finally stop puking as he passed out face down in his own internal filth. The house was so jam-packed full of squished human bodies that when someone came in, they would, without a doubt, condemn it. In that case, I figured, why not have some fun? We couldn't leave until the following sunset anyway, because it was presently light outside, making it way too risky to evacuate the premises. I frisked the residence, taking anything hard, hammers, bats, and chairs. I made them useful by destroying as much O.P.P. as possible. I would never do it to my own possessions, so, now that I had the chance to do that to someone that I wasn't too sympathetic for, I did it. I examined as many x-rated tapes that I could fit into a day too. I was a kid with no sweetheart; I needed that. I did a little bit of dressing up as a woman, including the make-up. What I meant was that I put on a tool belt to build wooden racks to hold football action figures. I am a manly man. I just remembered. After dancing around, I blacked out in the middle of the floor. I woke up discovering that gum was holding my eye captive for not paying attention to it when I dozed off. It must have worked its way out of my mouth, onto the carpet, and then underneath my eyelids.

After putting many different solutions that I thought would help on the sticky substance I finally got the gum removed. I may have also permanently devastated the vision in my left eye. It fizzled and blistered a small volume of light red liquid down my cheek. I became somewhat concerned, but I had a high pain tolerance for self-inflicted trauma. I encircled gauze around my head, with a pair of folded undies underneath it over my eye. I presumed that it would soak up a lot more than some paper towels would (and I should know from how many times as I tinkled in my pants). I creased the whitey tightys enough so you couldn't determine what they were, because the last time I wore underwear on my face, I didn't hear the end of it...ever.

I headed downstairs for an update on if Grandpa had awakened from his slumber, which he had. He was licking the bones clean, setting them up to make a dinky house out of them with the helping hand of model glue. He wasn't too thrilled when I informed him that it was midnight, so we had to get a move on it. Gramps tried to take the bone house with him, but I told him no with a swift chop to it, shattering it into pieces. We washed each other up with a sponge again (because it's challenging to wash your own back). I alternated my clothes into a pair of fresh stonewash jeans along with a t-shirt that advertised pork - one of my favorite kinds of meat. We vacated the house, ducking behind miscellaneous trees and bushes until we managed to get across the street to our ride of destiny. There was a pair of parking tickets tucked beneath the windshield wipers of the car that we had no intention of paying off.

I twisted the key before I began to speed off into the distance, but I only made it about two inches before the car came to a dead stop. I stepped out of the car to see if I could fix whatever was wrong with the car. Those damn cops had installed a yellow boot onto the front right tire to hold it in place. I almost shrieked in anger, but I kept in mind that we were supposed to stay quiet. I hauled Grandpa out of the car and explained to him that we had to scurry somewhere out of sight before somebody identified us. It was a decent distance back to get a new vehicle; we were fortunate that we never changed the title on the car that we purchased.

We discontinued our stroll in an alley, where the bum who everyone knew lived. He greeted us with a smile that was crowded with three whole teeth, escorted by liquor in a brown paper bag. Gramps complimented him by separating his vocal chords from his throat. The chords rested in Grandpa's hand before taking a journey down his throat. The bum was still animate until Gramps boot stomped him, crushing his jaw into the greater part of his spine. It's fascinating how much strength he had after a day or two of constantly eating meals. He used to be weak, but, at the present time, he was like a one-man army action movie star.

I positioned my back towards Gramps as he changed into the bum's attire, because there was no way that I wanted to see an old wrinkly man bare it all. I'm all about the females, believe me. Grandpa dressed up in his entire wardrobe, complete with the brown stocking hat and the hefty brown jacket that was smeared with mud. I buried myself in the bottom of the shopping cart that was overflowing with aluminum cans. Grandpa used the shopping cart as an aid to assist him walking. It felt nice being able to be lazy while getting to drink the leftovers in the cans. It's true that the best things in life are free.

I'm guessing around five or six hours later was when I was rudely awakened by being violently thrashed about in the cart until it crashed into something that propelled me out onto the grass. My face was coated in dirt. I rolled over onto my back, where the tangerine stained sky came into view. I rose up to my feet, adding Grandpa to the scene, gawking at me with that lengthened smile. I tackled him to the ground, slapping him in the face, open palmed, multiple times. That evened us out to a satisfactory limit. I pushed myself off of him, realizing that we were back at the place with an inventory of cars. I moved inside and slapped down another wad of cash before we made our getaway in a big van. There were cops in the corner, interrogating a suspect, but they paid no attention to me. Who would suspect a child of such a ruthless act as tearing the leg off an employee? The van wasn't extremely smart, cost wise, but think of all the stuff that could be packed inside of it. We were going cross-country. I needed plenty of space for all of my trash and money. It reminded me that the first stop we had to make before going on our voyage was home to acquire the rest of the money. When we got to our living quarters, all of the doors were obstructed by yellow crime scene tape. Somebody had invaded our privacy by breaking into our house without permission. The investigators were still inside, but I had to fetch the currency somehow so that we could get out of town fast. I was the master of disguise, though, so I knew that I could construct a plan of some sort. I whisked my lovely behind down to the costume shop with the intention of purchasing some tall boots, a fake mustache, and an undertaker costume. After I obtained the items that I traveled blocks for, I went back into the house. I entered our place from the back way. As it turned out, I bought the costume for nothing; nobody was even watching the place anymore.

I snatched the money quickly along with some solution for my eye. Just as I was evacuating through the back door, I heard something advancing up the driveway. I swiftly crashed through the neighbor's wooden fence, not even attempting to leapfrog it. I acted as my own surveillance camera, searching for the vehicle. Of course, it reversed out of the driveway to park in front of the house. I swung like a monkey from tree to tree to the van. Realistically, I just skipped foot by foot to the van, because that way it seemed like I was an innocent little kid just having fun if they saw me. I would've swung from the trees, but it would've looked suspicious. We took off in the van leisurely until we got far enough away to pick up some eatables. Five miles and twelve tacos later, we were equipped to hit the highway.

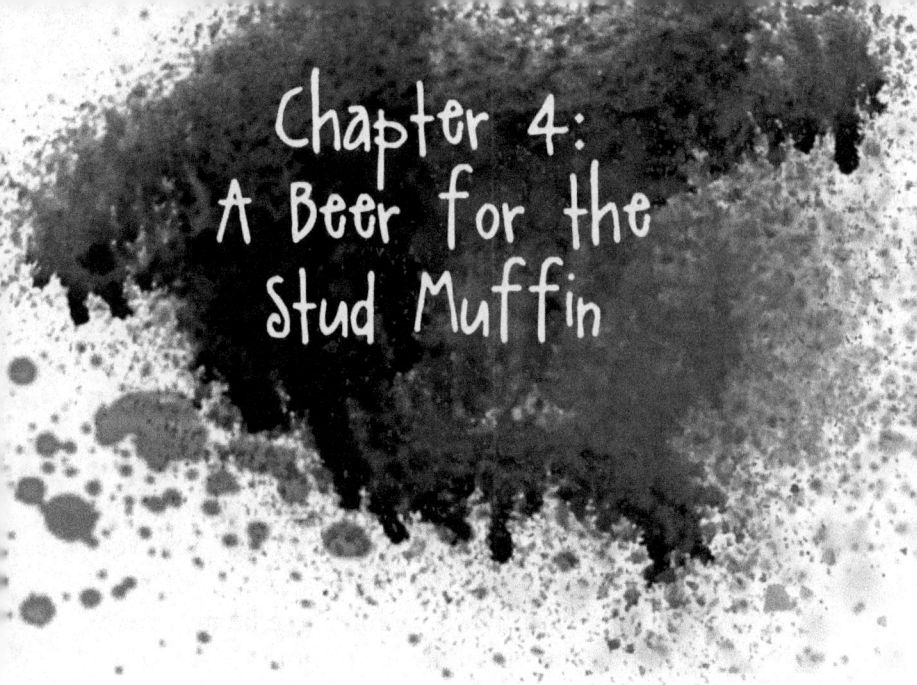

Chapter 4:
A Beer for the
Stud Muffin

It would be an especially long road trip if you factored in the bathroom breaks that I needed to take consistently because of the indents in the roads. We had to go from Burlington, Vermont (my hometown of great waters and Canadian neighbors, eh), all the way over to Oregon to find out what city Olaf was located in. That was if we didn't get eradicated by some suicidal guy that came from Seattle to take someone, who also had a meaningless life, with him. We reached the exit ramp to get onto the interstate, heading towards Montpelier. I was going to try to stick to the highways to camouflage us in the mass quantities of automobiles.

As soon as we reached the speed limit on the highway, the van shook like a kid with rabies. I inserted the only CD that I owned for the trip into the player: Europe's "The Final Countdown". Grandpa loathed it, since it was "heavy metal", but I didn't care, being that it was the only thing that could ever get me motivated to do something that big. If you were wondering how I could pull off an extended drive like that without anyone comprehending that I was only a child, lets just say that I had a great contact in the mustache dealing business. You couldn't even perceive how many mustaches I had that proved to be illegal in all of the 50 states. Driving down the road, you will find many different makes of them, but none of them will ever compare to mine in quality. It had been measured to the exact millimeter in width along with length. The hair was hand picked from the finest conditioned scalps in the world.

Anyway, that is enough about my intimidating mustache. I was taking the cruise of my life when we ended up getting stuck in the worst traffic jam of my two-day driving record. It was problematic being stuck around the same cars for a long period of time, because it was only a matter of minutes before they started to suspect something. Certain citizens could care less, but the others were those people that live to screw up other people's lives. We were in the middle of Montpelier. I drank too many refreshments, and my bladder was about to let loose after squirming about consistently in the front seat. The male that was coasting along beside us for some reason wouldn't stop taunting me about how he could see me. Wow, it takes a real man to see another man and not stop staring at him. I gave him the "I'm sick of you staring at me and if you don't stop I will cut open your abdomen, wrap your intestines around the axle of your car while you're tied to a tree, and I will drive your car away" look. After the traffic cleared up, the guy continued to follow us with no indication of letting up. The gauge in the van read that we were on empty, so we had to stop for gas soon because of the beast that we were driving. I said, "Screw it." We had to do what we had to do. We pulled over at the least lousy gas station that we could discover that still had six cars at the pumps since we were stranded in the center of town. I retreated from the van, making a beeline directly for this guy; I just wanted to get everything straightened out. Anyway, my Grandpa had my back, but, when I glanced back, Gramps wasn't there. He was next to the station, inspecting the innards of a garbage can. I guess motion sickness still affected a guy whose smell equaled the inside of an unplugged fridge.

I was on my own for that one. The stalker apathetically got out of his car, slicking his hair back before placing his hat on top of his melon. He looked like a giant compared to what I thought he was, definitely around six and half feet tall. It startled me for the simple fact that he could rip my spleen out with his pinky. He marched up to me with a pissed-off expression on his face telling me that I had a nice mustache. I was astonished, not because I thought it sucked, but because this guy followed us a long stretch of tar just to disclose that I had a nice mustache. Just how everything else seemed strange in the world, something had to be wrong. He spoke of a luxurious bar down the road. If we came with him to the bar, he stated that he would get us drunk to the point of vomiting, or else it was just puking. I wasn't quite sure. I asked him to hold onto his panties for a second as I ran inside to pay for the gas and to drain my mealworm.

When I returned, we tailgated him for a couple of blocks until we parked in the dust in front of pint-sized bar, where only the locals would go. According to the sign outside, the place was called "Big Johns Oats". We trailed behind the strange mustache loving man into the bar. The front door was guarded by a buff man who was checking ID's. He asked for my identification. Without it, he wouldn't let me in. I explained to him that I didn't have it on me. I confessed to him that I forgot it in the last bar that I was at on accident, due to me getting plastered at numerous bars all the time. I didn't sense that he believed me, because he was getting ready to force me to leave. Well, the mustache lover (let's just call him "Musty" – that's pronounced moostee) pointed out my mustache to the guard, questioning if he seriously thought that I was underage when I had a bushy one like that. The guard of the forbidden door agreed, because a mustache couldn't possibly look that good on a "youngin". When Gramps passed the guard, he muffled something about how Grandpa could go in because he looked like someone called Old Man Time, whoever that was.

When we passed the entrance into the bar, there were three people inside, all with beer bellies, sitting on cushioned stools by themselves. The only human interaction that those individuals had was with the bartender and their bottles. We seated ourselves in the farthest corner next to one of the singletons that was drinking alone. Everyone called him Fruit Cocktail, seeing that he only indulged himself with the girl drinks. I plopped down next to Musty while Gramps seated himself alongside Fruit Cocktail.

He proceeded to offer to buy Gramps screaming orgasms and sex on the beaches. Grandpa never accepted one of them because he would only drink plain beer – not even light beer, nothing but the original. I, on the other hand, would down any thirst quencher (or anything non poisonous) that I received without charge. I had an attachment to drinking anything that was free. I even guzzled an economy size barbeque sauce once, just because someone offered it to me. I began my alcohol binge with an average beer. I have consumed some disgusting things in my lifetime, but that was misery juice. I had to choke down every sip of it. Fortunately, I had a regular soda that I ordered to rinse out most of the repulsive taste. By then, I was already feeling kind of indisposed and dizzy, yet I was still offered more intoxicating fluids. Musty clued me in that if I added a pinch of rum to my cola, it would taste a hell of a lot more desirable. I figured sure, what was there to lose? What I had to lose was about a pint of stomach acid through my mouth. The corroded chunks flew, spreading across the counter. It crept towards the customers as they dodged out of the way, eventually it dribbled off the sides pooling on the hardwood floor. That was when the bartender decided to cut me off from my alcohol-inflicted addiction. I didn't even consider paying any attention to Grandpa through the whole ordeal, but, when I gazed over to him, he had a blue drink in a behemoth wine glass with an umbrella sticking out of it in his arthritic hands. I had a sneaking suspicion that once you tried it, you had to buy it. I began feeling normal again thanks to the projectile vomiting that I was coaxed into previously. But on the other side of this two-man crew, Grandpa was becoming a tad tipsy.

He was babbling on to each person about his days back in Vietnam along with displaying his affection for everyone. There was a gentleman exhibiting a winter jacket across the room, playing a solo game of pool. Grandpa strolled over, challenging him to a game. Winner took $50. I wasn't sure if Gramps could even fathom how to play pool. I mean, did they have pool back in the 1940's? The gentleman slapped his $25 on the turf that shielded the table. When Grandpa put his fruit stained bills down, there was no turning back. It appeared to be the most excitement that the bar had seen in a long time, being that all of the patrons indoors crowded around the table to watch. All six of us stood around the table, conversing about nothing as the match was about to get underway. Winter jacket man won the coin toss by calling heads. It was as if the balls were magnetically attracted to the pockets, judging by how many went in, one after the other. He didn't miss a single shot until his final shot to sink the 8 ball. Just as he advanced his stick onward to bump the cue ball, Gramps screamed out that the guy's fly was down in a piercing slurred voice. The man's eyes strayed to his zipper while he continued at a forward motion with his stick. He missed the shot by a mile, hitting the 8 ball into the wrong corner pocket. It meant that Grandpa had reigned victorious. Needless to say, the guy was pissed, since his fly wasn't really unfastened.

He started "Project: Shoving Grandpa Around"; that didn't sit well with Gramps. Gramps wasn't one to take crap from anyone, notably someone that he wasn't even acquainted with. The next time that he tried to shove Gramps, he landed his hand in a vice of soft dead meat. Gramps dragged him across the floor, back to the pool table, cramming Winter Coat's hand, wrist deep, into the corner pocket with the 8 ball. With Winter Coat's left hand, he took a crack at punching Gramps. Grandpa captured that hand, also sticking it into the opposite corner pocket. So Winter Coat was helplessly lying there, back side up, with both hands in the pockets of the table. Gramps got up onto the table placing the sole of his boot on the back of his cranium. He told Winter Coat that if he couldn't take a joke, then he would have to take the pain. Grandpa applied the pain leisurely by pushing his face into the table, accompanied by releasing the pressure from his boot a pinch. It was his example of how to torture another.

Every time that he hoisted his boot up, it came down slightly harder. Each time, more blood trickled from the pockets along with more gargling noises coming from Winter Coat's face. His breath bubbled, since it was immersed in crimson hemoglobin. Eventually, the noise's ceased to exist, but the blood kept exiting the orifices. The fuzzy carpeting on the pool table morphed from green to red, everywhere. Still, Gramps wouldn't let up. I fashioned a blockade out of my body, hoping to hold the populace back as they comprehended that it wasn't a brawl, it was a slaying. Big John Oat threw his oatmeal cookie to the terrain, making his way towards Gramps at a startling pace. I halted Oat by throwing all the pool balls at him. The 4 ball struck him smack dab in the jaw, knocking him onto the floor, comatose, or so I presumed. He elevated himself to his original stance in his oat stained overalls, approaching me, irritated by my defense. I surveyed the area, struggling to find anything that I could use to stop Oat with so that I didn't have to meet my demise that day. There was a hamburger (but that wouldn't work because there were no oats involved), a barstool (which might've worked, but, if a pool ball to the face didn't do anything, then a barstool was a bit questionable), and then I observed a shotgun that was fastened to the wall. I snatched it off the wall, ordering him not to move or I would shoot. He gave me the same line that everybody did when you threaten them with their own gun. There were no bullets loaded in the chamber is what I was informed. Except, that time, the enemy was right, because, when I pulled the trigger, the only thing that emerged was a click. No boom or big giant gaping chest wound, just a click. He had the laugh of Santa Clause, going on as he proceeded towards me, holding his belly, like a garbage bag brimming with douche.

At that instant, I was thigh deep in the survival instincts that I theorized learning in school, but I guess I forgot them. Big John Oat was three hops, skips, and a jump away from me when I rammed the barrel of the gun right into his mouth while he was in the middle of a sentence. The barrel broke through his teeth, placing white shards amongst the blood on his gums. It protruded out of the back of his skull, getting brain matter stuck inside the barrel. I shook the goop out of the tubes that delivered bullets when I extracted the gun from his mouth. Having no witnesses of the incident was a requirement. There were still four other innocent testifiers in the building fixated on Grandpa's butchery, so, most likely, everyone was still stationed there. I went over to the front door, lodging a worn wooden door stop underneath it so that nobody could gain entry or vacate the building. Gramps was still occupied with stomping on Winter Coat's head that was no longer a cranium. Instead, it resembled more of a discolored custard. Most of his thoughts were lodged against the sole of Grandpa's shoe. I came creeping up behind two of the innocents, conking their noggins together. The other two were staring at Grandpa, concentrating to the point where they couldn't pay attention to what had happened to the persons standing directly beside them. I had a sneaking suspicion that they didn't think that I posed much of a threat. I assumed that I would have to show them who was boss. I captured Musty by the hair, dragging him into the little boy's room. I appointed him with a swirley; the difference between my swirley and the original was that I didn't flush the toilet while doing it. I passed the time by stationing myself on top of the toilet seat while Musty's head was stuck in the freshly bleached toilet bowl. It was hardly a minute before his body quit twitching. I'm not sure if it was due to inhaling too much toilet water into his lungs or not being able to breathe from having his windpipe crushed when it was pressed up against the rim harshly. All I had to do was finish off the last individual, and we could be home free. Or should I say Oregon free? I think that was what I meant; it was not like I had an infinite amount of time to think about it. I scrambled out of the bathroom stall to acquire the last man standing, except Grandpa had already gotten to him. The mere mortal was lying on the floor with multi-colored darts lodged into different depths of his stomach. I imagined that it his belly button must have been the bull's-eye.

The last steps on the imaginary list were at hand. Make an escape and hide the bodies where a local drunk coming in for a visit couldn't see them. We resolved to carry them all into the kitchen so that we could fetch a prompt snack too. Once we got to the back, we overheard some footsteps scampering in the main area. After a hop, skip, and a jump, I was in the same opening where the sounds were created. I made it in time to spy a guy dashing across the room, only to leave an imprint of his face in the door. He must've been taking shelter in an adjoining stall in the bathroom. Gramps and I each took a leg, transporting him to the kitchen. He was kicking and screaming from the rug burn that must've been shredding his skin. He clenched the floor with his fingers for dear life, only to add more tribulation by breaking his nails off in the carpet. It took more energy than it should've to haul him into the kitchen. I busted him over the head with a glass bottle, sending tiny brown fragments into the atmosphere. I took the remaining bottle, using the jagged edge to penetrate the uppermost slab of his scalp. When he passed out from massive blood loss, Gramps clenched his head and twisted it around a couple of times until it popped off. Grandpa placed his teeth against the bottle top as he began drinking all of the syrup that was coming out. I assumed that brain juice was way better than OJ, but I wasn't about to try a sample.

We pitched the remainder of the Bathroom Man's carcass on top of the stockpile of human corpses that we were constructing. Gramps continued to enjoy his beverage straight from the gourd until the pile started to stir. It totally escaped my mind that I had never sacrificed the first two men. I had only administered them with the action-titled unconscious. Thankfully, we hadn't abandoned that location when we were planning on it. Both of the noses of the future casualties were scrunched against the tile on the bottom of the mound, so I relaxed on top of it until they drowned in the blood that was collecting at the base. The only way that I was going to reach the certainty of being safe was to be positive that all of them were dead, and I thought that numerous bodies equaled a tremendous bundle of free food. I ruled to split the food with Gramps, since I knew it benefited him by maintaining his strength. Being that there was a grill there, I was going to pig out, knowing that cooked human was better than a delicacy. Plus, if we devoured all of the bodies, we couldn't be convicted. The police can't identify the assailant by the victim's bones.

I grilled up my half of the cold meat on the griddle that must've been built by Jesus himself. In the meantime, Gramps strangled whichever part of the body that he could get his hands on molding it into mush. After the guts dumped out, he would slurp them up off of the floor. Black streaks were stranded on the tile, intertwined with the original blood color of a normal human. I had a scarce number of standards, but I wasn't about to willingly eat a raw cadaver. It was unacceptable that a toasted stiff was emerging as my regular meal. It made it better that I assembled mine into some sort of conventional meal, such as a hamburger or a roast beef sandwich fit for a foreign dictator, or a fat kid.

We were done consuming the nutrients some-time near dusk, but there was still housekeeping to be completed. The stains needed to be lifted from the main room. We got on our hands and knees as we scrubbed the stains out of the carpet, sending the leftover anatomy into the trash. It was a hell of a responsibility, but the payoff of not being confiscated by the police was worth it. They're a genuine boil in the ass to ditch once they desire you, which kind of makes them comparable to the peanut butter that fuses to your throat, after being pleased by a peanut butter and corn sandwich. At least that was what I repeatedly witnessed on the TV, except on the small screen, the people's faces were always blurry. I haven't ever spotted anyone with a blurry face walking down the street in my everyday life, but I wasn't about to take any chances. I snatched a hammer to sever the doorstop from under the door. I used the nail ejector on the rear to break it after finishing all of our cleaning duties to make the place look virginal. We stepped out of there, squeaky clean, not having to fret about our daily bread for a couple additional hours.

Chapter 5:
Doctors are Nothing but Liars and Crooks

I drove the vehicle back onto the highway, commuting at the permissible speed limit to be supremely safe. Gramps was in the passenger seat, snacking on finger foods, which on this occurrence actually happened to be fingers. It seemed like we were on the manufactured pavement forever. My leg was becoming inflexible along with my tummy that was getting all rumbly. The next thing that I made out was a sign that read "Boston - 5 miles". That couldn't have been correct unless I had a mishap, by-passing an exit or something, which wasn't conceivable on the account that I don't make mistakes, the sign must've been wrong. The next city we ran into was Boston, so I guess the city made a mistake by being there. Maybe I should've paid more attention in study group about east, west, and all that other illogicalness that I didn't think would ever matter. Since we were basically in the city, I reached the decision that we would go inside to find some place for me to score my forty winks. I pulled up to the front door of a luxurious hotel that Gramps swore was unnecessary. He suggested that we conserve our money and score our shuteye in the automotive. I refused to sleep in an air-tight vehicle with an oddity that reeked of fish sticks.

Later that night, I was making an effort of sleeping with my seat slouched back when I heard the window fragmentize next to me. The solid door opened as I was thrown from the driver's seat to the concrete. The engine was initiated as the van took off down the street with Grandpa remaining within it. The masked man who stole it probably didn't notice him in the backseat. Before the block even ended, the van started swerving from side to side until it entirely lost control, launching summersaults that eventually caused the van to catch fire in mid flight, altering it into a monstrous fireball. I sprinted down the roadway to ensure that Gramps was okay, but it evolved into a shuffle about midway there. When I got up to the van, Gramps was crouched over the burglar, mashing up his organs through the ventilated lesion in his thorax, while Grandpa's spinal column sustained its burning nature. I sensed that the cops and the ambulances were coming, considering that the wailing of the sirens was progressing. I took my best shot at wrenching Grandpa away from the mangled carrion, but he wouldn't budge. The ambulance delivered the stretchers to us just as I got Gramps to discard his grasp from the stiff. They wheeled us both away on stretchers. It took a total of four medics to elevate me when it only took two to raise Gramps up. They placed us in separate emergency vehicles so that they could interrogate us to get the truth out. I illustrated to them how I was propelled from the van, so I, in all factuality, didn't see what had occurred. All that I perceived was a mountainous fireball with a side of roasted Grandpa. I wasn't sure what Grandpa would state had happened, which they wouldn't inform me of either. It must've not been too far to the hospital since we arrived there a piddling number of minutes later. After a brief examination on me was done, I was stuck in the waiting room while Gramps was sent to the intensive burn unit.

I was educated that it would take at a minimum of a couple weeks in the hospital until we would be qualified to leave. Gramps had 3rd degree burns blanketing his body. The doctor's were perplexed as to how he hadn't perished yet. They were discussing how that in an abundance of locations the bone was sticking out of his structure. The doctor had done tests on him "confirming" that he wasn't taking in oxygen along with not having a heartbeat, yet he was still moving around fully conscious. They wanted to run more examinations on him before they would discharge us from the building. I figured that if I had time to kill, I might as well replace the good-for-nothing eye that I had. I forgot that the money went through the blaze in the van. I couldn't afford it if I didn't have the payment in my possession. I asked the nurse at the front desk if the medics had unearthed any belongings of ours in the van. Thank Jehovah that the money was sealed in a fireproof case that the rescue squad had toted in with them. I was off to get my eye transplant. I dug in my bag to retrieve the red and yellow vampire eye that I had invested in for Gramps. I was certain that he wouldn't take offense if I used it, being that he didn't need it anyway. The nurse and I went into the elevator, traveling up ten flights, to floor twenty-two. There was a formation of eyeless people in line. Some of the eyeballs were still drooping out of their sockets, but some of the inhabitants were respectful enough to cover them up. I seated my tushy down in the discrete seats, and I was stranded next to a meathead that had badly damaged his eye. It would've been fine had he not picked so deep into the socket; also, he didn't shut up. The conversation starter was communicating something about how his eye was still intact; it was just that he was fatigued, which caused it to become irritated. I didn't presume that as fact, considering that his socket was emanating puss near the inside corner, while his eye on the flipside was puffed out farther than it should've been. It sickened me how every so often I had to glance at him to act like I actually cared about what he was repeating. "Blah, blah, blah, I'm a moron." That's all that I ever heard escape his respiratory system.

Nobody else in the entire room was chattering with each other. How come I had to be situated next to the lunkhead that was dumber than a box of socks – dirty ones, too. Twenty minutes later, after masquerading like I had fallen asleep, he finally retired from annoying me. He was beckoned by the doctor to come in. Hopefully, I was saved from him for the remainder of my miserable life. After hours of harassment, I was assured that I was next up to get my uncontaminated eye. A few short moments later, they announced my name as I migrated up to the desk. I had forgotten to fill out my form, so they delayed my appointment until I finished filling it out. I was horrid at spelling along with reading, so I had to have the woman next to me help me out. I was blessed that she was friendly and had vision in one of her eyes. Her husband was there, too, assuring her that she would be all right through the exhaustive operation. I wished that I had someone who would do that for me, but Gramps would remark that only women needed help, not men. I knew that his statements were false because he was never right. She was a strong woman, so I felt certain that she didn't need support. But, I, on the other hand, needed a lot since I was a big baby. I was crying a large body of water, while kicking and screaming, when they summoned my name this time. I finally realized that they were going to carve my eyeball out of the socket with a scalpel, abandoning me with a gaping hole in my face until they plunked the artificial one in. I understand how that would make me a teeny bit uncomfortable.

When I got into the room, I was told by the nurse to lie down on the table that was topped with a white cushion. She removed the undie patch that was over my eye before getting this horrified expression on her face. She questioned how long my wound had gone untreated. I didn't even know anymore. Everyday resembled every other day, only with different lives being taken. The nurse chaperoned a mirror over to me so that I could inspect what my eye had altered into. My pupil was clouded over while the white of my eye was filled in with a yellowish type color. I dared myself to poke it to see if I had any sensation left in it. I totally forgot that there was something defective with it until that day. I smoothly caressed my eye with my finger. The result was not fatal, but my eyeball shriveled into a raisin, while a substance consisting of yellow suds spurted out of the gap. It should've administered agonizing pain on me, but it didn't. It was feasible that it didn't hurt, because that department of my body was already dead.

The nurse cringed, about to lose her cookies, as she rushed out of the room to snag a qualified doctor. My eye was suspended from a thread, hanging out of the socket, just like those people that I stated had no respect for others earlier. Three doctors paraded into the examination room all with shots the size of knitting needles. I suspected that they were planning on putting me under. I refused that option since I could take the pain. I requested that they numb me instead, considering that I'd heard stories previously where the surgeons put you under so they could do their damn-dest to molest you. I didn't yearn for that to happen to me, because I was so fragile. I was confident that they would try to carry out a scheme like that on me since I was so sexy. They agreed after only a couple of death threats to give me the numbing elixir. They injected two needles into me. With one, they stuck me in the temple. With the spare, they shot me up on the inside of my eye next to my nose. The needles outright delved into my tissue as they wiggled them around before tearing them out. They allowed it a couple of seconds to take effect, making me change into a hospital gown before they got their utensils dirty. They opened the surgery by taking a pair of puny scissors to snip my eye from the void from which it came. After that was a success, they began to scrape out the rest of the remaining eye goop. As I observed intently with my opposite eye, I could see the yellow liquid squir-ting on the doctor's hands along with his protective eyewear. I watched as the film slowly changed from yellow to red. As soon as the fluid turned red, they welded the wound shut to reduce the blood loss. They scrubbed down the lint-covered eye that I had been keeping in my pocket before they popped it in. The surgeon's imparted that I would be in excruciating pain for a couple of weeks until the wound healed up. They took a cheap shot by torturing me with a shot that would put me to sleep. I forced myself to get up so that I could put up a fight, but I plummeted to the cold floor, out for the count.

When I awoke, I was dressed in my street attire in an empty room that was so sanitary that it was impossible to conceive that it had ever been used. I knew that it wasn't an operating room at all. It was the place that they transferred the patients to when they wanted to feel them up. My blood began to boil. If anyone was going to violate my figure, then they should've consulted me first or executed it while I was on guard. At least, then, I would have enough proof that I got some action. When the doctor entered the room, I provided him with what he had coming to him. I made it known to him that I gave them no permission whatsoever to use my physique for their own sick and twisted fantasies. He claimed that in no way did he even consider touching me in anyway, so I believed him. The doctor had me follow him into his office to discuss how the operation had gone. I was informed that there were some minor things that went awry with the procedure. We ventured down the long hall where every inch of the structure looked duplicated until we got inside his headquarters. It was a freakishly plain office for a seasoned doctor. All there was in the room was a desk that was matchlessly cheap with a wooden school chair on each side. There wasn't a thing on the walls, not even a diploma or his license to practice medicine. It made me a tad uneasy that I was recently sliced up by a man that wouldn't even display those papers. I questioned him as to why he didn't have those on the wall. The "doctor" disclosed to me that it was because he wasn't a legitimate doctor yet. The hospital was a hellhole where they sent the trainees to learn how to carve up the mortals. That would've explained why the ambulance failed to turn on its emergency lights when it picked us up. It was not like we were bankrupt or anything. They could've taken us to an authentic medical center.

As the "doctor" had mentioned before, the operation didn't quite go as planned, he reminded me. My eye was heavily infected, they tried to discard all of the infectious matter from within, but they couldn't. They were unsure how much longer I had to keep my vital signs, because the infection soon would span through the remainder of my cranium, which would eventually kill me. This made my hopes and dreams scarce. There was so much stuff that I still yearned to do (for example, like participating in a chili-tasting contest, trying out to be a sumo wrestler, and watching every episode of "Guts"). I was too young to die. I was not the happiest little boy at that instant. The "doctor" instructed me to calm down by walking it off. As I was following his instructions, he punctured me with another needle that broke off in my neck as I scampered away. I stabbed the other end of the needle into my palm when I attempted to relieve some of the pressure from the wound. I banged my head against the door, falling over as I tried to open it. I woke up in a room identical to the one that I was operated in. Only this time I wasn't willing to delay for a doctor. I got up, without hesitation, bolting for the knob that led to my escape. I bid the room farewell as I moved on to the hallway. It appeared to be the same as it did before, only I didn't spot any inhabitants around. I hooked myself around the next corner where I spied all of the workers huddled in a circle, gossiping. I yanked myself back behind the corner to steer clear of trouble. They were chitchatting about a specimen that was in the hospital that none of the doctors could get a reading on. It was supposedly deceased but still up and moving about. It didn't take long for me to decipher who they were talking about. A big man in a business suit was claiming that he was going to get into contact with another character, higher up, so this fellow, with a secret identity, could come down to sort everything out. That may not be a good thing. My mission was then to explore the lower levels of the facility, searching for Gramps to get him the hell out of there. I had to dig inside my cranium to remember what floor he was on; I had nothing.

I wandered around; exploring an over exagg-erated fifty hallways, I turned up with zilch. I asked people around the hospital that consisted of nurses, doctors, and anyone that I anticipated would've had a tip to where my Grandpa was. Nobody knew. It was as if he had dematerialized out of the atmosphere. I began another expedition, tearing every hallway inside out, while calling his name, but still I found nothing. Even though I gave up on my spree, the security continued to pursue me, commanding me to come with them, but I disapproved of that idea until I found out my Gran-dpa's whereabouts. They carried me away, throwing me in a locked room with a couple of secure chairs that were screwed into the floor. I spent a lot of down time in there before I even identified another life form. Then two businessmen arrived, asking me a collection of questions, wondering who my Grandpa was. They asked why, if he came to that spot with me, how come nobody knew who I was speaking about. I was getting really peeved off. Somebody in existence had to have observed something. I snagged the one gentlemen's ballpoint pen, which he was conveniently using to write in his notepad with, shoving it into the core of his chest. He plummeted to the polished floor, grabbing the pen, struggling to pull it out, only to have his hands slip on the liquid, leaving a bloody handprint on his face from slapping himself. I progressed from the table to his side to stomp the pen the rest of the way in his chest with the heel of my shoe. Once the blood dripped from out of his orifices, I knew that it was time to finish off the other enemy. I apprehended the other gentleman, pressing my thumb up against his throat. His skin sunk in as I told him that he better squeal to me where my Grandpa was or that I would assassinate him too. He revealed to me that he didn't have information on where Gramps was at, but that it was somewhere on the 14th floor, between rooms 1426 and 1430. Of course, I strangled the bastard to termination anyway, because he shouldn't have aided such a mean and hurtful plan in the first place.

I wasn't even sure what level I was on at the time or how to glide past everyone to the 14th floor while exploring every one of the rooms when I got there for any indication of Gramps. There was a vent in the ceiling that I could presumably crawl through without being spotted by the masses. I stacked the bodies on top of the desk to form a stepstool. I was barely able to reach the vent even when I stood on the most towering point. I unlatched the side of the vent, pulling myself into its innards. It was too much work for a boy of my stature, which was why I needed a stunt double. There were also too many years of relishing myself with ham sandwiches that went straight to my bottomless pit, not into my biceps to generate tons of man muscle. But, following a high volume of struggle, I made it up there without anyone noticing. As I gained entry to the air conditioning vent, a handful of persons rushed in the room. I guess they must've overheard all of the bawling and shrieking (took them long enough, huh?). They all went racing out the entryway, instructing the others to sweep the area. They were making an effort to find me as soon as possible. The guidelines included bringing me back alive. At least, they didn't want me inanimate, or else if they caught me once more, it might've made it slightly complicated to get away. Little did they know that I was a genius. I wouldn't be hanging out in the hallway when people were searching for me. Most of all, I wouldn't do it after I had performed something so naughty. I squeezed my sweaty behind through an opening in the air duct where I was able to catch my breath. I peered through the grate, locating an elevator that only had a down button next to it.

My perception viewed that as a splendid situation. Then I took a moment to think it through; it really wasn't a neato burrito thing. I realized that it meant that I was on the floor below the roof as fudge nuggets would have it. I was going to need something to moisten my vitals, since I was already sweating out more water than a thirty-five gallon fish tank. But I would just have to deal with it for that period of my existence until I ran across a drinking fountain. I squirmed farther and farther down the aluminum passageway, and my migration became easier and easier, as I virtually slid down the shafts. It might've been because I took off my shirt, due to of all the heat, and exposed my perspired body to the walls. As I was coasting along on my way to find my decrepit old Grandpa, I almost tumbled into a drop that was straight down. Just when I thought that I was fine and wasn't going anywhere, I descended appropriately into that same downward air duct. I was snappy enough to snare one of my hands on the ledge before I altogether fell down. I was left dangling by one hand with my body flapping against the cold aluminum. (Surprisingly, it was a nice change after sweating down to dehydration.) I reached for the ledge with my free arm, grappling onto the freezing surface, striving to pull myself back up. The weight of me together with the condensation that coated my hands was just too great for me to manage. If I plummeted to my demise, at least I could say that I gave it my best shot. My fingers would've slipped, one by one, had I not purely given up letting myself go. I descended swiftly down about two floors, which would've been painful had my ass not cushioned the fall. I heard everyone around chattering, wondering if something recently had detonated in the building. Nope. It was just me: King Twinkie. I was astonished that the whole damn shaft didn't come down with me.

While I glimpsed through a neighboring vent, I observed that I was on floor sixteen. Either the structure wasn't that towering, or I had zoned out while falling. Either way, I was within a closer range to get to where I needed to be than I was before. An inconsiderable span down the way was a vent underneath my position. I calculated that if I could get out through that skinny grate to yank the fire alarm that was established on the wall, then maybe I would have a piddling chunk of people to evade. Then I could do it effortlessly and take the stairs down the rest of the way. I made it to the grate where I discovered that it was screwed shut from the reverse side. I didn't exactly have my tool kit on the opposite side or a servant to unscrew it, so I was literally screwed. Maybe if I held up for the perfect time when there was lots of racket, I could simply kick it open. There must've been a janitor's closet next to me or a wood shop class, considering that it sounded like a hammer that was banging on metal. I guess whenever would've been an appropriate time then; nobody would've even noticed.

I administered to the vent one kick. At the exact same time, a pedestrian strolled by. I seem to have the worst of luck. The grate snapped off its hinges, clipping the guy in the ankle, which caused him to topple through the open door to the stairs. I had to be prompt before someone discovered me, so I whisked myself away to the fire alarm. I pulled down on the lever until the annoying siren went off. I darted back to my newest hiding spot (another vent), waiting for the public to pass by and go down the stairs so that I could make my move. After approximately ten minutes, I ducked out of the shadows to stop at the water cooler, seeking bland refreshment. After my distasteful treat, I began to maneuver to the stairs when I was blocked by a man in a dirty jumpsuit.

I shouted at him to let him know that he better get a move on it. I disclosed to him that there was an inferno in the building. Furthermore, I heard that it wasn't amusing to be burned alive. He recognized who I was; I could tell by the look in his eyes. I found it to be no problem to read the bad looks from the good looks; it definitely wasn't a good one. I attempted to dash back into the vent, but I only made it partway in before his hand enclosed on my calf. I stomped him all over his face, yet he still would not release his grip. He eventually dragged me out, flipping me onto my back. My posterior was burning from it being tugged across the itchy carpet. He grabbed me by my hair, bringing me to my feet. He motivated me to walk away from my location to somewhere that wasn't even remotely close to where I wanted to be. As this sorry prick was lugging me down the hallway, I expanded my arm out trying to hook anything that would be of use to me. My hand ran into a picture frame of a kick-ass sailboat. When I used to take baths, I had this roomy steamboat; I wouldn't scrub myself without it. My army men would travel across the ocean on it to deliver new fatigues to Barbie. When I say fatigues, I really mean pick-up lines to hit on Barbie. Anyway, I took that large painted frame and bashed the corner of it into the janitor's chest. It shattered the glass along with splitting the frame in half. I wasn't afraid of that homosapien. It was not like he was going to try to execute me or anything. He attained a screwdriver from the utility belt that he was wearing crooked around his gut. It was disclosed to me that he was instructed to leave me with vital signs. He could still destroy the remainder of my body as long as I could speak. Well, damn, that left me in a concrete pit of misfortune. I started throwing a barrage of glass from the frame, saving the biggest shards for last. None of the fragments affected the guy, but, then again, my aim was horrible. I don't believe that the glass even made contact with him. When he lurched himself closer, I snatched a colossal piece of glass, waiting for him to make his move.

When the janitor reached me, he took a swing at my throat with a screwdriver. It was a wide swing from the right. When he was in mid swing, I parried, stabbing the sharp shard into a vein inside of his arm. It dismembered a nice portion out of the innermost region of his elbow. He gripped his arm, striving to seal his blood loss with his fingers as he fell to the grimy carpet like a big baby. I noticed that I had an incision on my pinky finger, so I had to cutoff my daily life to suck on it for a second. I towered over the janitor as he lay on the floor becoming pale. I explained to him that I had no choice but to do what I had to. I bound him in electrical cord, locking him in his own closet. I couldn't outright kill a man that put up an honorable rumble, especially while he was laying there relatively lifeless. That would not be proper, even for someone with standards as low as mine.

I made my way back down the hallway to the stairs. The hall was littered with debris from people who had gone into a panic over nothing. Fire alarms have always been taken way too seriously. I made my way down the ultra shiny stairs, watching out for wet floor signs. There were dozens of trampled remains that I had to tiptoe around or tread on to get down the two levels that I needed to go. I wandered aimlessly about the floor that Grandpa lingered on to find the room that he was parked in. There was one last hallway that had gone unturned. It was lit by only a single, flickering, non fiber optic light bulb. Since it was the final one that I needed to go down, I took my time going appropriately slow until I heard people crowding the halls once more. They must've waited long enough to predict that it was safe to gain entry to the medical center again. I rushed to the end of the hall, sheltering myself inside a randomly selected room. It was not like I needed to hide anyway, because I don't think that anyone had been down there for a long time, judging by the thickness of the dust particles on everything that I touched.

The room that I accessed was pitch black inside. I couldn't catch a glimpse of anything, so I had to feel around for the light switch. I couldn't find it anywhere. Every second that shed while I looked for it, the more intense a noise in the background got, almost like a low groaning sound as if someone were dying. I finally found the switch a foot from the ground, along one of the other walls. The light powered on, revealing that there was a bed that was occupied by a man who was attempting to rest. He was twitching uncontrollably in distress under the clean white sheets. I scurried over to him just to get a better observation of what the hell was wrong with him. His face was stitched together with what appeared to be scraps of other humans. I shifted the covers to the bottom of the bed, showing that the rest of his decayed form beyond the collarbone didn't exist. Just molded sheets with a pair of mangled ribs, but that was it. Not even a skeleton, which would've ruled out the verdict that it wasn't skinned alive. At the foot of the bed, there was a huge battery that was running jumper cables up to his ribs. It must've been low on juice, so it only powered him enough to jolt around.

The doctors, I imagine, were making their own trial version of a living dead guy or something. Maybe that was why all of those evildoers were holding my Grandpa prisoner. Something happened to him by misfortune that they had perhaps been struggling to decipher for a period of time. Whatever the creature was, he had to have been in an extreme magnitude of pain. I had to put it out of its misery.

I unplugged it from the battery, anticipating that it would cease to live, but, instead, it began to breathe on its own – just slower than before. The groans that it composed had increased in volume, so I had to cover his mouth to muffle the sounds. I deposited as much of his own blanket in his mouth as I could. I pried open the window with my broken fingernails. It was there that I tossed the inhuman creature out, watching him fall to the pavement. His bone fragments fractured into splinters, shedding raggedy entrails in between the cracks. There was not a likelihood that it could persevere after that. The cold meat looked awful nummy from where I was standing. To me it resembled strawberry pancakes with powdered sugar, and, boy, I could've gone for some of those. I was distracted from my starvation by the gossip that was coming from the opposite side of the wall. I placed my ear up to the cold dry paint, trying to understand what they were talking about, if it even mattered to me.

They were conversing about Gramps in the spare room. I could hear him in the background, cursing at them for being young whippersnappers. I carefully crept out of the room to get through the door Grandpa was behind to nab him, but there wasn't any entrance to the room. It was at the end of the corridor, yet there wasn't even space for a room there. Well, I was stumped on what to do then, to say the least. I toured my way back into the room that I resided in, examining the walls for a secret passageway or book that pulled out. There was nothing. I didn't see how anyone could've gotten into that territory that was beyond infinity.

As I was curled up in a ball in the corner crying (I mean regaining my strength), the door blasted off its hinges, diving to the linoleum. In came a horde of those man-made zombie things, only faultlessly built. They were incredibly slothful, but, undoubtedly, they were mighty, too. I had no clue as to how to diminish the large numbers of those creatures. My only chance would've been to leave a flaming trail behind me. I held up around the back wall of the room until they cleared out of the doorway; only, they never did. The creatures just kept coming and coming until I was stuck in a room that was overflowing with these things that were in desperate need of plastic surgery. The creatures came to halt just as they got to me because the voice of someone outside of the room commanded them to. The voice came from a man who strutted in, telling them to seize me, but not to harm me.

He appeared to be a doctor, except his entire outfit was black, including the surgeon's mask he wore. This man clearly loved blood. I could tell by the twinkle in his eyes, or else he was just affectionate towards teenage boys. I stayed optimistic, trusting that it was blood, though. His eyes reflected the originality of mine, well, one of mine. They had the red and yellow intertwined within them. I proclaimed that my Grandpa would annihilate him if he learned what kind of experiments were going on around there. I vented that if I had the ability to tear free, I would severe his head from his exterior myself, if I had the power that is. He lobbed a sparkly form of dust in my face (probably fairy dust) that knocked me right out.

When I gained consciousness, I was already strapped to a table beside Gramps. The room was loaded with all sorts of business-type dressed people, except the surgeon guy was there, too, but he was of interest. They were cross-examining us with an assortment of questions about how Gramps was transformed into the undead. Grandpa wasn't tattling, so neither was I. I didn't regard myself as a sellout. My only intention was to help out Gramps. I was a dead man already. They did not fail to bring up that Gramps couldn't be tortured for answers, but they could explicitly torment me. I may have mentioned for them to bring it, seeing that I wasn't afraid of any breed of torture. They initiated poking and carving all over my body with radiant pins and scalpels. My skin was peeled from the muscle while they plunged needles into my flesh, deep enough to where they barely missed my organs. My tissue was tender at first, but, once I got beyond the opening hour, the pain became less relevant, becoming more of a pleasant sensation. I would've appreciated it further if they were schoolgirls doing it to me rather than gentleman, but beggars can't be choosers.

The businessmen thereafter set out to torture me by abandoning the project altogether. They departed the room except for a team of surgeons that were there to make sure that we weren't going to run off. It grew to be the most uninteresting stage in my history. I was settled on a table in silence with two men that were wearing shades indoors, supervising me, while keeping their arms crossed at all times.

I requested to see some tricks if they knew any, but they wouldn't stop commanding me to zip it. If the two dimwits unstrapped me from the table, I made it known to them that I would show them how to roll their bellies. They disputed over if I would honestly do it. I would. Not at anytime would I pass up the chance to show off my ravishing stomach. After numerous minutes, they concluded by giving into the power of me. One of the shades came to unstrap me while the other stood back, playing it safe so that I didn't pull anything. The man took off his tinted shades since he was struggling to find out how to release the straps that encompassed me. He eventually got the straps undone and retreated backwards towards his partner. The taser gun was shed from his belt to ensure that I didn't try anything funny. I settled to my feet before I jiggled my belly in a wave-like motion.

It was working. They were becoming hypno-tized by the waves of flab that were rippling down my cellulite filled stomach. I energetically clutched a single enemy around the neck, holding him face to face in front of me. The other shot his taser at me without even comprehending what was taking place. He struck his buddy in the vertebrae, leaving him squirming on the floor. The remaining shaded man came dashing at me, denying himself of being competent enough to brake. I grappled his arm, flipping him over my back, where he landed soundly on top of Gramps. Grandpa instantly removed the meat from his throat with his front two teeth when the guy descended upon him. The disease free contents flowed across Grandpa's face. Since both of the fashion victims were either breathless or zonked out, I unloaded Gramps from the table so that we could actively make a run for it.

We made it out of door #1 and down one continuation of the corridor before we detected a surgeon coming with our observant corneas. With him were additional gentlemen in suits, marching in a band formation. We took a detour to get back to where we came from, but the hall was completely flooded with those Frankenstein-type zombies. The family duo was trapped in the center of a big heap of trouble. The wrongdoers took notice of us right away, fearing the Helty's, and for a good reason. They darted the opposing way, except for the Frankenstein's, but that was due to them being slower than an old lady without a walker. When we arrived back at the room, we slammed the door shut, barricading it with a steel post that we jammed in the door handle. The way that we accessed the room was the way that went into the main hallway. I wondered how I didn't find it earlier. Oh, well, there was no use in crying over spilled cookies. I rotated to the opposite area where I distinguished the bodies of the dark dwellers motionless on the floor. Gramps was already on top of one of them, squashing its brains against the floor. The palm of a hand is the ultimate tool of destruction. As the gray matter was being mushed, I witnessed steam rise up from the corpse's interior.

I pondered to myself that if the leftover body had been tasered wouldn't that somewhat make him cooked, just like being in the oven? I figured what the hell, I was famished, plus it was likely that I wasn't going to get out of the building that performed malpractice on a regular basis anytime soon. I plucked one of the scalpels that were used to torture me up off the tile. It was lounging in a puddle of blood, so I made it squeaky clean by rubbing the crustiness off on my shirt. There were no fresh utensils around. Anyway, it didn't matter; that one was elegant enough for the time being. I opened by making an incision along the man's bicep, since I was craving some muscular Canadian bacon. I stripped the skin from the bacon, revealing that this guy had a ton of muscle that he was concealing. It wasn't prepared as well done as I liked it, but I can tolerate rarely done meat. I could've tasered it more, but that would've equaled extra effort.

I was concluding my meal with the bicep of his right arm, preparing to move to the left side, when he triggered his brain cells that enabled him to wake up. Logic told me that he was dead, but, since he wasn't, I guess that made me a warm blooded cannibal. You're only an anthropophagus if the specimen was still alive. He glanced at me before the pain rushed through his body. My face was laminated with his hemoglobin. I had a smile plastered on my melon that was the size of an enthusiastic greeter's that worked at the front desk of a lavish hotel. He filled up his lungs with oxygen as he attempted to scream, but I backed him alongside the wall as he gripped a scalpel in his palm. I begged him for forgiveness expressing that I was sorry. I had theorized that he had expired. He continued to stay stationary without even blinking. What did he desire to get from me? I had already mentioned that I was sorry. That frustrated me; I was regularly advised that if you confessed to someone that you were regretful, and you meant it, they would forgive you. Oh, that might've been the complication – I didn't mean it.

I walked up to him slapping the scalpel out of his hand. I induced the torment upon his physique the same way that they gave it to me. I poked him repeatedly with my fingernail on the bone that was unearthed from beneath the skin on his arm. I landed his cranium in a headlock as I pulverized his head against the wall using repetition until he discontinued the movement. There was a splatter stain on the soiled wall from where I had run his head into it. There were small nuggets of cerebellum bonded to the splatter where short hairs hung off of the particles. The shell of what was once a man laid there peacefully, spurting juice from the rupture in its skull, constantly. I had to attentively creep to the carcass to be careful that I didn't slip on the huge puddle. Considering that he was being such an incredibly bad person. I decreed that I should gorge myself in the remainder of his flesh, just as punishment to him, not because I yearned to. I admittedly didn't want to, on account that it was a large portion of food, even for me. Oh, and because it was a raw human, gross. But, in the end, I disposed of the whole thing, even the coagulated blood that dyed the wall red that was sort of the equivalent of dessert. Grandpa had finished long before me, becoming supremely furious that I didn't share any with him. Why did it matter? He was only a geezer, and nobody wanted to share with those types of people.

I eavesdropped on the hospital members outside of the door that were plotting a strategy to breach the entryway. We were trapped in an opening some fourteen stories high with no way out besides through a hoard of businessmen and creatures. We were relaxing, cross-legged on the floor, putting effort into creating a strategic plan when we noticed that one of the ceiling tiles slid to the side. The surgeon in all black lowered himself with one arm until he reached a range that was close enough to the ground. Then he disengaged his grip, dropping to the floor, where his slick shoes somehow bonded with the tile. He maneuvered to extract the bar from the door handle, but I shoved one of the tables that slid across the floor at him that knocked him back onto the bed where he tumbled backwards onto the floor.

He rose to his feet briskly before proceeding to come at me. I tried to dodge him so that he would leap straight out the window. Instead, he predicted that move was approaching, so he dropkicked me accurately in the kneecap, sending me down to the ground. Gramps pounced on the surgeons back, wrapping his arms around the surgeon's neck. The surgeon snagged the collar of Grandpa's shirt with one hand, tossing him over his head. Grandpa collided with hard floor. In a daze, he stared up at the ceiling. He rolled out of the way in the nick of time before the surgeon could stomp Grandpa's head in with his shiny shoe. While he was attempting to crush Grandpa's cerebrum, I dug a pair of scissors into his spinal column. The surgeon kept reaching for them, but his efforts failed since I had lodged them in the uppermost section of his back where it was challenging to touch, also limiting the radius in which his arms could extend. Grandpa was stationed on his backbone in front of the surgeon. He kicked the surgeon in the "package" region, knocking the wind out of him. He was driven backwards to the floor, and the scissors wedged all the way inside of him. Through the pain, the surgeon still would not perish, but it did make him exceptionally weak.

When he arose from the fall, one of his eyes had been adjusted to blue. They were contacts. The surgeon was a phony. I guaranteed that if I removed his mask he would merely be an ordinary guy. I had Gramps deliver a roundhouse sweep to ship him to the floor for an encore so that I could dispose off the mask. I removed the mask along with the black latex gown. I was incorrect with my declaration. He wasn't an average human being at all. The surgeon ended up being a computer nerd that came complete with the pocket protector accessory, escorted by the nerdy black-framed glasses. The supposed badass was only an egghead with protection from ink stains, not death. I kidnapped the gel pens from his pocket protector without feeling any sympathy. The pens gained momentum as they sunk in between his ribcage while I assisted them with as much force as I could contribute. Vital fluids leaked from the clickers on the rear of the pens as he prepared to cough up blood.

In light of his situation, he was still dealing out knuckle sandwiches left and right. The surgeon of calculus catapulted us off of his punished anatomy so that he could rip the pens out of his chest. The refreshment from his crimson streams spritzed out when the plastic damns were lifted. I snatched some surgical needles off of the nurses' table. The tip of his finger was my prey as I grasped it, thrusting the needles to unknown depths within its interior. I maneuvered him to the nearest electrical outlet where I submersed the needles into its shocking home. The scream that echoed through the shafts was more like a high-pitched shriek with a whimper weaved within it. The orifices on his head began to drain the hemoglobin out at a breakneck speed. The aroma in the air from the scorched meat became so ridiculously strong that I contracted a case of lightheadedness. If I hadn't eaten earlier, I could've feasted on a medium rare meal.

The antagonists outside of the entryway became aware that their leader was no more, which made them generate increased violent behaviors. The wooden door began splitting vertically down the middle while the doorframe was discarding splinters into the room. The only exit that we could find was the nailed shut window that would lead us to a fourteen-floor splash onto the pavement. But, then, I remembered that there was the removed tile in the ceiling that the surgeon infiltrated the room through. I presumed that we might've been equipped to reach it if we stacked the tables on top of each other. We promptly got them stacked on top of one another in stable condition before I climbed to the top of them. From the tallest point, I still couldn't touch the ceiling so Gramps had to scale it to situate me on his shoulders. I was able to flop down onto my belly to stretch my arms out so that I could pick Grandpa up without tumbling over the edge. The villains came crashing into the room at the same moment that we immigrated into the ceiling. There was a trapdoor that we dead bolted shut beneath us. When we got our first glimpse of where we traveled to, we were astonished. Our location was centralized within a spacious metal room that reminded me of the interior of an oven. The walls were lined with giant cabinets from the ceiling to the floor. Every single one of them had a heavy-duty padlock on it. There had to have been something of use to us in them, so we devised a scheme to open them. There was a fully automatic assault rifle on a table that was attached to the floor.

I took action, snatching the weapon up from its resting place. I surveyed through the scope with my good eye. I pulled the trigger, firing at the padlock on the closest of the cabinets, but a bullet didn't exit the chamber. Gramps confidently stepped over by me, and, with a little more of a production than I felt was necessary, he turned off the safety on the gun. It was just like him to strive to make me feel like a moron. I aimed at the lock, again, through the scope and fired. The gun had so much backlash that the handle slithered from out of my palms, flying upwards. It swatted me in the jaw, which caused me to stagger backwards while opening fire on the floor. I was qualified enough to get the gun under control so that I could cease the barrage of bullets after a couple of seconds. I examined the padlock that I shot at up close, realizing that I didn't even put a dent it. The cabinet encompassing the lock had many minor dents in it that made a path down to the floor. Maybe I didn't hit the lock at all, I hoped. I was determined to give it one last try before I renounced my idea. For the next time around, I perfectly placed the barrel against the lock on the side of it so that a stray bullet wouldn't blow my head off. Before I pulled the trigger, I mounted my legs at a power position so that I wouldn't be knocked over or crippled that time. When the first bullet came blasting out of the chamber, the lock collided with the cabinet, leaving a bigger sized indentation in it. The remainder of the bullets sailed up to the ceiling. I maintained my stance, but I still couldn't dominate the firearm to keep it straight. I was finished doing my best to demolish the room with unadulterated firepower. I inspected the lock for the final time to note what I had inflicted upon it.

Nothing. Still nothing. I didn't even leave a scratch on it. The only technique that we could use to open the cabinets was to shoot literally in the same spot repeatedly going through the entire clip, then repeat about a thousand times, until a hole was punched in it. I'm positive that there weren't that many bullets in the gun either. It was essential that we saved all of the ammunition that was left in the gun, considering that we weren't going to make it out of the hospital using hand-to-hand combat. There had to have been a skeleton key for the locks hidden somewhere. Then I meditated on it (only without the sealed eyelids or humming to myself). The keys would most likely be on the surgeon that was in the room beneath us. But how on earth or, for that sake, on any planet, would we get down there, capture the keys, and then scale the tables back up to our current location? First, we reviewed what we had to deal with past the trap door. All of the humans that I labeled businessmen had disappeared. They must've wandered off, struggling to figure out a way to run us out of their highly armored room. The room below us was still burdened by tons of those homemade zombies that were either aimlessly roaming about or peering out the window. My assumption was that they were curious of what having a life was like or what was beyond the hospital walls.

The sizzling cadaver of the surgeon was in the far corner still plugged into the electrical input. I was convinced that we couldn't even hold hands with the guy without getting electrocuted. It was credible that there could've been a way to get the Frankenstein beings to cooperate with us. I yelled through the trapdoor to see what they would do. The entire troop reluctantly shifted formation, gazing around the proximity. They appeared to be really confused, considering that they didn't suspect that the noise was coming from above. I yelled more intensely, which caused them to look up. The creatures originated a strategy by setting up the tables that they had knocked over once again. They must've had at least a fraction of their smarts remaining if they remembered how to set up the tables.

I slid the trapdoor shut as I attempted to devise a plan. Grandpa was dead; they were all dead. If I could talk them into trusting that we wanted to help them get out of their institution, maybe they would assist us in our battle to get back to nature. We had another member of the undead for them to relate to. Grandpa was undergoing mortification, and they were made up of the freshly deceased. They were roughly identical to each other. I slid the trapdoor back open when I witnessed the creatures keeping themselves busy by struggling to set up the first table. I used Gramps in my presentation as I spoke preposterously slow so that they could have an opportunity to understand. I illustrated to them how we could work together to break out of the area.

They renounced their attempt to get upstairs while one of them reached his or her arm out as if it wished to shake hands. Grandpa and I battled over who would descend to the lower floor. Eventually, I emerged as the loser because of threats of death. Grandpa lowered me down by clutching the palms of my hands. In the end, I tilted him right over the ledge with me as he crushed my ribcage with his bodyweight when we hit the bottom. I propelled his skinny behind off of me as I cautiously stood up; I didn't want to make any sudden movements so that they wouldn't slaughter us. I extended my arm to the rejected craft project to shake its hand. It didn't behave like it craved to kill me, so either they were caring creatures or else they intensely needed to breakout of the place. I leisurely drew my hand back without releasing my grip. The creature's skin was stripped from its hand as it bonded to mine. The other craft projects stretched out their hands demanding handshakes. I had to shake every damn hand in that room before I was able to get out and do what I was obligated to do.

I had Gramps rescue the keys off of the surgeon since the electricity only tickled him. I announced to the creatures that we would return to pick them up after we had burglarized the cabinets. We completed piling the tables back up as we got back into the secure space. I took the massive key ring, placing a single one in the first cabinet, but the key failed to insert itself inside the lock. I then realized that the keys were numbered. The key and cabinet number didn't match. I acquired the correct key and then unfastened the first cabinet. It was overflowing with guns, from pistols to shotguns to more assault rifles. I freed the contents of all of them just to spy what else there was. A cabinet that strived to be unique had a collection of currency inside of it that was probably ours. I had Gramps pack as much as he could into his pockets, while I did the same with mine.

We uncovered the trapdoor, instructing the zombies assembled from leftovers to hold onto our guns until we dropped to the ground. We tossed an abundance of the weapons down the trapdoor into the faithful hands of the creatures. I took a semi-automatic pistol with me, because, at that point, I knew that I couldn't manage a gun any bigger than that. Gramps brought with him a double-barreled shotgun. It was the exclusive weapon of choice for the old geezer. It must've been because he didn't feel like a man unless he could manage to blast a hole large enough in his prey to crawl through. After we gathered an extra stock of pistols, we decided to use the effortless hallway down to the next lowest level. We crept at a steady pace, paying attention for any form of noise that could've been someone trying to eradicate us. There were a plentitude of doors on both sides of us, so we stood back to back to cover all of the angles. Every once in a while, a team of fancy dressed men would pop out, so I would have to fill them with lead. After every individual had emerged, we had to intensify our speed, considering that we were positive that they were going to send more up after us. The dead bodies were strewn across the floor behind us as we made it into the downstairs room.

But, when we entered the room, we found that all of the creatures had swiped the weapons that we supplied to them. Worst of all, they vacated the premises without us; all except for one that is. He was calmly sitting on a chair, aiming his gun at the door. I requested that he please withdraw pointing the gun at us. The creature gawked at me while tilting his head to the side. Confused, he terminated targeting me with his weapon as he moved it over to Grandpa. I told him no, notifying him about the relations between the old dead guy and me. I made it clear that I would not murder him unless he focused that stupid gun on me one more time. He disposed of his weapon by placing it on the ground before he hung his head in shame. I immersed him in the tenderness of my arms and told him that it was alright; it would just take him a bit to get used to having a brain that claimed residence in his skull.

A solitary man in a suit struck Gramps in the back from the doorway with the wood-finished stock of his gun. Grandpa's whole anatomy was downgraded to the floor. From the sound of wrinkly skin, I knew that something wasn't right, so I spun around firing off shots. My bullet impaled the businessman in the shoulder as he soared backwards against the hallway wall. He began to aim his gun back at me when I heard a shot. The guy's torso disconnected from his lower half. The gore showered itself about the hall as his upper entrails dropped onto his lower severed half. The barrel of Grandpa's shotgun was smoking, which I presumed meant that he was having a real splendid time. I wasn't. I had the urge to get out of that building before I engaged in an encore by wetting myself again.

I asked the monster what his name was so that possibly he would be able to listen to me better. He raised his finger upward pointing to his chest. There was a patch poorly sewn on his shirt that read "Nazm". I suppose that the name on the shirt should've been pretty easy for me to spot, but I certainly never paid too much attention to anything. I recited to Nazm that we had to add speed to our departure if we wanted to make it out alive. It at least applied to me. After plenty of hand movements, accompanied by repeated explaining, he convincingly comprehended what I was attempting to get across to him. All three of us strolled into the hallway together. My hand clenched my pistol as we hiked down the corridor. Following almost being shot, I started to get a little on the twitchy side. We had a massive number of steps to journey down before we would reach the front door. The elevator could've been faster, but, plausibly, they would've had it heavily guarded.

We approached the steps, and, just as our feet landed on the protective, no-slip padding, we caught a glimpse of two men in suits, sprinting up the stairs, carrying big guns. We ducked out of sight under the low wall, pausing until they turned around the corner. At the instant that they drew their guns, we would neutralize them. When they did surface into view, Grandpa gave a personal bullet to an individual in the head. His cranium erupted, splattering chunks of cerebrum across the wall and into the eyes of another bad guy, blinding him with vital fluid. While the man was removing the obstruction from his eyes, Nazm fired his rifle which launched slugs into the trooper multiple times from his collarbone down to his thighs. The gun was unloaded while it was neighboring my ear, so I was detecting a blaring ringing in my eardrum. I was mildly grumpy after that, but I ultimoately got over it. Moments later, I found myself in need of regaining consciousness, apparently after surviving a nasty spill down a flight a steps. My vertebra was sensitive. But all I had to do was crack it back into place, and I would be a-okay.

We became aware that a flock of men were marching up the stairs from the base of the building. I was making a legitimate assumption that it was because they may have overheard all of the gunfire. I had a tactic in mind, so we concealed ourselves off to the side of the stairs, appropriately behind the doorway. My crew and I delayed until our opponents made it midway onto the immediate set of steps. I nabbed the fire extinguisher from its holder on the wall as I sprayed it in the optics of the intruders that were leading the pack when they got to the top. They slanted backwards, knocking over all of the other enemies on the steps. They were all fidgeting about on the ground from the quality domino effect. There was a single male still standing that was slouched against the railing, determined to get to me, so I delivered the fire extinguisher to his face. It crushed his nose as it flattened him to the floor with the rest. Afterwards, we opened fire on all of the helpless victims that were crippled on the stairs. Blood sprayed in the air, like the splatter effect when raindrops hit the pavement. When the fire extinguisher was struck by a stray bullet, there was a humongous boom that emitted scorching heat. The caliber of the explosion heaved us back into the hall.

I leaped to my feet, being the happiest that I had ever been. That was the coolest phenomenon that I had ever witnessed. The stairs were completely demolished from the explosion. There was no additional way to get down to the foundation of the hospital either, besides the elevator. The property where stairs remained existent was crowded with maimed stiffs. Pieces of corpses were fused to the walls along with in every nook and cranny. Settled on top of the bodies were more functioning enemies waiting for us to undertake the burden of escaping that way. I had fathomed that we couldn't ride the elevator to the main floor in plain sight; we needed a better procedure. We spread out, rounding up an assortment of flammable or explosive items to bring them over to the elevator. None of the operatives down there were making their way up that way either; I presumed that they were thinking the same way we were. I pressed the button for the elevator, accelerating it up to our floor. I inserted myself inside of it, bringing it down approximately half a floor, where we loaded all of the flammable materials onto the uppermost installment of it. I then released the emergency brake, ascending the elevator back up to floor eleven, where we were lingering. I bid farewell to the elevator, making sure that we had plenty of spare flammables before dismissing the elevator to its descent to floor one. When it was almost to the base, we unloaded all of the flammable liquids that we had left on top of it. A Molotov cocktail that was placed in my hand was thrown to chase the liquids down the shaft. Gramps and I shielded ourselves around the corners of the elevator shaft while Nazm practiced occupying space in the center of the future firestorm. I altered his position out of the way just before the flames shot out of the shaft.

We wasted time for a while before even taking the chance of retiring downstairs. We bundled our hands in random fabrics that we'd discovered before we activated our procedure to coast down the cable in the elevator shaft. It exhibited identical characteristics to the rope climb in gym class. It was like climbing miles and miles of the rope except for navigating downward. It was indistinguishable in difficulty. Also, there was the added bonus of effortlessly being able to rip your hands to shreds if you unintentionally slid down it.

We only had around three floors left to shimmy down when Nazm lost his embrace on the cable. He took a dive flat on his face, breaking through the roof of the elevator below. He hoisted his arm up giving us the much deserved big thumbs up, informing us that he was all good. We hopped down to the edge of the elevator that was corroded with ash plus miscellaneous smoldering objects. We invaded it through the Nazm shaped puncture in its roof, careful not to touch the flames. It was impregnated with the simmering corpses of innocent bystanders. The main door had endured the blast, remaining shut. During that moment we had time to prepare ourselves. So we gathered our weapons to get ready for war.

I pressed the button to open the door, and, as the door reluctantly unsealed, it presented more and more people with hi-tech weapons every inch that it moved. I shoved Nazm to the side, and we all took cover while the back wall was being stocked full of bullet holes. We all glanced at each other like we were positive that it was the day of our extinction, ruling out Nazm, who gazed at us, wondering why we were hiding. He stepped out into the flying bullets as he confiscated one of the soldiers, using his body as a shield. Nazm positioned the petrified soldier in front of him as he shot the remnant of the soldiers down. An equal amount of bullets injected themselves within Nazm as well as the enemies. I hadn't anticipated that even someone assembled out of body parts could possibly take that many puncture wounds. But, after the whole ordeal was over, he was the last one left standing, only oozing out a lot of what appeared to be molded blood. It only took a short period of time for Nazm to coagulate his blood before causing it to expire.

We wandered right out of the front entrance of the medical center into the cloudless brown skies with the harmony of many sirens coming our way. The objective was to find a car and a fast one at that. There was a black vehicle that was parked across the street that appeared to be fast. I wasn't too concerned about what brand it was, thanks to me not knowing much about cars. I was usually more interested in home economics than shop class; I didn't get beat up in home economics because of it being populated mainly by girls. When I say that it was populated by girls, I mean that it was populated by the ladies, and the ladies love me, kind of. Granted that Nazm wasn't the smartest thing, it still wasn't logical for him to try to get into the driver's seat when we got there. At least, Grandpa knew his place, always sitting shotgun wherever we went lately. I commanded Nazm to hurdle his ass into the backseat; I was always the wheelman. I got into the car, outraged because, of course, I had to choose a vehicle with leather seats. Leather seats had never been a friend of kids that were drenched in perspiration. They happened to be one of those things that clung to me and wouldn't let go, especially when it had no air conditioning. But it was not like we were permitted all the time in the world, not like we had a relentless amount of spare time. Before we made our departure, I took one last look at the architecture that we had just come from. It wasn't a hospital at all. All that was stationed in that location was a plain building with nothing marked on the surface. Everybody was indoors. Even the general public must've been there to set us up.

Chapter 6: Torture Tickles like Poorly Constructed Scarecrows

I got the car revved up, ready to go before we made our way to the most accessible highway that we could find. I didn't suspect that anyone had seen us leave, so we must've been home free. That was until Grandpa let me know that he had observed a couple of all black cars that were pursuing us. He stated that it would presumably be best if we attempted to elude them. I gradually sped up, just to check if they were really following us. Every time that I got distant from their vehicles, they would end up tailgating me like a prison inmate. We instigated alternate options, such as swerving in between automobiles, but they continued to keep using inconsistent driving techniques to catch back up. I slammed on the brakes, getting behind a two-door sports car. Like a rerun of a 1980's action show, I rear-ended it multiple times, but they always gained control of the car again. I swerved into the neighboring lane, setting my sights on pulling up alongside them. When I progressed to the back bumper of the sportster, I jerked the wheel quickly to clip the car. That time, the opposition persisted to swerve from side to side until it lost control. The car advanced onto two wheels until it flipped onto its roof, and it commenced rolling. It sustained rolling down the road until it was struck by a semi that fashioned jam out of the youthful teenagers that were inside. I anticipated that the combustion of the car would've thrown our sadistic stalkers off, but they maintained a close range to us until it was definite that we wouldn't live through the adventure. I instructed Nazm to position himself behind me before they opened fire. They prepared to shoot at us, so I struggled to stay directly in front of other cars so that they would have to waste ammunition on them first. As it turned out, the preposterous stalkers didn't mind doing it. I was forced to be seated through the horrific events of all this fresh meat behind me, being shot up previous to crashing into the barrier. There was an exit approaching that I was contemplating taking, seeing that all of the other vehicles that were hunting us were in the left lane. So, when it became accessible, I suddenly pulled into the exit as I watched the other guys slam on their brakes only to get nailed by a heap of additional cars, which originated a mighty pile up. Who knew if they survived or not, but the real question was who cared?

We took a joyride for a while on the illuminated streets that were packed with strip clubs and eateries. My two favorite things, if I could get into the first one. Eventually, we ended up in this territory that had extravagant Chinese restaurants that were connected to one another. It had been decades since I had gotten an authentic feast that didn't consist of the flesh of human beings. I demanded that we go there to attain some food. Then I became aware that there wasn't a shirt covering my back, plus we had a creature relaxing in the backseat that resembled a man that had been minced in a lawnmower and sewn back together again.

We commuted down the avenue to where there was a clothing shop. When I went in, I abandoned Gramps and Nazm in the car since it was evident that I was the most decent looking one out of all of us. Before I stepped inside, I scoped a sign hanging on the door that read "No shoes, No shirt, No service". I never understood that rule. If you had no shirt, such as me, and it was essential that you got one, you couldn't get inside the business to purchase one. I swear that these corporate bastards never thought that stuff through. I inserted myself inside of their business anyway. The instant that I treaded through their door, I had the manager instructing me to get my behind out of the store. Without looking I plucked a shirt off its hanger to put it on. I explained to the manager that I would buy it if they withdrew from nagging on me, doubling as an overprotective mother. It seemed like they were doing their best to hold back the laughter when they notified me that I could stop in anytime if I bought the shirt.

After they disappeared beyond the clothing racks, I examined what I was wearing. It was a pink polo shirt that said, "I can still kick your ass". It just figured that out of all the shirts in the inventory, I had to bag something like that. Then I noticed this green and white plaid shirt that would've looked sweet over it, so I snagged that too. I obtained a plain white t-shirt along with jean overalls for Nazm. For Grandpa, I landed a black suit, since what more of an excellent attire for a zombie to wear than something that a dead body in the soil would be clothed in, which was what Grandpa should've been. I also acquired some stocking hats, too, for the individuals with exposed brains. Lastly, I picked up some shades to conceal their true identities from the public, well the lesser observant ones. Not so much for Gramps though since he resembled a burn victim. I escorted it all up to the checkout that everyone was meeting around, giggling like immature schoolgirls. I had to abruptly interrupt them from the excuse that they called work so that I could receive some damn service. A single female employee came over to check me out, and, when I say checked me out, I mean checked me out. I gave her a wink, but no more because I was so busy.

I made it out to our transit with all of the apparel, and I protected my eyes with my palms while they switched their outfits. I didn't desire to spy any male nudity; I strive to avoid that at all times. I ended up having to pressure Gramps to lend his helping hand to Nazm by putting on his clothes for him, being that Nazm made the mistake of plopping his pants on over his head. We drove back down the avenue, stationing the automobile a block away from the restaurant that we were going to. I concluded that the "hospital staff" may have been searching for the car still, so we should've kept it at least on the next block. Close enough that if we needed the vehicle, it would still be an option to work with.

The interior of the restaurant reeked of clams. There was a buffet that was embodied with edibles that were based on rice and noodles. I was certain that I would have a hankering for more ten minutes after I dined at the place, but I didn't stress. Asian food rocks! I was affectionate towards buffets, because it was a plentiful supply of food that you could eat for a low price. I opened with a plate that had different types of lo mein cradling it, and then I went onto my second that had the bottom loaded with white rice with assorted classes of stir-fry on top. It was a nice change of pace besides the usual human corpse. When I was transporting my third plate that was brimming with random meats back from the line, I accidentally bumped into this Asian guy dressed up in a suit and dark glasses. He dispensed a dirty look at me as he paced over to a lavish table in the corner that was crowded with numerous guys being stylish, just like him. I paid no attention to it, due to me still being hungry.

By the time that everyone had left to their place of residence, I was maintaining my animal instincts. That was until the waiter revealed that the congregation in the corner had invited us over for a drink. I confirmed that they were getting me food, too, prior to agreeing to join their sausage fest (a lame name for a boy's night out). For summoning us over for free food, they sure didn't emit happiness when they met us, but I was pleased to see them. Their servants pulled the chairs out and everything for us. When I parked my butt down, there was already a steaming bowl of egg drop soup. How could a boy become more satisfied?

That was until they reported that I had disrespected the people that were attempting to do business in the restaurant. I struggled to describe to them how I didn't try to nudge the guy. It was the simple fact that a pair of people attempting to fit through a small spot doesn't always work the best. They expressed to me that it wasn't the reason. It was due to me gorging myself in the edibles from their family restaurant since they couldn't afford to have their relatives lose that much money. I made it known to them that I forked out my earnings for the all you could eat buffet, and I had an appetite to get as much as I could for my money. They then chaperoned me to the cash register where they pointed out a warning to me that reported that the buffet was a three plate maximum. What the hell was the purpose of a buffet if it wasn't an all you could eat one? They might as well have made it some sort of combo meal, so they didn't waste my time. I expressed my feelings towards him, but I don't quite think he sympathized with me. He motioned my face closer to the sign, seeing that he couldn't comprehend that I knew what it meant. But, deliberately, it got too close to the sign for comfort before he abruptly banged my forehead into it. I reached up to clutch my head when I sensed something drizzling off of it. They had either recently washed the sign or else I was hemorrhaging. The color confirmed that I was in fact bleeding. I straightened my arched back, directing his focus to my shirt sending the point across that he shouldn't mess with me, or I would have to kick his ass. I didn't stand a chance, but I decided that if I threatened him, then perhaps he would just surrender. Instead of withdrawing, he got into a stance that he had conceivably memorized from disputes before; something I had no training in. But I held up my fists, according to how I had learned from my mentor Mason Storm. He never genuinely educated me about how to block flying tables and chairs.

I was doing a decent job though of evading furniture by seeking shelter behind the counter; that is until he sprung on top of it. He grappled me by the neck, tossing my slimy body into the grilled chicken on one of the buffet lines outright destroying perfectly good cuisine. For not wanting to prepare for his family's bankruptcy, he sure didn't show much concern about wrecking the restaurant. The squishing of satisfying edibles probably conjured up the most violent emotion out of me that I had ever detected. I ran full force at him, ramming my shoulder into his gut before taking him down to the ground. I bit a hulking glob out of his cheek while I was situated on him. He flung me off like I was a crumb as he produced legions of swear words that were way over what was considered sociable at that instant. He had a similar amount of animosity that was comparable to what I had. I could recognize this when his facial expressions went emotionless. I was pressured to take him down before he roughed me up some more. He leapt at me with an awesome spinning roundhouse kick or something that struck me unmistakably in the jaw and hurled me through the atmosphere. I was hammered through the brick wall into the domain that was next door. There was a gentleman in the next room that was dressed up as a woman. I extended a finger to him, proclaiming that I knew that I wasn't alone in that exercise. I bounced back through the structure fracture, equipped for extra punishment. I didn't catch a glimpse of him at all until I caught a fist to the chubbiness of my cheek that transferred me into a sickening state of dizziness. I rotated to the direction that I was punched from and broke new ground by swinging without even feeling concerned about what I was delivering impact to. When I desisted to swing, I identified a dented menu board overlaid with the blood of my knuckles. Everyone was laughing at me, even Nazm, but I don't think that he positively conceived what was going on. I pardoned him for being an idiot.

It was precisely time to mobilize something that I had a chance to reign victorious with: my smarts. I really did have smartness; I just lead on like I didn't. 99% of the world is made up of water, told you. I pinched the skin on my knuckles, tightly struggling to get as much blood out of them as I could. I drained the hemoglobin into a pool on the tile floor. I withdrew a couple of feet, mocking my opponent to piss him off so that I could get him to rush at me. He was tricked by it. As he came strictly for me, he lost balance on the blood. The kung-fu fighter slid on his rear side into the enormous glass window that was permanently fixed in the front of the restaurant. At the halfway point, he sighed in relief since he didn't drag along the concrete outside. His fate became agonizing as the glass that was still suspended above came down on him, lacerating him across the torso. I couldn't accept that I had actually defeated someone that should've been qualified to obliterate me with no problem at all.

I was in the middle of my victory dance with the spinning around and everything when I was interrupted by some purely mean people that pushed me over. They restrained me face down on the floor as they trailed my expression across the blood that belonged to me. My nose was crunched up in the liquid that was mixed with shoe filth that made it an uncomfortable place to unwind. Those guys didn't have any manners. I had clearly been a victim of physical assault. Furthermore, I was only experimenting with defending myself. But, instead of cooperating with me, they pinned me to the floor acting like I did something erratic or uncalled for. They elevated me off of the ground. It took four of them to control the weight of my body, okay, one, but he was powerful. Fine, it was a hot female that I couldn't take a swing at (no matter what Grandpa's opinion was). She hauled me back to my seating arrangement at the table in between Gramps and Nazm.

They knotted some rope around me so that they could be confident that I couldn't elude them. That didn't stop me from putting effort forth into escaping. I still shook the chair rapidly, attempting to tip it over to splinter the wood. Even if I did become triumphant, I would have to save Gramps as well; he was always holding me back. Rescuing him was a never-ending job. It became old and tiresome, much like him.

There suddenly was an old Chinese couple sitting across from us at our table. They notified us that the man that I had recently butchered was their one son that now only existed in their hearts. I was educated in how I would suffer through a considerable extent of pain along with my two sidekicks. I wasn't too concerned. It wasn't like I couldn't endure it or anything. It was more like a minor discomfort to me if it would be anything like the preceding time. Plus, I didn't believe that Gramps or Nazm would acknowledge the torment anyway. As Gramps was snoozing, Nazm was preoccupied with being amazed by his reflection in the table. If it wasn't for me, no one would know what was going on.

The Chinese couple liberated my wrist along with Grandpa's as they held our wrists together keeping us back to back. They impaled this huge shred of metal between the size of a needle and rod through our forearms. Our flesh got caught in the rivets that plagued the metal. After it intruded our tissue, they bent it sideways on both sides so it looped around our arms making it impossible to purge. The couple duplicated the technique with my opposing arm as they connected it to Nazm. It wasn't comfortable, considering that I could sense the maggots from Nazm's inner space tickling my arm. I presented to them some uncontrollable giggles, which infuriated the family because they concluded that I thought that they were all a joke, which I did. They guided us into the storeroom, which was a roomy freezer loaded with meat slabs. Beyond the chilled storage was a locked door that they accompanied us through. Inside was an additional freezer, except, instead of containing animals, it consisted of bodies that were hung by meat hooks from underneath their jaws (talk about frostbite). The frosty cadavers looked almost like I did one day, following a sledding expedition that lasted for over two and a half hours straight in a snowstorm. Boy, did that sting!

They then shoved aside a column of cadavers that unearthed another door behind them that was also latched shut. Once we passed into the opening, there was a sudden heat blast that burned my skin when it drafted against my face. After a few seconds, it initiated a sauna type feel to it. I despised those things for the self-explanatory reason that I would sweat such an excessive amount in them that I would form weird shaped rashes. After the cloudiness evaporated from out of my eyes, I found myself in a dark, steamy room. There were an abundance of newcomers in the room also, but they were all strung from the ceiling by hooks and chains. They were also suspended by miscallaneous sections of their anatomy. Some by the throat; others had steel rings in their backs with hooks running through them, restricted not to execute an action or the affliction would worsen. Some were dead, and some continued to gasp for their final breathes.

The torturers tossed me onto a table, where they pierced hooks through the muscle in my back. I could hear a pop every time that a hook intruded or protruded from my skin. While they were working on that, Gramps and Nazm fought to get me down, but they were tackled by a mess of heartless human beings that held them against the floor until it was their opportunity for torment. The blood slid down my sides trickling onto the table below me that was already saturated with someone else's vital fluids. My innards created inconsistent sized pools of hopelessness below me as I watched a tear fall from my eye where it landed on the table, spawning a pink swirl. I thought I knew pain, but I didn't. I was beginning to go numb, so it wasn't as sore after a slight amount of blood loss.

The torturers intended to hook Gramps up, but, when they removed his shirt, there was no meat left to hang him from really, except for his spine. Rather than wasting moments by locating a new spot, they just punctured the hooks beneath his vertebra. As usual, he showed more boredom than us. Perhaps, it was because I was in misery, and Nazm appeared to be excited. They confiscated Nazm, hooking him up traditionally by his back, but, when they commenced lifting him up, the complete meat package on his back tore off. He dropped onto the solid table below him where he barreled off. His muscles dangled from the hook, creating the illusion of the shadows of raindrops. He discontinued moving, so I expected that they concluded that he was dead. That was until he severed the leg off of a single torturer that was controlling the chains.

In a fit of irritability, they maneuvered Nazm to the corner where they fastened each of his appendages into cleverly placed clamps that were united with the wall. They triggered spinning the crank that took two figures to rotate. I could distinguish the stitches stretching out from where his limbs conformed to his torso. Nazm was dispassionately swiveling his vision about the entire time, not even paying attention. Motivated, he struggled to roll his tongue suitably before his stitches snapped. His appendages dislocated from the body while the remnant of him collided with the floor in a puddle of liquid darkness. Of course, they detoured their attention away, assuming that he had passed away, since what mortal man could've persevered after that? When they approached me, I saw Nazm's head hoist itself up, and it embarked upon rolling around like a croquet ball. As soon as they peeked back to identify what the noise was, he would pause. Eventually, they desisted in putting any of their focus towards the sound that they believed to be their imagination.

There were two of them; one was at Grandpa's table, and the other one was pacing around where I was hanging. The both of them treaded over to a workbench type of thing that was built into the wall. They tugged on these strings that came from a rolled up scrap of fabric above them. Down came this giant section of fabric that had distinctive compartments fashioned into it for unrelated classes of tools. It was comparable to the world map at school, except that that map lacked the deadliness. When the opposite torturer's cloth descended, a large blade spilled out, splitting his skull in half. The recently deceased's body dropped to the floor, allowing the blade to split his entire face in half. His lacerated brain flopped onto the cold cement, drowning in what formerly kept it alive. My torturer for the evening snapped his fingers, calling out to a couple of guys that quickly arrived in the room. One lugged the battered carcass out of the way while the spare man took over the prior guy's position.

The newbie didn't wear the proper garments. He didn't dress himself in the gloves or mask, which was strange. Since when they dismembered us, how would they be certain if one of us didn't have HIV? A morsel of plasma would tap them and BAM! They would be part-time owners of the epidemic that traveled through my veins. I warned them that I had drunk gallons of spit, which may have indicated that I had contracted HIV. For some odd reason, the newcomer backed away from me, going over to the workbench. He snatched up a pair of gloves together with a mask. I didn't assume that he would actually fall for that, but it was beyond believable compared to declaring that I got it through intercourse. But still, drinking a gallon of spit? It was impossible to get past a pint. I directed their attention over to Gramps, revealing that he had HPV. I forgot what that was, but it could work.

The original torturer paid no mind to me as he prepared to use his profession on Gramps. He obtained a tool from his bench that looked something to the effect of a nail gun. He pressed it up against Grandpa's bicep where he pulled the trigger. A needle that was the caliber of a chopstick shot out, passing the tip through Grandpa's arm. When he drew the gun away, the needle was poking out from both sides. Gramps didn't even demonstrate a facial expression that showed that the needle had affected him, which I anticipated frustrated the guy, since he performed the act a couple more times without being as polished about it before moving onto something worse. He took a blade that was measurable to the size of a machete out of the cloth. It curved inward, but it didn't have any ridges on it. The sharpness of the blade made up for that. The original torturer moved onto Grandpa's alternate arm, pushing the point alongside of it. He sliced skin-deep encompassing Grandpa's wrist as he did with his upper arm. The torturer then made an extensive incision from the wrist up connecting it to the shoulder slit. He grasped onto the piece of skin that was sticking out and jerked. He peeled all of the skin from Grandpa's arm, exposing the muscle that was coated in a darkish red-green paste. It looked roughly like this spaghetti sauce that my friend's mom tried to serve me once; I told her to shove it.

My personal torturer walked over to his workbench where he went ahead at digging through his unsanitary deformed medical instruments. He was inspecting certain tools, and then shook his head as he tossed them over his shoulder. He eventually found something, too bad it took the life span of a fly to acquire it. I could tell that he discovered what he had been rummaging for, thanks to the grin that was plastered on his face. It was the diameter of Grandpa's permanent smile. He strolled along towards me with something in his left hand. It appeared to be a flat skillet. It was a skillet that he undertook bashing me in the face and sides with it – how unprofessional! During the time that I was getting the tar beat out of me, I heard a high-pitched scream. When he wrapped up lashing me, I identified that Nazm's torso had rolled over to Grandpa's torturer, biting a generous chunk out of his leg. This diverted both of them as they struggled to repress the limbless form that was trying to gnaw at their legs. They ultimately dominated Nazm's head and body, driving it into the floor where the head was divided from the torso. They swiftly chopped it off with a misplaced blade that was propelled onto the cement. Being that it was a clean cut, the floor flooded with Nazm's neck juices. In that period of time, when they were busy dealing with Nazm, I noticed that Gramps was attempting to get loose. His arms were straining to reach around as he put effort forth into seizing the chain that was hooked underneath the spine in his upper back. The situation became a conflict, due to the needles that were driven in between Grandpa's muscles. They punctured his sides along with ripped the muscles when he shifted them. Blood trickled from the needles every time that Gramps even moved an inch. Once Gramps was capable of latching onto the chain, he elevated himself up a sufficient amount to where he could manipulate the hook from out of his lower body.

After his lower end was detached, he was able to make contact with the table on his tippy toes. It supplied him with plenty of leverage to erect himself high enough to where he could get the remaining hook out. While the torturers maintained crouching over Nazm's form, Gramps sprung off the table splashing down onto the newbie's back. The weight of Grandpa's skeletal frame made him crash against the floor, producing the sound of snapping bones. The spare torturer hobbled towards Grandpa at an accelerated pace. Grandpa upheld the torturer with one hand clamped onto the front of his shirt before he was planted on a hook that was hovering in mid air. The chain dangled from the ceiling where it was attached to a hook that intruded the torturer from under his mandible. Grandpa oscillated his body around until the cranium twisted off, similar to that old fashioned root beer, delicious. Showering hemoglobin on his coworker, the head continued to spin on the hook as the remains plopped onto the table. The newbie torturer was still functioning. He attempted to crawl out of the room when Gramps dragged him, which caused him to lose ground. Gramps stationed him on the table, where he reenacted what happened to him on the newbie. When the hooks passed underneath his spinal column, the newbie screamed like a pig. Gramps climbed up onto the farther table, where the severed head was overhanging, taking a stance that was bursting with leverage. He bounded from one table to the next, bearing down with all of his density on the newbie. It ripped his vertebra promptly from out of his carcass. His spine swayed on its executioner while his guts flopped out of his back on impact.

After Gramps had finished handling those guys, he came to help me down. He exerted all of his might as he attempted to raise me up all at once, but he couldn't do it. So he had to detach the top half of me first, followed by the bottom. I swung upside down for a bit since Grandpa decided to do it the hard way, instead of freeing my bottom half in the beginning.

When the curved objects were evacuated from my flesh, the lacerations bled twice as profusely as they did when they were planted beneath my exterior. It was fine, though, because I was currently over the pain by that point. I stayed motionless in the corner for a minute before I was equipped to go into action again. It also could've been due to that buffet I had an immense bulk of; it wouldn't have been rational if I hadn't eaten until I felt like I was going to hurl.

Once I regained my stamina, I proceeded to make my way over to check if Nazm had perished. He was lying on the floor lifeless, yet he never ceased to squirm about. I set Nazm's head on the table along with the single headless anatomy of one of the torturers, which I credited to be of the originals. I approached the workbench to examine what they had for utensils, hoping that there would be something that would cure him. I didn't know if joining the head to a separate body would even work, but it was worth a try. I collected a thick wire that they had draped over the workbench along with a skinnier, hook-like tool. I punched holes through the muscle in the neck together with those around the collarbone. I ran the wiring through the puncture wounds that I had arranged in a zigzag motion, constricting them together as tightly as I could. He appropriately played dead on the table with nothing moving but his eyes; he was striving to teach himself how to play ping-pong with them. A comm.- otion made its way from his head, declining into the body; it sounded like the body was altering its structure to accommodate with the head. Nazm's new embodiment generated a twitch, almost like he was having a seizure from snacking on some bad nachos. Every time a fresh section would begin to function, it would move in a wavelike motion until it got to the end of the segment. After a few shakes, he was up and looking more goofy than usual. A stitched together cranium, that was diseased looking, was secured to a healthy Asian body.

I situated one of the fluid deflecting masks over his face so that, possibly, we could elude catching the attention of spectators, moreover to get out of the building. Perhaps, he could even convince the family that he was one of them. I steered him towards the main seating area so that he could tell us if anyone was still out there. Along the way, I caught a frosty breeze from traveling through the freezer. Nazm embarked on his journey by walking halfway out of the door before taking an alternate route to backtrack. Nazm scratched his head in confusion, which tattered one of the stitches that frayed, creating a portion of artificial looking hair. A yellowish sap streamed down the tip of his nose. There was no way that scenario would ever work. I turned him around, shoving him out the door as he stumbled onto the ground. He set himself upright, parading back again, shrugging his shoulders, while throwing his hands in the sky, like he was trying to do a one man wave; it just didn't work.

I decided that I would go and check it out myself. I didn't expect him to understand how to act out the instructions even after hours of coaching. I snuck out into the dining room to observe that no one was there. They must've all equally concluded that we were going to meet our demise. Boy, did we deceive them! I was about to step out of the front door when I heard a bunch of chatter coming from the street. It was pitch black outside, and there weren't any automobiles around. So I didn't see why there would be anybody out and about. I glanced to my left where there were cars lined up across the street which blocked incoming vehicles from accessing the road. There were three guys, equipped with automatic rifles, bordering them. I glanced over to my right to behold how far it was to the car. It was parked a block down; too bad it had been outright destroyed. The tires were flat; the car persisted to flame; and surrounding it were approximately fifteen men that were all organizing a roadblock on that side of the road. I assumed that they had information about the escape plan that we had perfected, up to that point.

Chapter 7:
The Escape from
Buffet Heaven

I went back into the abandoned restaurant, reporting to Gramps that we had to discover a way out besides by way of the roads, being that they were all out of service. The only method that we could think of was if Nazm navigated himself down the street to the three guys that were stationed on the left and was competent enough to convince them that he was with one of their family members. Then he would have to steal one of their personal vehicles to pick us up at the restaurant, prior to somehow outrunning the other cars when they chased us. It was worth giving it a shot. We gave him accurate instructions on how to walk properly down to the men to get a lone personality to drive the car back to the building. He was counseled to tell them that we were seeking refuge inside. The last step was to neutralize him while we, Gramps and I, dashed out to the car. Once inside, I would put the petal to the metal. I'd speed away so fast that you could legally change my name to Mr. Ironfoot. His shoes stomped loudly against the tar on his way over. Nazm did alright until he started turning around multiple times to exhibit his thumbs up skills to us that he couldn't get enough of. Nazm made it over to the target, where he initiated a conversation with the guys who harassed him while he scratched his scalp in confusion.

I suspected that it didn't go too well, considering that a couple seconds later he was making an effort to retreat, but his quickest speed was an incredibly slow shuffle. The automatic rifles fired at him impregnating his body with lead. I could see the bullets bursting out of Nazm's chest after passing through his back. A family member that was not bombarding Nazm with slugs jumped into a plain black car that continued to run. He hit Nazm with it, tossing him onto the hood where he dented in the new paint job. They slammed on the brakes, launching Nazm from the cold comfy steel to the ridged rocky road, adjacent to where we were. Of course, he had to stroll his ass in to where we were waiting so that the enemy actively followed. I was certain that if the foe got a shot off, the whole faction would know where we were. At the exact time that he arrived at the restaurant was the same time that he started spreading bullets all over the place. He passed me, because I was hanging out beside the door when he entered, so I ambushed him from behind while he was producing a racket. I kicked him in the back of the leg so that he would drop to his knees. When he reached the position that I was waiting for, I snapped his neck with a wrenching motion.

I could hear more cars starting up along with the others that were already driving down the street to trap us in the building. We had to find someplace to stash ourselves and quick. We ascended up the stairs to take a look around. The first room that we invaded had a block cut out inside the wall the diameter of a door on a bathroom stall. It was covered by a cloth that had a dresser obstructing entry. Nazm pushed the dresser to the side as I shifted the sheet out of the way. The interior reminded me of a hallway except for that it was in between the walls with plaster decaying off of the ceiling. The boards holding up the foundation also ran across diagonally, leaving only enough room to crouch. We smuggled ourselves inside of it just before the bad guys came up the stairs to our current level.

I could hear the leader ordering his minions into different sections of the building. We had to put a rush on it. I was absolutely positive that it wouldn't have been long until they found out where we had gone. While we lurked down the extremely narrow hallway, we could hear people ransacking the rooms around us. I bonked my head on just about every other support beam that rendered me not quite as dumb as Grandpa. Lucky for me, he couldn't read my mind, or I would've most likely have been put in a headlock by then. We came to a spot where the hall split left or right; there was no straightaway anymore. A decision was agreed upon by me to go right down another dark passageway. As we headed down that way, I could hear the bad dudes knocking on the walls from where we had infiltrated the hallway as they entered our sacred territory.

We began moving at hypersonic speeds (not really), struggling not to compose any noise at the same time, but Nazm had some troubles with that since he couldn't carry out an action without attempting to make sounds like a speeding car. Grandpa bitch slapped him every time that he started up the noises again. We arrived at a staircase with unreasonably narrow stairs that only the front half of my foot would fit on, even with my small shoe size. The steps seemed to go on forever. There was no railing on either side and we were constantly catching each other when one of us would start to fall backwards.

When we finally got to the highest point, there was no door. There wasn't even a hatch to go into the ceiling, but there was a tiny trap door that was level to the top step. I opened it, but there was only a space around the proportions of a sandbox. The room's ceiling was as tall as it was if a man was cowering under his bed, not that I had ever done that before. The three of us crammed in there since we became aware that a team of people were coming up the stairs.

After the clock passed five seconds, I had enough of that crap. The B.O. power in that confined closet was ridiculous. It felt like I was in a steamy sauna with the entire homeless community of New York. I was being rubbed up against, which got crusty blood all over me. It mutated once the moisture from my sweat mixed in with it. I tried to pay no mind to it as I waited for the threat to leave. The footsteps got closer and closer until they arrived at the top of the stairs, where they stopped. There was no movement between any of us, like we were all holding our breath. We all stayed as silent as possible until Grandpa began to choke back a sneeze. Everybody knows that there is no way that you can control a sneeze, so why even try? I just prepared myself for when we were found. I wasn't definite on what I was going to do, but I knew that I had to do something.

The instant that Grandpa let out his mist, formulated of saliva, that shook the spiders out of their cobwebs, the personality behind the door snagged it, sliding it open. A smart guy would've stuck his gun in the area that was known to have an intruder and shot it up, but this guy was different. He moved his head down to survey the innards of the room to be confident that we were still in there, I guess. After his eyes adjusted to the light, I gauged them out with stubby fingers. His eyeballs erupted on my fingernails, mucking up my flawless skin. He fell back, knocking the other guy down the mini stairs with him. His gun sailed through the air, while he toppled backwards. I was talented enough to grab the barrel before it tumbled down the stairs with him. Talk about unnerving! Having a gun aimed straight at my face, while, in the meantime, I was struggling to lure it up to me was practically like I was trying to threaten myself with execution.

I squirmed out of the wall, peering down the stairs to check where the figures had fallen. My eye had adjusted to the dark so that I could watch them clearly, but they were having trouble on account of them having to draw out the flashlight from under their belts. I comprehended that if they shined it up at our position, I wouldn't be able to see anymore. so I had to cancel their activity first. I instructed the boys to hold onto me so that I didn't plunge down the stairs and fracture my femur. They controlled my movement as I brought the weapon up to my chest. I slanted the gun to the bottom of the steps where the men were beginning to stand up.

I generated gunfire, while my entire body shook and rippled like I was the high tide. Bullets sprayed everywhere. A majority of them punctured holes in the stairs or struck the ground towards the bottom. My vision started to go, due to all of the bright flashes when the ammo deserted the barrel. I didn't see the flashlight turn on from below, but I also couldn't distinguish if anyone was stirring about either, since my ears were still ringing from each of the loud bangs that damaged my eardrums.

I inserted my finger into my ear, swishing it all around, like I always did. It gave me a helping hand in scraping out the excess wax. It worked out alright, I guess, but my head still ached. I learned that ear wax doesn't produce headaches though. Once my vision began to operate well enough, I communicated to the others that I supposed that we should slowly head down the stairs, trying, once again, to avoid an agonizing death. I maneuvered the descent by placing one foot after the other, exactly as they had taught me in kindergarten. The stairs creaked louder with every that step I took, until I collapsed through the wood cascading into the stairwell. I somersaulted in the air and dropped back first on top of these special boards that had nails sticking out of them. I could only pray, since I had never gotten my tetanus shot. The planks were cloaked with cobwebs that were evacuating spiders from their homes onto my untouchable figure.

From what I sensed, I only had four nails lodged in me, which wasn't unacceptable for such a fall with dangerous obstacles. The spiders were munching on me, but I wasn't intimidated by anything that was petty enough to crush between my fingers. From the darkness within the stairs, I could spot that Grandpa and Nazm were squinting down at me through the opening above. Gramps was shouting at the top of his putrid lungs, telling me that he was going to assist in my departure from the unknown darkness. He instructed me to work my way to the lowest part of the staircase, while Nazm pursued drooling in the hole that dripping saliva on my forehead. I kept attempting to dodge it, but, somehow, his aim was miraculous. I strained to get myself up off of the nails before army crawling my way towards the base of the stairs. I could hear Gramps and Nazm walking above me, paying no mind to their surroundings. I took notice that a few steps down from where they were heading was infested with bullet holes. I felt certain that it would for sure break if they put pressure on it. I screamed up to Gramps, but he didn't hear my cries.

When his first foot settled on the step, it formed an extensive crack. His foot went ankle deep through the stairs, which left him stranded in place as he strived to regain his balance. It wasn't long before he totally lost control and toppled over through at least half a dozen additional steps, during his downward tour. He landed conveniently on a mountain of insulation. It was humorous how even a dead man got it easier than I did. After the soft fall, he still griped about how he couldn't get the fiberglass particles out of his skin. Nazm looked down and viewed a shaggy rat that was scampering around below him. There were sounds of extreme joy coming from Nazm's vocal chords as he plummeted to the floor and landed on top of the rat's leg. It hobbled a bit, briefly attempting to get away from Nazm, but he was snappy about capturing it. He began to pet it gently as if it was a newborn with scoliosis. When he realized that the rat was injured, a teardrop nearly withdrew from his eye, but he sucked it up, moving on. He deposited the rat in his right pants pocket before we forged ahead to our destination.

The closer we got, meant the closer the roof came to collapsing on our heads along with a greater amount of cobwebs that we had to breach. After endless spider bites, accompanied by sharp objects stabbing into our skin, we finally made it to the lowest point of the stairs. The good news was that we were there. The bad news was that so were a lot of the naughty guys. There was a gap in between the steps that I could peek through. There were two more extra naughty gentlemen that were examining the twisted remains of the men right before my eyes. They knew that we had to be within the vicinity, because we never passed by them and because there was no alternate way out.

They climbed up the stairs, kind of anxiously, in the way that we had gone up them, only slower. We hiked down them, which was more dangerous, yet they were whimpering about thinking that they were hearing something – which they were. It was me stretching out from underneath them reaching for a gun that was next to the deceased so that I could blast a tunnel through their domes or anything the slug could get a hit on. I had Nazm punch an outlet in part of the stair so that I could extend my arm through to abduct a weapon. They caught the noise within the silence as they began their descent down the stairs, swiftly, but while also still trying to be cautious. I dragged the gun inside of the shadows with me cocking it, ready to commence gunfire. I aimed upwards, firing consistently, a couple steps ahead of the noise. Once there was a thud, followed by a collection of tumbling, I was positive that I had assassinated one.

Strings of blood were seeping through the warm bullet holes. Gramps angled himself beneath the streams and outstretched his tongue as far as he could. I guess for him it was an endeavor, just like trying to catch the falling snowflakes in the middle of winter. It was enjoyable, but it also quenched your thirst a little bit. I relocated sideways alongside the wall, getting as close as I could, because the second guy was coming down fast. But, at the same time, I wasn't worried. He was firing his weapon into the stairs right in front of where his feet touched down. Eventually, gravity overwhelmed this victim by bringing him through the wood and making him putty in our hands.

He arrived pretty hard on his back. His gun was thrown from his hands, which left him alone with us with no defense. Life for him was not a likely option unless he knew some top-notch jokes, but they never did. All of us huddled around him ripping him apart like we were a pack of wild animals, like maybe a cross between that and a bloodthirsty cult. Grandpa punched him in the abdomen until his fist infiltrated the flesh, breaking into the vault of internal organs. He then mashed them all up into a sphere of guts before he fed off them like a popcorn ball dyed with pink food coloring. Nazm simply picked off the skin together with the muscle layers using his fingernails, spawning a treat that resembled flaky crab that had been soaked in mustard sauce, while I rightfully gorged myself with all of the leftovers. To me, it wasn't an issue so much as long as I acquired something to eat. Raw meat didn't bug me as much as it did before. With my fist, I hammered at the inconsiderable opening that we had made in the stairs, trying to break it apart more so that we could shimmy our way out. All that happened was I ended up manufacturing cuts and bruises on my knuckles. I aspired to show Nazm what to do to crack the boards, but he stuck to pulling the wood towards himself. I repeatedly punched the wood and demonstrated to him how it would break if he copied me. He replicated my actions once, and the board flew out farther than I could've thrown it. Again and again, he pummeled it; until, in conclusion, we were free to leave the rat-infested cobweb.

We crawled out onto the dusty floor, heading for the opposite direction from the stairway to hell. I listened in on the people that were wandering around in the hallways along with on the flipside of the walls; there was nothing but useless babbling. I collected the other two guns that were distributed around the bodies and handed them over to Gramps and Nazm. I was certain that they were still searching for us, and, furthermore, they wouldn't stop until they found us.

We made our way along the cold dark hallway with our guns drawn out, leading us onward, except for Nazm's, which he dropped a while back but refused to pick it back up. When we made it to the middlemost point, where we could've traveled left to get back into the restaurant, we perceived that there were increased numbers lining up inside the narrow hallway from which we had snuck in through.

We took cover around the corner as we blindly commenced blasting at the oncoming enemies. I made out the screams of numerous people, but we didn't cease-fire until the commotion ceased. I checked to see if they were all breathless, but, then, I witnessed that some of them were merely wounded on the ground. I reloaded my gun and unloaded my ammunition downward until there wasn't a movement left. I heard an immense amount of car doors slamming from outside of the structure, so I directed the boys to assist me by pitching the corpses in front of the opening to the restaurant to erect a blockade. They sent them to the head of the heap, one by one; while I supervised, making sure that it was being constructed properly.

When the bad guys finally made it to the upstairs, I could see them taking their best shot at getting in. The attempt was made by shoving the bodies out of the way, but there was no place to push them. They were stacked from the doorway to the wall that was on the counter side, which was only a few feet away. I was confident that there was absolutely nothing to worry about then (if I ever worried), except for the opponents that inhabited the other side of the wall with us. Nobody else would be intruding upon our domain. We advanced along the left hallway, but not as sluggishly as we did with the right. Gramps and I towed Nazm by the arms to make him go faster. After I thought about it, I wasn't too concerned about anyone magically popping out in front of us. Like all of the previous ones, we would be able to spot their flashlights from a mile away before they even heard us approaching.

When we journeyed along the pathway, instead of running into steps, it seemed like we were walking on a gradual downhill slope. I was positive of this after the floor and walls were warped into concrete. The atmosphere got so chilly that my nostril excrement began to drip onto my lips. No need to fear, I didn't lick them. I was not a booger eater. There was a whole lot of splashing going on ahead of us. It sounded like there could've been at least twenty people treading water below. I became slightly more careful as I made the smart move of using Grandpa as a human shield, which I preferred to do when circumstances arose that were too sticky for me to handle. It became so dark that even though our eyes were adjusted, everything still went black. The stench was rancid. We undeniably had to have been in a sewer of some sort. We sustained our pace moving forwards until Gramps nearly broke his nose by smashing into a wall, face first. I ran my fingers around the surroundings and deducted that the place was like an oversized open domain, I thought. We could see the brightness coming from the flashlights that were encompassing us and reflecting off of the quivering water. There must've been various paths along the walls that we didn't inspect.

I signaled for the guys to follow me up to one of the floating flashlights. We played the stealth card by delaying behind one of the corners until the glowing orb passed by us. I struck the flashlight obtainer in the rear of his cranium with the grip of my weapon. Before he had the time to make any clamor, I beat him with repetition in the head until there was crimson slime stringing off the grip of my gun. I removed the flashlight from the tightly clenched hand of the carcass, too, for my own benefit. When I didn't spy any other glowing objects around, I tried to focus the flashlight up at the ceiling to scout for someway out. There was never much luck, considering that everything that came into view looked about the same.

Another light was drawing near us, asking what we were seeking that could've been on the ceiling. I didn't say a word in return as I navigated my light so that it shined in his eyes, which caused him temporary blindness. He so-called "demanded" me to surrender my flashlight, but I didn't know the meaning of direct orders. Once he got close enough to us, Nazm smacked the gun upward out of his hands. He snapped the figure's neck with one hand, just by bitch slapping him in the jaw as hard and as quick as he could.

By the instant that situation was all wrapped up, I heard someone yell, telling everyone that he had discovered a body. I predicted that it must've meant that we were still in the vicinity. Now we were really searched like mad to find a way out of that God-forsaken place. It seemed like every single minute that we ran we came into contact with someone else that we had to slay. At least we were granted the permission to shoot the attackers afterwards, because they were already informed that we were hiding out there. We eliminated the battery power from our flashlights so that we could concentrate on shooting whatever light was coming towards us.

After awhile, there weren't enough guys left that prevailed to really worry about. We ended up finding a ladder in the center of one of the corridors that led up to another trap door. Grandpa and Nazm ascended up the rungs first to check it out while I relaxed by avoiding an additional risk. I didn't catch the sounds of any guns going off above, so I began scaling the ladder. Scarcely, had I reached the third rung, when my ankle was latched onto by a powerful hand, and I was yanked back down to the cold-ass concrete. It was an elderly man with a supremely long snowy beard, and he had a samurai sword point-blank against the tip of my nose. He was reciting a prayer for me, so I kicked him in the groin. I rolled sideways before he dove forward with the sword that would've gone right through my fragile throat. While he was in a stage of weakness, I stomped with both feet on his spine over and over, until I felt his vertebrae separate.

As I was climbing back up the ladder, a beam of light illuminated me from below. I rushed up the rungs without paying any attention to the environment around me, but I ended up snapping the brittle steps. I instead chose to do two steps at a time; it worked quite well. Gunfire went off that only missed me by mere inches. I executed the most challenging push-up of my life to get into the upstairs. I didn't even pay any mind to where I was; I just stayed focused on getting the door shut below so that the levitating flashlights wouldn't be able to follow us up.

The pair of oddities and I, the supervisor, pushed a heavyweight safe on top of the door, just before the bullets started to fly up at us through the hardwood floors. Nazm leisurely shuffled his feet and moved away as he got clipped with an abundance of slugs that flew out of his head, while Gramps and I dove out of the way as soon as possible. The safe happened to take a spill through the floor, presumably because the bullets crippled it, just like it did to the stairs. The firing was cut off after our dear friend, the safe, took the plunge. We raced over to the hole that now lived in the floor to make an analysis of the damage. The ladder was totally crushed along with the jumble of the guys that stood directly below their target.

In the blood that had pooled on the floor, there were footprints that led away from the crime scene that left a trail of crusty shoe designs back from where they came. My gut instinct told me that they weren't going to give up; it also reminded me of meal time which wasn't far away. There was the far off commotion of a semi pulling up to presumably drop off more fighters. It missed the parking spot in front and drove directly into the restaurant that we had exited not long before. It was only a matter of minutes until they figured out what our location was then.

We were about a block down the road in what appeared to be an abandoned drug manufacturing facility. We were blessed that none of the chemicals were shot in case they were flammables and not cough syrup. Nazm had already made his way around the home for the addicts as he carried a brimming bag full of a white powder. He was dumping it down his throat like he was trying to destroy the miracle cure for cancer. I advised him to quit being a bad boy by not making contact with anything else. He nodded his head that had white foam bubbling out from under the stitches in his neck, which meant that they were going to get all soggy. All of the gaps in his indestructible frame were now seeping the foam too that left him standing in a puddle of what resembled fluffy pee because of the moldy, pussing chemical in his blood.

By the time that I got done dealing with Nazm, I turned around just in time to witness Gramps with a needle halfway in his neck as he injected something inside of his veins. What did they think; I was their damned babysitter? The bastard opened his performance by shaking like an autistic child. Gramps was still mounted on his feet, but it seemed like his blood vessels were bulging out of his skin, preparing to burst. I ached to ring his delicate neck being that he should've known better, but I was afraid that his veins would explode on me, leaving the unkempt old man smell clinging to me for days.

My choices were either that I deserted them there to quest for a new ride, or I waited for them until they became useful again. The outcome of my thought process was #1. I was going to prowl around the block and hunt for a vehicle after I relocated them out of sight. It took a lot out of me to drag Grandpa all the way to the closet, where I camouflaged him behind a cluster of hanging suits. Acting like a crazy maniac, Nazm ran off out of my view. I should've been getting a double cheeseburger for that one later, and, by double cheeseburger, I meant a minimum of four of them. After using up my blood, sweat, and tears, I surveyed the territory outside of the walls to uncover which way I could get out of there. There wasn't anyone in sight; it seemed like it anyway. I darted out of the exit and headed for the nearest car that was located on the curb a few feet away. At the same instant that I got my first foot to touch the concrete, I heard someone shout that I was going for a car. I slid across the hood to the driver's side door, where I fumbled with the handle, before I realized that it was locked. I smashed my hand through the window and unlocked the door. There were no keys in the ignition, which would've been great had it ever happened in a hopeful situation. I lowered the sun visor and cupped my hands, waiting for the keys to descend into my palms, but they didn't. I guess the movies lied.

My noggin had run clear out of ideas, so I aimed my fingers at the sky and declared out loud that I didn't have a white flag on me. Just when I had enacted that response, something clamped onto my hands and uprooted me through the non-existent roof. Maybe I should've noticed that it was a convertible before I went through all of that labor. It was Grandpa who was rescuing me, but Nazm was nowhere to be found. Gramps pointed, revealing to me that Nazm was the gentleman who squealed that I was going for a car, but he indicated to the professional fighters that I was in the opposite direction so that they were telescopic from where we were. I guess from a distance, they couldn't tell that he wasn't one of them. It must've been the expensive suit and sunglasses that he was exhibiting.

Nazm approached from down the road and swerved all over the place in this monstrous pick up truck that vibrated deafeningly, like it was about to fall to pieces. He wasn't the individual we should've relinquished the decisions to. When he pulled up, he came so close to molding us into jelly that we had to dodge the truck. I opened up the driver's side door after brushing my shirt off to shove Nazm into the passenger seat only to have him pushed back into me. I guess priority was reserved for Grandpa.

I took my best shot at acting casual when I drove away. I didn't know if the clamor was as thundering outside of the truck as it was on the interior, but, even if it wasn't, we were pretty screwed. The only route of escape was going through the enemy's barricade. The backup end of the road was littered with automobiles that had ignited an inferno over our path to freedom. As we coasted down the road, like a monster truck with snow chains fastened to the tires, we passed the guys that were parading back from the fake location. Those goofy bastards never had a clue. I advised Gramps and Nazm to duck down, while we drove past the remaining adversaries, because it was obvious that there weren't too many zombies in town that had their driver's license. Once I accidentally made eye contact with the antagonists, they drew their guns out, like it was a showdown. I put all of my weight onto the gas pedal so that we could accelerate from 20mph to 30mph in less than ten seconds; what a beast it was. They launched "Operation: Unload Weapons" from behind and hit the massive trunk on the truck. I could hear the cries of the vehicle needing auto mechanic attention as sparks showered the pavement. I dipped down as the rear windshield shattered from behind me, while Gramps relaxed, taking a bullet in the shoulder.

We started to get shot at by snipers from the rooftops that were encompassing us. The hood of the truck began to take fire, which motivated it to heat uncontrollably until a blaze erupted, that left me a tad panicked. Suddenly, the steering wheel jerked to one side; maybe it was because one of the tires had popped. I fought to gain control over the truck once again, but it swerved sharper from side to side, like a senior citizen behind the wheel, until I lost what handle I had on it. That resulted in it flipping sideways repeatedly. We were tossed around inside, except for me, because I remembered that seatbelts save lives, not the undead.

Chapter 8:
Everybody was Kung Fu Fighting
(Not Really)

By the time my knowledgeable mind came back to me, we attempted to exit the truck. We were outlined with guns that were equipped to blast our innards out. Gramps and I put our hands up, while Nazm had to be taken down with force for attempting to consume a bug that was crawling on the ground. The foreigners with automatic rifles blindfolded us and ushered us somewhere unknown with our hands tied behind our backs. We were prodded into a car, or else it was only me, since I didn't hear a voice besides mine, crying for my oven. I craved my homemade meals that consisted of stuff that didn't bleed when I poked it with a spork. I detected that we had came to a halt many times, along with taking a number of turns, until we finally came to a standstill.

I was ever so harshly plucked from the car as if my bones weren't delicate at all. My appearances meant the world to me. I only had one eye, plus my skin was covered in recent scars and flesh wounds, but that didn't signify that I wasn't drop dead sexy, pardon the pun. I was guided into a door before being brought through one that clattered, like it was king sized and sealed watertight. It sounded like it slid from the side, but, on the indoors from the entryway, it felt like an oven that was large enough to cook for my appetite. As my arms were being liberated, I struggled to break free, but I got manhandled. The meager mortal flung me backwards into what felt like a thick gas pipe. Someone confiscated my hands, placed them behind me, and circled them around a pole to fasten them together. I fought to get free, even though I didn't expect to. All that I achieved was ripping my forearms to shreds (or it at least gave me rope burn). The voices in the darkness explained to me that they couldn't let me live, and they couldn't just let me die. I needed to suffer. Why must the world be such a sick place to exist on? A habitat where a boy has to suffer just because he exterminated a few people in self-defense? I should've been granted death; there was no suffer penalty in prison.

From someone behind me, I got a sensation that they were separating the two ends of my blindfold. I was thankful that it was the only thing coming undone. I squinted to make the blurry figure in front of me become visible. I then outright peeled my eyelids apart, which made all the more sense to do if I desired to plainly watch what was going on. There was a dangerously overweight guy in front of me that was wearing a suit. The coat installment in the attire was open and unearthed a brown-stained, white tank top underneath. They must've been those icky gravy stains. That consistently happened to me whenever I ate anything that involved meat. His presence was painstakingly offbeat compared to the backup fighters that proudly displayed crew cuts. They have never been manly unless you were in the army, well, not even then. This beast could've crumpled me up with his bare hands, but I wasn't intimidated. I just sprouted a leak in my pants for the fun of it.

Throughout the questionable boiler room was steam, mixed with wetness that dribbled from the pipes overhead, that were hooked up to a giant stove; it absolutely had to have been a boiler room. It for sure wasn't a cookout in the park. The boiler room was as pleasant as a pudgy man rubbing oil all over his naked body. His minions exited the room as The Beast lumbered passively over to the stove where he snagged a worker's glove that was nailed into the side of it. He sunk his arm towards the center of the stove only to extract it with the emotion of displeasure on his face. What did he envision was going to happen, a bunch of kittens were going to pounce out and cuddle all over him? I let out a small laugh, just a small one, yet he freaked out as if I had slaughtered his entire family right before his eyes. Some people got their panties all in a bundle for the dumbest reasons. He must've been one of those crazies that got drained of all feeling when they were in a rage, considering that he dragged the protective glove off reaching his clammy hand into the stove as he slothfully stole a coal from within. The Beast pulverized the red-hot coal by enclosing it in his exposed hand, which left a nasty blister that was peeling off of it. I mentioned to him that he should perhaps whisk himself away over to the doctor's office quickly to have it checked out, or it may get tainted. But, for some reason, he didn't trust me; like I would stress over it, it was his health. But, for God's sake, there were chunks of coal lodged within The Beast's hand that he had to present to me at point-blank range to prove that he was a man or something. I booted him in the shin, but it didn't appear to faze him until I bagged a faithful slap across the face from the boiling hand. The blisters were striped off as they fused to my cheek, forsaking a translucent shedding that sagged near the corner of my eye. I continued my effort to blow it off with the large gusts of wind that were expelled from my lungs, but it just wouldn't work. The Beast pointed at me with his bratwurst sized fingers and laughed his oversized noggin off with the occasional snort. I hawked the biggest loogie that I could procreate from out of my nostrils and aimed for his forehead with a direct hit. He stuck his hand into the stove once again and crumpled another coal within his palms. I clarified that the act was getting old, and, if he was intending on murdering me, he might as well of done it before I died of boredom. My reaction pissed The Beast off royally, which attracted him closer to me.

I saw him wrench his arm back to punch me in the dream box, so, when it conclusively made it next to my face, I dodged sideways without haste. It always seemed like the big bad asses were the slowest mothers in a fist fight. His knuckles collided with the pipe and constructed a deep dent that misted steam into his eyes. He held his palms over his eye sockets and stumbled all over the place, almost tripping backwards. After achieving so many near misses, The Beast did, in reality, end up losing his balance and settled flat on his spine, former to striving to thrust himself back up. I calculated that it would be my sole opportunity to make an escape, but it was awful troublesome. I was forced to keep my head cocked to the side so that I didn't fry my hair off on the emitting steam that was behind me. I tried to pick at the rope that bonded my wrists together, but, the further I fiddled with it, the more it frayed and split into mini ropes, which made it a complicated puzzle that I sucked at. The Beast managed to raise himself back to his feet, where he began swinging his fists around in mid air in an attempt to hit me; too bad the loser was across the room. He dashed in the correct direction towards me, like he was going to tackle me to the ground. When he got adjacent to coming in contact with me, I elevated my legs so that he would secure impact with the pipe below me. I almost timed it wrong and nearly got plowed into, but, instead, he unintentionally ducked under me and crashed through the pipe that I was bound to.

I lost my sweaty grip on the pipe and was reduced to the ground on my buttocks. The steam was spraying everywhere. It engulfed me and singed my skin. The only way that I could've conceivably gotten loose was to transport my arms through the disconnected pipe that was shooting out the steam. I didn't even want to attempt that stunt, so I wouldn't turn out looking like some freak of nature. I was already missing an eye, but if I just sat there, I would most likely meet my demise. I abducted a deep breath, locking it inside my lungs, as I swiftly angled my arms through the steam, but not without establishing a gash on the uppermost installment of my forearm. It didn't bleed profusely. I imagined that the heat must've sealed the wound enough.

The Beast was only then awakening from his unconscious slumber party that he celebrated by himself. My wrists were still knotted behind my back, so my goal was to find an item to cut the rope with. The boiler room, remarkably, wasn't filled with many sharp objects though, just pipes. It didn't help that my foe refused to give up; he forged ahead and charged at any region of the room that produced a noise. That meant that I had to be excessively mindful to not make a sound, which was challenging to do on a floor that was composed of metal grates and concrete in an echo bearing room. I spotted a single fragment of the coal that The Beast had crunched within his palm lying peacefully in between a grate still glowing red, which usually promised that it was hot. The only problem with getting to this negative solution to torch the rope was that The Beast was positioned immediately alongside of it.

I searched high and low for something to chuck, but everything was fixed to the wall. Somehow, I was obligated to formulate a noise from across the room, but the only way that I could do that was if I was over there, which would've defeated the purpose. I shuffled to the side a bit when my foot got caught on a section of grate that ejected from its resting spot in the floor. I had discovered that they weren't stable. That was what could be thrown. I delicately hoisted it up and aspired not to make a peep. I made the soft screeching noise from metal trailing along the concrete, but I don't think that he even noticed. The Beast generated a facial expression, like he thought that he had heard something, but he went back to doing nothing. It was a nuisance to put effort forth to boost the grate up behind my back. I kept escorting it along my skin, fabricating those microscopic cuts that stung, but that I probably couldn't see. Next came the tough part, pitching a not so light grate across the room from behind my back.

I stationed my left foot back farther to get some leverage, while I slanted my back at some degree of an angle. I happened to launch it over my head, only grazing my scalp slightly. It proceeded to descend immediately upon the tips of my toes and produce a clamorous impact. It didn't take him a second to charge my way. I spun around and dashed in circles along the walls, because it was the only thing that I believed I could do. While I was exercising my sweat glands, the grate that I had dislodged clipped me on the reverse side of my ankle and flattened me to the warm floor. It skidded along the concrete and halted beside me when I scanned the meat and hair that was wedged in it. I never realized that I had so much leg hair. In fact, I didn't have any in general, especially the gray ones. I glanced behind me, where I beheld The Beast disposed against the ground. He was drowning in a pool of blood with no breath remaining in his body. There was a rip along The Beast's hairline that was exposing his cracked skull. The brain matter was beginning to seep out from the tiny crevice that was manufactured. He established his resting place prox-imate to the coal that was being drained of color.

It didn't matter to me where he was positioned as long as he was defunct. I couldn't grasp the handle on the door with my hands restricted behind my back. I hobbled over to the coal as quickly as was possible with an injured leg. I rolled the coal up against the rope, but it didn't demonstrate that it was doing anything. I twisted my physique towards it to deploy a gust of carbon dioxide upon it, which caused it to shrink. All of the dust blew off of it so that it could glow red once again. I situated the rope up against the coal again and prayed for the best without praying; I didn't do that too frequently. Since my entire family passed away and the last one to "survive" still cursed me with his presence, I didn't see the point. After totally misplacing hope, I felt the rope give a little and no not cookies. It wasn't scorched all of the way through, but just enough so that I could reject my hands from each other and the rope would snap. I performed my upright stance before I began to skip (which I did whenever I was freed, by the way) towards the door when my abused ankle was ensnared. The Beast fought for his existence, but he didn't fight hard enough. I put him out of his misery when I demolished the rear of his head with the sole of my shoe until his skull caved in. I scraped the pink muck off from under my shoe, since it smells like rotten formaldehyde when it clings to something for a long period of time. It was an honorable demise for someone who was misusing a great amount of their life.

I smushed the bar between my hands that bolted the exit shut as I slid it open with ease, bringing me to the reverse side. It introduced me to an enormous open room with many doors that led to what I supposed to be offices. I peered through the viewing glasses that were welded in the doors to make an attempt at finding Nazm and Gramps. I discovered the hidden worthless treasure that was Gramps first in a room that was stripped of everything besides a metal chain that was fixed to the wall. The clamp at the end was secured to Grandpa's leg, which prevented him from vacating the premises. I didn't observe anyone else in the vicinity with him. The level of difficulty suggested a trap, but I wasn't the type of personality that would think of nonsense like that.

I stormed through the door and did a single legged hop to slow down myself, while I looked everyway for someone, but there was nobody. There wasn't even a challenge for me. And it wasn't that hard to give me one of those. Gramps was shaking his head at me as if something was wrong. Seriously, what could've gone awry? The key was deposited on the wall in the far corner of the room. What a bunch of muttonheads! They abandoned the key in plain sight without having Gramps guarded at all. Gramps was doing the frightened routine as if he had a concern about death, plus there was absolutely nothing to get his panties in a bundle about. I transferred the key to the opposite corner that Grandpa was in and inserted it into the padlock after quarreling with him. Talk about a spaz attack. I rotated the key and heard the clasp release off of Grandpa's leg. I started to make my way towards the door, but I paused when I didn't hear Gramps treading behind me. He remained in the corner, huddled in a tightly squeezed ball. I elderly napped him by the arms and hauled him over the floor to the exit, while he was thrashing about making an effort to get loose. In the long run, I ended up being his companion on the outside of the door to demonstrate to him that there was nothing beyond it that would harm him.

Once he witnessed for himself that there was nobody there, he brushed himself off and lifted his head up high. He was seriously acting like not a thing had happened. But, at the exact moment that I explained to him that we still had to rescue Nazm from the evildoers, he flipped out taking a stab at freedom. I advised him not to scamper away without aiding me, or I would leave him stranded there to rot, while I invested in a house in the suburbs, somewhere where he couldn't locate me. After that discussion, he was, to say the most, decent. He was promoting himself as a baby, but, at least, he wasn't cowering in a corner. He persisted with his comments about ditching Nazm, but I couldn't do it. He was only a stupid kid. Maybe stupid parts of a kid, but, nonetheless, he was someone who entertained me.

We searched plenty of doors, while keeping watch for any sign of him, when we noticed a diverse piece of glass. It appeared to be quite thick, so I went up to the glass to review it and confirmed that it wasn't an obvious hiding place for a genetically engineered mutant. Sure enough, there Nazm was strapped to a table like some sort of test patient. They could never leave a mystery alone; it always had to be "resea-rched", which honestly meant poked a million times with no results coming out from thousands of dollars of the tax payer's money. There were seven of them in the room with him. Every time that somebody gazed back, we crouched down.

Whatever we evoked from our brains had better of been a good procedure, considering that I didn't envision them just letting us suffer by that point. I scratched my head as my hand wandered down to my chin, which was the way that I got the best solutions out. Then I had it, my first hair was protruding from my baby-faced chin. I couldn't control my urge to play with it until I was slapped by Gramps. That was right, a plan was what I was supposed to be thinking of. Then I thought of it; we could build an explosive to blow the door from its hinges to make a surprise entrance. There was a desk in the main room that we were in. We began checking the drawers for anything that may've been beneficial. I found a scrap of unwrapped, original flavored gum that I stuck in my mouth to chew the hell out of.

I relocated the pistol that was in a drawer to the side, where I exposed a baggie of gun powder that I abducted and wrapped it tightly inside of Grandpa's shirt, well, part of it. After discovering a few wires, I merged them together with the gum and the gun-powder. I set the bomb alongside of the entryway. I didn't have the slightest clue on how to wire anything, so I lit the cloth on fire in advance to diverting ourselves behind the desk. I waited and waited until the section smoldered to ash so I had to relight it, stashing myself again. Finally, it made the intended boom, but it was not as intense as I had expected. It left the impression that it hadn't done anything. All I had done was fabricate a homemade firecracker. That was what years of being a pyromaniac, and not being a chemistry geek, got me: crap.

Seven suited Asians came out of the door, while Gramps and I stalled, huddling underneath the desk. We heard them inching closer to us until they were situated on the other side of the desk. I had to seal Grandpa's mouth with my moist palms so that they wouldn't overhear his whimpers. Everything was muted until the desk roughly divided in half when a guy downgraded through it and collapsed on us. I tried to wiggle free, but I just couldn't suck my gut in that far. I directed Gramps to help me elevate the evil on the count of three so that my organs didn't liquidate from out of my nostrils. He forced the guy off of us without even putting any effort into it. It made me wonder why it was so strenuous for us the previous couple of seconds. He must not have been trying, as usual. The wrinkles didn't bring the wiseness; they brought the laziness.

We carried ourselves back up to our feet to watch Nazm fighting off seven guys at once. He must've broken free from the straps somehow when the testers abandoned him. They had to have been idiots, considering that they were all approaching him without weapons. The foes were being catapulted all over the property. The rival that descended upon us and attempted a poorly planned attack, while he was still on the ground (because a dive is not the way to initiate an assault), received a kick from me in the cheek, like I was going for a field goal. Gramps came back with a punt just as solid from the opposite side. It was similar to a recipe; we beat him until his face became creamy. The skin seemed to mash into the muscle and developed a mixture that children could get slimed with if it had been green.

By the time that we got done pounding the guy's face into jam, the attackers that Nazm was combating had possessed some weapons from a distant room. They must've had a human sacrifice distract him while they retrieved the weapons, seeing that there was what appeared to be a man ripped to shreds that had been scattered throughout the room. I hoped that nobody slipped and shattered their spinal columns throughout the whole ordeal. Homicide was more enjoyable to watch. The only resource that those guys had were knives that were dwarflike, compared to a butcher knife, which would do zilch to a corpse who has had his entire body ripped from his head and remained one of the undead. They flawlessly encircled Nazm so that no matter which way he rotated, he would be challenging at least two of them. Every time that he would physically assault a particular one of them, the spares from behind would trot up and stab him in the back repeatedly until he backhanded them to the floor.

Eventually, Nazm deciphered what was going on, so he faked them out by making a short step towards a guy. But, when the two behind him rushed up, he spun around and immediately grasped each of their throats before fracturing their necks. With his four fingers, he crippled their vertebral column, while he crushed their windpipes with his thumbs. Following the eradication of the other two, space was added around Nazm, where the enemies could spread out to outline a circle again. Nazm lunged at the one in front of him and elevated him up above his head. The last pair pursued stabbing him in the ribcage, but his body language suggested that it didn't faze him. The meat peeked out from the wounds that were spitting on his clothing. Nazm dropped the opponent in his grasp onto his knee and clearly broke the guy in half. That action propelled splintered bone fragments through the air. He orbited his arms around to his back and captured the other two by their shirts. He reduced them to the ground and modified his clutch to their ankles. Nazm then had the control by suspending them upside down as they swayed about and strove to escape by using their fists. He lowered them onto their craniums repeatedly, until there was enough blood loss hanging out on the floor to suggest that they had died. They were plunged into their own bodily fluids, like they shouldn't have been permitted any respect. Not even the dead should disrespect the dead.

There wasn't another soul around, so we wandered outside to collect an automobile. The only thing disregarded on the street that wasn't overturned was a tiny compact car; we got lucky. I fantasized about how much money could be saved on gas. We immigrated past the doors into the car, where the keys were already in the ignition. I was content with finding a trespasser, but there was no one in sight. I guessed that the owners weren't planning on their car being in that neighborhood when they returned. We disappeared from that town for forever without any further complications.

Chapter 9:
Child Molester's
Fear Elderly Men

All I did was maintain commuting west, until we had to make a stop for the black sludge: gas. I liked to go to the least busy gas stations on account of us regularly attracting a sickening degree of the spotlight. We discontinued our journey at one that appeared to have been resurrected in the 1950's. It still had the access point to the powder room outside around back. I authorized Gramps and Nazm to wait in the car, while I obtained the key from the tool that was working for the gas station. I arrived at the counter inside and inquired about it when they explained to me that I needed to lease them my driver's license until I escorted the key back. Seriously, what was I going to do, keep it in storage and return whenever I needed to use the bathroom? I handed the clerk a hundred dollar bill and plead for her to accept that instead until I got back. She gladly welcomed my proposition as she presented me with the key that was joined by a chain with an old shoe. It seemed like the clerk yearned for me to take it. I mean, who wouldn't want another shoe? I dismissed myself racing around to the back, where there was a group that was categorized as bullies that were loitering.

I had never been fond of clusters of youngsters that hung out around bathrooms. Nothing productive ever came from it, but I had to creep past them to get to the door. I made it beyond them to the entrance when I became aware of the twigs that were cracking behind me. I turned around and stared at the three of them that had pressed their bodies up against mine. I mentioned to them that I felt more comfortable going to the potty when I was the exclusive member of the room or else it made it difficult for me to urinate. I didn't suspect that they took my feelings into consideration, since they just stood in place and crossed their arms. Not that mankind doesn't look cool when they cross their arms, but, when they were trapping a guy near a men's bathroom, nothing was cool.

They were beginning to nudge me softly towards the opening. When they got inappropriately close to me, they letup and shoved me back into the brick wall. The bullies expressed that I needed to give them my stock of belongings. Everything I owned was perched on the dashboard of the car, so I stuck out my hand that was dominating the key attached to the shoe that was aged enough to retire. One of them swatted it out of my palm while another slammed me against the bricks and held me there by crinkling up my shirt. The last bully commenced to search my pockets for valuables, but he couldn't find a thing. The youth that was restraining me socked me in the stomach. I speculated that he predicted that I would slump to the gravel from getting the wind knocked out of me, but I was still standing tall without wet underwear. How come he got to have all of the fun? So, I figured, what was the worst that could happen if I packaged up and delivered a punch to his gut? He lessened forward to the ground and shaped clouds of dust while he coughed. That was probably the motion that he was waiting for. The two left standing sprung up on me, so I gave them the same thing and left them both on the ground. While they were catching up on breathing, I went into the restroom to catch up on getting rid of the nutrients that I didn't need anymore. They started to bang on the door while I was in the middle of doing my thing. I didn't understand why everyone longed to disrupt me at the most relaxing part of my day? When I finished tinkling, I twisted the doorknob, while bearing my density forward. I was going to teach those guys a lesson in manners. But my primary objective was to pull the door open, since that was the way it became ajar. I didn't get to cleanse my hands, but I rejoiced whenever I had an excuse to not do that. I was doubtless that there were more germs in the air at that instant than on my hands, so what was there to stress about?

When I drew the door, near me, a single bully slipped in, so I slammed the escape shut as I heard his buddy scuttle into it. The man-loving bully lunged at me as I sidestepped him, and he whisked his face into the concrete wall. I entangled him in a headlock as I delivered blows to his abdomen in repetition until I got bored; then I transported him over to the sink. The guy was being foul-mouthed towards me, plus he called me nasty names, so I dropped him on the tile below the soap dispenser. He was out of wind, so he didn't struggle to move. Still, I placed my foot on his chest just in case. I pumped the soap out as fast as possible and squirted soap all over his face, along with in the interior of his snack consumer; the sinners needed to be penalized. After the soap refused to come out, I tore the dispenser off of the wall with one hand and chucked it at his face. He stayed laying there as the blood cuddled with the outer layer of skin on his forehead before cheating on it with the scum in between the tiles. I was afraid that I may've killed him. I was only trying to teach him a lesson: that soap was not one of the food groups in the pyramid.

The final couple of bullies were still outside a hootin' and a hollerin'. I made the passageway accessible to let another one in as I locked the last one out. Before the next big, bad bully could even react to identifying his friend on the ground, extensively blood-splattered, I gave him a right hook to the jaw. His head collided with the rim of the toilet, which knocked him out cold. I enabled the last teenager an opportunity to gain access, but, when he did without delay, he flipped out when he distinguished that both of this friends were lying on the grimy floor in a comatose state. I didn't feel bad for him, though, I bet they contributed in the paralyzing of a ton of children before attempting to pull the same old crap on me.

The Final stood back, cranking his neck back and forth to abort the stiffness. He charged at me, but I dodged him, snatching his momentum by the long beautiful locks of hair that was joined to his scalp. I mean, it was girly hair, perfectly un-manly. The propulsion from him running led us to the sink, where I bashed his face against the faucet over and over until a majority of his teeth plopped into the drain. I shoved him to the ground, where he became motivated to crawl backwards. I progressed over towards the toilet to unscrew the stick off of the plunger; in the following moment, I beat him with it until he terminated all movement.

I exited the potty with my pride in tact as I peeked around the corner of the station and waved

Grandpa over. After he vacated the compact car, I recommended that he go into the bathroom, so I relinquished the dirty shoe. It had been awhile since he had disposed of a lifeless corpse, so it would reduce his crabbiness later on. I went back to the indoors of the store to seek out adhesive bandages so that I could wrap Grandpa's arm up (from when the anti-food eating Asians had skinned him as a form of torture). The woman at the counter wouldn't stop nagging me no matter how many times I announced to her that I granted my Grandpa the use of the key. She pretended to care an awful lot for the bathroom that reeked of moldy tuna fish. The clerk persisted in threatening me by flashing my money in the air. I would get it back; she would see.

I gazed out of the glass doors, blinding myself on the glare. I was puzzled as to why it was taking Gramps an eternity besides his sluggish eating habits. I contemplated checking on him until I realized that I sheltered a dollar in my underwear, which meant that I could invest in a candy bar while I waited. After I ingested the first one, I had enough leftover money to purchase one more, so I did and inhaled it, too. I got the clerk to supply me with a couple more with the promise of paying her back when the key was recovered.

At last, I sighted Gramps on the flipside of the glass ready to come in, but there was a problem. He still had flesh hanging from his teeth. Furthermore, he was thoroughly drenched in blood. I attempted to get to the door before he could gain entry, but I slipped on a freshly mopped area of tile. I complained to them from across the room about not having a "Caution: Wet Floor" sign up. Gramps pranced inside with that stupid smile/grin on his face. He accompanied the key over to the counter and distributed it to the woman, while he continued to slurp down whatever was still pasted on his face. He nodded and wandered away, not even comprehending that his presence was a wee bit suspicious.

I spotted the clerk reaching for the phone to do what I was guessing was to call the cops. I got up off of my saturated butt (from water this time) and ran straight for her. Once I was within a proximate radius, I jumped the counter, like a hurdle, and plucked the phone cord that ripped out of the socket. The landing was harsh, since I clipped the hurdle with my knee. Grandpa drifted to my direction and shouted about how I wasn't being courteous. This guy consumed his food sloppier than any wild animal I have ever seen, and he was trying to tell me how to be polite. I extended my pointer finger straight up, bending it back and forth, letting him know to get over to me, or I would have to strangle his windpipe. He actually came; I was presuming that he'd be a total doofus about it by crossing his arms before telling me no.

When he made it over to me, I picked a sample of gore that was bonded to his chin off and unveiled it to him. Gramps confessed that it was there because he was hungry, not registering my point at all. I flung it back in his face, where it clung over his eye. A panicked innocent bystander plus a phone call equaled the police, I advised him. When he sympathized with me about screwing up, he imprisoned the woman by the upper spinal column assaulting the counter with her face once before tossing her to the ground, where he was arranging to rip into her. I booted him in the kidney and commanded him to vacate the mounted position on top of her. He already had three people for dinner. That was an appetizer, meal, and dessert. There was never such a thing as two desserts in a meal with the exception of mine, but a gallon of ice cream came in much smaller serving sizes than human beings.

Grandpa poised himself upright again without me having to pester him anymore. There were a couple random customers left in the store that I detected were attempting to leave, from the corner of my eye. The sole thing that I had always been a firm believer in was not enabling any witness to leave unless you were already out of sight. I went over to the door and accelerated like a bullet train to implant a broom through the handles. Grandpa must've came across a gun under the counter, considering that he was swinging it around and declaring to everyone that if they made a step towards an escape he would open fire. It was practically like he was a seasoned robber. I had never learned what that meant on account of seasoning not making food better in general. Really, it should've been is a condimented robber, considering what it would be like without condiments: hell on earth. Everybody obeyed Gramps as they backed against the freezers in the rear of the store. There were only five people nested in the store, including the woman at the counter. There was a child about six years old who was with his mom that was undoubtedly hot. The other two were men that had the appearances of lumberjacks. They had the big bushy beards that I was terribly jealous of, along with the awe-inspiring 100% cotton plaid shirts. I felt awful for holding them there, away from the rest of the world. It was selfish of me to hog them; they deserved better. Everybody was shivering because of the freezers, except for the lumberjacks. They had enough protection from the frigid weather. I wouldn't release anyone until I attained the gauze for Grandpa. The clerk directed me to the aisle that I required. Once the gauze was in my custody, we approached the entrance that was soon to be an exit.

When I was extracting the broom handle from within the door, I noticed that there were two police vehicles outside of the station. They were anticipating our departure so that they could send a flurry of lead into our guts. The darn clerk must've pressed some kind of alert button to contact the police. I burglarized the gun from Gramps as I paced over to the clerk resting the barrel against her forehead. I asked her why she would do something so irresponsible when all that we had to do was buy an item and leave. She stuck to her story and denied my accusations, but, moreover, she wouldn't give me back my money. The sweat cascaded down her forehead at an increasing rate the longer that I held the gun there. I could've taken a life like that, I was only panicked and overreacting, though. My behavior was out of line; I couldn't seem to take my finger off of the trigger in my state of pure and non-filtered rage. My finger slipped down on the trigger on accident and caused the bullet to evacuate the chamber as it traveled through her head and penetrated the milk carton behind her, shattering the glass on the refrigerator door, too. The clerk's anatomy dropped to the floor, while her neck tilted backwards into the cooler. The milk drizzled through the grating of the shelves into her head injury and invented a tasty looking treat that I didn't have the time for. The innocent people cowered, while the scruffy lumber-jacks stood there unaffected. I had never experienced such guilt in my lifetime for a mishap. I mean igniting a girl's hair with butane was nowhere near as emotion-ally scarring as killing her. The first thing that I reflected on was whether or not she had kids. How would I ever deal with myself again? I had to find out though. It would just suffocate me if I never got the information.

I took a trip into their break room and authorized Gramps to handle the gun so that I could seek out her purse. Once I discovered its location, I rummaged through the innards for a wallet that usually should've had pictures inside of it. As expected, in the innermost section of her wallet was a flipbook of photographs. There was a picture of her positioned alongside of an elderly man that appeared to be a lot older than Grandpa. When I flipped to the immediate photograph, it was of her kissing the same senior and not as if he was a family member either. Well I supposed that the planet could always do without one less pervert, but, if she was in love with him, I guess it wouldn't be that immoral. Then I saw her student I.D., which let me know that she was only a sophomore in high school, which meant that she was like 13. (I'm not mathematician, though.) I loathed the decrepit abomination that sustained vital signs so that he could walk the earth instead of her. I situated the wallet back in her purse, throwing the strap over my shoulder; I agreed with myself that I needed to find that old bastard later. I arrived out of the back with a purse on my shoulder, so everyone ogled me.

Even if it wasn't my purse, a man should've been permitted to have one if he needed the extra space. Those burly lumberjack men still stood there not even shedding a laugh. I got up in the youngster's face, challenging his guts by asking him what was so funny; he shut right up. It's impressive how cool I am that I can shut people up by getting in their face. I attempted to make it perfectly clear that I was only trying to get out of there without receiving any puncture wounds. So if I had to employ one of them as a human shield, I would.

I looked to where the rays of sunshine were coming from by peeking through the door to watch for where Nazm was. He remained seated in the car still, waiting for us to come back out. It was astonishing how he never even considered that the cops could be there for us. Lucky that we were entrapped in a tiny village, being that the only two cops in town were presently there. My goal was to find an additional way out. I remembered distinguishing that there was a back door when I was in the break room.

I ordered the lumberjack heroes to retire out through the back doorway, and I would dispense my gun to them. They were instructed to run within the visibility of the cops away from the building with the gun waving in the stratosphere. This was to mislead the police into pursuing them so that we could make an easy retreat. The lumberjacks said that they would complete my task only if I let one of them run out holding the axe that was in the emergency casing, along with the fire extinguisher. It was fine with me if they honestly needed to satisfy themselves. I directed them to run left with their weapons held high when I unfastened the door. When the alleyway was revealed, they held their weapons high, but they sped off to the right by preference. That's what the results are when you put your trust in another mans hands, especially bearded men in plaid shirts. Those ones are nothing but a nuisance.

My foolproof plan had run dry. They only ever went incorrectly because other people just don't get it. I came out of the back hanging my head in shame; I was screwed. It was simply a matter of time before the cops got indoors and shot me dead. I took a peep through the door to behold how close my death was when I saw that Nazm had gotten out of the car. The cops turned around to see what the pitter patters of footsteps were.

There was an officer that revolved, facing towards us, while the other one kept his gun drawn at Nazm. The officer ordered him to return to the vehicle and leave the crime scene. Nazm never failed to be slightly delayed when it came to conditions like that, so he stood there with the seemingly routine puzzled look on his face. He lumbered ahead closer to the cop. The police officer extended his invitation for him to stay back, or he would shoot. Nazm still progressed forward, leaving the police officer with no other alternative. He discharged a slug into Nazm's kneecap. He reviewed the physical harm done to him, while a tear slid down his cheek, not because of pain, but due to the lack of trust.

Nazm pounced at the officer who'd shot him, while the opposite one spun around. He brought the base of his palm up to the cop's expression, forcing his nose into his brain. Even though the blood was rushing down Nazm's arm, he still wouldn't let go. He only tightened his grip further on the officer's forehead putting on enough pressure that his fingertips began to burrow through the skin. I heard the cracking as they penetrated his skull and squirted mush out of the wounds. Nazm placed his unoccupied hand up against the cop's thorax, while he yanked with his other hand and severed the cranium clear off of the body.

The surviving officer was glued in place in a complete daze, perhaps not believing what he was seeing. As soon as he snapped out of it, he spared no time in unloading his gun into Nazm's chest. He did it in the fit of a temper tantrum for feeling unloved, I assume, since he devoted his entire existence to all people, until they tried to murder him. Nazm brought his arm back towards him that possessed the deceased officer's cranium and followed it with a prompt motion forwards that left the head spiraling through the air into the surviving cop's face. The cop toppled to the tar from the velocity of the throw, stained with blood that was not his own. Once he caught a glimpse of the blood on his hands, he freaked out, going into a state of shock. Nazm advanced towards the cop, while the officer maintained his position on the ground staring at his hands. Just before Nazm reached the cop, he awakened from his daze and attempted to run, but it was too late. Nazm was already immediately next to him as he ensnared him by the collar of his uniform. He elevated the officer up by it transporting him over to our compact car. Nazm snatched one of the gas pumps and lifted up the lever before depositing the nozzle into the cop's mouth. It obligated him to get to his knees, holding absolutely stationary. The cop kept attempting to take the nozzle out, so Nazm placed one hand on the top of his head and the other on the bottom pushing together like a vice until his teeth cracked. After that occurrence, the cop suspended himself there, doing nothing wrong, except probably hoping that he could ascend to heaven if he prayed before he passed away. Nazm put pressure on the handle pumping fuel down the officer's throat. It didn't last long before he pulled away, due to the burning sensation that I had felt first person when I wanted to see what gasoline tasted like one day. The cop started to crawl away, depending on a medical center that wasn't next door.

Then we saw Nazm make a pink translucent lighter appear from within in our car. We became a bit uneasy as we darted out there to stop him as soon as possible. We were not able to make it to him before he flipped open the top spinning the coil that established the spark. He threw the lighter at the cop that had now crawled at least out of the pump area. Nazm lobbed it at the officer and made the contact that torched him like a human hamburger. The aroma was delicious, but deadly, since he still had live rounds on him I was predicting. Gramps charged into Nazm, propelling him into the vehicle, while I entered the interior from the driver's side. The key twisted in the ignition, but the car protested against starting for an abuser. I watched in the rearview mirror as the flames were coming in our direction. I gave it one last try, holding the gas pedal down, while I turned the key. The car took off into the middle of the street. Thank the ghost of Jesus that no one was using it at the time. Behind us, the blaze had reached the gas pumps that were exploding a single one at a time. One of the pump's carcasses flew onto the gas station, changing it into an inferno. The people that were sheltered inside came stumbling out, bursting in flames, along with my hundred dollars. I had a feeling that it might magnetize some unwanted attention, so we sped off down a span of blocks to another gas station that had a payphone where we could drive up to it to call someone without having to get out of the car.

I seized the purse that I still had over my shoulder to inspect the clerk's address book for the over-aged child molester's phone number. I was pretty sure that I found it the moment that I distinguished the name Herman with a bunch of hearts around it; a crystal clear sign that he was elderly and that she was a loser. I rolled down my sheet of glass before apprehending the phone that didn't spin, instead having buttons. I dialed the number, waiting beyond the ringing for a voice. A male answered it that positively didn't sound like a creature that had a whole lot of days left in his worthless existence. I impersonated the representative for Uh-Ohs (an off brand of adult diaper), notifying him that he had won a two-year supply of old folk's diapers, so it was essential for me to gather his address so that we could drop them off.

After waiting past five minutes of him struggling to catch his breath from too much excitement, he conveniently handed over his address. The only botheration would be locating the street.

I snagged the phone book that was attached to a chain from the phone. I flipped through the first quarter of the white pages, looking for the city street map. I didn't check the index, because I wanted to save time. I ultimately found them, along with finding the correct city that we were in. So then all I had to discover was where Birch Street was. It took me a brief moment longer than it would most of the public, considering my trouble with letters. So it happened that it was only a few blocks away from where we were earlier. The sirens were approaching the location, so I figured that it would doubtlessly be a good proposal if we fled the scene. We commuted down a block, then another, then back one, and then to the right, without getting lost. Finally, we pulled up to a house that had a flower garden in the front with bird feeders that were hanging from every tree; I was confident that it was the residency that we were questing for. No respectable dinosaur would've had a home like that and certainly not a middle-aged man.

I parked in the driveway behind his van, just in case he felt the need to use his walker to duck out. We stepped out of the car to walk suspiciously up to the entrance. I struggled to unlatch the screen door so that I could knock on the actual door, but it was locked. Not at any time have I ever known anybody to do such a thing. With no other options left, I knocked on the screen, being optimistic that someone with such a large lifetime would detect me.

After scraping my knuckles raw on the covering for an extremely long time, a guy finally answered the door, but he only opened it a sliver with the chain still joined to the door. He yelled at us just because he couldn't identify who we were. I updated him that we were there to distribute the Uh-Ohs that he won. He refused to believe me since I didn't have the merchandise in my hands. I proclaimed that they were held within the trunk, which he actually fell for. I couldn't understand it either because the trunk wasn't even grand enough fit a mutilated sheep in let alone two years worth of adult-sized diapers. In all actuality, I had no idea how much two years worth was, but, if it was one per wee wee time, it had to have been a hefty quantity. He shut the door, which wasn't a bad thing, since I could hear him unchaining it.

The fossil in the doorway was the same guy in the photo. He unlocked the screen door only to walk away without greeting us. I was assuming that it was an invitation in. If not, it really didn't matter, being that he was going to expire either way. We disengaged the screen door from its latches, but the instant that we entered he bickered at us, while pointing to our footwear, trying to make us evacuate them.

Like I gave a crap, I never ceased my motivation into the bowels of his home with plastic covered furniture, but I overheard Gramps and Nazm letup to take theirs off. I marched back to the duo to open palmed slap them in the backs of their heads. Without hesitation, I shifted around to my previous route, heading back towards Herman the Skin Covered Skeleton. He continued to point his finger at me, giving me that common ancient being attitude. Once I advanced my way to him, I knelt down punching him in the hip. I didn't kick him because my leg wouldn't rise up to that altitude. He slumped onto the linoleum immediately, clutching his hip and grumbling about how he recently had to have hip surgery. What a rarity: an over aged man having hip problems.

Gramps and Nazm belatedly came over to me, but they didn't obey my orders and had taken off their shoes anyway. Herman should've let them keep their shoes on since presently they were only dragging blood and mold along the floor, instead of just mud, and mud was considerably easier to get out of carpet. I directed my fist back to Herman and mentioned to him that we were there to donate to him a homemade execution. He queried why we were going to do that in a frustrated tone. It was as if he didn't even want to make an effort into getting us to let him live. It must've been because he only had a year left before his expiration date anyway, which made it not worth the energy.

I notified him that his execution would be for having dirty fornication with an underage girl. He attempted to argue with me that the only motivation behind my actions was that I couldn't get a woman myself, and he could get a voluptuous one at such an aged adulthood. It was too preposterous for it to be true. I wasn't prepared for a serious relationship. I had too many goals for my career before I had to contribute my entire life to a partner. I had been taught that you have to sign everything over to them, even how much you devour is in their custody, and I wasn't equipped for that yet. If I did that, I would never be able to claim victory at a hotdog-eating contest. I booted Herman in the kneecap before he grasped it, falling over onto his back. I planted the sole of my shoe on his chest, situating weight into it. I hardly had to put any leverage into it before I detected bones that were beginning to fracture. They honestly didn't display deceit when they said that the older you got, the more brittle you became.

He still exhibited no sign of pain really, only anger. I heard the door being struck by bare knuckles.

Herman let us know that he invited some acquaint-tances over for supper. I suspected that if I had him not answer the door the visitors would call 911, fearing that he had passed away. I counseled him to say that we were relatives, or we would be compelled to slay his friends, too. He responded by declaring that he wouldn't show any dismay if his acquaintances dropped dead. So, instead of that, I reported that if he didn't cooperate with us, we would skin his cat alive within his vision perception before we assassinated him. That was his introduction to the mayhem he would be forced to endure if he didn't agree to go along with it, which he did.

I proceeded to answer the unpleasant noise as Gramps and Nazm assisted Herman in making his way to the door. I opened up the cause of the racket, where I was confronted by not one, but two old people. The statue on the left was a wrinkly old lady with excess-ively curly hair, while the other was what appeared to be an old man being, serviced by an oxygen mask that was hooked up to rolling a tank that was situated next to him. The elderly lady asked where Herman was, so I explained to her that he would be to the door in a second. When Herman got near the door, I whispered in his ear to get rid of them. They interrogated Herman with a single question, asking who we were. He enlightened them that we were young friends of his. He was doing well until he prompted them to come in.

After they accessed the living room, I followed behind Herman, shoving him into the wall to ask him what the hell he thought he was doing. He didn't seem to register the vital information too well, so I translated it to him one final time. He revealed that he was only wearing a hearing aid in the opposite ear so that was why he didn't catch what I was saying. I supposed that I would let them remain active, since it was my error, but, the next time, I wasn't going to stress over whose mistake it was. I would kill them all, no doubt about it. It was not like I would have a profuse amount of trouble finishing off three old folks that couldn't even get out of the chairs that they were relaxing in without help.

They quizzed Herman on what we were gorging ourselves in for supper. Being the wiseass that he was, he announced that he wasn't sure, since I was going to compose it. I was about to disfigure all of them, but I considered that it may be considerably more amusing if I messed with his acquaintances to make him be remembered forevermore as a jackass. I ransacked the cupboards to find the easiest thing to make: macaroni and cheese. When I prepared it, I substituted all of the milk in the recipe with butter (none of that margarine crap). I chopped up some cold hot dogs straight from the freezer before dumping them in the pot. To top it all off, I squirted ketchup and mustard in a spiral on the pinnacle of it to add some class. I accompanied it out to the table in the pot. I wasn't going to serve it up to any of those fossils. They were a bit stunned when they examined what I had fixed for supper, also because I dished myself up first without pausing for everybody else to get their rations.

They requested that I say grace first. I told them that I would after finishing my primary plateful. They didn't wait for me to announce their gratefulness to their Lord and Savior. Gramps smacked me when I didn't pay attention and started to eat. I desisted for him, but I was not thrilled. When everybody began to dish up, they resembled the anxiety emotion, except for Nazm, who didn't stop scarfing down to breathe, if he even had to. It was priceless watching everyone being polite and struggling to choke down my elegant meal. I couldn't believe how much the property reeked of that new car smell. It's weird how certain people have certain scents.

The elderly couple asked me how Herman and I met each other. I informed them of how we previously both got serviced from the massage therapist that we paid a small portion more to receive a little extra attention, more like a lot extra. They were undeniably offended. For a visual effect, every time that Herman wanted to expose my lies, I brought out the cheese grater and held the cat, because it wouldn't stop constructing dreams on my lap. There wasn't a time where he wouldn't seal his trap and go back to feasting upon the food the repulsed him.

Once we all finished digesting, I was ready to send the couple out of the front door, but they "had" to do their weekly crossword puzzle first, talk about a fun time. The cat sprung off my lap; I guess he predicted the boredom ahead. They pulled out a book that had to have been at a minimum of 600 pages long. I flipped to the middle, considering that they had already completed the first half. Grandpa asked to be excused from the table; I didn't understand why, though. Crosswords were his expertise, especially if they had questions about soap operas. There was no way he would've known; he didn't even take a peek at it. I stayed settled in my chair next to them and placed my cheek against the table in an attempt to doze off, but I was repeatedly getting asked questions, along with nudges when someone made a corny joke. After the constant call of suicide rang in my ears, I couldn't take it anymore, so I concluded that I should to go check on Gramps, since he had been missing from the scene for an extended period of time. I wasn't a wuss. I didn't ask to be excused; I just disappeared. I wandered down the hallway to where I prophesized the bathroom to be.

The door that I foretold to be the restroom wasn't; it was Herman's bedroom. It had a bright pink interior with an array of flowers plastered all over the wallpaper. If it wasn't meant to lure in underage girls, I don't know what would; although, I think he overshot the adolescence to about six instead of sixteen. I departed the room in pursuit of Grandpa again, not underage girls. I inspected the whole main floor, yet there was no indication of him, not even in the waste dispenser room, which meant that he was telling a fib. It was only a fib to me, since I couldn't think of another place he would've been. I overheard a commotion that came from the basement. The gateway was open a crack, so I traveled down the staircase. It was a nice finished basement with chains prefixed to the walls that had particles of skin bonded to them. When I got to the foot of the steps, I rounded the corner to view Gramps knelt on the ground. I interrogated him as to what he was doing down there. He spun around quickly, wiping the gore from his mouth, to confess to me that he was doing nothing. Whenever someone says they're doing nothing, they're always doing something wrong.

If he wasn't going to reveal the facts to me, then I'd to find out for myself. I maneuvered around him to take a peek at what he was doing, but, every time that I got in a satisfactory angle, he would position himself in the way. I ended up having to push him over to discover that he was in reality feeding upon the feline. I didn't care how sorry he claimed that he was; it didn't comfort me that our only form of having an upper hand on the geezer had dissipated. I became aware that the door at the highest point of the staircase opened and, furthermore, someone was toddling down them. We had to conceal the cat's carcass immediately before he saw that Gramps had slaughtered it.

I got onto the floor, scooping up the leftovers and shoveling them down Grandpa's shirt. I got rid of most of it before the old geezer reached the same level as us. Sure enough, it turned out to be the old man that sported the oxygen mask who was led astray while questing for the bathroom, even though he had visited it a hundred times. I took my stance and blocked the sight of the lower half of Gramps, while he slanted in front of the stain in hopes of it not being spotted. I pointed and steered the fossil upstairs to the lavatory inn, which it only took an over exaggerated hour to get him to reverse and head towards the top of the stairs.

After he had migrated away from us, I turned around and socked Grandpa in the gut on accident, spewing kitty guts onto his face. I advised him to clean it up during the time that I got washed up. I brought him a shirt to dwell over the bloodstained one that he was wearing. I delayed for a couple of minutes until I expected that the oxygen man would be out of the bathroom. I ventured upstairs to the waste depository, where the door remained locked; so I proceeded past it, going into Herman's bedroom, where I explored the closet for a shirt. It was loaded with outdated clothes from the 1950's. The closest thing that I could find to ordinary was a hooded sweatshirt that was laced with flannel on the inside.

Once I had cleansed all of the blood clots off of my hands onto his hanging outfits, I secured myself the hooded sweatshirt. When I passed the bathroom a second time on my way downstairs, it was still sealed. It sounded silent on the interior, but, like I was concerned that he could've had a stroke, he wasn't my fellow comrade. I navigated my hefty buttocks to the downstairs, where Gramps had his belly against the ground, licking the remainder of the carpet dry. I didn't care how famished he was, that should've been plain embarrassing, but Grandpa didn't seem to mind at all. I hurled the sweatshirt at him and instructed him to put it on over his head and get upstairs as soon as possible.

When I got back to the dining room table, Nazm was there getting hardcore into a crossword puzzle as if he had the facts to answer even a single question. That guy still couldn't figure out how to knot his shoelaces. The only way that he ever produced a meager amount of smarts was if he was in the heat of madness, but he for sure wasn't in one at that instant.

After squatting on the chair, I heard Gramps stomping up the stairs, but, instead of treading towards the table, he took an alternate route in the opposite direction. It was not like it was essential for him to freshen up. He had already brushed over his body with his tongue "sanitizing" himself before he came up. I stood up and strolled over to where his footsteps were heading. When I reached the hallway, I noticed that the washroom door was partway open. I situated my hand against the door and pushed it open, like a slacker, revealing to me the image of Gramps with his fingers inside of the old guy's mouth putting effort into tearing his jaw off. The circumference of his lips extended until the skin expanded too far to the point to where gaps were forming in between the flesh in his cheeks. Eventually, the pressure could be taken no more, and, when the tissue let go, it designed half a puzzle piece that was united with his face. The other half, along with his jaw, rested in Grandpa's scummy palm. I could identify that Respirator Man was still struggling to inhale, but he continued to suffocate on the bodily juices, while Gramps tore his tongue out and stuck it in his own mouth. After straining to squeeze another breath out, he finally resigned from his efforts. The only motion that he made thereafter was the death shuddering within the bowels of his innards.

Well, I knew that the lady wouldn't vacate the residence without her husband; so, legitimately, there was no substitute to committing carnage upon the woman, even though I admittedly didn't want to. I retired from the bathroom to arrive at the entrance, where I chained all the locks on the door. The lady stared at me with a hint of confusion as I advanced towards her placement. I expressed to the lady how I had no problem with her, but another mistake was hatched. It wasn't one that could go unpunished. I acquired the wooden spoon that was rested in the pot of nearly inedible macaroni and cheese as I plunged it handle end into her mouth. I grasped the back of her head previous to slamming her face into the table and hammered the spoon through the back of her gore soaked throat. She came back up, gushing blood like a two spouted sprinkler, but not lifeless. I felt God-awful because that had to have hurt like a bitch. Before she had the chance to turn to me and give me that "why would you disfigure me like that" look, I rammed her head into the table a last time so that the remnant of the spoon would discharge from out of the rear of her neck. She was arranged there, face down, with the blood flowing over the edges of the table, like a tainted waterfall.

Just when I presumed that death had taken over, she raised her head back up, swinging it in my direction. I drove my knuckles into her cranium, which resulted in her tumbling off of her chair. I hoisted the wooden chair above my head as I continued to beat her with it until it broke into fragments that were so small that they were unusable as weapons anymore. I felt horrible. But I couldn't be delivered that expression, or else it could've driven me to suicide.

When the woman left my focus, I directed it at Nazm who was awarding me with the worst look that he had ever given me. He captured me by the windpipe that he began to squeeze on. I rationalized with him and clarified that it had to be done, considering that Grandpa had already murdered her husband. If she was granted life, she would've went promptly to the police, which meant that we would've had to establish genocide with the police as the ingredients. He deduced what I was getting at, following me pointing out that Herman was making an escape attempt.

Herman would take one step, and then pause in anguish, only to take an additional one, five seconds later. He wasn't incredibly swift with his movements as they only measured out to approximately two inches apart. I leisurely shuffled my feet up to him simply to push him over. I notified him that my plans were foiled, being that I wasn't able to skin his fellow feline in front of him. I felt remarkably pleased about it, since I still got to do what I wished with the fossil. He fiercely declared that he was going to strangle me for that, but who would've paid any mind to such a threat when the person couldn't even boost himself off of the ground. Nazm exerted effort into stealing my kill from me before I cut him off dead in his tracks. I was certain that he meant well, but it was a specific thing that I had to achieve myself.

I got in Herman's face and reported that Grandpa had disposed his cat, and I shot his girlfriend right between the eyes. That was the first time that Herman had ever demonstrated any emotion as he sobbed like a girl, similar to the age of the ones that he was striving to fornicate with. There's nothing better than reducing a man to a whimpering baby before you put him out of his misery.

I obtained a knife, which I used to cut him from the center of his wrists to his forearms by trailing the vein. The skin split as fluid gushed out to escape the prison that it had been entrapped in for a lifetime. It was a necessity for him to have a short moment to comprehend that he was going to perish; also so that he could process the recent tragedies that had occurred before his vision went black. I didn't leave his sight until I admitted that there was no way that he wasn't truly dead and wasn't going to revive himself like the woman did.

I went back into the urine depository to get Grandpa to let him know that it was time to go. When I reached my destination, there wasn't a spot on the wall that wasn't splashed with hemoglobin. You would assume that after sixty years of table manners' experience, he could've at least kept the mayhem in the bathtub or a specific corner. I instructed him to get out of the bathroom since everyone was decomposing, which meant that it was time to go. He tried dragging the mangled carcass along with him, but I assigned him get rid of it before I would tolerate his behavior outside of the residence. He dropped the stinking corpse, and we all together said goodbye to the house.

We got into our automobile when we saw that the ancient couple had parked behind us so we couldn't get out, talk about being rude. I knew that if we had to retire to our households, they wouldn't have moved their car for us. I went back inside and plucked the keys from the woman's purse, along with all of the cash that was in it. I also abducted a bag that was overflowing with the garments from Herman's closet for Gramps to change into later so we didn't appear grotesquely suspicious if we had to exit the car for some reason.

I voyaged outside again where Grandpa and Nazm were throwing those white sparkly garden rocks at each other. They were skipping them against the cement driveway at midpoint, while the other one attempted to catch it. The rocks were banging up against the cars, while also striking each other in the face with them. My hypothesis was that they were striving to magnetize the most amount of awareness towards us. I commanded them to knock off the child's play and get into the car before anybody else could identify us. When I accessed the cushioning seat of the old couple's vehicle, I noticed that Grandpa had stubby white scuffmarks on his face from where he had been nicked with the rocks. He suffered the loss a few intelligence points in my book, which wasn't many to start with. I pitched the bag of clothing onto Grandpa's lap and lectured him to put them on whenever we came to a standstill, because he looked like a holocaust had hit him.

Out of one of Nazm's random acts of stupidity, he attained a rock that he had supported in his pocket and heaved it at the back of Grandpa's scalp, only to miss as it collided with the windshield, leaving a colossal fracture in it. I backhanded him without looking, but I knew I'd hit him when I made contact with something itchy that I distinguished as Nazm. I was optimistic that it got the point across.

Before we left, I had to shift the seat way back because of how short the crippled old man was. They had a newer automobile that when you pressed the handle down, it automatically drifted backwards at a supremely slow speed, but it was still neat. I put the car in reverse, but I must've shifted it down too far. When I put pressure on the gas pedal, it bolted forward, rear ending the car that we previously were mobilized in, not that it was a serious loss or anything. I evacuated the driveway, but our bumper must've been hitched on our prior vehicle, since we took the bumper with us. I had Gramps get out so that he could remove it. I was the driver, so I shouldn't have had to do anything apart from dominating the automobile's functions. Gramps fumbled with the bumper until he got it off before entering my domain once again.

It was definite that everybody in the surrounding region had acknowledged that something was going on, meaning that it would seemingly have been in our best interest to get the hell out of town. I took a spin back towards the gas station, being that it was the only way that I knew how to get back to the highway. When we passed the station, it was still spewing flames every which way, even catching an adjacent building on fire. There weren't many fire-fighters there. They must've not had any in the town. Foreign cities could've been importing some that took a while to get past the state border patrol.

Nobody recognized us when we drove by, not even the cops. The leads on who had committed the appalling felony may not have yet been surfaced. A tragedy always ensues when you mess with the Helty's.

We hit the onramp up to the highway, but, unfortunately, it was not busy. It only brought all the more attraction to us, which never implied a happy time. A majority of the Monday morning drivers were speeding around us, which indicated that they should get arrested before we ever did.

Chapter 10: Frisking Someone is Sort of Like Third Base

There was a police car heading towards us from the oncoming lane that flipped on its lights as it whipped a donut half into the no u-turn gravel spot that was enclosed between the lanes. I crossed my fingers and prayed to a specific cereal mascot for a miracle that would cause him pull over someone else other than us. He was accelerating rapidly behind us, but, thankfully, he switched into the neighboring lane. When he got a car's length in front of us, he slammed on his brakes, abusing them like a skinny albino orphan, as he pulled up behind us and made contact with our tailpipe. I didn't know what to do: pull into the creviced section of the road to get arrested, since we couldn't eliminate the cop behind us, or attempt to make a get away and have further police along with helicopters in pursuit of us? The unequaled option that was placed before us was to discontinue our pace and try to convince the officer that I was of the legal driving age. At least if we got arrested, it was manageable to break out of jail.

I pulled the car over and searched for the emergency blinkers, but I couldn't find the button. Grandpa pushed it for me, while I checked my pockets for a lesser quality fraudulent mustache that I anticipated I still had, but could've forgotten it in my other pants. By the time that I was done with my exhausting exploration, the cop was strolling along the white line up to the car. When he arrived at my door, he knocked on the window, so I supposed that I would roll it down for him. He asked me for my I.D., so I entrusted him with it, as he immediately handed it back and enlightened me that a library card doesn't pass for a valid I.D. Well, that may've construed a teeny little problem that would undoubtedly happen.

The policeman quizzed me on if I knew why he pulled me over. I explained to him that the only excuse that I could think of was because something so beautiful, such as myself, shouldn't be allowed to be viewed by the public. I guess that my prediction was somehow incorrect, but some things just shouldn't have been admitted to. He falsely informed me that there were a couple reasons. Reason #1: I was driving 35mph in a 70mph speed limit zone, and the minimum speed was 40mph. That wasn't even a decent reason. What was so erratic about me having a desire to be more cautious than the other crazy drivers on the road (even though I would've been one of them if I had observed how fast or slow I was going)? Reason #2: The windshield was cracked, which also wasn't a superb reason. How much does a crack in your windshield really affect your vision of the road? None, especially when it was on the passenger side of the car. If a glass fracture in the windshield was so bad, then why not start fabricating them out of plastic with a film over it that you could replace? It was the entire car manufacturer's fault, not mine. Reason #3: I appeared to be a teenager behind the wheel. First of all, I looked like a stud. Second of all, why should my age deter someone from encountering how capable I was of handling a spacious hunk of metal? It wasn't rocket science. Right, left, gas, and break. That was all you needed to be educated in. After my logic, he still wasn't willing to let us go.

I swept through the contents of my back pocket and uprooted $200. I've always heard that money can buy you anything, excluding love, but I wasn't trying to fall in love with the cop or have him all romantically entangled with me. So I was hoping that maybe it would bargain my way out of a ticket. When he requested my I.D. a second time, I extended my arm as to bestow upon him a handshake, which I sort of did just with currency on the interior. He inserted it into his pocket, so I got a running start on rolling up my window, until he ruled that I had to retire from the car. I stepped out of the car and asked him what the problem was. He said bribery was illegal, so he was going to lock me up behind bars for it, along with all the other laws that I had broken. I commanded him to provide me with my $200 so that I could put it towards the bail. The corrupt officer acted like the $200 I gave him never existed, what a stupid dummy. Boy, oh, boy, did I not fancy those classifications of cops.

He pounded me up against the car door and locked the handcuffs around my wrists before towing me into the backseat of his squad car. The oinker then paraded back to our car with an ego trip and installed Gramps and Nazm in handcuffs, too, before heaving them into the backseat with me. The cop set out on an expedition down the highway at a routine speed to take us back to the county jail. I noticed that Nazm was separating the handcuffs behind his back until the chain snapped. I indicated to him with my eyes to tug on mine to split them too. He seized my hands and began to pull them apart with all of his strength. I muttered to him to use the chain as the location to pull apart at, not lacerate my hands clear off of their tender wrists. He said, while not whispering, that he couldn't even strain to hear what I was communicating. The cop shouted at us to shut up, but I delivered him the finger, where he couldn't see it to teach him a lesson. I whispered to Nazm once again. Thankfully, he sensed what I was getting across that time as he yanked my chain until it broke.

I didn't stress too much about Grandpa getting free at that moment, so I authorized Nazm to breach the bulletproof glass barrier or whatever component it was constructed out of in between us and the cop. Nazm created a high velocity impact with his fist, thrusting it out of its designated enclosure into the neck of the cop. The glass was knocked out of its alignment as I stretched my arms through and wrapped my curled fingers around his throat. He veered in miscellaneous directions for a bit before being forced to pull over so that he could attempt to exercise some type of self defense. He struggled to turn around because my grip was strangely stronger than he figured it would be. I was assuming by the way he lost consciousness and nailed his head on the steering wheel.

I plucked the keys off of his belt to unlock the handcuffs on Gramps. He shoved me out of the way and transported the cop into the backseat with him, where he began to devour everything behind the officer's rib cage. The sticky feeling of blood flooded over the interior of the car. I mentioned for Gramps to save the head for me, so he tore it off, rupturing the tendons from the spinal column, before handing it to me. I pitched it onto the floor on the passenger side as I clambered through the space into the driver's seat. I had to make a brief pit stop before I got to do the only decent thing that I would get to do out of the whole expedition.

I pulled off of the highway onto a desolate gravel road, where I brought the car to a standstill on the side of it. I exited the patrol vehicle and walked around to the trunk. I pried it open, forgetting about the lever in the car when I discovered that the decent had turned into the wondrous. There was a sack in the center of the trunk that had a spare change of uniform in it (perhaps in case of the ever so often jelly stain). I shook my fist at the visitors in the vehicle, advising them not to sneak a peek while I changed.

The gruesome twosome sustained their attraction to me, so I had to swap uniforms in the corn field that was bordering the road. It was saturated with cobwebs, but that didn't bother me on preceding occasions, except for that time I could feel the sweet caress of the spiders crawling inside of my pants. I have mixed feelings about that incident. On one hand, it felt kind of erotic, but, on the other hand, it was not acceptable to admit it. The uniform fit properly around my midsection, but the sleeves and pant legs were too long. So I had to roll them up.

I wandered out of the corn field, but there wasn't a soul-less form that remained in the car. I squinted, gazing down the road, coupled with every-where surrounding me, yet I didn't spot Gramps or Nazm anywhere. I got back into the driver's seat and intended on waiting for them to come back. They most likely just stopped to snack on a farm animal or something; it was no big deal. There wasn't a point in my life expectancy that I couldn't handle myself. A hand grasped me from the backseat, where I swore nobody was and held me back against the warm cushion. A single arm was wrapped around my chest,

while the other was placed beneath my chin, controlling my head movement, so all that I could see was
the ceiling. I thrashed my legs about, doing my
damndest to get loose, when I encountered the shaking
of the shocks on the car from something thumping onto
the hood. The phantom arms relieved me a bit and
granted me permission to witness what activities were
going on beyond the windshield. Nazm was crouched
on the hood of the car and was pointing and giggling at
me with an expression similar to being man tickled to
death. My eardrums detected Grandpa in the back,
laughing his ass off, too. I sprained my strenuous
muscles until I peeled his arms away from my body to
say goodbye to the automobile of hilarity as swiftly as
I could.

I put up my dukes, forewarning them that I
could take them both on with my fists of steel, but they
just stood there and snickered. I went into the backseat,
subtracting the belt accessory from the cop to settle it
around my waist. I removed the pepper spray from its
holder and depleted its contents into Grandpa and
Nazm's corneas. They embraced their eyes in astonishment as I directed my finger at them giggling to
demonstrate to them what funny was. I ordered them to
get back into the security vehicle without hesitation or
I would beat the excess crap out of them while they
were blinded. When they undertook the task of getting
back into the car, they promoted stupidity by running
into the door, since they couldn't find the handles. It
cheered me up watching them in such a humiliating
situation while performing a personal play with a
brilliant portrayal of foolishness at the same time.

When we entered the state vehicle, I acquired a
small knife out of my utility belt and snatched up the
severed cranium of the policeman that was deposited
on the floor. I stationed the blade up against his

mustache as I began to slice it off by a few layers of skin underneath of it. I examined the glove compartment and rummaged for anything that could paste the mustache to my oily skin. There was an array of stuff. Vaseline, a stuffed animal bunny, a container of green fluid that looked like, at one point, it could've been in gelatin form, and that was only the start of the weird stuff. The lone thing that I found useful in there was super glue. I swear that I heard somewhere that you shouldn't let super glue make contact with your skin, but I was constantly learning fictitious information from the world that was out to kill me. I squirted enough of it onto the raw flesh behind the mustache, where I believed that it would hold. The cheap tube trickled a bit, allowing the leak to cling to my hands as I put them up to my face. Once I stuck the average mustache to my face, it was fine until I had to strip my palms from my cheeks. I only maintained a mild burning sensation for a couple of minutes until it matured into an extremely itchy feeling. Itching always meant a rough time.

I required Grandpa to toss me the badge of the police officer. He was rubbing about the crust of the cop searching for it since his eyesight still wasn't up to par after the mace incident. I demanded that Gramps quit feeling up the cop. I knew that he was deceased and all, but that was about the end of the things that they had in common. Gramps attempted to explain himself as he handed me up the badge, but I wasn't impressed by his excuses. I pinned the star to my uniform as I positioned the officer's shades over my eyes and left the disconnected head to ogle me with a single eye cocked to the side. It creeped me out, so I had Nazm roll down his window so that I could catapult the noggin into the corn field. I could imagine that it was a good enough burial for someone as disconnected as he was, get it? He was disconnected, because his head wasn't attached to his body anymore.

I deserted the gravel wasteland for the luxury of the highway to return to our adventure. Grandpa had remained in the back, composing squishing noises with the cop. He did that stuff just to irk my nerves; I knew it. Meanwhile, I was driving along, sensing the power of the badge soaking through my shirt as I longed to collide with a flock of punks who were feeling lucky. I halted on starting anything until I was out of the county, just in case they put out a search on the license plates. You never know with those fraudulent police; sometimes, they actually tended to brainstorm.

Ahead of us was a sporty car stuffed with teenage cuties. It was a convertible that was way too expensive for them to afford. It aggravated me when people gathered such a huge ego from their mom or dad sustaining a better job than the normal, hard working American or non-American. I had a sweet car when I was a kid. It was called a "working girl convertible", but you didn't see me sprinting around everywhere, bragging about it. I changed my course to follow behind them, where I waited for them to pull over. They ignored me as if the badge didn't exist. Then I remembered to turn on the flashing lights. They pulled over without stalling, and I parked my vehicle directly behind theirs.

I unfastened my car door slightly just before I was almost obliterated to smithereens by a semi. After that experience, I decided to move to the opposite side of the white line for enhanced safety. I had to shimmy myself back and forth a couple of times before I perfected my skill to enter the parking spot. They probably presumed that I was a doofus, what a group of unsmart sissies. I glanced both ways before exiting the car the next time. When I thought it was all clear, I stepped out and shut the door behind me. I initiated my confident strut as a car drove by, so I pressed my back up against the police vehicle to make sure that I wouldn't meet my demise. Just like I knew, I didn't die. I made my way to the convertible and pulled out my nightstick along the way. When I got to the rear of the car, I bumped one of the taillights with it, breaking the plastic along with the bulb that was inside of it. They initiated me with screams, asking me what I thought I was doing. I declared to them just how it was. I had no clue what they were conversing about, and they shouldn't talk back to an officer of the law. I tell you, a good man undeniably can't make a decent living without being accused of doing wrong.

When I got up to the driver, I demanded that she provide me with her I.D. She was dressed in a mini skirt, and she bent over in the opposite direction to reach for her purse that was located in the back on the recently vacuumed floor. I was obligated to withhold what I was feeling to do by what I was going to do: screw over the rich girls. I just capitalized on my biggest turn off, using it to my benefit: a girl that doesn't like to ingest anything but pure crap, for example, like yogurt. There is nothing worse than a fine female who doesn't enjoy eating. That single thought made me so passionate about my hate that I longed to take them all in for the homicide of a fellow police officer right away. I would plant evidence against them, of course, so it seemed irrefutable. She sat up with her wallet in one hand, escorted by an extended smile on her face that was abruptly reduced to a sad puppy dog expression that I was a sucker for.

My violent temper matured into love for a female who was most likely made up of plastic. The rest of the girls in the car were winking at Gramps and Nazm and waving at them like they hankered to take

them home to bake them fresh poppy seed muffins. I
soon realized what they were trying to pull one on The
Gary, and The Gary never falls for that sort of crap
unless he's trying to fool you. I counseled my love (I
mean the source of all my hatred) to supply me with
her driver's license. She dispensed it to me while
grazing her fingers along my hand, remodeling me into
a nervous mess. It was to a sickening degree of
intoxication for one minute, love intoxication. I
struggled to read the identification, but it was challenging when it felt like a Richter scale breaking earth-
quake was going on.

Her name was Candy Cox, which didn't sound
like an actual name at all. It showed on her license that
she was twenty-nine, but she didn't even appear to be
eighteen. Something was up. I didn't expect that an
I.D. could be falsified until I remembered that my
original mustache dealer was doing his best to get me
to invest in a reproduction of an I.D., but I rejected the
offer because then I would've been too tempted to
purchase naughty magazines. Could it be that she went
through my dealer to get one of them? Just to test her I
questioned why her mother would name her Candy.
She explained to me that it was her mother's stage
name at the office that she formerly worked in. The
girl was dumber than a box of charcoal, and I say
"charcoal" instead of rocks because charcoal sucks and
rocks are amazing miracles.

I requested that "Candy" step out of the vehicle
for me. She agreed with hardly any hesitation as she
settled her brand new high heels on the harsh tar. After
shutting the door, she seductively relocated herself at
the rear of the convertible where she bent over putting
her hands on the trunk. I wasn't certain on how long I
could deal with the flirtatious behavior before I would
have to extract my pistol to blow the thought of her out

that existed within my skull. I asked her what she was gesturing, and, through some analysis, she came to the rationalization that I needed to frisk her. Seriously, why would I have suspected her to have a weapon? Oh, I got it. She didn't want me to frisk her to check if she was withholding any weapons. It was to seduce me, like in "Guiding Light". So, in other words, she was the weapon. That may have been my lone opportunity to caress someone who wasn't asleep or trapped in a coma, so I couldn't pass it up. I motioned in behind "Candy", instructing her to spread them. I was only following what I had witnessed on the boob tube. I patted down each of her legs individually at a slothful pace. They were so silky that they could've been a baby's bottom; at least, that was what those professional baby butt feelers make it sound like. My palms were excessively sweaty, so I had to halt my efforts or else it would've been too humiliating for my fragile mind to endure. I bent over stationing my hands on my knees to hopefully heal the insanely heavy breathing problem that I was having. It felt like my lungs were going to implode while the feeling in my left arm wouldn't seem to come back.

When "Candy" rotated herself towards me, that petite hussy kicked me in the chest before rushing for the convertible. She was awful slow though on account of the high heels that she was wearing. All I had to do was reach over to get a grip on her wrist. When I restrained her, she was still running, which composed the sound effect of a loud pop. She shrieked in pain as she embraced her shoulder, which I was predicting had popped out of place. She proceeded to bawling; asking me why I would hurt her, so I told her straight out that no one outruns the law, especially when it was Sheriff Helty.

That's right; I promoted myself. She tried to state that she thought she overheard her phone ringing and accidentally kicked me in a panic to get there. She followed her lame excuse with those puppy dog eyes once more that made me melt like pudding on a bagel. It was a requirement that I gave her a breathalyzer test to detect if she was drunk. I instructed her to recite the alphabet backwards, but I just stood there nodding, since I had no clue what she was blabbering about. There was another test that I wanted to do before I forced them to donate all of their money to me. The last basic test was walking the white line. I guided her to the white line, where she would have to walk, toe to heel on it, down to the cop car.

When she began to perform my task, I kept one eye on her while using the other to hint to the other girls about my bribe. They handed over approximately $300 even though I was still scheming to arrest them. It didn't make me corrupt, considering that they sucked, and I didn't. When she was returning from walking the line, she gave me this smirk, while strutting all provocative, which wouldn't allow me to arrest her. I ended up permitting her to get back into the car with her friends. I hustled back to the squad car, getting there short winded to no surprise.

When they left the side of the road, I trailed right behind them, since I couldn't let go. I drew the pistol out of my holster as I shifted into the right lane. I directed Grandpa to take control of the wheel to maintain us going straight down the lane. If I couldn't see her face, she couldn't make me feel like mush. I fixed the sights of my gun out the window to fire at their back tires. I pierced the rubber on a tire with a bullet, making sparks fly from the wheel, while the car spun out of control, running into the barrier that was dwelling there to protect people from flying off of the bridge that was up ahead. The entire front end of the car caved in as a single female in the backseat was launched through the windshield. The glass shattered before she slid across the pavement, abandoning a trail of crimson muscle and tissue along the way.

I came to a screeching halt on the side of the road. I floored it in reverse until I hit the speed bump and made contact with the bumper of the convertible. All I needed was to be certain that she was breathless before we vanished. When I got to "Candy's" door I identified that there was still some movement coming from her figure. She elevated her head a bit, begging me to find her a doctor. I informed her that what she needed was an executioner because there was no way that she was going to survive with her whole lower body tangled like that. The gore was intertwined with the twisted steel that was in front of the seat. I pressed the barrel of my pistol against her temple and asked her what she wanted on her tombstone. The moment that words formed from her vocal chords, I pulled the trigger. It could've been that I couldn't take the sadness in her voice, or it could've been that I just didn't care. The bullet traveled through her head and fragments of brain splattered on the face of her confidant in the passenger seat. At that instant, I began to regret the day that I was born, for I had already concluded the lives of so many people. Many were in self-defense; others were for the protection of Grandpa. It was the first time that I believe that I murdered on purpose, but some humans waste the life that they have and don't deserve to feed themselves with the food that could salvage a good person's survival.

I proceeded to the car with my chin to my chest praying to God that I would be strong enough to make it through the venture without getting the urge to murder another living creature. It was already too late for me when I realized it. When I accessed the navigator's seat in the car, I glanced at Grandpa and understood that I had done not a thing wrong. The entire trip was all for the sake of him, considering that all through our lifetimes we had been the outcasts, so we were just getting even with the world, which justified it. After my glance to Gramps, I attended my vision towards the backseat at Nazm, who had a childish smile on his face, while playing thumb wars against himself. I comprehended that I couldn't have killed her in cold blood. I remained a child at heart, exactly like Nazm. It was a circumstance of terminating the dreadful suffering that I knew that she was going through. There was no need for mourning as I drove away into the night sky, pursuing something that would bring me back to my typical mood.

As I was patrolling the open road, I spotted an actual drunk driver swerving into every lane. On several occasions, he came close to making an exit into the muddy ditch. It was a sign so that I could redeem myself by saving innocent lives instead of taking them. I flipped on my lights and waited for him to pull over, but he still speeded along, dodging the few cars that had lingered on the road. I turned on my siren, having faith that it would spark an interest in Deputy Gary's orders. I had to demote myself after the last incident, but, don't fear, I will get promoted again after this. He pulled to the side of the dirt path, knowing what he had to face if he didn't comply, I was assuming. I discontinued my hunt directly behind him. I withdrew from my steel travel machine and jacked up my pants, like some classification of badass. I didn't do it to be a badass though. It was just that those cloth leg protectors got incredibly prickly after a while.

When I got up to the driver's window, I asked him if he knew that he was swerving all over the road. He was a clean cut breed of man, the kind that wore khaki pants with the ironed crease in the front. He apologized, confessing to me that he didn't notice that he was performing that poor of a driving job. He was only struggling to tear apart the plastic casing on a string cheese package. When there was no other alternative, he was forced to use his teeth, being perfectly aware that it was not good idea. I grasped what he meant, too. I struggled on a daily basis with packaging that was too powerful for the average man.

The scene foiled my whole plan for redemption. I couldn't off a man that fought the same battles as I did. He was me, only freshly showered, which I was in a desperate need for. I advised him from that point forward to carry a knife with him. It would satisfy all of his unpackaging needs. I released him before I ended up doing something foolish like asking him if he wanted to have a dance off in the street. Not the most intelligent activity to do at night in the middle of traffic.

I came back to the squad car, feeling like a new man. I had string cheese in common with someone. I unlatched the trunk, removing my old clothes, like a boring magic trick before I went into the ditch to change. I maintained my focus on the car and stared over the small hill, while I dressed like I was blind-folded. For some reason, I couldn't seem to get my head into anything besides where my arms should've been. I also stumbled over one of my pant legs while putting them on. I crash landed in the mud, which made me undeniably messy so that I smelled like rain water, and not the fresh scent rain water, like you can get in detergent. By smelling of rainwater, I meant that I reeked of day-old, rotten animal carcasses.

When I reentered the car, Gramps and Nazm plugged their nostrils shut by sinking their fingers deep inside. As if I didn't have to deal with a worse stench that ejected from their sweat glands. I caught a glimpse of my face in the rearview mirror, which reminded me that I still had that mustache on, and it looked ridiculous. I tugged at it, but it only tightened my skin. After a couple more tries, it snapped off, leaving a burning sensation underneath my nose.

I shifted the vehicle into drive so that I could head for someplace to chow down. It had been at least a day since I had consumed my last supper and around a week since I had been consuming human flesh. A giant billboard with many mounted lights shining up at it captured my attention. It spoke to my stomach with a burger on it that they claimed was impossible to eat. Just because it had ten beef patties on it didn't mean that it couldn't be done, and I was going to be the first to prove it. There was no way that something man-made was going to show me up. I took the exit that was flaunted on the billboard when it came up; it only guided me onto an additional highway. I had no concern over how off track the eatery was. It was something I had to do.

Chapter 11:
A Brawl So Tough that it Could Make a Grown Man Eat His Liver

After precisely five miles of intense excitement, we finally reached the place. It didn't appear to be a restaurant, considering that it was only a brick building around the size of your mediocre fast food joint. The sign on the outside told me different. The place was called "The Massive Meat Impound". They had so much meat that they give you extra; at least, that was what the sign read. We took a spin around the back, where we parked the automobile so that no one would sight us getting out of a cop car; it might've been a dead giveaway that we stole it.

Still, someone rushed out of the back door and witnessed us evacuating the car. He viewed the area for a while, acting like he didn't notice us, while at the same time creeping towards the door from which he came. I dropped to the ground and held my knee while letting out a cry for help to the man so that he would come over to us. He peeked over his shoulder at me, but he continued to walk. He then stopped, and then he kept walking again. I shouted at him, asking if he would make up his damn mind already. In conclusion, he came over to me to assist, like any compassionate gentleman would. He asked me with concern in his voice what was wrong. I used the excuse that I sensed that the bone connected to my leg was fractured. I uncovered my leg, and, when he was leaning over to examine it, I thrust my knee upwards, causing it to collide with his face, which stained blood on my pants. I presumed that I had broken the bone that was affixed to my knee and the one that was inside of his face. I was troubled as to how I was supposed to get the stain out; it was not like I carried stain remover with me everywhere I went. Not like it mattered, due to the fact that I had already stunk as if I had recently ran the fifty-yard dash, and that was about as repulsive as it got. I would've been in a coma for life had I ever attempted the mile. That poor guy was just in the right place at the right time.

He was reduced from being most likely the greatest trash taker outer ever to another guy that was lying on the pavement after getting a taste of the wrath of Gary. I had followers like Charles Manson, except my followers were labeled friends, and they didn't literally do anything that I instructed them to do. There was an autobiography written about it; it was titled "Helty Skelty: The Ever So Awesome Man That Should Have Been a God and Ruled the World or Even the Universe". It's the truth.

The man was putting effort forth to shift his nose bone back into place while rubbing the blood from out of his eyes. I traveled over to the dumpster and leapt inside of it, while lecturing Gramps and Nazm not to damage him but to make sure that he stayed there and stayed silent. I started to part the plastic of the garbage bags, exploring for some sort of cloth to keep him quiet so that I didn't have to commit another homicide. I discovered a treasure of some perfectly ripe leftovers that I stowed away in my pockets for later. How do people waste such superbly awesome food?

I found a grease splotched rag in one of the bags that I pulled separate ways, attempting to rip it. My hand slipped off of the rag, and I slapped myself in the forehead. I took my best shot at it once more, only to end up with a similar result. I hauled it out of the trash bin to transport it over to Nazm. I figured that if anyone could split it, he could. Nazm had the roughest skin in all of the land. If he could be a superhero, he would be Captain Sandpaper Man, and his superpower would be to bolt up to the bad guys, where he would rub up against them until they perished from blood loss. I strategically placed his hands on each side of the rag. It was easier than trying to explain it to him. With my hands, I motioned for him to pull his two hands apart; he did that but let go at the same time, letting the rag float briskly to the moist concrete. I picked the rag up from the location that it would mold at, situating it within Nazm's palms methodically how it was before. I positioned my hands on top of Nazm's, gripping his knuckles, as I struggled to demonstrate how tight to hold his hands when he swiftly pulled them apart. It tore the rag into the desired size that I wanted. He did an acceptable job, but, also, I sensed the tingle from when he harmed me in the process. My hands were still in a fist, facing the ground, as I concentrated on my hemoglobin trickling from them onto my shoes. I rotated my wrists around and unclenched my fists to find that my palms were skin free. You think I would've felt the agonizing pain when it happened, but, lately, I wasn't affected by anything that didn't go more than a couple inches into my interior.

I seized the cloth that was split into a pair of mini cloths and fastened it around the guy's head. It went in his mouth so that he wouldn't be able to produce a sufficient amount of noise. It must've been the most disgusting taste for him. Plasma and grease, if only they manufactured raw hamburgers like they do with raw steak. I knotted the other half of the rag around his wrists behind his back, leaving him settled belly first on the ground. I decreed that Gramps and Nazm should drag him into the shadows on the opposite side of the building so that they wouldn't be spotted. Their additional task was to maintain surveillance on him until I returned.

There was a gas station neighboring the restaurant that I strolled to, only to collect something to shield my lesions. It wasn't a petty gas station either. Instead, it was one of those larger chains, but I wasn't in a predicament to be picky. If I ended up bleeding on my meal, it would make it less enjoyable. That particular service station was called "The Quickie", which I had learned about from Grandpa, but I couldn't dig far enough into my memory to remember why.

When I arrived at the front door, someone opened it for me, considering the condition of this poor fragile boy. He asked me if I needed any assistance with anything, so I politely gave him the finger. He stomped his feet while wandering away, having a hissy fit about my so-called "poor attitude" towards helpful people. The domain had everything that was located in any gas station. They even had a minuscule bed in the bathroom. I wasn't sure who could fit on the thing, but it was still rather handy.

I headed into one of the aisles, where I landed a few boxes of band-aids along with some gauze. On the way up to the counter, I caught a glimpse of these winter gloves that reeked of awesomeness. They were black with pink stitching, and I know what you're thinking: Isn't pink a little non-manly? Ponder about it for a second, though. Didn't they all state that pink was the new black? So, technically, wouldn't that make the gloves all black, which would morph the gloves into cool. Or would it make it like the gloves were pink and the stitching was black? All of the contemplating was making my brain ache. I had never been the type to be up on the fashion sense and concentrate on runway models. Ok, I watched models, but not for the fashion, I swear. I snatched up the gloves anyway and headed up to the cash register. I hoped that they could still scan the UPC codes, considering that they were smudged with the blood from my hands.

When I got to the front of the store, I saw that the line was considerably long and I didn't feel like waiting. I scampered up to the counter, slapping my hands onto it, wailing about the distress that I really wasn't in. I bitched about how much I needed the products at that exact moment. I slid my hands across the smooth surface, streaking blood, for the sheer amusement of grossing people out, along with being certain that I got the speedy service that I was entitled to. A lady that was in the middle of getting checked out sheltered her mouth with her palm as she made a break for the crusty toilet bowl. I assumed that it meant that I was next.

The cashier began to scan the products, while I extended my hand into my back pocket to snag my wad of cash money when I discovered that it wasn't there. It must've fallen out within the confines of the police vehicle. This caused me to have to put on a second act to get the items as a handout. I knew that I could do it, but it was so much trouble for such a small cost. He had to have been the slowest employee working there, considering that following all of the pondering he was still scanning the merchandise. I might as well have filed my taxes while waiting for him if I had a job. Once he wrapped it up, I acted as if I was confident that I had the money on me by reaching in my back pocket and feeling around with a look of confusion plastered on my face. This was followed by the frantic searching through all of my other pockets. I was going to have to pick off the lint that was glued to the scrapes on my palms after the whole scene was over.

I sent my hands into the atmosphere clenching them in a fist while descending to my knees, challenging God on why he had forsaken me. My boo-boos were starting to become dehydrated so I struggled to undue the fists that I had formed. The cross between gelatin and rat poison was difficult to detach, but I pulled it off. A noblewoman stepped up to me, handing over the currency to pay for my items. I uttered indirectly to her that it was about time; I had only been pulling the rehearsal for a minute. In Hollywood, that was nearly $5,000 worth of labor, and I was better than anyone that was contracted there. I snatched the money out of her hand as she gasped, for what I was presumeing was how long she realized that she had paused to contribute the almighty dollar. I dispensed it to the cashier as I grappled the plastic bag containing the products.

The cashier guy stayed poised there, counting the money, like he was going to present the lady with her change. I made sure that he understood that I was delaying for my change by stamping my foot on the floor and generating sounds of exhaustion. My actions didn't even make him strive to go faster to get me my money at the speed of lightning. Instead, he shot for the goal of Uber slow. Once he got the change prepared, the lady established her hand in place to take it, but I swiped the money and announced that if it was essential for her to acquire the change, she should've requested for it back earlier. I retreated from the store, leaving a whole bunch of annoyed customers behind me, but I also came out of the store twenty-seven cents richer. It was well worth a few pissy people.

I figured that Gramps and Nazm would be alright for another few minutes while I put on the bandages. When I got into the dimly lit parking lot, I took a seat on the curb at the edge of a parking spot. A car pulled up, attempting to park in front of me, but I had my legs stretched out as far as they would go. If I didn't do it, I wouldn't have been comfortable, and I couldn't have that. The car pulled up halfway into the spot, inching forward, maybe trying to get me to modify my position, but that wasn't going to happen. He ultimately gave up on the battle for a closer parking space. He ended up parking on the farther side of the building since there were no other open spots. I listened to the door forcefully shut as he commenced his walk to the front door, but he never made it there being that he halted at me. I heard him cease all motions behind me, where he pushed me forward and lead me onto the pavement.

I turned around, perceiving that the kid couldn't have been a day over forty-four. He was striving to appear all cool by pushing me over in front of a million people, but there was no way that he could look amazing as long as he was joyriding in a teal compact car. I stood up brushing off the small rocks that had clung to my shirt. I put up my dukes and equipped for some one-on-one action, only of the violent sort though. I wasn't in the proper mind-set for my customary victory hug afterwards. He hopped down into the parking spot with me. There were automobiles on both sides of us. Where a car wasn't blocking us, there was an outraged mob of civilians keeping me in there, wishing that I would get the crap kicked out of me. They could've just maintained their wishing career since this man refuses to go down. The bully didn't seem so tough anyway. He was just another normally proportioned man, out to prove himself worthy.

I paraded up to him, taking a wide swing at his ugly mug that he blocked, returning with a fist to my sternum. From that specific region, I experienced a feeling of numbness that ran through my intact anatomy. I remained mounted in place in a state of shock as I was struck in the face, but I sensed nothing except for the pressure from my jaw shifting about. The ensuing time that he went for a shot, I was stationed next to a car; so, when he swung, I parried. His fist collided with the door as I witnessed his knuckles disappear into his hand with a loud snap. He pulled away, clutching his fist, while in the background I overheard someone yelling in anger that he put a dent in their car. While he was shaking the hurt out of his hand, I dashed at him and knocked him into one of the concrete polls that were in front of the sidewalk so that dumbasses couldn't crash into the building. Following my defense, he leaned his back up against it with a sign of extreme agony slapped across his face. I withdrew from my position back to the car on the opposite side, where I placed myself in front of the passenger side window. When he approached me, swinging with his other hand, I evaded him again and enabled him to shatter the glass so that he could carve up his arm badly. The shards of glass that stuck in place drug along his lacerations when he brought his arm back out. I listened to someone that came out of the store sniveling about her vehicle not being insured.

A scarce amount of citizens rushed the bully, overwhelming him down to the ground, while I masked my true self behind my hand when I composed a high-pitched giggle. I couldn't let people find out how big of a girl I was on the inside. They would never discover my flaws though, considering how manly I appeared to be externally. I gathered my bandages and gloves that were distributed throughout the tar to bring them behind "The Quickie", where I had a better chance of putting them on in peace without a walking mound of guts interrupting me. That was what he was, because he needed a lot of them to approach me like that.

I ripped the band-aids from their package and spread my fingers so that I could put them on correspondingly. I wiped my hands together first since they had accumulated pebbles along with lint and dust. I didn't get them squeaky clean, but it was good enough. I wrapped the band-aids around each finger until I couldn't see my fingers anymore. Then I cloaked my hands and fingers with gauze until there wasn't any remaining. For the final step, I put on the magnificent gloves that I had discovered, like a hidden treasure chest stocked with bologna. They were a tight squeeze with all the first aid bandages on my hands, but I still got them on, which was all that mattered. Who, honestly, in this day and age, is concerned about blood circulation anyway? I positioned myself on the soles of my shoes and constricted my hands into a fist and then back into an open palm to stretch out the bandages. It was to be certain that I could still man-euver with them being so restricting. I could feel that my fingers were being strangulated, but they would get used to it after a bit.

In the period of time that I was in the middle of my finger exercises, the guy that I beat to a bloody pulp (I liked to address him as Compact Car Man) approached me. He was significantly nicer than the last time that we had met up, but that was perhaps because he uncovered that my fists should've been outlawed in all the other states on account of the sheer deadliness of them. At that point, they were only on the list waiting to be banished in ten states, but, someday, I will work them up those lists.

Compact Car Man put forth his palm to me as if he wanted to shake hands, but I had been warned about that trick, where they would perform that action and then they would strike you in the throat with their unoccupied hand. It would leave my air tube crushed, making me suffocate on reused oxygen, already existing in my lungs. Well, I wasn't going to be fooled by something as simple as that; I am a thinking gentleman. When he got closer to my hand with his own, I slapped it, delivering a down low (the opposite of a high five). Compact Car Man provided me with a strange look as he spun around to walk away, but I knew that wouldn't be the grand finale. He was up to something. There was a dirt-riddled glass bottle upright on the ground that I inadvertently knocked over with my foot. I picked it up as I crept very quietly behind him. He must've detected me (but I didn't understand how, considering that I was trying so hard), so he rotated to my direction, demanding an answer as to why I was following him. I got slightly nervous for the fact that I was caught red-handed with no explanation, so I panicked.

I grasped the bottle and tightly bashed it on the top of Compact Car Man's cranium. Instead of everything going as planned, he remained upright and conscious. It didn't make him too chipper as his face changed from peach to a deep red. A drop of blood didn't even leak down his face. He only stood in place until I backed up, then he followed me. Compact was becoming a hypocrite, since he was coming after me. The bottle top magically lunged my arm forward, attempt-ting to penetrate the jagged edge into his throat, but praise the Lord of Lords that he blocked it, sending the leftover bottle flying. He apprehended me by the scruff of my shirt and proceeded to heave me against the wall behind me. Even with the beastly back pains that haunted me, I made a mad dash in the direction of the bottle. I needed to protect myself.

I had a notion that Compact Car Man wanted to cause me harm for some reason. While my leg was in the air during my getaway, he snatched it up and began dragging me along the hellish pavement (yet another reason I was oh-so-thankful for my gloves). He elevated me off of the ground, placing one hand on the back of my shirt and the other in my back pocket. He rocked me in a seesaw motion, like my rocking horse, until he relinquished his embrace, which was one thing that my rocking horse would *never* do to me. He launched me clear across a parking spot into a wire gate that was entrapping the dumpster. One of the wires was a stray that came untangled. It punctured through my skin as it wriggled about, scraping against my collarbone. I had to pop it out previous to the moment when the mound of a man darted full force into me.

I wasn't able to get it out in time, so I was tackled through the gate with Compact settled on top of me. It was not like we were playing the lame-ass game for losers: football. That result is the reason why I always competed in touch football. There were no players extending their stay on top of me, plus then my clothes never got dirty, which, in turn, left my delicates lasting remarkably longer. When he finally got up, I was greeted with an additional slam up against the thick green steel. He went for an uppercut, so I secured my eyelids, waiting for some kind of miracle, when the sweet sound of victory sailed into my ears.

That music to my ears was the blood-curdling whimper of a big giant wussy. When I gained the courage to unfasten my eyelids, I distinguished half of a hand waving around, cutting the air as it flung blood cells back at Compact's face. The other fraction of his hand was barely hanging onto a sharp piece of metal that was improperly molded on the dumpster. I plucked his hand off of the stagnate object to pitch it at the cranium of my adversary for the time being. At mid scream, the hand went in between his upper and lower jaw down into his throat. The focus went from his hand to his neck almost instantaneously. It was like his hands were cemented to it as if he was making an effort toward concealing a hicky from his mom.

I felt sort of responsible for the mishap, so I tried to get near to Compact to provide him with the Heimlich maneuver, but he managed to boot me away, while he turned a tint of bright-ass blue, increasingly, by the second. This didn't end my obsession with salvaging an innocent life though. I nabbed a metal bar from inside of the dumpster so that when he attempted to kick me away, I would smack him in the leg with it until, eventually, he was on the ground not capable of operating his legs anymore.

I snuck up behind him, while he was crawling away, and situated my arms around his structure. I explored his body downward until I couldn't feel his ribcage anymore, which was when I activated my kindness with Herculean hugs until the divorced knuckles bulged out from between his lips. Compact deposited a heap of slop that had come from his gut onto the filthy pavement. I didn't know if I could ever do something like that unless it was something I had

just swallowed an hour before. Yet he implied carele-
ssness and didn't even make an effort to move. Then I
realized that he wasn't even stirring to breathe, so
either he was sleeping or dead; my bet was on dead. It
served the moron right for not approving of me helping
him. I grappled him by the arm as I towed him behind
the dumpster, where I showered a couple of trash bags
over him. I wasn't even going to take a shot at
throwing him into the dumpster. My muscles needed a
bona fide challenge, not one that I could simply do
with one arm.

I propped the gates back up against the steel
posts to give the illusion that they were still hitched to
the fence. Maybe, that way, nobody would discover the
secret before we took off, so I could still get to gorge
myself with the mammoth burger. I progressed across
the sharp blades of grass to the restaurant parking lot,
where there was no indication of Gramps or Nazm. I
figured that they must've gotten part of my instructions
right and chaperoned the trash taker outer to the
reverse side of the building. When I got to the opposite
side of the building, I identified Gramps and Nazm
angled against the brick wall with the guy plopped
down in between them. I could only make out the
outline of them, since it was lightless. But, when I got
closer, I could see them well, especially the man that I
requested them to watch that only had meat hugging
him from the ankles down. The rest of his anatomy
was made up of bone with a few nuggets of meat here
and there, but, generally, he was only red tarnished
bone.

I swore that my brain was spurting fluid from
all of the pressure that I had been dealing with. I tried
to explain to them that if they watched someone, it was
difficult to eat them with a stare, but, if they could, go
for it. They attempted to convince me that they did,

which made them the grand prize winners in my punch to the gut contest. I didn't terminate my blows until I made them bleed something out of an orifice on their faces. Who needed a punching bag when a zombie never deflated from too much abuse?

Chapter 12
Grease—
Nature's Orgasm

When I was finished, I had Gramps toss the leftovers into the dumpster underneath some bags. Nothing was going to stop me from eating the burger of royalty. I hooked Gramps and Nazm by the earlobes and towed them to the all access front door. I had the pre-school speech with them by encouraging them to behave, or I wouldn't fetch a treat for them later on. They shook their heads in excitement as if they were wiener dogs waiting for those repulsive pig flavored treats. Actually, those were tolerable, but, for some reason, the beef ones just don't taste right.

After all of the bickering that I had to do, my stomach initiated the growl off. It felt like if I refused to meet my belly's need to be satisfied, it was going to shut itself down to torment me, so I rushed to the door. By the looks of the place, it couldn't have had too many customers in its prime. It was a terribly sloppy place with a tiny dining area with only about ten tables in it. It must've been the busiest time for them, since the interior was packed. The only customer that I could picture eating in a dump like that was me. I would lick food off the floor. My standards were not that high.

We paused by the entrance for someone to come and seat us since the sign lectured us to. I was a pushover, which was code for "I didn't take crap from nobody besides people with the nervous eye twitching" or everybody, really. It didn't take long before an immeasurably lanky guy with long scruffy hair approached us with a meat cleaver in his right hand and a greasy apron below his misshapen skull. He authorized us to have a seat in their waiting domain until one of their tables cleared out, which was reportedly soon. At any other location, I would've marched straight through the doorway, but that day was the day that I would secure a reputation in history. We relaxed our clammy butts down onto the bench that was assembled with wood from the forest of hell. There were legions of splinters in it, reciting that there was no way that it wasn't brewed from 100% pure evil. I did my best to stay tranquil, striving not to anger it.

When I was surveying the territory, I noticed a whiteboard that had a number on it of how many mortals had attempted to digest "The Massive Heart Attack" and failed. "The Massive Heart Attack" was constructed triple cheeseburger style and prepared with ten all natural beef patties, ten cheese slices, twenty-five pickles, twenty strips of bacon, twenty onion rings, and a multitude of condiments that combined BBQ sauce, mayo, ketchup, and mustard. A mere two hundred seventy-two mortals had partaken in the challenge and reigned unsuccessful, but I would be the earliest to finish it and leave with clogged arteries. It declared that if I finished it that, along with fame, I would also inherit a spectacular prize. I figured that it would be a piece of cake. From that day forward, they would call me "The Man with the Expandable Iron Stomach" if more of the community knew me.

The dwelling was also stocked with all different sorts of cows. There were cow toys lined on shelves, along with wallpaper that had "moo" printed across it. Even the ceiling was covered with extensive pictures of cows, only the white was shaded brown from all of the years of built up cigarette smoke. In fact, when I resigned focusing on the sign with The Massive Heart Attack stats, I noticed that they were being possessed on the patchwork of a hulking ceramic cow that was taller than me.

The same slender, dented-headed man came up to us and announced that there was a table organized for us. We pursued him until he guided us to the opening into the kitchen, which didn't seem appropriate that we would be dining back there. A random customer arrived, updating us that the table that was prepared for us was in the corner as he pointed us in the correct direction. I came to the conclusion that the employees didn't find it appealing to go into details. We toured the restaurant into the corner, where our table was prepared, but it didn't appear to be ready at all. I didn't really care anyway, I'd eat a meal off anything, but Gramps was having his biggest hissy fit ever and rejected the notion of dining at the grody table. He left me no choice but to play the "you ate the garbage man" card and the "you owe me a bucketful of good behavior or I will have to pull out the belt and whip you until you wish had never come back to life" card. He gracefully sat down with us at the table.

The light in the corner above us was burnt out, making it strangely dark, as if the table was only used for the albinos, so they wouldn't get torched. You would suspect that the rest of the bulbs would help illuminate the final stretch, but they didn't prove to be of much use. It also didn't help that our table was the sole one approximate to that corner. Conceivably, it could've been because we were out of towners, and they all had to be seated at the bastard table. It was cloaked by dust, combined with particles of moldy food, but, worst of all, they hadn't even presented us with the menus yet.

I sunk my two fingers into my mouth to attempt to whistle, but then it came from deep in my memory that I had no clue how to do that. I whistled in the most common procedure by puckering my lips, but I was convinced that Grandpa couldn't even make out the commotion coming from my actions. In conclusion, Gramps got the clue and whistled with the two fingers method. The racket from that, I swear, was going to cause me to go deaf. Everybody stared, yet no one came over to serve us. I spotted that the waiter with the misshapen skull was peeking out from the kitchen and was thinking that I couldn't pinpoint his position.

I picked up the morsels of moldy rations from the table to squeeze them all together into a spheroid. It turned out to be a special liquidy ball, too. It consistently dribbled this light brown fluid from it that smelled like the innards of seasoned work boots. I had never sniffed them. It was only a sneaking suspicion. I chucked the mold ball at the kitchen, where it splashed against the wall adjacent to the waiter. I beckoned him with my finger, advising him to come over. He literally crossed the restaurant to get to us, which put me into a state of bewilderment. I anticipated that I was going to have to implant a boot into somebody's ass. I mentioned that we needed an employee to come over to disinfect our table and deliver us three menus. He acknowledged my orders as he nodded nervously (more than he should've been) before heading straight into the kitchen again, hopefully, to do something.

Practically at the instant that he went into the kitchen, another male exited it, while exhibiting one of those apron things with the pockets as he approached our table. He extracted a white rag that was heavily stained out of the pouch, which he wiped the table down with, briskly leaving streaks that were half an inch steep. He flopped down the menus onto the remaining dust before departing without even speaking a word. Nazm was the first to lift up a menu, followed by Grandpa who landed one. I would've likewise went for one had there been an additional one settled there. I could've accepted that had it been thirty menus, but, when we undeniably said three, I didn't consider that any human being older than the age of two would've been capable of miscounting that.

I didn't even have the desire to go through the trouble of getting the waiter back, so I gawked at Grandpa's, while he hunted through it. There wasn't much of a menu at that restaurant either. There were only two different soups that's ingredients ranged from stuff that was made up mostly of beef or beef stock. All there was for burgers was a hamburger or a cheese-burger with bacon and The Massive Heart Attack. Luckily, I had a ton of money that I neglected to snag from out of the vehicle since The Massive was $35. Not having enough money wasn't going to cutoff my attempt to consume it. I would just reimburse them with the prize money that I won from finishing the complete burger.

I traveled close to the entrance to secure a pen along with a piece of paper to write down what I wanted to eat, considering that I wasn't going to remember what all of it was. I wasn't only going to order The Massive, because it was essential that I got some variety in my meals. I ended up adding three additional delectable items to my list. Two of which were appetizers, so I wouldn't be in the "I'm so hungry that I'm going to dry heave" phase when I embarked upon making myself perish at a young age. The other was a dessert that was a brownie, stockpiled on top of ice cream that had another brownie smushed above it, drenched in a tremendous volume of chocolate syrup.

This may have sounded like more than could fit in even a bulky stomach, but it wouldn't become a predicament for me. I had an accelerated digestive system. I had found everything that I craved before Grandpa had even picked out his opening entry. He was still struggling to decide between a cheeseburger and the beef stew. Nazm was settled on the opposite side of the table and was holding his menu upside down while pointing his finger to stuff in it, pretending like he was reading it. I was intending on writing whatever down for his order anyway; he wouldn't be able to tell the difference. I sat there, twiddling my thumbs, until I lost my patience. I scribbled on the paper that Grandpa would be having the beef stew while Nazm would be ordering spaghetti.

I bellowed for the waiter to come over, so, yet again, everybody stared at us like they were primitives. I presumed that we were that rowdy table that everybody disliked in a restaurant, furthermore, wishing that we would get salmonella poisoning and die. I was basing this on personal opinion, not fact, like you may've been anticipating. That same goofy headed greeter glanced at us from the kitchen as the waiter appeared quickly after. It kind of startled me.

I was pretty sure that they were going to perform an unsanitary act on our meals, and I loathed people who tampered with my food. He didn't utter a word to us as he took out a pad and pen. I revealed to him that we had already written down everything that we wanted, so he could disappear and fetch it for us.

He rolled his eyes like it wasn't even his real job. The consumers were only citizens, asking favors of him, but this guy generated more in tips, possibly than I would produce at my first job, whenever I decided to get one.

He kidnapped the list from me as he sluggishly walked away while scanning it with his retinas. It took him awhile, but he was imaginably striving to figure out the big words like spaghetti. They weren't misspelled either, since had I copied them straight from the menu. The waiter then came to a standstill as his face morphed into an expression that appeared to be a state of confusion. He rotated his route to aim towards us. When he got up to us, he appropriately pointed to our list where it said Massive Heart Attack. I shook my head as I shooed him away with the back of my hand. I couldn't care less how flabbergasted he was that I ordered it. All I wanted was my appetizers for an introduction, and then they could deal with being astounded by how risky they envisioned I was. He fast walked at the pace of my running back into the kitchen.

As if it was routine, almost at the exact moment that he entered the kitchen, someone else exited it and headed towards us. It wasn't an individual that we had seen yet; it must've been the chef. He was a bit of a chunky man, so I was impressed that he could migrate as rapidly as he was. He had a hair net on that couldn't even contain all of his hair. It was still curling out from underneath every side of the hairnet, not like it was an issue, since his whole face was contaminated with facial hair. When he arrived at our location, in a terrifically demanding tone, he asked us who placed an order for The Massive Heart Attack.

I raised my hand without hesitation, like we were back in 4th grade, because I wanted to look cool.

I could never pull that off back in school, considering my lack of brains. He disclosed to me that he couldn't retrieve it for me, being that I wasn't good enough to try it. He obviously had no idea who he was speaking to; I was The Helty. Man of the hour, every hour. I erected myself upwards, poking him in the chest with my pointer finger, decreeing that he better get in back to cook me my burger, since I was a paying customer. The situation suggested that there would be no way that I was going to be able to get the burger. The chef maintained his stance there, with his arms crossed, shaking his noggin from side to side, as if he was a bobble head doll that got its spring put in the wrong way.

I had to up the ante to make it worth their time and mine. I put up a proposal on the spoiled table that if I didn't swallow and digest everything that I ordered for myself, I would be obligated to make a payment of $500 to them. If I did finish it, all they would have to do is install a photograph of me on the wall and retire The Massive Heart Attack so that I would be the lone human being who was skilled enough to consume it, ever. He seemed to be pleased with that suggestion, most likely because he presumed that there was no way that I could ever pull that one off, but I could. He jiggled my hand with his, disclosing that we had an arrangement. He strutted to the kitchen executing an overly confident walk that made him resemble someone that had a majorly uncomfortable wedgie. It was one of those that couldn't be picked through the pants. He would've had to go into the lavatory to physically get it from the root of the problem. When he reached the kitchen, there was a considerable amount of excessive laughter, which I was speculating was about our immature deal.

With all of the monologues about wedgies, it cautioned me that I had to go to the potty. Not for a wedgie, only to dethrone some liquid from my anatomy before I had to load my bladder up with more. When I made it to the center of the room, I noticed that there was no indication of a restroom anywhere. I questioned a person seated at a nearby table, and he pointed me in the direction of the kitchen after a brief coaxing with my pink-, I mean, black-gloved fist. It's truly pathetic how much of the populace was fearful of an underage boy. It must've been the scars together with the reproduction of an eye. I walked to the path that led into the kitchen, but, when I got under the doorway, I didn't spy a single sign of a bathroom anywhere. I ended up wandering into the kitchen, thinking that it might've been one of those cheap places that you had to prance through the kitchen to get to the tinkle station.

When I got into the kitchen, I became concerned, though, considering that there was only one person working in it. He was chopping up slabs of meat, furiously, like a madman. He would pound the cleaver into the cutting board to trim off a chunk of meat. Then he would catapult it behind his back onto a heavyweight grill. He was literally throwing meat back over his head, highly unprofessional. Some would crash land on the floor, but he picked those up to place them on the grill.

Once he spotted me eyeing him, he grunted, asking me what the hell I was doing back there. I commented that I was only wondering where a toiletry might've been located. Like any other disgruntled employee, he neared me assaulting me in the direction that he wanted me to go. I ended up being shoved just beyond the doorway that led to the kitchen. He pointed up above the doorframe that had a sign that was united with the wall; it read "unisex bathroom". You know I should've spotted that, but I was not greatly observant – or so I've been told.

I swung open the door below it, where I was piloted into the twilight zone. There were no urinals inside of its confines; they were all stalls. There was only a pair of stalls, but they were both taken up at that occasion, which caused me to become meagerly distressed. I contemplated scrubbing my hands while I stuck around, since I was trained by the lies in the television that I should before and after I went to the bathroom, being that it spreads fewer germs. However, they were already so tidily bandaged and gloved, I decided against it. I did take note that at least this particular establishment was a teeny bit updated by having the soap that was foam instead of that boring pink gel-like substance. While I proceeded to pump the foam out of the dispenser and watch it plop into the sink below, I overheard the two entities in the stalls having a full out conversation about what breed of puppy they considered the cutest – a strange topic for toilet talk, I believed.

After emptying both dispensers of its mesme-rizing contents, the Chatty Cathys had finally fulfilled their needs. It was spooky that they both got out at the same time. They must've delayed until their dialogue was finished, too. One of the gentlemen that appeared was the chef who lumbered around like he had a wedgie. I *knew* that he would have to go in there to fix it so that he could sidestep the embarrassment of doing it in front of fresh faces. They together supplied me with some dirty looks before leaving the waste management terminal without washing their hands. What a sickening bunch of people that were occupied inside of that airtight building.

I opened up the stall door, but I couldn't take the foul odor that was lurking in the air. I tried plugging my nostrils, but, somehow, the ghastly aroma still got by that. The dilemma was that there were only two toilets, and they both reeked of something awful. I mean it was no problem for me, but it might've produced some trouble for the cleaning crew, since I had terrible aim at long ranges.

With discretion, I went over to the sink, unzipping my pants, aware that I was about to do something that was frowned upon. I staged myself about a foot away from the sink where I angled my pee pee more upwards than I usually would. When the time was merited, I fired, making as much as I could into the sink. It became a bit of a game, attempting to make the soapy foam within the sink melt like cotton candy. I credit myself for doing a pretty swell job, but that didn't mean that I didn't sprinkle tinkle it all over the mirror and floor, too. I left that potty station feeling a whole lot better than I did before. I didn't wash my hands afterwards either, on account of someone having vandalized the soap dispensers.

I headed back towards my table where Gramps and Nazm were sitting, happily sipping on some sodas. They actually remembered to get me one, too. I sat down, peering at the drink that was planted in front of me. I considered siphoning it through the straw, but instead I withdrew it from the soda to stone Grandpa with it. He should've been familiar by then with how I never sip a soda with a straw. I liked to rot my teeth at any opportunity that I had. I asked Gramps what brand of soda he got me, but he wouldn't inform me. The anticipation was killing me. Not really, I was just in a sarcastic mood. I raised the soda up, establishing my nose next to it, sniffing it to be confident that they weren't attempting to pull some cruel prank on me by catering me with an alcoholic beverage. It smelled nothing like an alcoholic beverage but preferably more reminiscent to pink lemonade, yet it was a grimy brownish black color. I entrapped a sip within my mouth so that I wouldn't appear to be wussing out. It was my favorite beverage of all time, a suicide; a mystifying title for something so impressive. They should revise the name of it to heaven, seeing as that's what it is: heaven melted into a cup. Unless they were striving to suggest that suicide is beautiful, and everyone should attempt it once. I gulped the whole thing down. Afterwards, I promptly slammed my cup on the poorly finished table, pleading for another, which they were snappy to bring, supposing that it would end up spoiling my appetite. If it spoiled anything, it would end up spoiling my bladder, which was no big deal. The primo thing about a suicide is that it tastes totally inconsistent every time, but I was still a sucker for it.

Right after I received my drink, they delivered my first appetizer: potato boats. They were fashioned decently, except for that I didn't acquire any sour cream with them, and so I asked the waiter to fetch me a bundle. I was blessed, since he brought a plentiful plastic container of it out. Every time that I ate one of them, I would dip them in the sour cream beforehand so that they would be extensively masked by it. I wish that there was some way that they could spawn a bacon flavored potato. I might just have to invent that one myself. After defeating the six of those, I was still in excellent shape, since I wasn't quite out of the "I'm so hungry I could dry heave" stage.

I tapped away with my fingers on the table until they brought out my second appetizer: a steak prepared rare. I understand that one might not be considered an appetizer, but I had to possess a steak. It was perfect, prepared the exact way that I enjoyed it. When I dissected it with my knife, the whole bottom of the plate overflowed with the clearish color of blood. The center of the steak had the complexion of a raw liver, dark red with the slimy/mushy consistency. It was fantastic; whenever I took a bite and chewed the flavor of undercooked meat, it squirted all over my taste buds. It never once left a nasty aftertaste. Another great thing about raw meat is that you never have to fight to get it down your throat, since it slides effortlessly, making chewing more of an annoyance.

Following the finishing of my steak, I got out of the dry heaving stage, so I was feeling more up to a challenge, if it was even possible for me to come across one. I acknowledged that everybody was gawking at me, even though none of us were originating any noise. We were only sitting there in one of those silences where nobody felt like saying anything. I guess someone must've spilled the beans about the ordeal that was going on between the chef and me. Still, if anyone had manners, they would comprehend that it wasn't polite to stare. I held my pinky down with my thumb, sticking my other fingers up, telling them to read between the lines. I thought that it was an appropriate saying for that situation.

After my speech, I realized that the waiter was at our table, setting The Massive in front of me; it was an insult to call it a burger though. It was the size of my head, which was already abnormally oversized. I swore that they built the meat patties on it larger than usual just for me. They appeared to be bigger than the ones on all of the signs. Then I witnessed the fine print, where it stated that the sandwich maybe larger than it was pictured; I didn't sweat it. It only meant that it would be an extra adventure for me, which was never a negative thing. It kept my life exhilarating or, in the case of Grandpa, decaying. They had administered me a fork along with a steak knife to dispose of that abominable snowman of the burger world. There was no way that I could've even hoisted the thing up without it collapsing all over the contaminated floor. Everybody crowded around me to gander at me, while I accomplished the feat, so I had to announce that I needed some space. Too much pressure could cause me not to take pleasure in what I was doing, much like the case of when I tried to learn how to figure skate. What I mean is play ice hockey with no pads.

The crowd backed up, but they still retained the spotlight on me without stressing that their own meals were getting cold. Now that was just crazy. An individual's nourishment should've been up there on the priority list along with staying alive. I carved the burger into eight slices like a pizza, only a zillion times thicker. I then separated the top and bottom apart on each slice. It would still be a stretch, but I was all about the risky business. I began to inhale each section, one by one. It was fortunate for me that they lined the condiments along the foundation of the burger, too, so I wasn't devouring a plain hamburger. I'm not claiming that plain meat is atrocious, but I favor globs of ketchup on my burgers, accompanied by everything else. In truth, I had to add extra to my burger, only to insult the chef.

After I made it halfway through the burger, it embarked upon wearing on my stomach. It was a good thing that I wasn't to the stage where my stomach was expanding. When I got to that point, I regularly had to poke my fingertips underneath my ribcage in an attempt to rearrange my organs to produce further room for my stomach. The grease was beginning to get to me a bit though. It was a downer, but there was an upper to it, which was that everything slid down with ease.

I was 3/4ths of the way to conclusion when I started to get to the full stage. Everyone's frowns turned upside down, since they envisioned that it meant that I was finished; but, little did they know, I don't surrender even when I start to experience sickness. I annihilated the remnants of the burger with ease, and I was only full. I cracked my knuckles with my arms extended in front of me before I established my hands behind my head as I leaned back in my chair. The chair must've been really aged, considering that the rear two legs snapped, motivating me to flail down to the carpet. That shook me up, leaving mounds of food together with drinks juggled about inside of my belly. As was customary, everyone stood there laughing, including the douche bags that I came with. It was nothing new, but, that day, I would be the sole person chuckling my head off. So that was what I decided to do at that exact moment. Everyone was confused as to why I was giggling excessively (and yes my chuckle mutated into a hysterical giggle, I constantly got overly excited), until I retired it, proclaiming that they should put my gorgeous mug up on the wall. The entire room went silent.

I glanced up at the table, where I scoped the one thing that I dreaded but adored at the same time: fresh food. It was that ice cream brownie dessert that I ordered. This also was oversized, compared to what the menu displayed. I understood that they were striving to screw me over with all of those enlarged items that they were serving me. I was not the type to be proven wrong, so I rose up, replacing my chair with the one that was stationed beside me. I plopped down on it, and it ruptured beneath me, leaving my keister planted against the floor once again. I commanded that someone get me a functioning chair so that I would be equipped to achieve my mission in peace. No one confiscated one for me, so I shoved a patron off of his chair to use it for my own self gratification. It ended up being more suitable than the previous two, which meant that it was powerful enough to hold me up.

I began to stuff my face quickly, hoping for the best, but, halfway through, I was taken over by a brain freeze that could've sent a snowman into a coma, if they were alive in the first place. I sat there for the biggest waste of two minutes that I had ever had occupied by caressing my forehead, which did nothing, but I, at least, somewhat, looked cool.

I could sense that my stomach was stretching out, so I realized that it was the time for the shifting. With one hand, I searched for my ribs, and, when I reached the bottom of them, I jabbed my fingers in as far as I could, driving anything solid that I felt upwards. With my alternate hand, I continued to shovel down the remaining balance of sweetness, because, if I got a brain freeze when I was done, it wouldn't be an issue at all. It hit me a couple mouthfuls before I was finished, but I was still able to choke down the last bit before the freeze took over. I slowly released my fingers from beneath my ribcage so that I couldn't cause excessive destruction to my innards all at once. Thank Jehovah that my heavy organ at the time was my stomach, so only the slender ones descended upon it, not inducing me with that much discomfort.

I clenched my belly, commanding the staff to get a picture of me on the wall. I wanted to see it there before I scrammed. They accompanied the Polaroid out, taking a picture at quite possibly the time where I looked the worst. It projected out of the camera as they began to shake it violently until I advised them not to because I didn't want the colors running on my victory photograph. They pulled it out, posting it on the wall proximate to a picture of The Massive Heart Attack.

Then something happened that made me a tad bit weary. One of the other employees escorted out a labeling gun as he began to type something into it. He put the sticky strip below the photo of me. The words were too long to read "Awesome", like I had requested, so I got a little frisky and chose to investigate. I went up to the atrocity, which was the unprofessional picture of me. Underneath it, I read the words "World's Largest Loser Head". Talk about having an imagination with wording phrases; those guys were geniuses. That wasn't part of our understanding. I wasn't too pleased with the persons who relished in screwing me over. I explored the encompassing sector until I found the man infected with hair that I made the agreement with. I demanded that he adjust the picture from embarrassing to super cool, politely, but he rejected my request. He replied that the deal was only to install my photograph on the wall not that he couldn't scribble anything under it. He understood what I meant, yet we had to run around and play that game.

I hated it when someone denied being smart so that they could acquire what they wanted. Before he could do anything, I transmitted a right hook that made contact with his face. All of the beard hair cushioned the blow as my fist was forced back to me, pulling a muscle in my arm. I encountered a strain that rendered my arm worthless. From what I could see of his face, through all of the hair, was that it was reconstructing to red in the heat of outrage, which I favored over passion. Like anytime that I was stuck in circumstances similar to that, I sluggishly tiptoed backwards, while frantically seeking the aid of Grandpa. He was standing there, concentrating on us, without it even manifesting him that I may need some assistance on that one. I called him over to help me out, so he arrived point blank in Beardy's face. Gramps took a swing that didn't have any effect on that guy either. It implied that every time something ferociously collided with his face all that occurred was he would revise himself to become redder than before. Other than that, none of it seemed to faze him.

Beardy secured one jab at Grandpa that struck him in the abdomen. His fist went through the thin skin that sealed Grandpa's internal organs within his brittle frame. Beardy's eyes widened up when he comprehended what had happened. At a prolonged pace, he extracted his hand out, which was painted with coagulated blood mixed with intestinal fluid. He vibrated his hand, struggling to rid himself of the goo. A majority of it plopped onto the floor, but, from the wrist down, it was still coated with the fluids, which left the bearded man shivering uncontrollably, like a deaf puppy.

I acted like it was going to kill Grandpa as I questioned Beardy as to where I could get something to wrap his wound in. One person captured Grandpa by the arm, accompanying him into the kitchen. I followed since I would be the one to rehabilitate Gramps or, at the least, engineer the quick fix. When we arrived at the kitchen, the stranger initiated his rummaging through drawers before he got to what we needed: cling wrap.

I stole it from his hands when I directed him to buzz off; I could control the situation myself. He reclined his head forward as he pouted, stamping his feet all the way out, what a big whiny baby. I never imagined that I would utter these words, but I instru-cted Grandpa to take off his shirt. I gathered a sour taste inside of my mouth just from muttering those words. Grandpa hiked up his shirt, revealing the decomposing flesh that had warped into a gooey texture. It was tinted brown from the common flesh tone color. Everything that was internal spilled out through the gaping hole in his midsection onto the recently greasy tile.

Someone intruded upon our privacy by coming into the kitchen to check if everything was going alright, so I located myself in a position to block her view of Grandpa. I reported that everything was going fine and to get the hell out before I had to ask her again. She spun around to leave, heeding my warning of the second time.

I didn't want to be handling any quality of foreign organs, so I notified Gramps that he had to shovel in his own so that I could quarantine the expired organs. He began to pick them up, one at a time, impaling himself with his own arm to create room for each one. When all of this was said and done, I quickly drew the cling wrap, like I was back in the Wild West. I even shouted out draw when I yanked it out from underneath my zipper. It dumbfounded me that such a slender layer of plasticy miracle could support such a bulky weight.

I must've zoned out being that Grandpa was beginning to get impatient standing there with his hands over his stomach, imprisoning all of his guts within. I told you that he was a baby. I pulled the cling wrap out an inch or two and slapped it onto Grandpa's side. It fused to his slimy skin, and I didn't even have to cradle it, due to all of the vital fluids. I played ring around the Rosie with him repeatedly until there was enough bordering him to support the poundage of his organs, and, thankfully, they didn't all fall down. I wasn't certain on how many there were, so I put on reinforcements just in case.

The only dilemma with applying cling wrap as a medical instrument was that you could clearly see the injury underneath it. It was not a pretty sight. Hopefully after awhile though the blood would harden over the wrap and make it more difficult to view the entrails of Gramps. I authorized Grandpa to put his shirt back on so that we could blow that popsicle stand.

When he was distributing his shirt onto his withered figure, I focused my attention on a ruckus coming from the eating block that had to have been disturbing the peace. Well, I wasn't going to have any reckless clamor unless I was a factor in it. I snapped my fingers and lectured Gramps to put a hustle on it as he stalked me into the birthplace of the commotion. I paraded out there, thinking that no one would touch me, considering that they all believed that they had recently butchered a man. What I was presented with was a human with a switchblade, backed by another man carrying absolutely nothing, robbing the place. The other guy must've been the tag along that didn't think anything through before doing it. In their defense, they were both decorated in all black clothing, even with black nylons shielding their identities. The main robber had his switchblade stretched across the counter with the point up against the jugular of Beardy. It easily could've been swatted out of his hand, but, because of the dramatic experience that the bearded man had just been through, he couldn't, seeing that he was presently too shaken up. He was trembling enough to be tracked on the Richter scale as he struggled to grab the money out of the cash register. He was unloading fifty percent of it onto the floor. The robber boosted the blade up to his throat harder, prompting him not to dump anymore, or he could kiss his trachea goodbye. I thought that was a tendon in the leg, but whatever.

All of the pressure couldn't have been sitting well with the bearded man being that he was shuddering more than ever as sweat drained out of him like acid rain in Canada. He pulled off a worthy accomplishment though when he handed the wad of funds over to Nylon Head who deposited it into the innards of a plastic grocery bag, also not a good choice. When the robbers turned around to head out of the front door several cop cars pulled up proximate to the entrance.

Nylon Head urgently shifted his course, thrusting his switchblade into the larynx of Beardy. He tried to remove it, but the robber continually twisted it, ripping the meat encompassing it until Beardy ceased to move anymore. Like a raving lunatic, he effectively shouted at the corpse, making it known to the deceased that was what he had earned for calling the police.

At that moment, the stupidest thing I had ever seen in my miserable existence transpired. I saw someone that wasted half of a sandwich. I only spotted it, since it was in the garbage. Besides that, this lady announced out loud that she had called the cops, because a man was hurt and needed medical assistance. Nylon Head insisted that he didn't behold anybody that was wounded, and that he was correct. Grandpa was nowhere in sight. It came to me as no surprise that he wasn't attentive to me again.

Grandpa retreated from the kitchen with an eight pack of jumbo frozen hotdogs that were in loose packaging within his embrace. He was punishing one of them by gnawing on it; with his other hand, he struggled not to lose his grasp on the packaging. Nylon Head ordered him to relinquish the hotdogs, or he would be tempted to carve a sculpture out of him. Gramps discarded them with quickness as he placed his hands in the air. When the hotdogs bonked on the ground the ice shattered off of some of them, which left Grandpa eyeballing them, but he was too afraid to do it.

I didn't see why; it was not like he hadn't been cut before. I mean, come on, all of his entrails spilled out roughly five minutes previous to this incident. I imagine that would've been more agonizing than getting stabbed.

The robber's concentration broke away from Grandpa as it went directly to the door. By the time that he rotated back, it was too late. The police had materialized through the doorway already drawing their guns. The robber glanced around frantically looking for an obvious way to escape, but the only other exit was beyond the kitchen. He took captive the closest person to him by the collar, pulling her in front of himself and obstructing the officer's line of fire. He clung his blade to her neck as he warned the police that if they didn't remove themselves from the building, while leaving the average, hungry Americans inside, he would slit her throat. The cops lowered their guns, while they backed out of the door.

The tag-along robber took off his nylon mask, tying it in the innermost part of the handles on the door. He evidently did it to make sure that no one could get in or out, but, during the procedure, he exposed his identity to everyone. He wasn't the best shaped cookie to come from the cookie cutter.

The tag-along robber turned out not to be a man like I had foreseen. Instead, it was a manly looking woman that I hoped had taped her chest down. Not that it would've been the only defect about her. It might've been had her face not had a fine layer of dark mustache hair, which also would've been fine had she appeared to be her age and not like a fifty year old.

I revived memories of seeing pictures of people comparable to her in the newspaper. It was supposedly caused by drugs, but I was betting that it was, in reality, a conspiracy. I expected that mustache hair on women was provoked by an overabundance of performing the backstroke in public pools. I always had a feeling that the pool water was malicious.

The robber formally referred to as Nylon Head threw his nylon to the floor in a fit of rage; he was a man. He released his arm from around the woman that he was brutally bear hugging, shoving her to the floor. She fixed her hands against the carpet alongside of her, striving to propel herself upward when Anti-Nylon Head stomped on one with his heel, crushing the bone beneath the sole of his shoe. She cursed at him, utilized words that I had never even heard from my fellow classmates, and they all should've had their mouths washed out with soap. Not the fun foamy soap either, bar soap, unscented.

This did not please Anti-Nylon Head who stamped his foot down viciously on her opposite hand. No one dared come to her aid in fear of the same thing happening to them. She struggled to raise herself up with her feet, but she wasn't capable enough to pull it off, making herself a vulnerable target. She still squirmed around on the floor, making an effort to escape, but there was no hope. Everybody was fastened within the room, having to watch as he buried his knife deep in between the ribs into her heart.

The first time that he sunk the blade in, it collided with the bone, so it didn't go all the way in. It frustrated him as he lost control, submerging it into her chest, not grasping when to desist. The knife only penetrated the organs about a fourth of the time on account of her ribcage acting as a barricade. She lay inanimate for a short period of time before her chest resembled a mangled unidentifiable body. His manly woman sidekick had to wrench him off, since he had snapped into a demented state of mind.

Then, I appreciated that he was the specific person that I shouldn't mess with (while he possessed a weapon). You had to tick him off plenty beforehand, considering that the sole reasoning behind him exterminating the lady was thanks to her contacting the police. I learned that, because he still wasn't done screaming at the deceased. She-man shouted at him to shut up as she burglarized all of the jewelry that the loved one had been wearing. She didn't dismount the body after stealing her jewelry though. She pressed her nose up against the corpse's nose examined up and down her features. Then, she fixated on her lips, plausibly attempting to unravel what shade of lipstick it was. It was considerably obvious that it was dusky rose colored. What I mean is that it was some shade of red. Instead of only analyzing the corpse's lips, she scrunched hers up against them, maybe to resolve if it was flavored lipstick. I wasn't entirely convinced by that conclusion, since I didn't see how running her hand up the cadaver's shirt and massaging the tattered flesh or the service of her tongue could've helped determine that.

Anti-Nylon Head hoisted her up off the dead body, clarifying that there wasn't time for that at that moment, which was true. It took an extensive period of time to discover the perfect shade of lipstick. They were both coated in blood, acting like complete nutballs.

Through this exhaustive ordeal, I must've not had my head on straight. I realized that Nazm wasn't anywhere in the crowd when I got bored with the reality play. It pestered me, because if Nazm made it out onto the streets, I was positive that he would get lost. I situated my palm flat above my eyes like I was trying to block the rays of sunlight so that I could make out something in the distance; it worked too. I concluded that it wasn't only to see far away in the light but also in the dark. I pinpointed Nazm's location where he was still seated in the corner at our table in the shadows finishing up his feast. I used my best judgment to come to a verdict. It was to leave him alone over there until the whole event was over with. He really shouldn't have been left unattended. He was a carbon copy of a child that needed to be supervised 24/7 or else he would commence the nibbling of boogers (which Nazm was in the process of doing) the minute you drifted away. It was great to unearth that he was still producing mucus.

After the two bandits had finished their coaching sessions with each other, they decreed that everyone have a seat except for the one personality that they urged to enlist as a hostage. The captive would have the fine duty of tolerating a knife that would be held up to their throat as the robbers strived to figure out what to do. The crowded room went voiceless. It was essentially because the robbers had decided to muzzle their opinions for a second. Nobody put their hands to the sky or volunteered for such an honorable role in a hostage situation.

I sure as hell wasn't going to do it. I was going to enable one of those poor schmucks to get stuck with it. Eventually, they had to settle on somebody at random, seeing that nobody was up for the task. The specimen that they selected was not somebody that a respectable human being would've elected. Then, again, a respectable human being wouldn't have ravaged an innocent in a rage or felt up a ripe cadaver.

Their recruit was a mere stud of a child, around the age of five, who rightfully came to have a meal with his parents. Now his mommy was snuffed out, but, furthermore, he was being hugged by a stranger - not for comfort, but for a threat. With the single movement of an inch, the kid could've been wasted, and kids are famous for being fidgety. The exclusive purpose for why he grabbed the child was because no one cared, since they were all going to perish in the near future anyway.

She-man recommended that Anti-Nylon Head go to test if the backdoor was free for a withdrawal, while she babysat the rest of us in the main area. He agreed, so he made his way to the backdoor while maintaining the placement of his switchblade connected with the youngster's throat, becoming satisfied as nobody made a motion towards him. After the burglar had made it through the doorway to the kitchen, Grandpa felt the need to misbehave.

We were sitting beside each other at a square table with two additional people. Gramps grasped one of them, winding up the innocent's shirt within his palm as he forced him backward, capsizing him and the chair. This guy laid there vulnerable on the floor as Gramps bit into his jugular, swinging his head from side to side to rupture the veins within the body. Gore flung throughout the surrounding area until Gramps made his way into the throat. She-man attempted to pull Gramps off with no success, basically because she had no nuclear weapon on her. She screeched out irrelevant words in an irritating tone at Grandpa until he curved his focus. Gramps glanced back at her while shrugging his shoulders before going back to consuming the neck on the stiff.

It seemed that because she had no weapon, Gramps didn't sense the menacing atmosphere at all. I estimate that after a couple of minutes the robber had deciphered that. It may've been the incentive of why she abducted a meat cleaver from the table in front of us. Why nobody ever fathered the impulse to snatch it themselves to slaughter the robbers was beyond me. She-man started screaming at Grandpa all over again until he rotated once more. When he did, she threatened him by remarking that she would mince his body up into itty-bitty pieces. Before she even concluded her sentence, Grandpa had his hands in the air surrendering.

The cops weren't able to behold anything that was going on inside because the blinds were down on the few windows that were in the restaurant. They might've been competent enough to tell from the sheer volume of noise coming from inside though. The pay phone rang, which was odd. How many customers got calls on a mysterious phone when they went out to eat? Plus, everyone nowadays owned cell phones that caused brain tumors. Everyone looked at each other, waiting for somebody to pick it up, but no one was man enough for the responsibility. So I sucked up all of my fear (which was none) and uplifted the phone with a confident hello.

After all of that, it presented itself to be for the robbers. I couldn't conceive as to why they would keep anyone posted as to their whereabouts, furthermore providing someone with the number, especially the police. I entrusted the phone to She-man, but she dodged the offer to take the call, which was not friendly, since I had already confessed to them that she was there. I plugged up the receiver on the phone with my palm, indicating for her to handle it, but she wouldn't, since she wasn't supposed to form decisions without the other guy. I mentioned that she needed to prove herself by not forevermore listening to those male chauvinistic pigs. Finally, I said, "You go girl!" and that was all it took for her to gain enough confidence to clutch the phone. As soon as she settled the phone alongside to her ear, she hung it up. I questioned her as to what that was all about. She replied that the cops were going to call back in five minutes to get the list of demands.

Now that wasn't a decision that she could assemble by herself, but I concluded that if I could persuade her to by repeating that it was, perhaps the two burglars would end up neutralizing each other over their own stupidity. I attained a notepad and a pen from the counter when I stressed that she should start by writing down her demands. She was hesitant to do it, wanting to delay until her partner returned, but I debated her out of that.

When I paused to take another breather, I witnessed Gramps slurping guts down like lo mein. This guy had to have been bloated, yet he had to feast upon the spare consumer at our table. I strolled over to Gramps, swatting him in the back, reciting that he was being a bad boy as if he was a dog. He whimpered and scampered back to his seat before I had to get brutal with my actions. I skipped back to She-man so that I could checkup on how the demands were coming, and she dished me a list, showing me that it was completed. The list read:

1. *Not able to get arrested for the crime.*
2. *Lots of money.*
3. *A brand new car.*

It was a fitting list for someone who couldn't think for themselves, or, in that case, at all. I took the liberty of contributing my two cents to the list, so the final draft ended up like this:

1. *Nice muscular prison mates.*
2. *A full hundred dollars in food stamps.*
3. *1990 Dodge Dynasty (must be brown).*
4. *Peanut butter filled pretzels.*

I had guidance in the spelling from She-man, which was pathetic, but, sometimes, you've got to do what you've got to do. I couldn't digest how she thought that all of those suggestions were valuable things to ask for, even the pretzels. I convinced her that a Dodge Dynasty was the most luxurious car that existed on the planet.

The phone rang again when she dispensed an expression at me like she was puzzled as to who it could've been. I refreshed her memory, and her pain went away. She answered the phone with the officer on the line and leaked her demands. She had to repeat peanut butter filled pretzels twice, but, other than that, it went smoothly. She hung up the phone before springing on me to give me a meaningful hug. It would've been breathtaking if her arm hair wasn't tickling me, also if she didn't have the fragrance of a year-old avocado. I thought, what the hell. I participated by bouncing up and down while we were hugging in celebration.

As we did that, Anti-Nylon Head emerged from the kitchen. She-man nudged me away, collecting the cleaver, spouting that if I ever made an effort towards attacking her again that I would become sushi. He didn't believe her for eight seconds as he forewarned her that if she screwed up one or two more times, he was going to extract the plasma from her body himself to exchange it for money at the hospital. So far everything was going as intended. She-man asked Anti-Nylon Head what happened to the little boy that he was holding hostage. He responded that when he unbolted the back exit, there were tons of cops guarding it. After he refastened the door, his grip slipped on the innocent as he raced off. When he started the hunt for the hostage, he was spanked in the back of the head with a frying pan. When Anti-Nylon's head whirled around, he was bonked on the face with a boiling hot pot that riddled him comatose. When he arose from his dreams, there was no sign of the kid, so he must've retreated through the back door. A grown man getting outsmarted by a whippersnapper, what a sweet deal.

To cheer him up, she reported to him about how she had given the cops their demands list so that he didn't have to put any concern into it. He requested to inspect the list, so she willingly forked it over. Strike two. He nodded seeming like he approved of it before his expression went sour. He close-fisted punched her point-blank in the face. I realize that she appeared to be a male, but that didn't mean that he could strike her like one. She acted like a concrete wall, not even blinking as the blood gushed from her nostrils. He went for another swing that made contact, but it had the same overall effect. It was admirable to observe a woman being capable of receiving that much tribulation without even sensing it.

That was until he took his next swing with the blade in hand, slicing her from ear to ear like a pickled herring. The blood surged from the arteries as her jaw stayed in place while her cranium bent backwards, severing the cheek fat along with it. The blood sprayed in my face, resembling a quality efficient sprinkler, but, then again, I was in the closest range beside Anti-Nylon Head, staring in disbelief. My vision was blurred pink from the hemoglobin discoloring the moisture coating of my eye. At least it didn't cause as much irritation as spilling salt in the eyes. I poured salt in mine once, because someone lied to me, claiming that it got rid of pinkeye.

What a sucker that liar was. I purged myself of that pinkeye within the next day after showering the salt in them every hour. To get the blood out as well as to clear up my vision, I kept in mind that you were supposed to cry whatever it was out. So all I did was reflected on how plastic bags were beginning to replace the paper ones. It hinted to a conclusion that nobody cared about the environment anymore.

While She-man's corpse was plummeting to the outdated carpet, the robber landed her by the hair to hold her up. With his other hand, he swiped the blade back and forth into her neck like a credit card (except you don't put those in necks), until he arrived at her spine. He then relinquished his hold on her hair, grabbing the spine that was exposed inside of the throat with his bare hands and snapped her head off. He chucked the detached head out through the sealed window on the side of the building.

I carried Anti-Nylon Head's knife in my hand after snatching it from his loosened grip. When he wrapped the slaughter up, he charged at me a whole two feet between us, snagging it from my hands. I clarified that I was only making sure that it wasn't one of those cheap free-fair knifes, because, if it was, I could've sold him a genuinely authentic one. However, since it was legit, there was no need for my services. I didn't think that he was grateful of my offer, since he delivered a maddening look while stroking the blade provocatively with his fingers. He was advancing towards me until I was saved by the bell, I mean the ring. The phone had rung again. My deduction was that it was the police, once more, wanting him to release a hostage to demonstrate good faith. I raised my hand when Anti-Nylon Head said that someone needed to be liberated. I was notified that there was no way in hell that I would be released, because he was going to strangle my esophagus later. If he did that, I wouldn't even get to attempt committing suicide once. He seized a senile lady, dragging her over to the front entrance.

When she was shuffling her feet out the door, he planted his boot on her ass, providing her with a proficient thrust. Anti-Nylon Head held his finger up, telling the cops to wait a second. He popped back in, picking up the headless body of his former partner in crime. He flung her out of the front door, encouraging them to dispose of the human waste.

When Anti-Nylon Head dropped by a second time, he asked where all of the other hostages went. I viewed the rest of the room, realizing that he was correct. Only about half of the blameless that were originally there still were. He stepped up to the hostages, inspecting the immediate area that we had been settled in when I watched him tugging Grandpa up off of the ground. I whisked my physique towards him to ensure that nothing was going to happen. When I gawked at the floor, seeing that it was scattered with dead bodies. The corpses had portions absent from each of them, always fatal. Seriously, it was like I had never coached him about not wasting meat. Anti-Nylon Head used his knife to his advantage, stabbing Gramps in the midsection a few times before he plopped down in a chair, protesting movement.

Little did the robber fathom that Gramps wasn't moving only because he was depressed that he got in trouble, not due to him being deceased. He was cradling his stomach over his shirt like a man who was bleeding to death. I could imagine though that the knife had just clipped the cling wrap, and he didn't want all of that fresh human meat that he devoured to spill out. The robber clutched his own skull as he went on a rant regarding to how it was everybody's fault that nothing ever worked out for him. It became a splendid time for me to hide, so I sheltered myself behind the tallest individual in the room. I envisioned that if Anti-Nylon Head apprehended me in the state of mind that he was in, he would sacrifice me without a doubt. I crawled from behind the tallest fellow over to the corner, where our table was joined to Nazm, when the robber wasn't squinting in that direction.

I turned to Nazm, who was still calmly trying to absorb his dinner and guided him to leap out of the window to freedom. Expecting he understood that, I stashed myself underneath the table, out of sight thanks to a tablecloth, wasting time until he made his move. Nazm lifted up his plateful of nourishments pelting the window with it. The plate fragmentized, but so did the window, launching spaghetti noodles and meatballs all over the officers outside. The robber snapped out of his angry ranting before lunging at Nazm. When Anti-Nylon Head made a connection with Nazm at the edge of his knife, Nazm mounted himself against the floor until he realized that he was being physically assaulted. Then Nazm knocked Anti-Nylon Head down with one hand and sprung out through where the window used to exist. I suspected that Nazm escaped because of his hatred for selfish people.

During the whole ordeal, Anti-Nylon Head never once saw me, since it was so dim in the corner that it was almost impossible to spy underneath the table. I had to extend my arm out from beneath the table, when the robber wasn't keeping watch, on account of Nazm standing outside of the window waving to me. I had to try to shoo him away, but the police tended to that for me when they escorted him away from the crime scene. I uncovered that the cops came in handy every once in a great while.

After that point in history, Anti-Nylon Head unquestionably lost it. He started going down the wall where all of the prisoners were lined up shanking them into extinction. Grandpa studied while this was going on by noting that the robber squandered a considerable amount of time on each victim, so he visualized that it would be alright for him to initiate his reign of terror on the opposite side of the hostages. Without Anti-Nylon Head even showing concern, Gramps began to chomp and mush down on the first hostage. It was astonishing how much Anti-Nylon Head didn't care. Usually, when someone murders a fellow man and he comes back from the dead with cannibalistic tendencies, they tend to be concerned. It could've been that Anti-Nylon Head had transformed into a lunatic, so everything was justified. Who knows for sure? All I know is that he showed no remorse. I swore that maturing into a zombie made it so that your belly could never get stocked. That was until I beheld, during Grandpa's feast, that whenever he digested something, it would trickle out of his abdomen into a pool of the slightest processed goop. This must've made it so most of the nutrients didn't soak into his body, so his stomach only stayed partially full, leaving him famished shortly after he ate, never capable of getting stuffed. After the puddle reached the diameter of a human being, he would progress to the next batch of hostage.

The line diminished quite slowly, yet everybody still poised themselves there. Maybe it was the fear of dying with their back turned to their attacker while struggling to disentangle the cloth on the door. Or maybe it was the fear of fighting back and losing to become the example of a weakling who couldn't stand up for themselves. Whatever it was, no one could suck it up. When it came down to the last person, there was a huge conflict. Who was going to make the kill, Grandpa or Anti-Nylon Head? The tension mounted as both men stared into each other's eyes then shifted towards the hostage as if that was the trophy. It was similar to a quick draw in the old Wild

West days, except that there was no dust, or guns, or a girl to romantically entangle with in the end. Okay, maybe it wasn't like a quick draw.

Every time that Grandpa appraised the hostage, he licked whatever section of his lips that hadn't rotted off, while Anti-Nylon Head wiped the blood off of his blade onto his shirt. They both put a foot behind them for leverage. When the first one flinched, so did the other to spawn a mad step towards the hostage. I couldn't distinguish who made the original move, because they were both feening for dead tissue from the bloodlust so much that they were virtually lightning bolts. It didn't matter anyway. As if it was the standard, the robber went openly for the chest, while Grandpa went for the legs. It was similar to chicken; you usually wanted the breast, but, every once in a while, you needed to switch it up with a leg. The captive was already dead from the total of puncture wounds in her chest, but Gramps was taking his time, working around the leg, nibbling every piece of meat that he could off of it.

When Anti-Nylon Head was spent from working on the shredded corpse, formally known as hostage, he put Grandpa in the spotlight. Anti-Nylon Head kicked him to the ground, followed by drawing near him with a blank stare, occupying his eye sockets, knife in hand, anticipating another murder. Gramps ascended, prepared for him to struggle to pull off the kill, because he was, at the present, enraged for being heckled in the middle of his feast. Blood marinated both of them as neither of them stepped back while stationed nose to nose. I wouldn't get that close to someone unless we were in a long distance relationship, not because I wanted to execute them.

The flinching was nonexistent. Not even when the cops came over the megaphone, which made me nail my head on the table, motivating it to do a tiny hop off of the carpet. The megaphone was blaring, so Gramps and Anti-Nylon Head couldn't detect my clamor. The police demanded that Anti-Nylon Head release another hostage, or he wouldn't reap his demands. I don't suppose that he gave a crap about the demands, seeing that he wasn't dismissing Grandpa.

They were still positioned face to face when I overheard someone brush up against the entrance and scurry away, like they had a moment ago shoplifted a candy bar from a gas station, or, in my case, a carton of cigarettes for Grandpa. He would always supply me with the funds, but, whenever I explained to him that they wouldn't permit me buy them because of my age, he wouldn't believe me and flip out when I came home with nothing. I had no choice; it wasn't my fault that back in the 1800's cigarettes were legal to minors and now they were deemed "unhealthy". It was nice to have extra money to spend on candy bars, though.

During my thought process, there was an explosion that blasted the front door off of its hinges and in rushed many, many officers. They were all wearing riot gear with their guns drawn, targeting the robber. I didn't see much of a point in the bulletproof vests. I was almost positive that those didn't cutoff sharp pointy objects from boring into the chest cavity. When they breached through the door, Anti-Nylon Head revolved around to the back of Grandpa, hugging the knife against his throat, while exploiting him as a human shield.

The cops prompted Anti-Nylon Head to abandon the weapon so that he could approach them with his hands up. If he complied with their orders, the cops pledged that they wouldn't open fire on him. Anti-Nylon Head claimed that the officers wouldn't do so either way, considering that they would also blow away Grandpa if they tried. I wasn't convinced that they were too anxious about that, considering that the whole room was littered with the bodies of people that were livelier than Grandpa. The tension was high, but neither side was letting up. I didn't suppose that the robber was too panic-stricken about dying, even though he should've been, seeing that all of the naughty inhabitants always went to hell.

With one hand, he reached around Grandpa's face, jerking his head to the side. In the meantime, with the other hand, he prolonged the slitting of Grandpa's throat so that everyone could observe it really well. After he lacerated Grandpa's jugular, he heaved him to the ground, letting him gargle on the blood in his windpipe. Anti-Nylon Head outstretched his arms, composing a free shot for the police, which they took without procrastinating. They pumped out bullets, impregnating him with enough lead to mold him into a giant pencil. One of the policemen must've taken the entire nightmare personally, whereas after the robber was obviously spiritless, he implanted him with more lead to bleed out his soul onto the floor. The crazed policeman was sent to the ground by the other officers to be handcuffed. They accompanied him out of the restaurant to squeeze him into the police car.

The medics rushed over to Grandpa with a stretcher that was covered with a white sheet. The assumption of death lingered in the air around Grandpa. The medics were near him when I emerged from my hiding spot running over to Gramps. Legions of guns were drawn at me on my way over, but, when they acknowledged that I was too brawny for them, they deposited them into their holsters. I pushed the medics away when I got there in fear that they would expose the condition that he was truly in. Then we would be stored inside of another hospital, dealing with more experiments. I was no match for the women in the fine art of nursing.

I was instructed to step back, or I might compromise his life. They rolled Gramps over as I stepped back to let them do their jobs. Gramps was acting like he was breathing, which looked decent, except for the slash that was crossing his throat. He peeled apart his eyelids, declaring to the nurses that he wasn't cut as deep as it appeared. All that he needed was something to dress up the nick. The hospital was not an option for him, not even if they were offering free cookies. The nurses took a tour of their ambulance again to get some cookies, since they didn't bring any in, deducing that Grandpa was dead and all.

I directed my focus at Grandpa when nobody was keeping tabs on us. I questioned how it didn't at least graze his trachea when it seemed to have gone halfway into his neck. He authorized me to come closer so that he could clue me in on how he managed that one. I happened to get adjacent to Grandpa when he tilted his cranium backwards, peeling apart the moderately scabbed laceration displaying the frontal of his spine to me. I couldn't believe that his head didn't disconnect from his body. His blood spurted into my eyes, blinding me with his dark green hemoglobin. A couple of chunks even bonded with my face that I scraped off, casting them to the pits of the ground, where they brought about a splat noise. Grandpa was giggling like a stunted schoolgirl, playing double dutch in a plaid dress.

It was the first time that I had heard Grandpa laugh in over five years. The last time was when I was sledding, and I lost control of my steering. I glided straight off of a giant cliff that was as tall as I was when I was in elementary school. I flipped over and descended upon my spine on top of jagged rocks, finally ending my journey with a resounding smash into a pine tree. He didn't reflect upon it as comical when he found out that my jacket was shredded. He made me travel by foot to school in a short sleeved shirt for a month before investing in a brand-new coat when spring dropped anchor.

What a demented senile man. No wonder where I scored the not so nice side of me. I heard the medics chitchatting, while they showed up inside of the building. I snatched Grandpa's hair (well the straggly ones that he had from before he went bald) and yanked it harshly towards me, uniting the two halves of flesh together for eternity, I could only have dreamed. He furnished me with a dirty look while shaking his fist at me, pretending that I was one of his boxing buddies at the senior citizens club. I was lacking the sagginess in my face. But Gramps had poor eyesight, so you never know.

The medics sprung back into the situation with some thick gauze that I snatched from their hands. It was swiped from me, and I was directed to no longer touch the equipment, stripping me of what dignity I never had. I wasn't informed that gauze was considered medical equipment anyway. It was only a towel with a fancy name and shaped differently. They politely asked Grandpa to sit up so that they could control the bleeding. They must've been mistaking other people's blood for his or else they were just idiotic.

The gauze was placed around his neck as if he was something special, using the utmost care to make sure that they wouldn't suffocate him. He grinned or smiled the entire time. I wasn't positive as to which one it was, considering that his face was becoming remarkably decayed. Everybody around him must've not gawked at him, because they credited him as a burn victim that was striving to be alive in a judgmental world. When he brewed up excuses on why not to go to the hospital or be established on the stretcher, the medics helped pull him up by his arms, ushering him to his feet again. The medics paraded in front of us steering us towards the outside, while the police department collected evidence, struggling to match what organs went to which body.

I tripped Grandpa down to his knees, where I went ahead putting him in a headlock, followed by a good old-fashioned wholesome noogie. He must've sensed the burn from knuckles on skin. I didn't stop until the friction caused too much warmth for my comfort. I wrenched him upwards by the neck that was at the present maimed by my triceps and biceps to teach him a lesson of why not to screw with The Heinous Helty. I brought about "the look", but like that had ever battered anyone.

We forged ahead on our tour to the great outdoors, where we were greeted by a crowd of spectators, along with reporters who were challenging us to illustrate the full story for them. I had memorized enough knowledge about reporters to understand that they would change up my story to make it look like I snapped the necks of gophers, and I was no gopher killer, only a squirrel killer (if I could capture them). All of the reporters flocked around us, asking what happened to the murderous robber, so I unveiled precisely what had happened. How I strangulated him with an everyday garden hose while freeing a pack of innocent children out of the back door.

I pulled away from the questions to go near Gramps by the cops. It was there that I plunked into the backseat of the squad car. Nazm was already in the car with us, except he was granted the front seat, as if he was gifted enough to wield all of that excitement.

Gramps was leaning back against his door, stretching his legs across to my side of the car, crossing them on my lap.

I realized that it was going to be an enduring and unpleasant car ride, regardless of the distance that we were going to be traveling. It didn't help that Grandpa was harnessing the same socks that he had on when we embarked on our journey. No matter how much I pleaded with him, he wouldn't change them, because they were his lucky, teal, flying elephant socks. Somehow, to him, flying elephants were deemed lucky. I couldn't even comprehend the thoughts of a senile man if I had a gigantic brain held captive in my room. Nazm seemed quite pleased to be in the front seat, and he continued flipping switches and pushing buttons.

The cop got into the car winding the key in the ignition. I was predicting that sirens and lights would to go off, but the exclusive thing wrong was that the radio was blaring some classic rock station. The officer reached over to the radio, I imagined, to poke a button to turn it off, but, instead, it jumped over to a country station. The cop leaned over to Nazm, uttering to him to never grope his radio again, or he would haul him in for destruction of property. Nazm started to reach his hand back over to the radio when the officer spanked it told him a firm no. Nazm peered back at him with a puppy dog look on his face that didn't even faze the officer as he turned the radio up even louder.

The cop squatted on that seat while driving, impersonating someone who played an acoustic guitar on his knee. He even got Nazm to join the hoedown that was going on in the front seat. At that point in time, if I would've had a weapon on me, I would've tested its potential on myself, not caring about the whole purpose of the trip anymore. It was too much acoustic for my sanity to manage, leading me to want my fictional girlfriend to break up with me and carry off my cowboy hat with her. There was an exhaustive volume of knee slapping as I attempted to ring my own throat to give me a shred of hope for the future. My hands deserted my throat to shove Gramps legs off of me as I scoped out the police station that was less than a block away. There had never been a time that I had been happier about then the one at that instant.

Chapter 13: Metal Tubes Remind Me of Aerosol Cans

We pulled up in front of the building, so I tugged on the handle, doing my best to break away from the confines of the devil vehicle before remembering that they locked from the outside. I waited impatiently for the car door to become ajar. Of course, he opened Grandpa's side first, but I played leapfrog over him, hopping onto the street before Gramps even made it out. I put my face up towards the ozone layer to inhale the fresh exhaust in the air. It reminded me of the day at the gas station, settled behind the cars that pulled in to huff down the fumes, until I was spotted and forced to gallop through the field of tall grass to avoid rehab.

Standing in the middle of the street, breathing in the atmosphere, was not a neato idea, I discovered, as I was almost struck by a car. It swerved to miss me and ran into a fire hydrant on the flipside of the street. Water bombarded the air and showered everything, while the furious citizen got out of his car and proceeded to shout at me, like it was my fault that he wasn't paying attention. He began roaming across the street, drenched equal to if he was in the rain, which would've been sexy had he been wearing all white and been a girl. When he got up to me, his fist made a line drive into my mouth and sent me back into the backseat of the cop car on top of Grandpa. He was stretching his grasp into the car when he was pounded against the cop car to be handcuffed.

It must've been for assaulting a beloved icon. The officer lugged him toward the station, while the convict screamed about how he was going to sue the entire police station. It seemed to be a requirement to do that when you got arrested. We were summoned to trail behind the cop into the station, so we did to elude being incarcerated or provoking a scene.

When we got internal, I obtained a seat in the waiting room alongside of a table disguised with magazines. It would've been slightly entertaining had there been more than two different magazines, also if they hadn't both been about fish. Dull situations always seemed to haunt me, but I consistently found ways to make them more interesting. So I read a couple of magazines about fishing, upside down. By the time they had asked us to approach the back, I lost consciousness from all of the blood rushing to my head. Someone must've pushed me over, since I regained consciousness when my head collided with the floor, bestowing upon me the boost to get back on my feet to barf on the floor. I spewed green and red Christmas vomit all over my shoes, but by that point I was so damn polluted that more puke wouldn't hurt at all.

After that, I felt fine, so I led the way into the back. We were all routed into three isolated rooms. I anticipated that it was so I could get an extravagant room, so I wouldn't be crowded by other people. But when I got into the room, it was kind of humble, only being occupied by a table with a chair on each side of it. That wasn't lavish enough for me; I was high maintenance. I resolved to make due with what I had, seating myself on the table. The officer expressed his true emotions, telling me to get off the table and install my ass in the chair. He relaxed in the cushioned chair across from me when I got off of the table. He retained a stack of papers in his hands that could've held my entire legacy. Just like my legacy, it appeared that the utmost of it still needed to be filled in. The officer stood the papers up, tapping them against the table to straighten them before we got into the fun stuff.

He reported to me that I was going to be interrogated about the incident that happened earlier. I was going to be held responsible to recite the truth, or I would go to prison. I agreed with him, but I crossed my fingers behind my back so that I could then falsify my story without getting in trouble. He extracted the pen from his pocket that had a fluffy pink ball on the end. I choked back the laughter, but it still muffled through my lips, causing him to hear me. He ended the countdown before it began by freaking out, since it was the only pen that was remaining in the desk drawer, but that's what they all declare.

He commenced the simple questions, such as my name and age. I lied about those to keep him on his toes even though he would never learn of my treachery. I told him my name was Magnar Solistee, and that I was nine years old. The age seemed a bit leery from the expression that I received from him, but I had a baby face that would've secured my status as a twenty year old when I turned fifty.

Right after that, he initiated the tough questions, like why were my shoe prints identified in a puddle of vital fluid behind the restaurant. I mentioned that it was because I donated my shoes to a starving child, but he gave them back when the hostage situation was over as a gift for my courage. Maybe he stepped in it?

The cop asked me why all of our fingerprints were discovered in an abandoned cop car behind the restaurant. I divulged that it was because we found it, appearing totally trashed. We only wanted to pinpoint the owner, so we searched the innards of it to find an I.D. It was all for the concern of my fellow Americans. Then the officer asked me why more than half of the remains were completely devoured. I said that it was just another whacko, cannibal, serial killer robber on the loose that we happened to run into.

He made it known that he trusted that I was full of crap. The cop accredited us as the murderers. I gasped in horror, wondering how he figured out what happened through all of my complex lies. The officer stormed out of the room, locking me inside when he shut it. I grabbed the handle, planting one foot up against the wall. I pushed with my leg, inserting some oomph into my arms when I pulled at the door, but my superhuman strength was no match for the door. I collapsed backwards to the ground, where I fought to regain my breath after my tireless attempt for freedom.

The door opened from the reverse side, bonking me in the leg. Gramps and Nazm squeezed through the crack that it was ajar, while Nazm waved savagely at me, acting as if we were separated at birth, and death. The officer came next, charging the door hard enough to slide me out of the way. When he got into the room, he took notice to me lying on the floor and asked me why I was resting there, causing trouble when he was only gone for a minute; it was tough love. Actually, it was because I cherished being a frustrating hyperactive son of a gun. But I construed that it was because something was striving to climb in through the floor, and I was the only thing restraining it.

He tossed a clipboard on me, informing me that I had to stain my signature on the piece of paper. I questioned what it was for, so he announced to everyone that it was to verify that I agreed that everything I stated in our conversation was true. I signed it under my pseudo while keeping my fingers crossed behind my back. I didn't think about it beforehand, but I had screwed myself over. By crossing my fingers while being asked the question, I proved that I was lying about lying, which meant that I was telling the truth. I was in a bit of a pickle. Possibly not even a bit of a pickle, but a whole one, even worse, a jumbo pickle, like the ones that came individually packaged.

I inclined my body from the floor to seat myself in my chair, making Gramps and Nazm stand beside me. The officer commented that Gramps and Nazm had both squealed the exclusive factual story. There was an assembly of prison guards coming to pick us up to pilot us to a maximum security prison in Washington. I jumped up from my seat, declaring that he didn't know the truth. But he insisted that he did, thanks to some new kind of technology, where you could determine who the killer was by fingerprints and teeth marks. He was bluffing, like I would believe something so preposterous. It was not like we were living in the 22nd century. I made it known to him that I wanted to speak to my lawyer. I was notified that the only one that was available was a free one, and he sucked. We couldn't afford one, because all of our money was disposed of in the abandoned cop car. I guess I wasn't the only forgetful one out of the bunch.

That became the end of the road. In reality, it was more like a fork in the road. Go one way, and it was lethal injection. The other way was surviving in a cell the remnant of my life with a guy who was nicknamed Jenny. There was without exception another way. When you reach a fork in the road of life, there are multiple ways to go, considering that forks have four points. That contributes two more options to sneak by, while the others are watching and waiting for the expected ways. The stupid road sign system gave the fork a bad name.

The officer vacated the interrogation room when he was paged to the front desk by the voice inside of the intercom. As soon as he fled the room, I got up off of my chair so that I could hoist it into the air to disassemble it over Grandpa's cranium. At least, that was what I would've done had it not been screwed to the floor, so I settled for a swift kick to his kneecap. When he slumped down to pop it back into place, I dropkicked him in the sternum, knocking him over so that he hammered his vertebrae against the floor. I asked him why he would confess the valid way that the events had happened to the police. He claimed that he didn't in a trustworthy tone that led me to suspect Nazm.

I switched my focus to him, pointing the finger. I poked him while requesting an answer as to why he would tell the truth until my finger sunk into his right ventricle. I pulled it out, perplexed as to how body rot could muster such a foul stench. Same as the former suspect, he claimed not to have told the truth. He was too engaged in "eating his food", which really meant picking his nose, to even notice what was going on around him. If it was all legitimate, that meant that I pretty much divulged what had happened just by denying everything and giving all of those unrealistic explanations. I hoped that they wouldn't be competent enough to figure that out between the two of them, since I did all of the thinking for them.

I wasn't that lucky as their expressions shifted, (well, at least Grandpa's did, since Nazm was playing with a bug on the floor) from a look of confusion to a look of the angry elderly syndrome type. Grandpa gripped me on my shirt as he shook me like a helpless infant. Then Nazm joined in from behind, only so he wouldn't feel left out, I'm convinced. I was being jerked about as if I was taffy that needed to be stretched out to dry.

This went on for a drawn-out period of time without a single punch or other act of violence developing. They said that the older you got the wiser you got when, in fact, it was the older you got the more soft you got.

They must've caught a flash of the retaliation from Grandpa and Nazm (if you could call it that) on the security camera, seeing that a cluster of cops and guards came busting through the door, dominating us to the ground off of each other. Once we discontinued the skirmish, they loosened their embrace while some of the inactive guards came up, struggling to furnish us with handcuffs. Gramps and Nazm went patiently while getting their arms clamped together, but I wasn't about to go down without a scuffle.

I cried out "Rape!" while kicking my feet rapidly as I strived to maneuver my arms against my chest. The only piece of the method that I achieved was the screaming, which I shouldn't have even bothered yelling, being that no one was going to believe that I was being sexually violated when I was already on tape. That awarded me with a solution, so I screamed out "Snuff film!", but the only ones who would know would be the sick bastards who were currently watching it. I was ultimately locked into the handcuffs when all three of us were raised to our feet by the brute strength of the boys in blue. I managed to break free from the grasp of the law as I scampered about the room seeking another exit, but, like I had predicted, there wasn't a separate one besides the heavy duty bolted door.

They allowed me to run around the room in a circle for their own personal gratification before I credited myself with an additional way out besides the door. It was through the two way glass that took up approximately the entire wall. I navigated my way to the far side of the room dashing as hastily as a wood-chuck could chuck wood (which I think is fast) and jumped shoulder first into the air, heading strictly for the glass. When I collided with it, I anticipated a walloping crash, but all I got was a walloping thump. My anatomy came to a dead stop as I bounced back, tumbling over onto my ass. Everybody had a super jolly moment over it as I struggled to get back up to dish out a second go. I may not have been the brightest color on a stain glass window, but I was no quitter. That was why I never sprung on the smoking bandwagon, because I never quit once I got started on something.

Once I stood up, I went for my second run to the window when I was apprehended and wielded in one place by a swarm of cops that were succeeding that time. Another cop came out of the wood works with a couple long chains welded to clamps. He fastened one of the clamps on my ankle after fighting with it. Then he connected that same chain to Nazm's ankle. The same crap was pulled between Nazm and Grandpa, too. I wasn't convinced that it was legal for them to send us to prison without permitting us to post bail or something. I had a theory, though, that our rights were stripped after committing a certain number of murders, combined with the bodies that were eaten.

We were dictated by the sheriff to walk out of the entrance that we came through. We were escorted by too many guards with assault rifles than three criminals should've really needed. When we got outside, there was another gathering of the population surrounding us. It seemed like they had not been there for very long, and had all just been imported there from the restaurant with a few armored vehicles added. A reporter broke through the police blockade before the cop closed it behind me. She bitch slapped me on the cheek, alleging that I was the reason why she got fired from her job. It was because I conveyed a false statement of what transpired at the restaurant to her. I predicted that the news spread quickly throughout the city. When the reporter turned to walk away, Grandpa took a big bite out of her cranium. Oozing gray matter splashed against the concrete, while the remainder of it was being swished around inside Grandpa's mouth.

I took a mad dash at getting the hell out of there, counting on that I would be pursued by the rest of my chain gang, but, instead, the metal rings plucked my leg out from under me, causing me to do a face plant on the ground. Blood evacuated from my mouth, while I drooled out a few teeth into the crimson stream. I experienced someone gripping the back of my shirt to usher me back up to my feet, but I had no clue of who it was, considering that I was partly unconscious at the current time. I could perceive Gramps pressed against the ground, getting beat with nightsticks and tasered without remorse. I would've taken a stab at lending a helping hand, but I didn't feel like it. Sometimes, people should have to learn from their mistakes with the beating of a lifetime.

I was shocked on the spine as I was instructed to start stepping forward into the armored vehicle, or he would crank up the voltage. There was no use in putting up more of a hassle. It would've only branched off into an additional riot, where only us, along with a couple other innocent humans, would suffer. I strutted toward the vehicle so that at least going in I would have the presence of someone who had some dignity left. Nazm entered it willingly, while Grandpa was thrown in voluntarily. We became so well behaved that, in prison, they could've addressed us as The Helty Bunch. We plopped down on the steel benches that were united with the side of the truck. They certainly didn't feel pressured about our comfort much, being that I could sit on jagged glass again and it would cushion me better. There were also steel hoops melded to the bench that they slipped our chains through to maintain us there. When they concluded with all of the security checks, they retired from the vehicle, except for two of them, who sat across from us, possessing their guns in a way to taunt us with the risk of witnessing death right before our eyes. Little did they know that I had death before my eyes for quite awhile. The officers shut the back doors when I heard them thrust the ample metal bar across them to ensure that we couldn't escape.

I was convinced that the chains wouldn't hold us against the wall. Most likely, we wouldn't attempt to drop out of the back of a moving automobile, but, then again, there was Nazm. It must've been that obsessive-compulsive disorder that made them upgrade the security so much. Another long period of waiting happened. The habitual topics ran through my head, such as people slipping on spilled baby oil and trying to remember three of the however many presidents we've had.

My thoughts were interrupted by the immense amount of heat that massaged my skin. It must've been due to too many oxygen inhalers in a confined place. It was too bad that corpses didn't exhale frigid air or else they could've been my own personal fans, but, instead, I had to burn up while the guards had their own hand-held fans. I made a request for them to point one of the fans at me for a second so that I wouldn't pass out. One guard gradually moved it in my direction, only to stomp the entrails out of my faith in him by turning it away. My blood boiled, like a lake after a warhead has been dropped.

I felt the tremble from Nazm as he snapped his arms out of the handcuffs. Nazm attempted a lunge, outstretching his arms as far as he could to reach for the guards, only to land on his face with his arms stretched out above him. Both of the guards darted to opposite directions, only to both be apprehended by the undead. Nazm grappled the guard closest to himself by the arm, but, while pulling him back towards his grubby body, the guard's arm was dislocated from the socket. Not only out of the socket, but not inside of the body either. The intact arm was unhinged from the soon to be carcass. He shrieked in terror, probably not even realizing that if the vehicle had been watertight, we would've been drowning in his blood. We ran over a bump in the road, so the guard slumped against the wall, slowly fading into a comatose state before introducing himself to the pits of Hades. I just assume that everyone's going to hell if they weren't preaching to me about our Lord and Savior, Jehovah. I wish that I could skin those religious door-to-door salesmen alive.

The second armed guard was bit on the hand, while rushing past Grandpa. That's when Grandpa latched on, biting harder every time that the guard attempted to break free. It originated with a teeny bit of blood coming from his teeth; then, it escalated to not being able to spot Grandpa's teeth through all of the red blood cells. Gramps worked his way up the arm, monotonously inflicting enough damage to cause a grown man to faint. That was exactly what presented itself once Gramps began chomping on the bicep. The guard's gnawed upon arm was blackish on the inside of the mutilation, because Grandpa's mouth was still bleeding from the nightstick beating before. There was a steady stream running down the guard's arm, which altered directions for every chunk of meat that was protruding from his skin. Gramps struggled to hold the guard up with his teeth, while he passed out. I saw that his jaw was quivering from all of the strain, but, somehow, he made it up to the guard's neck, which ripped almost instantly after Gramps sunk his teeth in.

While the body was on the downfall, Grandpa picked up the rebound. His teeth lodged into the guard's skull, which held for a second before the uppermost section of his cranium tore open, granting us permission to witness his inner thoughts that seemed to be about blood. The guard's remains descended down to the ground. When it received the impact, his brains popped out of his head, while shards of his skull shot out. Gramps and Nazm were both gobbling upon the parts that they had inherited from the bodies of the middle-aged men.

I instructed them to sit back and behave so that when they opened the door, I could have Nazm calmly put his hands in the air to not petrify the cops. Well, at least, only to petrify them at a respectable magnitude. The vehicle came to a halt when we paid attention to the officers getting out of the front seat, which were followed by the sounds of many more pairs of boots approaching from behind. Nazm positioned his hands in the air, signifying that he did listen once in a great while. The metal bar slid on the door before it became ajar. Outside, there were rows upon rows of the public that all had disgusted looks on their faces.

The disgusted faces soon lost all pigment as the crowd turned the airport into a heavefest. There was so much stomach acid coming up that it seemed to purify the road, protecting it like the lining on the interior of a stomach. When some of them were finished (perchance caused by a small meal), they wiped the leftover filth from their lips with their sleeves. They continued to march through the film of barf to us, splashing away with every step. I understood that it was going to suck, because, when I got out of that vehicle, I was going to be leaving my footprints in puke with my worn out shoes that had holes in the heels.

When the officers barged in through the back door, one of them slipped on the armless guy's blood. He belly flopped on top of the corpse, bonking his face on the stub, where the arm used to be. He was knocked out cold, but the other people didn't show any dismay over that as Nazm was getting handcuffed again. They pulled a lever somewhere that I couldn't sight, which liberated the clamps from our legs.

We were escorted out of the back into the film that looked comparable to the moss that covered expired sharp cheddar cheese. Dogs on chains surrounded us with an enormous amount of guns aimed at our heads just waiting for the signal so that they could pull the triggers. One of the dogs drew near, sniffing at my groin region. I attempted to veer away from it, because I had a feeling that it wasn't trained to be a criminal's best friend.

Instead of wounding me with its man hungry teeth, it angled itself onto two legs, where it proceeded to rub up on my ankle doing its thing. I would've much rather preferred the former. Laughter was something that the world had too much of. I needed to put a stop to all of the senseless laughter. First, however, I had to hold-up for the dog to wrap it up, since I couldn't shake him loose. I was forced to watch this atrocity go on, since there wasn't anything engrossing going on anywhere else. The dog spread out on the ground and cuddled with my leg after it was done, but the officer removed him from the romantic moment to have us forge ahead until we got to the runways.

It was a minuscule airport with only five runways. Two of them were being taken up by undersized planes that were being stored there. The only runway that had an aircraft on it had this humongoid one, which was constructed sturdier than the Leaning Tower of Pizza – about the same size too. That may've been the one we were going to ride in, but I wasn't confident of it. We were heading along that path, so the optimum guess was most likely yes. The chains clinked against the tar as we shuffled along on a trip, walking much farther than we should've had to when we could've gotten a lift right next to the plane.

I was hit with a double whammy. The whammy was a rock, so I presume that it was a single whammy. The citizens of whatever town we were located at were rioting and pegging us with anything that they could scrounge up; sucks that it wasn't soft stuff like clothing or pillows. I could go for a nap at that place and time. The guards restrained the citizens until we reached the plane that mechanically lowered the steps for us. I could see the pilot in the window teaching a little girl how to start it. It was a fancy plane until we got to the center of it where it had the complexion of a trashy movie theater with people enslaved in their chairs with their hands cuffed in front of them.

We were unshackled at the legs to be chaperoned to different spots miles away from each other. There were at least a hundred full seats in that thing, so they were rather far away. I was seated in the back row amongst some of the most ruthless killers that were out there. That was before they screwed up by leaving a bag of popcorn in the microwave at a victim's house. They then removed it, while it was on fire, engulfing the apartment building with flames. I suppose that they attempted to stomp it out with their shoes, causing so much racket that the police appeared. It was only my hypothesis on how someone got arrested, but it was a legitimate incident. The only reason that I realized that I was in the back with the worst was because all of the troublemakers always relaxed in back, while all of the sissies sat in the front. Also because a majority of the guards were towards the rear, while hardly any of them were keeping a lookout in the front.

I installed myself in between a large muscular convict with a bald head and a skinny prisoner with a lengthy beard and long scraggly hair. They imprisoned me with chains along with switching my handcuffs from behind me to in front of me. It still wasn't under the most serene circumstances, but, sometimes, you have to brush yourself off and get back on that horse. Wait. Never mind, that's the wrong quote. What I meant was that sometimes you have to take what life gives you. In this case, it was a plane loaded with psychopaths. I tried to act like it was identical to school, so I plunked my head down, cupping my hands together in my lap, wasting time until the trip was over.

The engine geared up, while the propellers started on the plane. A voice came over the intercom, directing the guards to inspect every prisoner to become confident that they were secured in their seats. All of the guards came around, tugging on the seat belts, checking to see if the chains were fastened correctly. After they provided the all clear gesture to the man in front, we began to depart at the speed of light, which was like a jar of mayonnaise rolling down a hill.

I kept modifying the angle of my cranium in hopes of a view to the outside, but all of the other heads were in the way. It was my first plane ride, and all I could see was the noggins of convicts that weren't informed on how to wash their hair. I got shouted at for my head bobbing around by a guy on the far left side, attempting to look out through the window on the right side, modern day Einstein. I reclined back into my seat, figuring that maybe I could catch some zzzs if I closed my eyes. I believed that I could dream hearty thoughts, dealing with marshmallow-filled forest animals, not chocolate covered ones though. Running around, hopping marshmallow-filled forest animals.

I must've fallen asleep, considering that I was transferred into a forest with the most beautiful wildlife I had ever beheld. A cute little bunny hopped in front of me and stared at me with its big eyes. I pet it on the top of its furry head, making its eyes close from the sheer sensuality of my touch. I prolonged the petting of it with my palm. I added another stroke to throw it off, which doubled the pleasure. I went for tripling the gratification by fracturing its neck with a twist and a pull, yanking its skull off of its spinal cord.

Marshmallow goo spouted out approximate to a water fountain, except for it was purified and over-flowing with marshmallow. I placed my lips in a position, where they touched the source so that I could suck the treat dry from its throat while squeezing its body to make sure that I got every last drop. I consumed the creaminess in record time. I was already induced by the sensation that I was becoming a fiend for the stuff. It tasted like there was some sort of addictive additive in it.

I comprehended that I was dreaming, so I was empowered to do whatever I wanted. So the first thing that I did was lavished myself with a shotgun that I could dominate, since I improvised the rules. It was comparable to one of those ancient video games, where different breeds of animals popped out from behind trees so that you had to blast their brains out. The only variance was that I shot anything that performed a motion, even the poor innocent bunnies. The small ones would explode, leaving marshmallow residue pasted to anything approximate to where they met their demise. But the big ones, such as bears, depending on where the bullet infiltrated them, would split in two. Gel like white fluid would spew out both sides, so I would run up and pounce on the pile it created. Slurping and rolling in it at the same time. Seeing that it had been ages since I had showered, plus I was extensively drenched in the blood of other people, it doubtlessly wasn't a smart idea. Can you get blood born viruses in your dreams? No...I don't think so.

I was attacked from my side by Bigfoot, who swatted me onto the grass from a backhand that sent me flying. I picked my weapon up off of the ground, aiming it at him, warning that I wasn't afraid to blast an endangered species. That strapping brown yeti wasn't listening to a word I said, so I pulled the trigger. I encountered a click, but no projectile traveled into Bigfoot. I cocked the gun, imagining that there were bullets in the gun before I fired it once again. That time bullets exited the barrel.

It nicked him, discharging only enough marshmallow goo to seal the cut. The marshmallow was heated from the bullet, causing it to become toasted over the laceration. That thing had to have had skin tougher than an orange. I emptied what bullets were left into his thick flesh, doing no more harm than I did before. Bigfoot approached me, wanting to knock my head off, but I arose from my nap in the nick of time.

I sat back in my seat with the big bald prisoner furnishing me with a dirty look. The chair in front of me was torn apart by what appeared to be teeth marks. He turned towards me asking if I was hungry much. If he meant what I thought he meant, then that meant something about how I chewed up the seat in front of me. I would've chosen to have been awake the first time that I tried munching on upholstery. He must've smacked me; so that would be what woke me up before Bigfoot annihilated me. I questioned what provided him with the right to make contact with me without my consent when I was in a peaceful sleep. He remarked that it was not like something that inconsequential would draw any attention in a plane filled with murderers and drug lords.

I attempted to squeal to one of the guards, but Mr. Employed by the State just recited the words shut up. I guess his opinion was final. Without even requesting the information from the convict, he rationalized why he was there. He described how he used to run drugs all over the country with bikes. Everybody who was employed by him rode a bicycle to transport the drugs. The justification of why the police had so many complications finding him was because all of his employees were school children that had no clue about what they were delivering. When one of them got too nosy or began snitching to people of what they were doing, he would slaughter them, leaving the mangled bodies on their parent's doorstep.

He didn't give the impression of being a nice guy, but I had always heard not to be quick to judge. I asked him how he got caught to check if it was because of the whole burnt popcorn thing, but, to my amazement, it wasn't. A police officer questioned him, seeing if he knew anything about the mutilations or the drugs, and he broke down and confessed everything the first time that they asked, due to a guilty conscience. Maybe he learned from the errors of his ways so that, the next time, he wouldn't be so ethical.

I must've been mistaken about how he was a bad guy when he had such a vast conscience that egged him on to do good deeds. Then he went on about how he would fork over candy to a baby without hurting it if he could maim just one more child. Jesus certainly wouldn't approve of him, even if he was displaying a cross around his neck. I mentioned to him that he should flip it upside down to show everyone the real him: a Satanist.

He hit me in the face with his cuffs, repeatedly beating me with them until a couple of guards were able to get over to us. They held onto him, stable enough to ensure that he couldn't break free when they unhooked him from the seat. They stood him up only to knock him down again. They hauled his motionless body over to a door that they hurled him into before locking it up. It must've been something to the equivalent of how they had "the hole" in prison, except this one was thousands of feet above the clouds. It could've been labeled "the broken elevator in the sky".

I turned to the raggedy convict beside me, disclosing to him how big of a chump I considered the other guy to be. His facial expression remained the same. Great, I got stuck alongside The Lord of Lameness, I thought. I waved my hands in front of his face, bringing them closer, like I was going to bash him in the face with my handcuffs a couple of times to determine if that would have any affect on him. I tried it, and some blood trickled down from the corner of his mouth to his jaw where drops of blood left him for the floor.

That time I got a reaction out of him. When the blood started dripping, his tongue slowly retreated from his mouth, sliding around, striving to get at all of the plasma droplets. His expression reeked of delight, while mine was burdened by disgust with a hint of confusion. The explanation for my confusion was how could the taste of blood get him in a sexy mood? Possibly, if it was a raw hamburger, but even that would make me full, which wasn't an arousing feeling most of the time.

He twisted his head, staring in my direction with one eye. The other one must've been lazy or impaired somehow. I hit him in his lazy eye with the handcuffs on the inside of my wrist. Loads more of hemoglobin materialized from this area of the head and ran down onto his shirt in less than a second. His smile only enlarged, and he never lost his concentration on me, while he was lapping up as much blood as he could while catching the remaining balance in his hands, sipping it out of them as if it was a bowl.

I called the guard over, pleading for release from the company of that sick bastard. The guard strolled over, gawking at the blood that was gushing from all over the sadistic bastards face, challenging my views on what the hell was going on. I spelled it out to him about how he must've had an itch on his face when he got over excited since he all of a sudden placed the cuffs against his skin, where he began to scratch with them.

The guard declared that I had to come with him as he started to unchain my legs from the seat. I asked him why he was taking me away instead of the sicko. His excuse was that it was because the marks on his face were clearly from a bludgeoning. I agreed 100% on that one. I could still pinpoint the indents from the handcuffs in his tissue without an indication of scratches. I played it cooperatively, allowing him to lead me to wherever he wanted me to go. He accompanied me back to where that room was located that they tossed Baldy into. I was told to have fun with my new cellmate. He shoved me inside, latching the door behind me. The room was only the size of a double stalled public lavatory.

The door was too solid to break down, so I assumed that I had to live with the fact that I was going to be murdered before I hit puberty. That was unless I stumbled upon puberty within the next five minutes. Baldy was still knocked out in the centermost portion of the room, which meant that the afterlife was at least a little farther away. I began to ponder…what if I neutralized him while he was unconscious? I would have to suffocate him with my bare hands, which could take quite a while. Also, I risked the possibility of Baldy waking up in the middle of his execution, which would surely make me experience a slower death in turn for it. On the other hand, if I didn't even make an effort, the last moments before my passing would be spent awaiting it, not having fun pulverizing somebody with my bare hands, which swayed my decision. I was going to tenderize his face with my knuckles. It was going to be similar to swindling candy from a baby that's parents left it alone in a stroller, neglected.

I intertwined both of my hands together so that they were in the shape of a wrecking ball of types. I stationed myself at the perfect distance to where my arms could be fully extended and my fists would sock him right in the cranium. I swung my fists, putting all of my strength into it, which spun me in a circle being that I didn't calculate the range precisely. I set myself up for the next swing, ripping it. It was a direct hit to the back of the skull. It bruised my hands more than it harmed his head, but he should've been dead from that one blow to the dome.

Unfortunately, Baldy wasn't inanimate, considering that after he was struck, I heard a noise escape his mouth that sounded like an "ouch". He became motivated, pushing himself up to his feet. In that moment, I developed a plan that sucked but was worth a try. I was going to take a crack at it, staying behind him the entire time until the plane landed, being optimistic that he wouldn't detect me inside of the room with him. Once Baldy rose to his feet, I was standing behind him. He spun to the left, so I shuffled behind him to the sound of his footsteps so that he wouldn't become aware of me.

I pulled a misstep once when Baldy moved again, so he caught a glimpse of me in the corner of his eye. He flipped out, reaching for me, but I backed away just in time. I ran for the door. I didn't realize how close it was to me, so I ran into it, which laid me down on the floor. I sprung up, banging on the door, yelling for the guards to let me out, because Baldy was going to strangle me. It conceivably didn't help any when I called him Baldy out loud. Nobody answered my calls of emotional distress as I parked my back against the door, pausing for my violent demise. He was advancing closer and closer with every deep breath that I took. It wasn't abnormal that my breaths were deep, though; a lot of fatty foods being consumed can do that to a person. For the first time in my life, I was sick of it all, meaning that I wasn't going to even put up a fight. I contemplated that maybe I deserved death, at that point, to end my legacy. No one heeded my distress, so it must've been meant to be. The sound of my fast food diet was interrupted by gunfire. There were multiple guns going off outside of the door.

Baldy and I quickly forgot our differences and rested our ears up against the door to see if we could decipher what all of the excitement was about. Just like how curiosity killed the cat, it also killed muscle bound bald men. We were facing each other with our cheeks pressed up against the door when I watched the interior of Baldy's cranium escape through a hole in the side of it. In a split second, blood and particles of gray matter jetted out of Baldy's ear, while a look of emptiness masked his face. He slumped down to the floor, leaving a streak of thick red juice along the door, all the way down it.

I noted that there was a hollow space in the door where his melon was rested before. I wasn't convinced that it wasn't caused by his brain wanting to escape at all. It was a stray bullet that traveled through the door, passing through his thick skull. Once my mind processed what had happened, it transmitted a signal to my awareness to step away from the entryway. It resembled a favorable concept, so I followed what my mind reported, for once, instead of pursuing my gut instinct as usual. The latter was to initiate the consumption of Baldy's body, while everything was still pouring out, because it was fresh. The predicament was that the cold meat was propped up against the door, so I wasn't that reassured by that idea.

I drifted beside the doorway as I curled up into a ball, practicing the tornado drill. I heard more bullets pinging against the door, so it was satisfactory that I got away from it when I did. Barrages of them created impact on the door, but then it all letup, except for the faint sounds of gunfire on the other side of the aircraft. I prayed that a bullet didn't penetrate a window or else

I would be sucked out of the plane through the hole. Somebody was striving to break down the indestructible door, because I listened to the rampaging beast on the reverse side who was using an immense amount of exertion to try to get in.

The door took a miraculous dive as it slammed against the floor, revealing that Nazm was the one causing the entire racket. I spotted that the guard was lying dead outside of the door with numerous bullet wounds. His keys were disposed of plainly in sight next to his soul-less frame. Common sense was something Nazm had lacked since the day that I met him. I told him that the next time that he wanted to shoot down or blow up a door that I was behind to let me know first so that I could get out of the way. He provided me with the double thumbs up of understanding.

When I rounded the doorframe, I made it back into the section with all of the chairs, where I discovered that divine intervention had taken place. I didn't have a complete understanding of that term, but I presumed that it was some form of execution in vein of the electric chair. Most of the prisoners were stiff in their seats from gunshot wounds, while the others were struggling to get free. All of the guards were rubbed out, and there were no other traces of life besides the prisoners.

Then Grandpa came lumbering out of the hallway that led into the cockpit, clutching a backpack in his hand. I announced that there was no time for us to go back-to-school shopping when it was only spring. He always made me go extra early, generally around December, so I already had all of my school supplies. He explained to me that the thing he secured in his grasp may have appeared to have been a backpack, but it was really a parachute. I didn't see why they would disguise a parachute, but, then again, some people disguise art with boobies.

If he had a parachute in his hand, that could only mean one thing. That he rigged it so when an imbecile yanked the string, instead of being floated down to safety, they would be bombarded with potato chips after they splattered against the landscape below. I got slapped and notified that it was a dynamic parachute. We needed to use it, thanks to Grandpa's assassination of the pilots.

The first thing that we needed to do was resolve who was going to wear the parachute, while the others rode on his back. I thought it should've been me, considering that I had more width to my torso, but, after being voted against in favor of Nazm, I lost. I suppose that it made more sense, since he was taller, but I wanted a reason to complain. I would've looked for an extra parachute, but that required effort.

I swiveled my peripheral vision, searching for an exit sign. There was one in the center of the plane that fastened to the wall, but it required a key. I scuttled over to the security guard that had dropped his keys, fumbling with them as I struggled to find the proper one. I tried every one that the key ring had to offer, but none of them were working.

We were doomed to go down with the airplane and a dozen prisoners that were left alive and crying for help. Sparks shot up from the lock as I shielded my eyes, falling to the floor for refuge. When they came to a halt, I uncovered my eyes to see Nazm throwing a gun to the floor. I got pissed! I asked him if he had ever heard of something called "ricochet". Of course he hadn't, so I spelled it all out for him while kicking him in the ass. He had set the record for the most times almost killing me in a day without even trying. Gramps only pulled that one off a max of once a day.

The door was now unhinged, leaving it gaping a crack. One more thrust was all that it would've taken to bust it down. I secured us together first, using heavy-duty duct tape that I had found on one of the guards. I also heisted some sporks that were spilled on the floor from one of the guard's meals, just in case I got famished somewhere where all they had were forks. Always be prepared is what my doctor constantly told me.

We marched together to the door, really close to each other, bracing ourselves to dive out of that hatch with our lives depending on the durability of duct tape. The plane was going down at a steeper angle every second that we stood there getting ready to jump. I took the ballsy move by driving us all forward through the doorway. Nazm didn't move, though, because I couldn't force his massive body weight off of his sturdy stance. The putrid flesh that he consumed must've still retained itself within his muscular physique. He turned back to me presumably curious as to why I shoved Grandpa into him. I instructed him to nudge the door open and take a nosedive.

Before we got the door open, I discovered a fault in our plan. If Nazm harnessed the parachute when we all rode on his back how would the parachute eject out of the backpack? Nazm pushed open the door and prepared to jump out, but, luckily, he heard me shrieking his name and peeked back. I directed him to pitch back the parachute; then he could jump out. We were fortunate that he didn't leap out, because he didn't even strap the thing on himself. He was only holding it. He heaved it back to me, but, at the moment that I caught it, was the moment that I got removed from the aircraft.

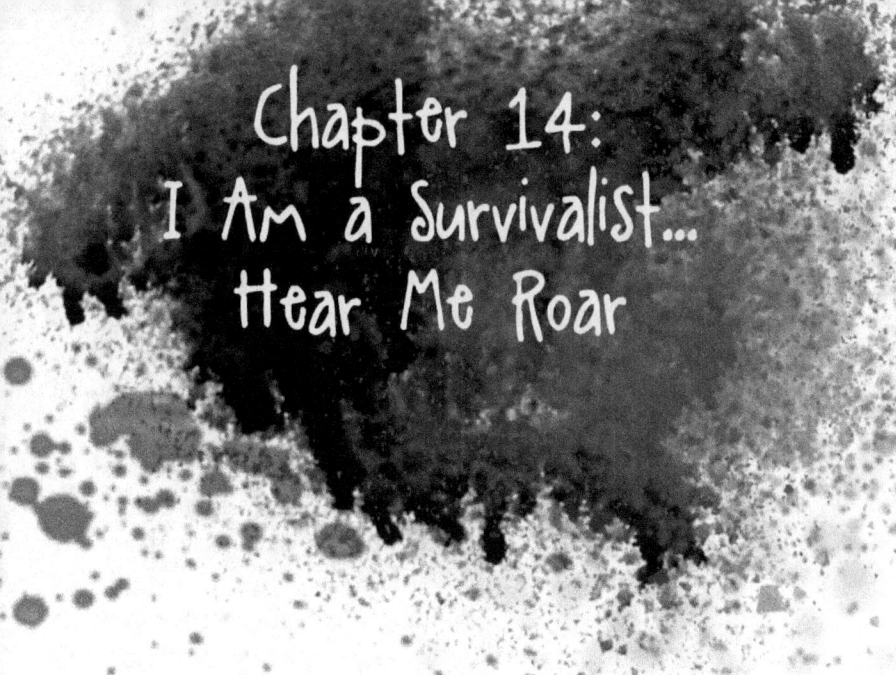

Chapter 14:
I Am a Survivalist...
Hear Me Roar

We began our venture downwards to the green speck below. The wind hit me in the face, almost knocking me out. It wasn't the velocity of the wind, but the odor of Gramps and Nazm being thrust into my nostrils. It was a stink that could only be summed up in a ten-page report that incorporated the word vile over one hundred times. I panicked, rushing to put on the parachute, but I got it around my arms fairly speedily. Around the same time that I installed the parachute and was about to commence tugging the cord, I perceived the loudest crunching of metal noise that I had ever heard.

I glanced over to witness the last half of our plane bringing about impact on the side of a mountain. Bodies were plummeting as sections of the plane broke off, only to emerge as balls of fire. When I observed flaming bodies plunging to the ground, I thought of only one thing: supper. It was cooked meat and a whole lot of it. I had to follow my gut instinct that time, since I followed my mind that last time. It was only fair. If we hadn't jumped out of the airplane at the time that we did, we would've been supper ourselves for a hungry pack of wolves.

I realized that if the plane ran into a high part of a mountain, then that meant that we were considerably elevated. I looked down, only to view a large body of water that I wasn't too fond of, due to how much moisture my skin takes in. It was just the look and feel of the wrinkly fingers in the shower that made me never want to go swimming.

I told Gramps and Nazm to assist me in steering the parachute in the direction of the plane wreckage for the free munchies. I didn't want them to presume that I was scared of the water, because I wasn't. I've always had too much self-confidence for that. We all shifted all of our weight in that direction when we began descending more quickly than we had been before. At the rate of speed that we were going down, there was no way that we were going to clear the water. The wind got harder against my face, while the parachute almost ceased to exist. I sealed my eyes, praying for land. I felt a splash of water stroke me before I was completely emerged in it. I unveiled my eyeball to make sure that there were no sharks coming to make me lunch. The floating molecules in the water got into my eye, making it difficult for me to see. I was holding my breath as we sunk closer to the bottom of the cesspool of a bathtub. I was still taped to Gramps and Nazm, and we sunk, resembling a shipwreck.

I didn't think that they remembered that I was the only one that had the necessity of breathing, being that they were discussing how entertaining the trip was. I pounded on Grandpa's spine until he took notice that I was on the verge of passing out from a lack of oxygen. They started pulling on the tape with me, but it wouldn't snap, due to the heavy dutyness of it. Then we attempted to all swim to the surface together, but, since we were uncoordinated synchronically, that plan also deteriorated. I became weak and lightheaded, eventually warping into eternal bliss.

Or it would've been eternal bliss had I not woken up on jagged rocks with Nazm on top of me with a smirk on his stupid face. The indoors of my mouth tasted like rotted fish chunks; it seemed like a fishy situation. I was back in my own personal living hell. It was consistently a great feeling to not be able to escape that. It didn't take a brain surgeon to comprehend what had just happened. Needless to say, I wasn't too pleased. In fact, I would've rather dropped dead.

I sat up, shoving Nazm off to the side, so that I could regain my breath. He sat back up with his legs straight in front of him, clapping like a little boy in thanks to me returning to the hellhole that I call Earth. My lungs felt like they were going to deflate, reminiscent to a cheap birthday balloon that's pumped with oxygen. I had to roll over onto my belly to push myself up, because, if I tried lying on my back, it was like performing a sit-up, which is identical to attempting the impossible. I could barely do it the push-up way either, but I made it to a standing position, eventually.

I rubbed my eye to get everything back into focus again. It worked, but only after a couple seconds of believing that I should've been wearing a pair of trifocals. When Nazm got back up, I pushed him over, just for the fun of it. I overheard a crack from one of his bones when he struck the rocks, but he got back up without even paying any mind to the sound. Near fatal injuries had never seemed to affect him anyway, only if they were emotionally related. I identified the plane wreckage in the distance. It was up the mountain a ways, but we had no choice. I was starving, and there was no way that I was going to struggle to survive off of berries and leaves when there was warm meat a short climb away.

I didn't grasp what I was in for when I said short climb, though. It seemed lengthier than running the mile at school, but I walked those every time. It still felt longer than thirty minutes to me. Halfway there was when my hands became raw and bloody on the surface of my tattered gloves, considering that they were practically disintegrated by then. I slipped them off before unraveling the bandages, because I was sick of getting the loose strings stuck in between the rocks and bushes. My palms had clear liquid coming out of them with no hint of scabbing. They were still as tender as the day my skin slid off because of the lack of oxygen. It tingled every time that I latched onto a rock to haul myself up, but it tingled a lot worse when I actually pulled myself up. I had to bare the unorthodox sensation, though; because, if I didn't, then I would never sprout hair on my chest, since I wouldn't be a man. At least, that was what Grandpa explained to me after all of the whining I did within a short elapsed amount of time. Gramps and Nazm didn't have any issue climbing that pile of prehistoric crap. They also apparently had no problem with abandoning me to fend for myself, seeing that they were not even visible to my naked eye anymore.

Some people declare that family is the most treasured thing in the world. I think that it's about as valuable as an eight pack of hot dogs: less than two bucks. The fact that I had been ditched only made me work harder to get to the wreckage sooner. I didn't want to get stuck disposing of the stiffs that they didn't want. I would be picking the fat off of the meat all night long. I don't mind fat, but the charred type wasn't too tasty. I visualized that with every blood-stained rock I created on my way to the top. I forged ahead at a steady pace, just so I wouldn't risk losing weight in the process. You never know. If I was starving to death, my body might've needed to digest the fat for me to stay animated.

The stones became steeper, while the smoke became thicker, as I made it to the final stretch of my adventurous climb. When I reached the final rock in my climb, my hand slipped from the puss that was accumulating on my palms. I reacquired grip with my other hand before that one slipped too. White liquid spilled out from underneath my hand as I held on tighter, while I brought my other hand up to get a firm grip on that rock again. That would've sucked had I fallen. What a bitch it would've been climbing that mountainous mountain all over again. I pulled with all of my might, plopping over onto the surface above, like a whale on land squirming around, striving to get back to its polluted habitat. My figure was dowsed in perspiration with no hope of drying anytime soon, since it was sprinkling out. From the clouds, it looked like there was going to be a storm materializing, but, then again, I was ordinarily as accurate as a weatherman.

I rested there, taking in the cool, soothing drops of rain, until I sensed that I had enough will power and charisma to go on. I also had to move because a puddle was forming around where my head was, as the rain became increasingly heavier. When I raised my head up, I saw Gramps and Nazm standing there, not feasting upon the leftovers of mankind; but, instead, they were conversing in front of the wreckage without any intent of eating. Only a portion of the airplane was on the level platform that we were staged on, which was the caliber of a football field. The remainder was either extensively mangled in the rocks or lost in the body of water below.

I walked up to them, questioning why they weren't stealing my food supply. For some unknown reason, they were afraid of the flames that the plane was engulfed in. I touched the metal on the plane, which was damn hot, but I played it off like it wasn't that bad. That was what got me stuck in the position of the guy who had to fetch the bodies to bring them outside. Sometime, I really should've made an attempt at learning how to keep my mouth shut so that I would quit getting stuck in those sorts of situations.

I needed a damp cloth so that I didn't suffocate on the smoke. It wasn't too much of a challenge to find that, since everything was saturated from the rainfall. I took a couple of deep breaths to equip myself for more permanent scars. I stationed the cloth over my mouth as I stepped inside of the plane. It was upside down, so the surface I trampled on was angled kind of goofy.

When I got into the main aisle, I beheld that some of the loved ones were suspended from their seats on the ceiling. Their arms dangled above them, some of them still steaming from them scorching in flames. The bottom of the plane was gashed open above me in some places, which aided in extinguishing most of the inferno in the main cabin. The smoke was essentially cleared out, so I put my shirt back on. My nipples were getting hard, so I needed to slightly warm them for self gratification. It bothered me when they got sensitive.

The corpses that were on the floor weren't burnt that bad, but most were deformed beyond the service of a plastic surgeon. I swore that I heard a cry for help from somewhere near me. I surveyed the area for a sign of life anywhere just so I knew that I wasn't losing my marbles. An arm was sticking out from underneath a cadaver, while one of the fingers was going into a spasm. When I removed the corpse from off of the arm, I found that there was an uncut body beneath it, which was a relief.

It was a young girl that appeared to be virtually untouched. I stated that I was going to get her out of there safely. I elevated her up, where I cradled her in my arms as I imported her outside of the wreckage. I handed her over to Grandpa, ordering him to watch her to make sure that she didn't perish. I directed Nazm to come inside with me to assist me in gathering bodies for the night's barbeque. With an expression of the jitters, he begged me not to make him do it. I mentioned that he had no choice as I prodded him from behind every step of the way. Once internal, I had him round up the dead, only to hurl them outside, while I collected quilts, along with anything else that could keep us heated through the blackness.

I had a heap of clothes handy that I planted in a dry place within the plane before Nazm even had a pile of rotting flesh outside. Talk about no motivation for the substantial tasks, but, once it came to mouth to mouth, he was all over it. I helped him drag out the rest of the stiffs by coaching him on where to place them. Sometimes, I wonder where the universe would be without me. When the mound was up to my chin, I ruled that it should be enough food for the remainder of the dark hours.

After I stopped paying attention to what I was doing, my worry went to the small girl that I had found on the aircraft. She was lying down on the dirt, while Grandpa was cupping his hands catching the raindrops inside of them. Once he filled them, he would pour the water into her mouth, for she could be terribly dehydrated. If dehydration didn't exterminate her, the water sure would from the tainted blood that relaxed in Grandpa's veins that occasionally got outside of the skin. She happened to gain some strength when her arms showed an effort to leave the ground.

It was too boring watching the process of reviving a person to hold my attention. Instead of caring for the girl, I decided to make myself useful by sorting the corpses out for who got what. The crucial thing to me was that my main group stayed in good health (or at least fully responsive). A stranger didn't mean much to me no matter the age or gender. I shouldn't even have spoken to her. I wasn't supposed to talk to strangers.

Nazm made an effort at quarreling with me about how his collection was smaller than mine, but I came back at him, conceiving the point that he had larger bodies then I did. Since I had a bunch of smaller corpses, it meant that I got less meat, because all of the bones were in such a limited space. He nodded his head, registering that I was right, even though I was lying to him. I traded him all of the bodies congested with lard, being that he probably wouldn't even notice.

By the time that we had come to closure, Grandpa sat down with us, holding the girl, who was now intelligent enough to vocalize more than one word. For some reason, she seemed slightly more interested in me than anyone else. She nagged to come over so that she could sit by me. It might've been because I was the only other vital being there, or else it was my stunning good looks. Either/or, it made me better than everybody else. She approached me, where she squatted on the king-sized rock that I was settled on. I snatched one of the moderately fried corpses by the leg, dragging it over to me.

The girl began to bawl hysterically as if she had never seen a dead body before. I mentioned that she should calm down before I got the urge to throw something off of the mountain. She asked me what I was going to do with her daddy. Apparently, she was hallucinating, believing that the cadaver was her dad. I planned to demonstrate to her how to lighten up in a stressful situation. I withdrew the spork from out of my pocket that I stuffed in there before we took our suicide dive out of the airplane. I asked her if she was hungry, since she appeared to be becoming diseased. She was vibrating with a glaze that polished her eyeballs, reflecting my face back to me, equivalent to a mirror.

I preached that she needed to seek nourishment, but the exclusive thing on the menu up in the mountains was dead daddy. At the same time that I said the dead daddy piece, I lifted the spork high into the atmosphere before driving it into the bowels of the stinking flesh. Blood spurted out into her eyes as the ridges went through the skin, but even more devastating than that, my beloved spork fractured itself. I never could've anticipated that it would've been practical, but it transpired. I weep for the future when they mold sporks cheaper than that. Salty water dropped from my eye in a moment of sadness before it was hindered by the screeches of a child directly in my eardrum.

I was being beaten to death by hands the diameter of drink coasters. I covered the side of my ribcage, attempting to block whatever I could that was being thrown by a master of the catfight. My eyelids cringed as I held-up for the sheer torture to end. It didn't last long, though, thanks to the hands of an elderly man. She was lucky that I never got to fight back, or, whoosh, she would've been chucked off of the mountain. Grandpa carried her back over to his post, where he held her back, while cradling her like she was some big, dumb baby.

I was starting to accept that there was a possibility that the body could've been her father's. It was a stretch, but I wasn't going to cross it off of my list. I paid no mind to my minor problems at that instant. The outlet I spawned with my spork opened up wider as I pulled it apart, ripping the skin to get to the superior meat. The intestines had the presence of ripeness in perfect shape for a new-found, raw meat lover such as myself. I nibbled on it leisurely to relish in every bite. I set out at one end of the intestine, chomping my way down the remnant of it. The great part about the intestine is that it has several clashing flavors to it from various foods digesting in different sections inside of it. My taste buds were submerged with flavors that couldn't be formulated by any class of chef. I avoided the stomach, because I didn't want the acid within it to rot my teeth.

Meanwhile, Nazm was pigging out like a slob, tearing the bodies, limb from limb, gobbling them up like they were turkey legs. He was at the equivalent of an infant that could only get a portion of his edibles in his mouth, while the other share sailed about in the breeze. While we stuffed ourselves, Grandpa starved to take care of the frightened young girl. He treated her as if she was the grandchild he eternally wanted, making me sound identical to a sack of moldy potatoes.

When I was done munching, I chose to go to the interior of the plane, where it was dry, to wrap up in some of those cloths that I had gathered. It was now raining more solid with the occasional thunder and lightning close together, which meant that the storm was nearby. I blanketed myself thoroughly so that my skin wouldn't be touching any metal. I was taught in school that if I was in contact with any metal and lightning struck, I would be one roasted goose. Or maybe I'd be the cooked meat in manufacturer prepared chow mein, since I was practically in a tin can.

The rest of them stayed outside for a while longer, plotting my demise. When they arrived in my shelter, I figured that I should make a move first. That move was to off the girl before she had an opportunity to do me in. She never took her eyes off of me, though, so it was a tad bit harder to get behind her so that I could hook her by the jaw to wrench her skull sideways and snap her neck. I didn't plan this out at all. I was fighting sleep to stay alive, but, after not catching my zzzs for so long, I just couldn't take it anymore. I ended up crashing, like the lazy-ass I was. The last thing that I recollected before my eyes sealed was the little girl (which I named The Little Wussy) gazing at me.

My thoughts and fears all became scrambled up in the inner recesses of my cranium when the lights went out. In my slumber, I acquired an unnerving dream that a platypus dined upon my brains, because he was hungry and didn't need a better reason. It was a giant platypus that devoured halved-bodied humans, one chomp at a time. After the feast, he would lick the guts off of the grass with his long clammy tongue. The next day, Platy went to the hospital, only to pass away from a brain tumor. The only doctor qualified for the job to do the surgery was a frog that pronounced that he was too far gone to operate. I didn't understand how to analyze dreams, so, if there was a message behind the whole thing, I didn't get it.

I awakened well rested in perfect condition, ready for battle against little girls that rode pogo sticks. When I gained consciousness, I noticed that everyone had shifted from where they once were into the internals of the clothes, curled up, as immediately as they could get to me. I loathed it when people got inside of my personal space bubble. I monotonously rolled everyone off of me doing my best not to wake them. I got outside without startling any of them, so I relaxed my tushie on a rock in front of the corpses to enjoy some breakfast.

The rain had come to a stop while the sun kept it heated enough to where I didn't need a blanky. I started gorging myself in more intestines, since they reminded me of sausage links. I judged that it was only appropriate that I exhibit some respect for breakfast. The Little Wussy drew near from out of the plane, so I armed myself with a sample of a ribcage bone that was stripped of meat. Her face looked so sweet and innocent, but I realized what lay behind those eyes, pure unadulterated evil. She approached me, so, when she got within swinging range, I swung. It must've been due to my nervousness from the menace, but the bone slipped out of my hands, soaring into the airplane, where it fell to the earth, composing an ouch noise.

Certain death, I welcomed it with open arms, and it hugged me back. It was like The Little Wussy was super glued to my leg. I wobbled it around while trying to pry her fingers apart, yet she clung to it like tough stains to a carpet. She activated her tear glands, claiming that she was sorry if she made me mad. "She just wanted to be my friend". I felt like butter, internal to my skin. She was the devil incarnate. I had to brace my powerfulness so that I didn't fall for her treachery.

I attended my sonic eardrums to the helicopters that were coming, which must've been searching for the wreckage. I didn't have the time to bother with The Little Wussy. I attempted to ward her off so that I could alert Gramps, but I had no such luck. I toddled back to the airplane with the girl fused to my thigh. I accomplished making it there to mention to Gramps and Nazm that we had to hurry to get out of that surrounding region. I instructed Grandpa to snag some clothes for when we got chilly at night. I lectured Nazm in order to get him to kidnap a cadaver for later when we felt omnivorous. I offered to The Little Wussy that if she released her grip from my leg that I would give her a piggyback ride. What young hooligan could refuse such a proposal? She hopped on my back, while we outset on our adventure into the vast wilderness.

Nazm settled a corpse on his back piggyback style, binding its arms together in front of him with one of his hands as he slapped his own ass with the other one, galloping along the way. Gramps was transporting a heap of clothes on his back with a batch also stuffed inside of his pants and shirt to get as many as possible. We headed back down the side of the mountain that we scaled, considering that it was either that way or the way that was down yonder, but I didn't anticipate that I had the stamina for that. I might've had the steam if I had a Captain Coke. It was this energy drink that Grandpa would've enabled me to have if I was a good boy. It made me dizzy. But Gramps remarked that it was because I was ladylike, so I couldn't manage all that caffeine at once.

It sure was a struggle getting down that mountain with a devil demon on my back. She was a max of fifty pounds, but, after awhile, it wore on my physique, leaving it feeling similar to grape jelly, not strawberry. I surrendered my firm footing as I took a dive, but I was able to rearrange the girl so that only I would get busted up from the fall. I wasn't certain why I did it, but I felt like a better person for it. And it felt splendid. I never even fathomed that taking the fall for someone, literally, could be such an amazing experience. I got the impression that I was a lame ass being and that I didn't think she really wanted to murder me at all.

I raised myself after crashing on my stomach with her still on my back. I wasn't even sweating the plunge. I pushed myself to restart the tumbling, because, if I didn't, we would be back on that aircraft to prison. I situated her in various positions to keep her safe from bonking her head on the rocks while we rolled around.

When we arrived at the bottom of the mountain, there was only a singular way to go, which was directly into those deep woods. We submerged ourselves in the leafy wilderness before the helicopters got proximate enough to spot us. Even though it was still bright out when we went into the woods, it was murky inside of them with the rays of the sun beaming through every once in a while. I supervised my step every time that I took one so that I wouldn't trip on any twigs or step in a snake hole. I hate snakes. They are so long and scaly. I was informed about this one guy that wasn't paying attention, so he stepped in a snake hole. The snake swallowed him whole, beginning with his one leg, disturbing. I wasn't about to tolerate anything resembling that occurrence.

The woods were completely silent besides the cracking of twigs beneath our feet, which never ceased to scare the living crap out of me. I obviously was not one with the wilderness.

Our excursion lasted all day, so, by the time we harmonized to letup for the day, the little girl had propped her head up on my shoulder and was sleeping. It was the cutest thing ever. I mean, I was glad that I could finally get that thing off of my back. I woke her up, letting her know that it was time to get down. I had Grandpa arrange a blanket over the sticks for her. I placed her on the blanket while situating another one over the top of her. She appeared to be in heaven, even though that would plausibly be one of the most emotionally scarring days of her life. She had us all comparable to putty in her hands. I ended up being a dummy by using all of the blankets on her when I had none. Gramps and Nazm didn't need any, seeing that they were practically cold blooded already. We needed to ignite a fire so that I didn't get metamorphosis cast on me to turn me into a banana popsicle by the morning.

We all checked our pockets for something to light the fire with, but, as expected, we came up with nothing. Then I recalled this thing that I mastered from the one time that I went to boy scouts. If you rub two sticks together rapidly, it will start a fire. I went around gathering twigs, while Nazm found the logs. When Nazm returned with the logs he had full branches cradled in his arms. I depended on him to break them down at a minimum of twenty times before we set it up. When he broke those down, I constructed it in tepee format that I taught myself along with the rest of the nation. I fixated all of the twigs underneath the logs, where my target area would be when I started the fire. I had two sticks of equal length that I kept out for the specific purpose of igniting. When I put the sticks together, I realized that I had no clue on how the operation was supposed to work. No wonder why I never went back to boy scouts; it sucked.

I decided that I would at least give it a try, so I had Grandpa clamp onto one of the sticks, while I spun the other one against it, wishing for the best. But the only thing getting close to setting on fire were my hands from spinning that stick in between them. I, in actuality, needed to quit using them since my scabs and blisters were reopening, soaking the stick in many forms of infectious liquid. I had to dig out another dry stick so that I could hand the royalties over to Grandpa, while I clamped the other stick this time. Apparently, Gramps thought that he was some sort of miracle worker, being that he had that fire blazing in less than an hour, thanks to the lighter he discovered in his back pocket. I guess checking your pockets never involved the rear ones.

We began to organize our food supply. In conclusion, I received the legs, since I regularly acquired the midsection. Gramps dug in with the shoulders that he overindulged himself with. He relaxed the head on the ground as he hollowed out everything in the center by slurping it down the throat. He finally had it to where he was rattling the entire thing over his slack-jawed skull, while struggling to catch the leftovers as they slopped all over him. I was delivered a double whammy when he gobbled up the organs that were smothered with dirt. Normally, he was a big baby about that. He must've been remark-ably famished. Since I had the option that time, I chose to roast my rations. I had begun to like it raw, but, sometimes, a change was needed. I clutched the leg by the foot, cooking the rest, because I would not consume feet that were that foul or any feet for that matter. I knew that it was close to done when the skin started to blister.

The scent of baked meat must've woken up the little girl. The look on her face stressed that she was starving. I gave in, offering her the leg that I was going to eat. She kindly accepted it with the politeness of one hundred retail cashiers, which was in actuality polite, once you added them all together. I felt guilty for distorting a young girl into a cannibal, but what else was I supposed to do? Either way, she would be munching on an animal, so why not a better tasting one? That was unless I wanted the girl to drop dead, but I didn't want her to so much anymore.

The little girl was severely cautious about dining upon it. She picked at the blistered skin, peeling it off, only to fling it on the dirty corroded ground. I hoisted it up reciting for her not to waste the skin; if she didn't want it, she could pass it down to me. I disposed of it without brushing off the dirt. It was not like dirt could poison me, unless it was contaminated with asbestos, but what were the odds of that? I didn't try to be a dick about it, but I ended up coming across that way as I always prevailed. It was perhaps, because, most of the time, I was trying to be one. She attempted to hand the leg back to me, but I wouldn't take it, confessing that it was my present to her.

The little girl provided me with a shy smile while drawing the leg back over to herself, cradling it up to her chest. Then she let her true colors show of how her hunger meant more to her then what the world calls sanity. She slashed into that meat with what fingernails she had left, lifting up whatever globs she could get out of it, inhaling them. It was adorable.

Lastly, I was able to snack feed the beast inside of me. If I didn't nourish my stomach, it would most likely commit suicide to make me croak. I tore into the other leg, like a man of an island, striving to get into a can of beans. I was through before Nazm could swallow the remainder of his corpse's midsection. I supported him with that, of course, like any real friend would. My belly punished me badly afterwards.

Either I scarfed down way too much, or the stiff had something gravely faulty with it. My assumption was the latter, considering that I hardly ever got stuffed, especially from that petty of a quantity of food. Whatever it was, I resolved to put myself in a slumber. Rest cures everything, or, at least, that's what the world wants us to presume is true. I swept as many of the sticks away from the dirt as I could to clear myself a spot to spread out on. I kept leaves on the ground for some extra padding.

I laid my figure down to rest for the night. The ground was as hard as a rock, and it was freezing cold. I damned the sky for hogging all of the heat, since heat rises. I tried to trick myself into believing that it was lukewarm outside, but it didn't work. I experienced someone situating a blanket softly over me. I opened my eye a slit to witness who it was. It was the little girl, tucking me in with one of her own blankets for ni-nite time. My eyelid wouldn't stay ajar for another second as I fell into momentary darkness. At last, I was fitted to doze off, uninterrupted by pointless dreams of animals.

I was awakened by a low growl of some sort. I reasoned that it was Grandpa snoring, since he was getting too cozy, but after numerous attempts to get him to shut up, it was time to get physical, physical. I revealed my eye, welcoming it to the painful stinging of smoke. I blinked a couple of times to wash it out so that I could get up to kick some ass. When I swiveled in the direction of the commotion, I spotted Grandpa, but bent over him was a giant bear. It was sniffing Grandpa, assumably because of the interesting smell that he emitted into the air. I wasn't for sure if Gramps was snoozing or just didn't mind, but he was laying there stiff as a slab of sheet rock, while all of this was happening. My sweat glands were on hyper drive as I tried not to manufacture any noise so that the bear wouldn't come after me.

But my quivering must've distracted it from its fascination with Grandpa, because it began making its way towards me. It must've been a portly bear by the crunching sound it produced beneath its feet when it stepped on the bones from our supper. I began shuddering recklessly in fear with nothing to defend myself with besides a blanket in case it attacked. I suppose that I could've affected its sight with that for a moment before it decapitated me with its paw.

The bear switched courses again with luck, except for that it was heading straight for the little girl. She had woken up as she started to stretch out. Allegedly, stretching pisses bears off a whole lot, seeing that it let out this gynormous roar. That made the two zombies arise from their slumber, but the bear still maintained its focus on the little girl. Something had to be done and fast, or I would be stuck, feasting upon the little girl's carcass off of the ground, considering that I can't waste meat. I gave Nazm the gesture to do something, because, if he got hacked up, all that we had to do was stitch on some new body parts. If it was one of us, it was pretty much an instant death. The blood of my ancestor relied on that, or maybe just the little girl's blood.

Nazm did his tiptoe walk up behind the bear, leaping on its back, not allowing it to reach him. This, in fact, misled the bear into attempting to maul Nazm to termination instead. The bear got up on its hind legs, only to drop down onto all fours, venturing to shake Nazm off of his back.

Grandpa threw a stick, wishing that the bear would chase after it, getting it away from us, but then I refreshed his memory that it was dogs that like to play fetch, not bears. He shrugged, responding that it was still worth a try, which would've been true if stupid ideas ever worked.

With each moment that Nazm remained on that bear's back, the more maddened it became, causing violent destruction to the trees encompassing it, breaking off the bark. Thankfully, not all the way around the trees, or they would've withered away - or so it was rumored. Nazm began to elbow the bear in the back of the neck in hopes of dismantling the vertebrae, I think. He held on with one hand while belting him with the other arm, generating a rodeo-type scene. The bear's skull eventually commenced the backwards lean, until after the final blow, when Nazm brought his elbow down to its neck. Nazm's elbow popped the bear's cranium off as it spiraled through the air, until it thumped against the ground and rolled to a stop. A head is not meant to roll for more than a short distance, due to the awkward shape of it, primarily on a bear with that huge schnoz. It must be toilsome scoring a date being a bear, since nobody finds a human with a big snout sexy at all.

   Then came the dilemma of the night: We had the bulkiest ration of food we may ever have, but we had dined out only a few hours before. We couldn't bring it with us because of its tremendous size, but, surely, we couldn't eat it all unless we put our all into it. In conclusion, we disposed of the whole thing, knocking everybody up to the point of full. We had to imprison our vomit within our organs just so that we could digest it all to absorb the proper nutrients from it. We all blacked out again until sunrise showed up, which wasn't that bright underneath the trees. The impounding of the puke didn't work, seeing that we all woke up with it painted all over our clothes. The little girl was face down in a puddle of her own. I rushed over to her aid, rotating her over onto her back to check for a pulse. I deposited my two fingers on her throat, like I did to that dummy in class. I'm talking about the dummy that I choked for too long in the hallway.

   The little girl still owned a pulse, but it was incredibly slow. She still had a chance of being revived though. I began pushing on her abdomen also plugging her nose while transferring my oxygen into her lungs. I wasn't positive that I was doing it correctly, but, at that instant, anything was worth a shot, except for throwing a stick. I stationed my mouth on hers again, deporting the oxygen from my lung capacity into hers with no luck, until she took her first breath into my mouth.

The problem was that her first breath was saturated with vomit. It launched out of her mouth into my throat, leaving me gagging on the chunks. I grappled my throat as I staggered backwards, tripping on a stick that made me land hard on my spine. The little girl's barf spewed from my air tube upwards and then downwards onto my face. Now I wasn't showered with only my own spit up. It's such a bore to only be exposed to your own excretion. I wiped it off of my face, like the sweat from my brow, as I went to check on the little girl.

She was still established in the dirt, coughing up a storm. All the throw up worked its way out of her system, as only minuscule scraps were coming out, clinging to the sides of her mouth and chin. Grandpa knelt over her, rubbing away the vomit with his shirt. I forced him out of the way so that I could look like the superhero when she unleashed the sight of her eyes, since they were squinted shut during all of the coughing. My plan was successful, too. As she unsealed her eyelids, she shouted out how I was her hero. I appreciated that she meant super hero, so I let it go. She wrapped her arms around me so snuggly that it seemed like she wanted me dead. I entrusted her with an uncomfortable pat on the back, while she clung to me when I attempted to stand up. I waited it off until she got sick of me.

I explained to everyone that we really should get going before another bear or random poisonous animal tried to eradicate us. They all complied as we packed up our blankets, squeezing as much meat as we could into our pockets for our next meal - a meal only big enough to feed a baby. You can't always have a snack fit to feed a king when you're wandering around in the woods, but you should be able to. It was not like it would break McOeltjenbruns to construct some low traffic restaurants in the middle of some woods. Or, maybe it would; it's not like I know anything about the fast food industry.

We strapped everything onto our backs as we made our way down the imaginary trail. That meant that we weren't even certain if we were going down the same route as before, since we had no clue what the hell the North Star was if we could've even seen it. Plus, we winded around trees, along with various other things, such as animal carcasses.

Then, I spied something that I had to stop for: a beehive. I desperately hunted around on the ground for rocks. I was only efficient enough to find two, so I had to make them count. Otherwise, I would be a disappointment to myself along with any other child in the world. I concentrated hard on the hive while gripping the rock like my life depended on it. I even put my leg into the pitch, lifting it up as I chucked the rock at full force, which was probably forty-five mph. I struck the beehive, but it didn't fall down. Instead, it punched a hole through it, causing bees to pour out of it, swarming around the hive as if the rock was the traitor. Insects are remarkably stupid.

I prepared for my next throw by kissing the rock. It was possibly more disgusting for the rock to be kissed by me than me kissing a rock that had been under a dead animal. I invested all of my oomph into that one, targeting the stem of the hive, where it was hanging onto the tree. When I pitched the stone, it was as if everything was going in slow motion. I watched it clip the stem, but only enough to break off a tiny scrap. The hive still rocked back and forth, leaving a dose of hope for me. It swayed, and, after each rotation, the stem cracked a bit more, until the hive finally snapped, leading it down to where it collided with the ground. It ruptured in a way that is comparable to an egg meeting my frying pan.

This made the bees plenty angry, and they took it all too personal and assaulted me. Another thing about animals is that they never learn to shake stuff off. I trotted as fast as I could away from the bees. To be productive, at the same time, I raced down the path that we were already traveling. The bees still wouldn't let up, even though I distinctly had forfeited. I didn't bear a white flag on me, so my next action was the second best way to show it.

I sprung into the nearest mud puddle that was extensive enough to submerse me. I twirled around in it, counting on the TV being accurate when it reported that bees wouldn't sting you if you were coated in mud. It worked, though; the bees refused to land on me, ultimately losing all interest in me before buzzing away. I laid there for a moment to repossess my pride for what I had achieved: one downed bees nest and eluding my own demise, thanks to my quick wits.

When I stood up, I saw my own personal bunch heading towards me, marching with pride. It seemed that Nazm had taken a liking to the little girl. She was hoisted up on his shoulders, reaching for leaves, flowers, and birds in the nearby trees. I underwent something that was creating friction against my leg. I peaked downward to identify a brightly sun-colored snake going up into a striking position. I did the only thing that I knew was smart, which was to kick the snake and run away. The only problem was that I missed when I tried to punt it, and I couldn't start step two before I successfully completed step one. I stood there paralyzed, like my shoestrings were knotted together.

The snake took its opportunity to attack in the turn-based battle, getting me with a critical hit. The snake's fangs were buried deep in my calf muscle. I strived to rattle it off, but it only flung around, holding on without remorse. Nobody came to my charity, since I wasn't a little girl. I ensnared the snake with both hands, attempting to fracture it in half, but it only bent, as snakes do not have bones like The Gary does. I took the leg that it was latched onto plunging it underneath the mud going for a good old-fashioned suffocation. I sensed the tension release when the snake tried to retreat, but I gripped it, restricting it underneath the brown cream until it ceased to move.

I pulled my leg up, sweeping the mud off of it, uncovering the puncture wounds where I was bitten. It was at the present beginning to swell up from the poison that was harbored inside. Somebody needed to suck it out and soon. I asked for a volunteer, but I got no response out of any of them. I couldn't do it myself since my stomach blocked me from performing such an activity. I picked Gramps, authorizing him to come over, considering that he was the least likely to horribly screw something up. He approached me cautiously, since I was in quite a panic. You would think that I would've been used to near death experiences by that point, but it's something that is hard to take in stride. He had the information on what to do, being that we watched the same snake program together on our ancient television at home.

Gramps reached inside of his shirt and plucked out a single rib. I wasn't sure if it was his or someone else's, due to him already being cloaked in vital fluids.

He occupied my leg with one hand to prevent it from flinching. With the other, he plunged the rib into my leg, almost an inch deep, dragging it along the swollen area. A cloudy liquid became exposed with a dash of blood. Grandpa established his lips against my leg as he began to suck the poison out. He spit three times before he started to drool 100% blood out. He kept going and going without even realizing that he was depleting me of all the hemoglobin that I had left.

I knocked Gramps off of me, challenging him on why he wanted me lifeless. Of course, he didn't understand until I displayed the blood polished leg that he had established to him. I got up, enabling the blood to drain into my shoe. It was more suitable than it all crusting to my "leg hair". I waggled as much of the mud and gunk off as I could, because I didn't want to become overly crusty.

Thus, our journey through the blackened wilderness began again with no trace of ever being permitted to leave. The wilderness seemed to go on in every direction for infinity. My feet were throbbing from tribulation, while my legs couldn't harbor the weight of my chunky behind anymore. I imparted upon the trio that we had to pause to take a breather or my lungs were going to implode. They reluctantly agreed.

We plopped down on the cold, moist ground. It was undifferentiated from heaven, except I don't think that heaven produced dampness in the butt of your pants. My eyes roamed aimlessly into the distance, inspecting many offbeat things that struck my curiosity, including a bird regurgitating a worm for its young. My interest was held very easily, and I stress the very. My eyes glowed like high beams at the sight of a small shack not that far from where we sat, shrouded behind a couple of bushes and trees.

I pointed it out eagerly to the others to see if they wanted to go check it out. It just so happened that they once again conformed to me, but, then again, if they didn't, they were all morons. Who would want to roam around more when there was shelter right in front of them? The anticipation was killing me, since they could have a TV without a supply of VHS tapes of "Guiding Light" to the extent of the ones that we had at home.

We moved the brush aside when we got up to it. It appeared to be a storage shed, a decrepit one. It had those goofy ripples in the metal siding where rust had taken over the once silver look. The door was padlocked shut, but that didn't bother me, thanks to Nazm being my own personal human jackhammer. I enthusiastically told him to sic it, like he was my golden retriever. He arrived at the entrance, smacking the padlock consistently with his hand, which was curled into a fist. The padlock broke off. I patted him on the head, feeding him an earthworm that I harvested from the dirt as a reward. He got so much of a thrill out of that. Just like his rat, he treated it like a pet before chewing it up.

I unlatched the door, opening it up gradually, just in case something indoors felt the need to physically assault me. There was nothing animate within the walls, but it did appear that someone was living there. The walls were decked out with illustrations of barnyard animals all done in green and purple crayon. Towards the back of the room, there were hooks dangling from the ceiling with one that had a baby critter impaled on it. I couldn't reveal to you what kind of critter it was, considering my lack of knowledge for the useful. Next to the hooks was a heavily stained mattress that had no pillows on it. It was complete nonsense. Wherever there is a mattress;

there is bound to be a pillow. So why not just take both? It wasn't much of a home, but it could've been, because the person who dwelled within was also misplaced in the vast wilderness.

Grandpa went over to rest on the mattress. I knew that he didn't refuse to compromise self respect for comfortability. Nazm walked around, blindly confused as to what he could do in such a humble space, while the little girl, whose name I unquestionably should've known by then, stuck by me wherever I maneuvered to.

I treaded along the trail of Nazm's confusion as of what to do while we were there besides pig out on the impaled critter. I jerked on it, struggling to purge it from the hook, but it wouldn't budge. I tried it, carefully and slowly; then, it slid right off without the use of effort. All of the exposure to the woods must've freed too much of my animal instinct, seeing that I ripped that poor critter into shreds.

I expect that my people were disappointed in the fact that I didn't share any of it, because they all strayed from whatever they were doing to back me into the corner. The little girl built a firm stance in front of me with her arms spread wide, ordering them not to harm me. I asked them if they would deny the voice of a child to inflict malice upon an innocent soul.

Suddenly, the entrance swung open as a man came in hunched over, stumbling backwards, rambling on to himself about how he swore that he locked the door before he left. He was hauling in the carcass of a larger cat-type creature that he must've sacrificed for his appetite. When he turned around, he jolted in shock from someone being in his home out in the middle of nowhere. He wielded a long knife from his holster and waved it around in front of him, asking us what we thought we were doing in his home.

I questioned if he meant shack, but I had a hunch that he truly did mean home from the red hot coals displayed in his eyes. I disclosed to him that we were lost in the woods, and we didn't know which way was out. He pointed to the back of the shack, which I assumed meant that it was the direction that we had to go to get out of there. Another shocked look came across his face when he asked which one of us ingested his dessert. It must've been the critter that I munched on, so I held the skeleton behind my back, tossing it beneath the table and out of sight.

When I began paying attention, I noticed that everybody was pointing their fingers at me, even the little girl. But she couldn't help it; all kids are tattletales. I put my greatest effort into letting him know that I wasn't informed that anyone was lodged there, or else I wouldn't have eaten it (when, really, I couldn't have cared less). He announced that he was going to let it slide because he could hear the sympathy in my voice as he withdrew his knife, what a sucker.

I suddenly became aware of radios and people strolling around outside that soon distorted into dead silence. I was positive that it was the search party, because I heard twigs snapping underneath their weight along with voices over the walkie-talkies. There was a lone way out of that place, which was the front door, which might've been too obvious. I was updated by the man that if we hurried we might be able to all seek shelter in his crawlspace. He pulled out this big wooden crate that was stationed up against the wall. Beneath it was a section of the floor, which was cut out. The area was visible by the metal shavings that encircled it. He quickly lifted the lid so that we could all drop into the hollowness. Once we were internal, he dragged the covering over us, which forsakened us into the darkness.

I asked him how they were not going to notice the square shaped carving in the floor along with the crate that was in the middle of the shed. He grabbed a string that was hanging from the ceiling that I could hardly see. He hung on it with all of his weight designing a vision of levitation. I heard the crate trailing across the floor above until it banged up against the wall. He pivoted towards me and told me that was how. It was frustrating when people I didn't even know got smart with me. I wasn't just some stupid kid. I was, and still am, also awesome.

The door ruptured upstairs when we overheard humanity yelling to each other over their radios, but we couldn't make out what they were verbalizing because the hole muffled the outer sounds. I was pretty sure that I apprehended something about how there was nothing of relevance there, but I could've been mistaken.

There was still a cluster of stomping going on above us, so I figured that I would do my damndest to embark upon a conversation about how much regular yellow lemonade sucks and how much pink lemonade rocks. Apparently everybody else loved the yellow lemonade so that one didn't go over to well. Instead of tolerating a deep discussion, we stood there in an awkward silence. Nobody offered a sound besides the guys upstairs, but that didn't count, seeing that they weren't part of our group.

I asked if a light bulb even claimed a spot down there. He lit up a match, exposing a wall of candles that were fixed upon some shelves. It was funny that he never thought about doing that before (and by funny, I meant dumb). The room warped to an orange hue from the glow. The shadows danced about on the walls around all of us from Nazm blowing lightly at the flame, pressuring it to jiggle but not extinguish.

The little things in death amuse some people way too much.

The whole cellar was surrounded by dirt, but there were boards up over it to humor the handyman-finished wall and floor. I was not impressed. All of the walls were lined with shelves that had canned goods on them. Most of the cans were baked beans, not even the diverse flavored ones, just plain baked beans. Not saying that there's anything faulty with the original baked beans. I bought the economy sized ones when we went grocery shopping back home, but having an assortment has never hurt anyone. That is except for this one guy, who I was acquaintances with back home that died when he switched from twist bottle caps to the ones that you have to pop off. But that was a freak accident. He attempted to pop the cap off of his soda with a knife, so he put a ton of force into it. When the cap came off, the knife was driven into his eye socket. It would've reached his brain if he had one.

Anyway, it was as if this freaky guy had moved out to the woods to avoid something. It seemed to me that he was plotting on living down in his cellar for quite a while with extreme internal pain. If whatever it was didn't get him, the beans sure would. I questioned the significance of the secret hiding place, coupled with the ludicrous volume of baked beans. He maintained his stance, giving me a look like it should've been self-explanatory what it was all about. Little did he know that I had a knack for neglecting the obvious. I granted him an equally rude expression, so he finally fessed up, letting me in on his paranoid delusion. He educated us on how he moved out into the woods to elude the mass quantities of zombies that would be taking over the world someday. As long as he had the underground cellar, he could hide out until the plague passed over. There were at least two things that guy had no clue about.

One: As far as I knew the infection couldn't be spread when you had your guts reamed from your body. Two: If it was possible for the infection to spread, then he ushered it down into his hideout with him. I would've felt safer stashing myself away from zombies in a barricaded house than a burrow in the ground with thin weak wood floorboards overhead. If a horde of zombies got in that shack and all stood at a close proximity, the floor would most likely collapse on top of us. What good would baked beans do then?

The footsteps disappeared from the structure, and the cellar went silent. I asked if I could have some baked beans, because earlier I only ate myself back into the "I'm so hungry I could eat a wild boar" phase. It took a lot of negotiating, but I, ultimately, obtained a can of baked beans for my bile soaked jeans. Don't ask why he wanted my pants. I acquired my baked beans, which was all that mattered. Then I realized that there was no can opener in the vicinity. I queried as to where there was one that I could utilize. He told me that he would let me use one if I provided him with my left shoe since his was worn out. Mine wasn't much better and was a significantly smaller size. His was a loafer and mine was a high top, but I don't think that he cared. The predicament was that there wasn't a shoe store anywhere nearby. I handed it over, but only because I was desperate for those beans. I snatched the can opener from him without haste as I began to open that sucker as fast as I could.

When I pried the roof off of it, I distinguished that I grabbed the wrong can. Inside were refried beans, which were a major step down, but still edible. Something began to shake the residence that we were in like a ketchup bottle. Not really, but there was a tremendously ample noise coming from within the room. Nazm would've been blushing, if he could, considering that the uproar came from his empty stomach. He cradled his belly, thinking that it would suppress the noises from us, causing us to forget all about it.

The hermit approached Nazm, wondering if he wanted to trade anything for a can of beans. Nazm's response was something of a giant clap that ended with the guy's throat being squished sideways. At least, it was an instant death for the clothing hungry bastard. His eyes bulged out from all of the strain on the sockets when I observed his Adam's apple shoot down into his stomach. Grandpa must've seen Nazm's actions coming, since he had the little girl distracted by explaining the differences of beans to her. Nazm forced him down face first to the ground, where he proceeded to rip into his shirt. Once he got past the material he dug through the skin excavating the spine with one hand. He heisted the refried beans from my hand without even minding me. He poured them inside of the humongous gaping wound in the man's back stirring them around with his hands. I strived to clarify to him that there were a lot more ingredients to a taco but he wouldn't hearken my word, even though I am the master of all meals. Grandpa looked starving, too, so he tried to get a piece of the pie (that's metaphorical pie). But Nazm pushed him away, like we hadn't ever done anything for him.

Feasibly, the reason that all of those things that were equivalent to him, back in the hospital (that was not), were so crazy was because they were kept hungry. I managed to get my pants and shoe back before Nazm noticed that I was neighboring him. My pants looked and smelled as vile as the day that I desecrated them. I installed the shoe on my naked foot, delaying until Nazm got done with his hissy fit. When he concluded, there wasn't a scrap of meat remaining for Grandpa. Nazm acted like nothing had happened, suggesting that we be on our way.

That was in the program, but it wasn't going to occur, just as Gramps had other intentions. It involved his fist, along with rapid movement, without connecting to anything. Nazm dodged them all, catching Grandpa's hand and controlling it, while Gramps swung his other one, which was also to be entangled in Nazm's fingers. Nazm dominated his movements there until he cooled down, so everything would go back to normal. Gramps seemed to be fine, but, deep down, I anticipated that he was enraged. I bet that it left a scar that wouldn't enable him feel the same about Nazm anymore.

I wasn't going to deal with their crap for another second; I searched for an exit. I remembered that the only way was to climb the rope. It wasn't in my field of expertise, so I permitted the others go first, while I watched them do it with ease. I latched onto the rope as I hopped up, but I lost grip, falling to my bottom. I never could've imagined that gym class would come in handy in all my life. I decided that I would make one more attempt at it. I wrapped my hands around it solidly, except, that time, I didn't hop up. I resolved that I would struggle to scale it from the bottom. The little girl was up there, leaning over the edge of the hole, shouting words of encouragement to me, while I ascended centimeter by centimeter up it because of all my nightmares related to gym. My hands were becoming covered with thin black layers of skin that were all rolled up, having just started to heal up.

Grandpa towed the rope up with me on it, refusing physical support from Nazm. He struggled, but did it himself after I spent so much time striving to climb up it. I absolutely adored how everyone thought of this stuff after I exerted all of my energy, both mental and physical. I thanked him anyway to help him calm down a bit.

I judged that we should wait a night before persevering in case we ran into that search party again. It was agreed that one of us had to be conscious to keep a lookout in case they returned so that we could drop back down into the bean room if need be. We all ended up staying awake, like sexy people do at slumber parties. That wasn't our intention, but we just couldn't sleep. There were no noises throughout the flawless night, except for all of the animals that felt the need to form the biggest racket possible during the dark hours, or, at least, that's what I blamed the noises on that were coming from my body as a result of having consumed a large amount of beans.

The next morning, I totally forgot which way we had to travel to make it back to the city. It was a noggin scratcher, but, after much thought, complete with spinning in circles, I verified which way to go. We departed from behind the shack, heading farther away from it, without looking back and hoping for the best. After walking a few thousand exaggerated miles, I questioned myself as to why I didn't ask how much farther it was to town. The terrain seemed to get steeper the further we went, leaving me to ponder if we were just heading back up to another mountain. Gramps lost all hope as he slumped over onto his knees, screaming to the sky, asking why God had forsaken us. I looked over to Nazm, who was holding a hook that he had swiped from the shack up to his throat, ready to commit suicide, even though he couldn't die that way. I figured that I should try talking him out of it anyway for his self-esteem.

I instructed the little girl to go and cheer up Grandpa while I chatted with Nazm. She was still clinging to my side, but I was certain that I should do it alone. I smoothly marched towards Nazm, interrogating him as to why he wanted to do this. He claimed that it was because the world could do without a monster. I delivered formulated reasons as to why the world needed a monster. Like how they filtered out the dingy oxygen so that the average human being could live longer. Also how they lend a helping hand by getting rid of the bad people, so, in a way, they're crime fighters. As usual he believed any nonsense that I threw his way.

The only thing left for me to do was cheer up Grandpa, but I had him in the palm of my hand. I spun around to brighten up his day when I saw him sitting on the ground cross legged, immensely saddened by something. I strolled on over to him, where I noticed that he was hunched over a mound of flesh, eating it like a savage. He wasn't depressed about anything; he was just starving. That meant that he lied to me, not directly, but close enough.

Then, I put two and two together, and I came up with the correct answer that I won't tell what it is. Not because I don't know, but because I don't want to. The heap of gore that Grandpa was devouring wasn't an animal at all. I comprehended this because I hadn't seen the little girl since I assigned her to cheer up Grandpa and because her cranium was posed on the top of the pile of flesh, untouched. I kicked Grandpa in the back, asking him what the hell he thought he was doing. He shrugged his shoulders, never ceasing the consumption. I booted him again for a better response, but all he could give me was that he was really, really hungry.

I abducted the head from the top of the pile, cracking it open on a rock. I plucked the brain out of the skull, feasting upon it like it was a foreign delicacy. It would've seemed cruel to do what I did, but I had my reasons. I didn't want her to meet her demise out in the middle of nowhere abandoned. I was optimistic that by absorbing her brain waves I would be able to take her soul with me so that I could transport it to wherever she wanted me to chaperone it to. If she wanted to hangout in my body for a while, that would be cool, too.

I mourned the loss of a fellow human being for the first time, ever. She was the only individual to ever show concern for my well being, so I envisioned that I had the right to. When the mournfulness that clouded my mind finally lifted, it was nighttime. I must've been out for a good period of time, since the rest of the little girl's body had already been devoured. I was not willing to take a break anymore. I reported to Gramps and Nazm that it was time to go.

While we were walking along, I heard Nazm teasing Gramps about how he had pissed me off, so we would be wandering around until we expired. Ordinarily, I would get angry, but I was flooded with so much emotion that I couldn't feel a thing anymore. I had persistence for once, so I wasn't about to enable anything to bring us to a standstill. We must've toured a quarter of a mile when I witnessed the sky glimmering with light, not natural light either. It was an unnatural glow. I confessed to Gramps that if that was town so close to where the little girl had given her life for evening snack, I was going to kick his ass later. I took a few more steps so that I could peek over the hill, and what did I see? It was a bunny rabbit, along with a town less than a mile away.

I said screw it to myself, punching Grandpa square in the nose, making him lower to the ground, where I straddled him and pummeled his head from side to side until his face was guised in that moldy blood type color. I dismounted his body, letting him know that I couldn't contain myself. I advised him to watch his back for at the least the next couple days. Flying objects may've wanted to collide with his dome. He got up, rattling his head back and forth, flinging his unknown blood type all over the place – except for on me – because I was presently on my way to the road. They followed once they realized that I wasn't about to wait up for them.

Chapter 15: Love is an Infection with Minimal Bodily Harm

When they got down to the road, I commanded them to hide out in the bushes, while I undertook the task of hitching us a ride. Nazm came over to the road to stick his thumb up while smiling like he was doing something merited. I ordered him to get in the bushes with Grandpa unless he wanted to be featured on an imaginary snuff film. I didn't give a crap if he was suicidal. If he provoked me again, it might as well have been considered self-inflicted. Grandpa accompanied him over to the bushes while clasping onto his hand. Nazm wept during the complete trip being Mr. Poutyface.

I stuck my frustrated thumb out, pausing for someone to give us a lift, and, yes, my thumb was just as frustrated as the rest of my body. A car passed us with no gesture of even pressing on the brake. I was repulsed by those irresponsible serial killers for branding us honest hitchhikers with a bad reputation.

Hitchhiking is so strenuous that it should be regarded to as a workout. Because holding your arm out for hours on end, while dodging the occasional vehicle that drove over the white line, is truly exhausting. It wasn't beneficial that it was dark out and I was saturated with the little girl's blood at that. I wish that I could've kept a pair of clothes clean for more than a day. I stirred into a sitting position after my legs couldn't accept anymore of the torture. It's more intricate to dodge cars sitting than when you're standing.

There was an automobile that somehow spotted me posed there and pulled over beyond us. I gave the signal for the boys to hop out of the bushes to get into the car. When the car made out the other two, it sped away as if we were going to butcher them. I wouldn't have, but, now if I ever recognized them somewhere, I would. I had the boys stay by the asphalt the next time with me to cause less astonishment to our ride when they pulled over.

The next car that drove down the road passed us, but they shifted into reverse, driving into the gravel on the side of the road, almost nailing us. I called out shotgun before anyone else could, because I being snug was the only thing that mattered after all the obligations that I went through. I secured the front seat while Gramps and Nazm entered through opposite sides of the car.

The driver was a beautiful girl that didn't act in the manner that she had been around the block a hundred times. It was a term that I had heard somewhere. I had no idea what it meant. This girl was more ravishing than anything I have ever witnessed. If you took a gyro and mutated it into a human, this would be it. Her eyes were as brown as the barbeque sauce that I poured on my beef sandwiches. She dressed classy, but not as classy as a businesswoman. She wore sweatpants accompanied by a worded shirt that advertised something that didn't even exist. Her smile was big and white, like heaven, when she asked me why I had the scent of an old work boot after a fourteen-hour shift. I had no justification, besides that I had gone through hell. She touched my cheek, calling me a poor baby. I frequently get bitter over such a name, but she seemed sympathetic when she said it.

There were two girls in between Gramps and Nazm in the back that implied that they were having a good time with them, which was unique, since they were pretty lame in all actuality. Credibly, it could've been because the two girls were dumb as doorknobs. I ignored the numbskulls in the backseat, turning my attention to the woman who could change or destroy my world.

I requested the name from the girl of my dreams. She told me that her name was Gertrude in a soft gentle voice without missing a syllable. Gertrude was the most attractive name that I had ever heard of in my life. It also reminded me of my Grandma. Her name wasn't Gertrude, but her mom's was. Considering that I was already on the topic of my family tree, I decided to talk up my descendants. I mentioned to her how I was a late descendent of Magnar Helty, ruler of the world at one point in time. I understand that some of mankind likes to call him God, but that was his full name.

Gertrude disclosed the names of her friends in the backseat to me. Olivia was the muscle bound minx that was getting hit on by Nazm. She wore a sleeveless shirt that exposed the arms of a male construction worker. Her hands were blotted with oil or grease or something from an engine. That was a field that I didn't know anything about. Olivia was sporting a pair of sunglasses even though the sun was crouched behind the clouds and had been the entire time we were out of the woods. People that wear their sunglasses at night are just plain creepy. It was not like they save your vision anyway, plus it makes you look like a doofus. So, what's the point? The only people that wear sunglasses all the time are the ones that get beat by somebody, because they don't want to show off their battle wounds.

Judging by the way this girl looked, there was no way that she could even get jumped by a couple of people and come out with a bruise. Her hair was slicked back into a ponytail, while her jeans had holes frayed in the knees – another pointless thing. However, I must confess that it looked badass.

The other girl that was running her fingers down the front of Grandpa's shirts was named Shaniqua. I swore that Gramps had a friend named that. He visited her constantly at some bar with the title "Juliet's Bedroom". It sounded like trespassing to me, since Shaniqua was there *all* the time, inviting Grandpa over without asking Juliet. I never registered as to why Grandpa had me run down to the bank with a hundred dollar bill to inherit all $1 bills though. I never challenged his motives, being that he, without exception, gave me my $2 cut.

Shaniqua in the backseat had fingernails that were longer than I conceived was attainable. She perchance had those fake extensions that people spent so much money on. I contemplated getting them once, but they were out of candy apple fingernail polish…just kidding. To maintain those things would be a bitch with all of the daily activity that I did back in the day, like reaching in the fridge. Shaniqua's hair was braided together back behind her being that it was so long that if she had it in front of her she would trip on it and shear the tissue off of her scalp.

Speaking of the skin on her head... Her face was good looking, except for that it was masked with teenage acne. Also, the fact that she didn't seem like an awesome person made her appearance worse. Inner beauty does affect the external, but it also makes me want to eat them up, literally.

I queried Gertrude as to how far along they were going. She answered back that there was a party going on in Medford. They wanted to go to it, striving to become the cool people if for only a day. I was about to ask how they were not cool, but then I witnessed it first hand. They were dressed in cheap thrift shop attire. When they announced that Medford was in Oregon, I sighed in relief. Gertrude asked me what the matter was. I explained to her that it was nothing. We just had to rendezvous with a buddy there (more like a foe, but I didn't say the foe part out loud).

Olivia inquired to Nazm if he wanted to accompany her to the party, so he said yes without my consent. Then Gramps also agreed to go when Shaniqua asked him. It was as if I wasn't in charge anymore. Gertrude then requested the same from me, so I melted like bacon fat. I didn't say yes, because I had no backbone. I said yes, because I had no backbone when it came to extremely gorgeous women.

We drove on into the night without stopping to get something to munch on. It was the first time that I established something higher than food on my priority list. We ended up stopping at a gas station, where the girls all needed to get out for gas along with a potty break. They asked if we wanted anything to eat from inside, but I described how we had misplaced all of our money, during our strenuous trip across the country. She told us not to worry about it, since she was going to pay for us. I loved a woman that invested in

Je Son Stryker

nourishments for me. I gladly welcomed the offer without hesitation.

They shut their car doors, heading off wayward into the gas station. None of us spoke a word to each other while they were absent. Nazm played the drums with his hands on the seat, but that was the only clamor from within the car. It could've been because all of us were certain that we were making a big mistake by getting attached to those girls like that, primarily Grandpa who was at least fifty years more elderly than Shaniqua. They were taking an extended period of time inside, so they must've been pigging out so that they didn't resemble slobs around us.

They evacuated the building with a few plastic bags crammed with purchases. If they bought us that much food, it would've been the coolest thing in the world, besides triumphing in a jalapeno-eating contest. And the reason for that coolness is because of all the complimentary milk you get afterwards. Milk is best curdled a bit, so it's a cross between milk and cottage cheese. The lumps add some considerable flavor.

When they arrived at the car, they handed a bag to each of us. Gertrude provided me with three hot dogs in a glossy cardboard tray. It was a smaller portion then I was used to, but, in that situation, it wasn't what counted. What counted was that she fully loaded every one of them with all of the condiments that were there. I questioned how she was familiar with what I liked on my wieners, but, supposedly, she didn't. She ate her hot dogs the same way. So there were enough condiments to make sure that you couldn't even taste the meat. I yearned to consume the wieners in a seductive way. One in which we both commenced the consumption of the hotdog on separate ends until we reached the middle together, but, I wasn't the outgoing type that would suggest it.

Instead of waiting for her to pull a move on me, I decided to scarf down my wieners before they got cold or, even worse, luke-warm. Ketchup and relish juices channeled down my chin as I attempted to gobble up those bad boys quickly before the luke-warm phase that sucked so bad came about. I finished with them remaining hot the entire time, but not without my clothing receiving some battle wounds. I was devastated. I wasn't absolutely positive if ketchup could be lifted from the fabric. I've heard that blood comes out with no troubles, though. I was also definitive that all of the holes could be stitched up too.

I plopped my head down for a second, spying the plastic bag that I had placed beneath my feet a few minutes before. I picked it up with the slight suspicion that there may be fruit flavored vitamins inside or gangrene. Inquisitively, I opened it by ripping a hole in the bottom of the bag, because I couldn't loosen the knot on the top. Possibly, if it was a single knot, I could have, but a double knot is next to impossible for me. I even struggled to tear through the plastic. It didn't need to be so durable. All you had to do is double bag it if you're buying bowling balls for God's sake.

When my fingers drilled into the bag, I spread it apart unveiling that there wasn't any gangrene in the bag. It was instead packed with material. Gertrude informed me that it was new clothes for me, since mine were all rancid and deformed. I asked her why she would squander so much currency for a hitchhiker such as myself. She declared that she didn't consider me to be a stranger, but she considered to be more of a friend. Plus, she got the clothes for free, because Shaniqua hit on the cashier. I knew it. It was cheap crap for a cheap person. I could take a hint.

When I brought out the shirt, I knew that I was mistaken for thinking that way. Only the best intentions were there as I was faced with a black screen printed shirt that read "Kill yourself. All the cool kids are doing it." with a picture of a kid that had his head arranged within a guillotine holding the rope ready to drop it. There was also a red and black flannel shirt inside to wear over my shirt. It buttoned up so that I could leave it open when it got too hot. Only a person that cared for me would get me a shirt that persuaded people to kill themselves along with flannel: the greatest gift in the world.

She asked me to try them on, but I filled her in on how it wasn't appropriate to change in front of females. She understood completely, remarking that she wanted to get a motel room for the night anyway, so I could change there. I was fine with the concept as long as no shenanigans went down. I was assured that the shenanigans would be minimal. Minimum shenanigans were close enough for me as long as they were TPing someone's tree or house or tree house.

It was a short cruise across the street to the motel or as the sign read "MO E ". It was one of those crappy ones that had the doorways to the rooms outside, and it required a key, not a card, to get in. They delegated Shaniqua to go in to acquire the room key, most likely because she could get it without charge. She came out with the room key in hand, minus $30 from her purse. She verbalized that the room wasn't on the house that time, seeing that the desk clerk was a married woman. Statistically, married women must grant ugly women less gifts.

We were room number 207. It was on the second floor, which had a twisted metal guardrail, so I couldn't fall off of the balcony as easy. We all trotted up the concrete stairs with plastic bags in our hands.

We went up a flight of seven stairs that led us to a brick wall. I was puzzled until someone grabbed me and spun me around to see another flight of seven stairs that guided us up to the balcony. I pointed to the wall behind me, claiming that I thought I saw a goofy looking bug as I attempted to save my dignity from taking a blow. I hiked up the stairs before I sprinted partway down the balcony to the door. I rested my hands on my knees as I bent over catching the wind that I had lost. I should've learned by then not to move at an accelerated pace unless it was actually necessary.

Something smashed into my back that had a poking feel to it. I looked to the ground, where I heard the clinging noise last. I sighed in relief as it was only the room key, not a scorpion. I managed to conjure up enough brain power to wonder how it struck me when I wasn't holding on to it. I peered upwards to behold two people looking away, masquerading as if they were engrossed in something that was invisible. The other one was Olivia who had her head slumped downwards, whispering sorry to me when, admittedly, she should've been in my face telling me to deal with it since she could kick my ass one handed. I was grateful for the apology though. I informed her that it was okay. The next time I wished that she could've yelled something first, so I could let her know about my gratefulness with a rough noogie. I'm talking about the kind of noogie that when I pulled my fist away it would have stray hairs in between my fingers. She wouldn't be too thrilled that she would have to redo her hair, but specific things deserve certain consequences.

I upraised the key, situating it within the lock. It wouldn't revolve, so I jangled it around until the lock moved. The door did unfasten once I used my body weight to assist the key in its purpose. There wasn't much damage applied to the doorframe. It was only cracked in the middle with a splinter the size of a broom handle sticking out. I had to apply all of my weight to shut it too. Once at the interior of the room, I began to ponder where all of us would sleep. There was only one, single-sized bed. There also wasn't a whole lot of floor space. I was thinking that perhaps if the motel supplied us with a ton of towels, we could use them for something to arrange ourselves on so the floor wouldn't be so stiff.

I was notified not to worry about it at the moment, so I could invade the bathroom to shower and change my clothes. I complied so that someone else could handle my problems for once. The bathroom door was ajar before I got to it. The toilet seat was up with either exceedingly potent unfiltered water inside of it or an inappropriate bodily substance that shouldn't be shown to others of the same species. I shut the toilet seat as I held down the knob to flush it, sweating that it may overflow. The gods were on my side that time, since I stayed clean and fresh smelling. As fresh smelling as I was before, which wasn't all that fresh, I suppose, or else I wouldn't have been inquired to take a shower.

I gripped the handle on the door to shut it when my hand slipped off of it. It took me a couple more attempts to quit, so I could lean against the door to fasten it. I am suspicious as to what could've been on the knob to make it so slick. The only thing that I could conjure up was mayonnaise, but why would anyone try to create a masterpiece sandwich in a tinkle station. It was not the right location to prepare something that would go inside of your mouth, after the ten-minute rule, when it hit the floor.

I began to take off my attire for the hot steamy shower that I was about to embark on. I had to peel every article of my clothing off of my body because of all the disgusting fluids that had made their way to my skin. My whole body was doused in red, along with black and yellow in a few spots. I was a walking splatter painting.

I opened up the curtain on the tub to expose a large black ring that was encircling the middle of it. It formed a stream of black down to the drain. That didn't bother me, because our tub at home appeared to be in the same exact condition. The only secret there was to taking a shower in such a bathtub was to always latch onto something sturdy. It was so you wouldn't slip on the black gunk, which would force you to crack your head open, letting the sewer rats feast upon your crimson vitality.

A bath would've been the easier choice under such a circumstance, but then I might as well have not washed up, because I would be stewing in my own filth. I can picture it now. Me, Gary Helty, settled in a tub of water that was guised, like it was dyed with random pigments of food coloring. It was not a pretty picture, except for me, arranged there in my underwear, since I don't take nudie baths. I never wanted to encounter one of those mishaps where someone walks in on me at one of my most vulnerable times.

I twisted the knob on the shower all the way to scorching hot. I paused for a couple of minutes and waited for the never coming steam to never develop. I positioned my hand underneath the spouting water, but it was still nerve-numbingly cold. There was no steady stream occurring; only a few seconds of water, followed by nothing, that was pursued by a few more seconds of water. The water was brown from its dawning and stayed brown. I had no substitution but to get in, though, if I wanted to impress my lady. She would be capable of indicating if I was still odorous.

My only way out would be if I applied some shower in a bottle, but I doubted that anyone there had cologne on them. I introduced myself to the rear of the tub to avoid the freezing water all at once.

It happened to work out the way that I wanted it to if the way that I wanted it to was to be sprayed by the water, since the showerhead was set too high. I shrieked at the sudden shock of below zero temperatures bumping into my bare exterior. I frantically spun the knob in the opposite direction, but the temperature remained the same. Gertrude opened the door a crack and asked if I was alright. I falsified my statement and told her that I was just testing if I could still do the Do Re Me Fa So La Ti Do. She advised me that I couldn't fool her as she shut the door without allowing me an opportunity to explain. It wasn't as entertaining as I thought it would be to have someone around who could figure me out constantly.

I pushed my worries aside as I was face to face with a bigger threat. Something that would make certain parts of me shrink. I bounced into the bulk of the water, expecting a quick, but not a painful experience. I didn't perceive what I was getting into. It still stung, making my nipples uncomfortably hard, so, without much hesitation, I ruled to make the shower the fastest shower in the history of showers, excluding the people that totally skipped the showers in gym class.

I snatched up the shampoo bottle, which was the caliber of a ketchup packet. My hands were already damp, so, when I went to twist the top off, my fingers slipped. I attempted it with my teeth for a last hope. When I bit down with enough pressure spinning the cap, it actually came off with ease. I dumped out some of the contents in my left hand tossing the rest onto the porcelain (I think that's what the tub was constructed out of). I rubbed the shampoo into my hair working it in between all of the crevices at a record amount of time. As a rough estimate, I'd guess that it only took approximately nineteen seconds to complete that task. I stuck my head beneath the water and shook it around a bit until I was ready for the soap.

When I got to the soap, I was heavily disappointed that it was bar soap, not the liquid soap with a loofa. But, what else should I expect from a cheap motel that bums could probably afford? I picked at the paper around the soap with the motel's name printed on it. The packaging tore off into tiny scraps, taking me a bit longer than anticipated. As soon as that bar was out of the packaging, it was on me like sauce on spaghetti (preferably not Alfredo sauce). I caressed my smooth, silky skin down without dawdling. The suds rolled down my body with ease as my fresh smell emanated into the air. Shades of rotten colors were falling onto my feet as they were carried away by the water. When the pigment vanished, I carefully turned off the water before extracting myself from the shower. I was completely chilled to the bone. Not because I was scared of bodily injury that was caused by the black slime, being that I don't get frightened, but on account of my body temperature being reduced to 57.8°F.

I wiped myself dry of all liquid with one of the hotel towels, which was originally white, but was yellow afterwards. I didn't stain it yellow either; that was from over usage. It smelled like bleach, yet it wasn't white. It could be that bleach has the same aroma as tuna fish sandwiches, but I can't tell the difference. I put my shirts on first that reeked of new shirt smell, which is a pleasant scent in small doses but not all day. I know it's weird to put my shirt on first while I was still wearing soggy boxers, but it's another issue of mine to sidestep being seen nudie.

I prudently dressed in my other boxers by first taking off my other ones, only after surveying the area at every angle and taking shelter behind the shower curtain. I was only being heedful. My body is a sacred temple that is not to be tainted by the likes of others. I took a glance at the latest jeans that would specifically accent my buttocks, which provoked me to try them on. I elevated them with my sweaty palms as I attempted to fasten them around my waist. Either I was getting tubbier or pants sizes were shrinking. I could usually fit into a size 36 in pants, but, presently, they were transforming into hip huggers.

The difficulty with wearing a 36 waist was with me being so short; I had to roll up the bottoms of the pants, since they didn't make anything in my length. I rolled them up inward though to divert myself from looking dumb. I couldn't have someone as impressive as me looking like a jackass. I'm Gary Helty; I have a reputation to withhold, somewhere.

I had accomplished the feat of getting the pants on over my ass when I was faced with a larger problem, getting them buttoned. I pulled up the zipper with all of my might. After the zipper reached my belly fat, I sucked it all in, making me look like more of a supermodel than I already did. I scuffled with the jeans, struggling to get them to expand enough for me to put them on. After that strategy flopped, I tried coaxing them with more love, which, in return, I received more love. They fit like a glove after I got them buttoned. I credit socks, since they always fit better than gloves. They should modify that quote to "fits like a sock".

It was an entirely unrelated story when I released my breath and my innards inflated with oxygen. My face altered to a bright red from the squeezing, which made me have to go tinkle. The quandary was that I couldn't remove the pants again to set free my stream. I had a personal wrestling match with my zipper to get that down before I unbuttoned the handy trap in my crisp boxers. I never foresaw that there was a purpose for such a thing, but I knew better thereafter. I gave praise to the man who ran into that predicament before I did so that I didn't make a fool of myself in front of my lady friend. The wrestling match didn't retire until I got the zipper back up, but, in the end, I remained the victor. Victor of the match...I wasn't changing my name.

I was so delighted to check out my ultimate sexiness when I got out of the room, so I neglected to waggle my wee wee, leaving that dribbling sensation inside of my pants. Even though dribbles don't make it through the pants, they're still not a favorable experience. I snagged my towel to rotate the doorknob so that my faultless physique wouldn't be corrupted with whatever substance was all over everything. There was no simple way out of opening those doors as it still took me some time to unlatch the lock.

When I walked out into the bedroom/living room/whatever it was, I gawked at my baby stretched out on the bed, sleeping like an angel without the wings, if angels even authentically had wings. Encompassing her were a couple of corpses, indulging themselves on the bodies of the ladies that supposedly were so fond of. Grandpa was squashing Shaniqua's stomach over his head while he held his mouth open as wide as inhumanly possible, seeing that all of the skin around his mouth was rotted, empowering him to open it wider. He was catching everything that trickled within it. I was supposed to be the one that played with my food, not the fossil who I deep down counted on to guide me on how to grow up into a respectable human being. I had the notion that my future was previously down the drain.

Nazm (the only friend I had) had Olivia torn apart limb for limb. He was poking orifices into her midsection that were the diameter of his fist, and he was consuming whatever he snatched inside of her when he closed his hands. He would refrain from it every once in a while, being distracted by the current television program: infomercials. It was the sole thing on at that time slot with only having a single channel. There's not much you can get in with an old fashioned antenna. It is such a primitive concept.

My love would never be my love if she viewed her friends slaughtered with no chance of last rights before their souls departed their embodiment. She began to stir around when Grandpa communicated to me that they saved me supper while pointing to Gertrude. I was getting ready to tackle the pathetic bastard when I heard Gertrude asking how long she was asleep for. She also added that my ass looked sexy in those pants, but that was beside the point at the moment. My only responsibility was to make sure that she didn't observe what was going on while they cleaned up.

I sprung on top of the bed throwing the covers over her head as I waved for the boys to start straightening up, but they wouldn't. Gertrude questioned the motive of my actions. I instructed her to stay underneath the covers, and I would explain everything to her. I crawled underneath the covers with her with a talk on the agenda when I sustained too much affection for comfort. She placed her hand on my stomach soothing it up to my sternum.

I situated her hand along her own side expressing to her that I was serious. I wanted her to be informed on how I felt, while, in the meantime, working in that her friends were horribly mutilated. I revealed to her how I had never met someone that made me feel so good and found me attractive. It was a phenomenon that I indeed told her the truth. I never did that, unless it was by accident. She let me know that she felt the same way about me, swearing that she was in love for the first time. It was definite that I was in love, which made the situation more complicated. A tear rolled down my cheek as I knew that I couldn't bring her along with us. If I did, it might've subjected her to her own demise, but I wouldn't authorize myself to do that to her. Anytime Grandpa got hungry, I was convinced that he would chomp her down without hesitation.

I must've been in deep thought for a while, because the next thing I saw was Gertrude, oscillating her hands in front of my face, asking me if I was feeling alright. I pulled a Nazm, giving her the big thumbs up, while keeping my lips clenched together to desist from screaming out loud in pain. I'm talking mental anguish, not physical pain. I instructed her to glance up over the covers and look at the floor, then the walls, and then the ceiling. I told her to just look at everything. She peeked her head out, ready for such a jolt that she would reasonably jump out of the bed, making a mad dash for the exit.

When she did it, instead of fleeing, she slowly put her head back under the covers, asking me who butchered them. I explained to her how Grandpa and Nazm did. She didn't seem to mind that her sidekicks were cold as a turkey, but, instead, she wanted to know if they were going to kill her, too. I responded to her that they most likely would as soon as I turned my back. She advised that I shouldn't turn my back then, as she pressed her lips up to mine, lavishing me with the best and only kiss of my entire, uneventful life.

I dodged my head to the side, questioning if she even had sorrow, since she found out that her friends were dead. She replied to me that they weren't even her friends. They were a couple of hookers who paid Gertrude to hang around with them so that they could feel normal for a few days. I suspect that a hooker is one of those lunatic fishing people that live out on their boats in the center of a lake. I understood then why she didn't care at all. I reported to her that I had to leave as I got out from underneath the covers. I shuffled towards the door, while grappling Gramps and Nazm along the way.

She nabbed me, hooking my arm to spin me around. Gertrude held me in her arms, pleading with me not to abandon her. I confessed to her that it was what needed to be done to keep her safe and that was all that mattered. She handed me her car keys with some money, telling me to find her when I was finished doing whatever needed to be done. I disclosed that it couldn't happen, because, if Grandpa was still functioning, in the end, I couldn't subject her to death.

She embraced me tightly in her arms, similar to how I hugged my teddy bear. What I mean is, how I wrung mortal necks. We both stationed our heads on each others shoulders, feeling the breath escape our bodies, along with our water content. We were perched like that as long as we could before we were interrupted with a tap on my shoulder. I surrendered my grasp from her allowing the words "I love you" to escape from my mouth one last time before I exited the door into reality, where everything sucked and I wished it all would die.

I stood slumped as I traveled down the stairs of my demise. Every step that I took brought me farther and farther away from the only place that I wanted to be. I missed her already and felt like it had been a lifetime in which we had been apart. When we got down to the car, I came to a standstill, dead in my tracks, letting my blood settle for a moment. After it calmed down, I pounded Grandpa's face into the car door repeatedly until splatters appeared on it. I then heaved Nazm face first to the ground without a sign of remorse. I scraped his face against the tar until I felt the need to permit him a break, which was a long ways away. I wasn't finished with him until slabs clung to the tar.

Jason Stryker

Chapter 16: Demons in Disguise as Librarians

I plopped down in the driver's seat and relaxed as well as taking in all of my mixed emotions until Gramps and Nazm got inside. I contemplated leaving them, but no matter how much I loathed Grandpa, sometimes I knew that I wouldn't be here today without him. I owed him a lot for that. It was a silent drive that Nazm insisted on trying to break with jokes that made no sense like, "Why did the elephant cross the road? Because he was too heavy for the crosswalk." Yeah, that was a great one. I just persisted on staying quiet and contemplated colliding with the sturdiest wall that I encountered. The destroyers of dreams changed clothes once again as I drove, but I hardly noticed it, since I was too focused on my grudges. The only time that we froze our Sunday drive was when gas was a necessity. When we stopped, Gramps would pump the gas and then pay for it without even verbalizing a word to me. At least, somebody knew how to shut up.

The stress mounted until Gramps finally snapped, asking me what the problem was in an unsatisfactory tone. When someone got fussy with me, while I had an attitude, like the current one, it was not pretty. I strived to explain it to him through his tiny prune sized brain why I had to reject the love of my life. They claimed that there was no way that they would've murdered her. But Gramps was sentimental towards that little girl, and he ate her. So, what would stop him from disposing of someone he didn't even care that much about? I left it at that with a bitter pout on my face.

Then I received word that we were all out of money, since Nazm had gotten a bad case of the munchies, spending the remaining balance on chips. Not even potato chips though. He paid for a mass amount of apple chips. Everybody knows that the only way apple chips are adequate is if you dip them in mayonnaise, but I didn't spy any in the backseat with him. I caught a glimpse of a sign that read "Salem - 32 Miles". We had no direction of where we were going, so the place where we would run out of gas might as well have been the first place that we started looking. The car chugged along, doing the best it could to make it within the city limits, but it died right outside of the sign with the population on it.

I then had to vacate the last thing that was related to my love besides her aroma, which absorbed into my clothing. It smelled like eggs on toast in the morning with a hint of strawberry perfume, delicious. I didn't want to try to hitch a ride with such a short distance to town. Commonly, I would've, but, at the present time, a walk might've comforted me into clearing my head.

I stuck my hands in my pockets as I strolled along without noticing a speck of the scenery. I was led astray in my thoughts without knowing where I was going outside of my head. Every once in a while, I realized that Grandpa and Nazm were trailing behind me. They still wouldn't speak to me, even though I began to block Gertrude out of my subconscious if only for a short period of time.

An idea popped into my head, which was a fairly new experience for me. Why were we wandering aimlessly, struggling to locate a grave in that state, for one deceased man when we could just go to the library to do research on the date of Olaf's death in the newspapers to find out where he was buried? Ingen-ious. It was a plan Stan! Or, so the other two in my group would've remarked. We pranced down the streets in the morning glow without the aid of the streetlights, because they had shut off a few minutes earlier. Not like I needed them; I'm a survivor. I could get stranded in the middle of the desert for three months straight and not even crave a drink of water. I was tough, maybe too tough.

As we moved ahead, I looked out for anything on the left side; Grandpa took the right side, and Nazm roamed about bumping into inanimate objects. I watched many things pass me by. There was a café, a shoe store, a library, and a gym. Once I hit the gym, I acknowledged that I spotted a library, but it hadn't processed in my mind that it was there until it was gone. It was an entire building behind us, which meant that I had to walk the length of a whole building, backtracking the steps that I had put so much labor into.

I snagged Gramps and Nazm both by the hair on the back of their heads, stretching the wrinkles on their foreheads smooth. I tugged them along behind me without allowing them to turn around. I was being stalked by two buffoons that were walking backwards and stumbling over their opposite foot every time that they took a step. That wasn't even the amusing part either. The fun part was when we got to the steps, where they had to try to climb those while sustaining their balance. After too many slips and falls, I forfeited my grip and let them fall down at least twenty steps, which were molded out of concrete. I was never worried that one of them would get busted up. But, one thing was for sure: it was enjoyable to see things happen to them which would deform a mortal man. Just as I had suspected, they weren't injured at all. I continued my way up the steps, contemplating how they constructed letters as gigantic as the ones that spelled out library on the building. They were the size of me, and philosophers thought that the pyramids were some great achievement. Underneath the magical letters was a big doorframe that influenced magical sliding doors.

I walked up to the doors, and they peeled apart without me even saying "open sesame". I was in awe as I witnessed rows upon rows of books. I didn't know too much about them, but I think that books were all rejected movie scripts. If they were acceptable, they would've been made into movies by now. It is a miracle that libraries haven't ceased to exist yet, being the bastard child of the entertainment business. I stepped inside, only to be nailed with the over abundant vapors of ink.

The walloping bundles of paper were always a hazard to me as I was extraordinarily prone to paper cuts. I desisted from making contact with anything in the place, and I treated it like it was a nuclear dump that could cause me horrible mutation, such as appendicitis. I didn't feel like exploding at the moment either.

Gramps and Nazm were on me like Labradors, following another Labrador of the same sex's ass. Every insignificant step I took, they were promptly behind, waiting for my next move. If that place were anything like our library, all of the newspapers would've been down in the basement, which is where all the extra boring material went. I thought that it might've been better if we all split up to search for the door, instead of hanging close together, like a bunch of cowards. I understood that when you split up, there's more of likelihood to be decapitated by some ravenous maniac. However, in our case, we were the ravenous maniacs, and, if one of the other ones tried something on me, I would thrust my sneaker where the sun doesn't shine: in the shade.

Nazm explored the upstairs, while Grandpa and I took opposing sides of the ground floor. We sent Nazm upstairs, because we were certain that he was too intellectually challenged to comprehend if he discovered the door anyway. I concluded that my luck was running out, considering that every path I took led me to a dead end. I felt like I was in one of those cornfield mazes; only substitute the corn with literature. Along my voyage, I was confronted by many demons in the librarian's disguise. One was a senile lady with glasses that had a chain hitched onto them so that she could hang them around her neck when she wasn't reading. I ran like there was no tomorrow when I identified such a horror, leering at me from such a limited distance. I don't know what it is, but elderly women, in general, creep me out.

She made me lose my course, so I was astray in the middle of the library with evil demon shadows that were threatening to eat my soul all around me. They could've been threatening to assist me in finding a book, but I wasn't about to risk my life over such a stupid task. I began to feel nauseous, and I prepared to arm my skill of projectile vomiting to my defense when I became aware of someone shouting out my name. For all I knew, it was one of those demon beings out to play an April Fool's Day joke on me in early May, which would've made the prank impractical.

I heard my name being called again, while the shadow demons were swirling around my location and preventing escape. I had to delay for the perfect time to break away. At first, my intent was to dart straight at one of the shadows, tackling it to the ground, hoping that it would dissolve in fear. But, then, I visualized that the smarter move would be to beeline it in between the shadows and keep going without looking back. My body went as rigid as a cement truck that's haul had quit rotating and mixing. My legs felt equivalent to mayonnaise in an unstable container as they gave out from underneath me and sent me to a little place I liked to call "carpet".

It was a relaxing surface for overnight stays, but it was not for a sense of dread. Nothing can cure that feeling besides death or resolution. The shadows got warmer and warmer to me until the blank shapes started to show some features. They were old lady librarians with glasses that had chains fastened to them that dangled from their wrinkly, old necks. My dread soon matured into suicidal thoughts as I panicked that there would be no end to the madness.

Just when my sense of failure kicked in, I had a sensation that told me that my legs were loosening up. I raised my heavy behind off of the carpet as I rushed forward through two of the lumbering figures with hunchbacks. I estimate that I broke the speed barrier, heading towards my name that was echoing in the dusty and dimly lit building. It couldn't have been too good for the readers to strain their eyes while fixating on a book. Improper lighting should be punishable by law to compensate for the consumer's vision bills.

After my random thought process, I found the voice that was calling my name. It appeared to have been a wall that my face connected with. It kept speaking to me yet my vision hadn't adjusted since the collision. Once it came back into play, I distinguished that it wasn't a wall; it was Grandpa on the other side of the wall. He let me know that he discovered the door that steered us towards the basement. I erected myself and urgently brushed the blood cells away from my face, flinging them to the now stained carpet.

I turned the doorknob, but I obtained no response in return. I questioned Grandpa on how he was so certain that it was the door to the basement when it was locked. He pointed upwards above the door to a sign that read "Basement". Ah. You would think that by then, I would've majored in reading the postings, but I'm not too keen on change. There was only one selection at hand, since we were trying to ditch Nazm for our expedition.

That verdict was to ask one of the depraved librarians if she could open the door for us. Grandpa wasn't strong enough to break down such a stable door. I got the fear again, which was never a pleasant reflex. Crossing the room was hazy for me as I ran into things while holding my head down to evade confronting another demon before I made it to their master: Satan. I saw the bottom of the counter out of the top of my eye and quickly halted before I could bang my funny bone on it.

I raised my head as accelerated as imaginable so that I would have the jolt instead of a long period of fear. I inherited my jolt, because, in front of me, was the oldest librarian ever with drooping skin and all. She had a wicked sneer for an expression. My tremors were soon lifted as her hostility distorted into concern when she took into consideration the blood smeared across my face. She ushered me into the back, where the librarians furnished their evil first aid kit.

I was asked what happened to me, so I admitted to Droops what had occurred. I confided in her about how I had recently finished defeating a whole play-ground of schoolyard bullies, along with how I only caught a jab once, but it was with an aluminum baseball bat. I couldn't believe that she fell for such a nonsensical explanation as she challenged me as to how I fulfilled such a great feat. It was all due to the sheer volume of my fists. I was equally grateful for each of them for doing absolutely nothing for me. The librarian dabbed my forehead with cotton balls marinated with peroxide.

Afterwards, she asked if I wanted a bandage to cooperate by preventing the scabbing process, but I kindly refused as I told her to talk to the hand. Then I had to retract my statement to get her to come with me to unlock the door. I asked Droops why they were obligated to lock the door. She disclosed that it was because citizens loved to steal the newspapers when they were in it, such as if they committed necrophilia. I conjured up the necrophilia part myself. Why would anyone want to commit thievery of newspapers and admit that they were emotionally attached to old wrinkly chicks?

When we reached the doorway, I found that Grandpa had dematerialized into thin air, or else he walked away. Either way, blood was going to fly when I found his crusty ass. I acted like everything was cool, putting one hand on my hip and portraying that I was, in fact, relaxed. I don't think that my acting skills were up to par, because the room suddenly smelled a bit fishy. Then I recalled what could cause such a stench; it was my body odor. I must've had a gland problem or something. On every occasion that I wore a shirt for over an hour, the sweat seeped right through it. Maybe I should've considered using deodorant.

The droopy-skinned librarian injected the key into the crevice when the clatter of the lock being disarmed brought me one step closer to freedom or death; both of them sounded great to me. I unsealed the door with quickness, not even letting the librarian dislodge her keys from the lock. My impatience was unhealthy, but it also led me to great things faster. In a way, it is comparable to fast food. It tasted delectable, but you die of a heart attack sooner than later. In the end, it was all worth it, though. Healthy foods are for losers.

I huffed, and I coughed all the way down the stairs into the basement that was fit for a king... which would be me. It was equipped with carpet that had an awesome itchy feeling when I rolled around on it, coupled with many chairs that had cold, sticky padding. It was too bad that the room was stocked with books in place of where the VHSs of children's game shows should've been. The door from upstairs had finally closed. I didn't hear anyone making their way down the stairs, so I was Scott free. Or maybe her name was Betty... It wasn't relevant anyway.

I rummaged through the shelves and looked for a sign of the newspapers, but I came up with nothing. So, instead, I examined the innards of a collection of binders, which were installed on the shelves. I discovered an entire section of binders that were dedicated to remembering exclusively useless crap from the past, such as the day they redid the tar on Cedar Avenue. Without Grandpa around, I had no estimate of what date to even start looking at to unearth when he had perished. It would also help if I could revive his name from my memory. I knew that I had heard it a thousand times, but I tended to block out stuff that didn't incorporate chicken tenders. My mind fixated on the name Maxine until I recollected that it was a girl in my class in which I shared the hobby of sticking pencils up my nose with. She definitely enjoyed sticking them up my nose as far as she could.

Then it hit me; the name was Olaf Guttenberg. I'm not sure how I remembered such a ridiculous name. It must've been all of that memory medicine that I had been swiping from Grandpa's nightstand. Lucky for me, the name wasn't an issue, considering that there was no way that I could read through every one of those binders and seek some out-of-place name in the obituaries. I didn't have that kind of time or that kind of willpower. My reading skills weren't the best either. I began making an extreme number of grunts as I savagely flipped the pages with no remorse.

I ended up generating enough of a ruckus that someone came downstairs to see what all of the fuss was about. It was another demon, but it was not the same one as before. By the sneer on her face, I could tell that the only thing on her mind was death and destruction. The demon insisted that I remove myself from the room at that instant, or it would call the police. I told it that I couldn't leave until I got something, but it didn't listen. The demon grabbed me by the arm beginning to yank me towards the stairs. I couldn't let such a vile being foil my plans without a scuffle. I broke free from the grasp of evil to run back over to the binders, flipping through them and wishing upon an imaginary star for a revelation. As soon as I started, I was finished, being towed away again. I took my free arm and socked the demon directly in its kidney. The affliction must've been unbearable as it slumped to the floor on its knees, holding its upper body up, while wheezing something awful. I was sick and tired of being interrupted in the middle of the task at hand, so I flipped the demon onto its back. I placed my knees on top of the demon's arms, weighing it to the floor, as I wailed on its face with my mighty god fists. Black blood flew as it cauterized anything that it touched, equivalent to molten lava.

I waited until enough of god's work had been dealt before I interrogated the demon. I asked what information the demon had on the Vietnam War and a soldier named Olaf Guttenberg. It declared that it had a bundle of knowledge on the war but nothing of the soldier. I described how I needed to find out where his body was buried or else I would have to invoke the wrath of Jehovah upon the demon. It divulged that there was a plaque only a few feet away from my placement on the wall of all the soldiers that had died in the war. Their burial sites were also listed in the book underneath.

For being a transgender know-it-all, I punched it in the face repeatedly. Its face met my fist, and then its head met the floor, speckling black blood onto the carpet, dissolving a void down to the dirt. Once the figure got to the twitch that it does when the embodiment passes away, I quit slugging it. I stood up and flapped the plasma away from my hand to elude my tissue, being incinerating to the bone.

I immediately walked a short distance over to the plaque to check on the listing of Olaf's tombstone. I researched the book underneath. It fascinated me as to how I missed something so obvious after inspecting the room up and down. Sometimes, there are downfalls to being oblivious to everything that doesn't involve me. I flipped through the pages and hunted for the name. But, they were all in alphabetical order, so I had to wait until I found the first letter of his last name, since I only retained the ABCD portion of the alphabet.

Once I spotted the name, I scrolled my finger across the line until it was under the place of burial. Sacred Remains Cemetery was the title that the graveyard was given. I felt certain that I would forget the name, so I searched for something to write with. There was a pen in the demon's pocket that turned out not to be a demon at all. It was only a feeble defenseless librarian, who had been bludgeoned to death by a child. Her face was completely annihilated with parts that were out of place. Her nose cartilage was jammed into her eye socket, which protruded her eyeball from its home. It was dangling by a vein, but the blood had concluded flowing.

I withdrew the pen from her pocket, since she wouldn't need it anymore. I ransacked the space for a blank piece of paper, but they all had text on them. I did the only thing that I could, which was to write on the skin of the librarian. I jotted down the name on her face, seizing the loose piece of flesh that was drooping from her cheekbone. With one swift tug I lacerated the outer exterior of the lower quarter of her face. I folded the chunky skin, nice and neatly situating it within my pocket for safekeeping. I couldn't risk misplacing such a vital segment of my ongoing quest.

I tediously erased all of the plasma that was on me onto the librarian's shirt, leaving her to resembled one huge blood smear. I didn't bother to move her out of the way or anything, due to clean up not being my forte. I headed back up the stairs to search for my wandering companion of unusually aged circumstances. I located him in the main area of the library. He was making conversation with some female before migrating in front of a group of children.

I strolled on over, questioning the lady on what my Grandpa was doing. She informed me that she had to leave for a family emergency, so Grandpa volunteered to take over her Spanish teaching class. It bewildered me how he could do such a moronic thing for the measly ten bucks that she slipped into my pocket. If I was stuck there to observe him, I might as well have enjoyed the show. I pulled myself up a hard plastic seat, settling down in the back row. There were a multitude of words on the chalkboard that I couldn't read, due to the foreign nature of them. I'm guessing that they were Spanish, since that was what he was teaching.

After Grandpa had initiated the educating of the class, I realized that he had a basic understanding of the language from the time that I locked him in his room with the Spanish channel on. I couldn't even conceive how he had learned something from that. Every time that I watched it, I was too busy snickering at the overdramatic acting in the soap operas to even pay attention to what they were saying.

I was marginally entertained by his teaching, but not enough to hold my attention. It just wasn't the same without the over the top acting. I was tapped on the shoulder, being disrupted – the story of my life. I turned around as Nazm waved to me with a severed arm that he was dominating. I panicked, since that could screw us over royally. I directed him to hide the damn thing before somebody caught a glimpse of it. He tossed it underneath the chair in front of me, which could've worked had he not over handedly thrown it, like a baseball. It bumped the kid in the back of the legs petrifying him to the point to where his chair slanted backwards until he banged his noggin. The kid rendered himself comatose from being a puss.

Fortunately, I was seated far enough back or his head would've descended upon my no-no area, which wouldn't have been a good time. The children all lifted from their seats, shrieking at the sight of a disconnected body part. What's the difference? Limbs didn't alarm them when they were attached, but, once they came off, there was something so horrendous about them that made youngsters wet their pants.

Either way, the kids all started to evacuate the building, so Nazm did the first thing that came natural to him. He captured as many children that were accessible and tattered them into scraps. He took two kids, one in each arm, and smashed their faces together so brutally that they exchanged brain matter. There were only about a dozen children that became spiritless before I got Nazm to terminate his rampage so that we could make our swift getaway.

We didn't want to retreat the same way that we gained entry, so we headed towards a door in the stern of the library. When we leaned onto the handle to get to the outside, an incredibly boisterous alarm went off, deafening my fragile little ears. There were no cops within my visibility, but the markings on the door represented that it was a fire exit. That must've been the basis for the alarm. I fathomed that a fire alarm enticed police officers and sexy firemen in a matter of minutes.

Chapter 17:
I Make the Decisions,
Not Cereal Mascots

The optimum option was to find a car and steal it. Outside the door persuaded us into the parking lot, where a young man was getting into his rusted junker. The mission was to hijack him, along with his vehicle, to drive us to the cemetery, because I couldn't even estimate on where to begin looking.

The youngin' accessed his car seat at the same instant that Grandpa thrust his arm through the passenger side window to unlock the door. The boy attempted to flee, but I shoved him back inside of his automobile, seat belted him (safety first), and closed the door behind him. Nazm and I got in the backseat, while Grandpa restrained the boy's arm and bordered his mouth to prevent him from struggling. I advised the boy that he would not be harmed unless he didn't obey my orders. If he refused to aid me in any way, I would have Grandpa ingest his entire arm.

I gathered the note that was bound in human flesh from my pocket, which was beginning to dry together. I separated the folds from each other, while strings and chunks of gooey blood stretched along, thankfully, though, not compromising the quality of the ink, making it as manageable to read as the time that I wrote it.

I wielded it in front of the boy's face, commanding him to take us there as hurriedly as possible. He responded, yet I only could be optimistic that he read it right, since he was cringing the whole time that he looked at it. The most natural portion of your anatomy is internal, yet everyone has a phobia of viewing it in reality. Grandpa kept his pose as I stayed with my head in between the front seats, verifying that he didn't initiate any false moves.

The cemetery ended up being on the outskirts of town, where we would need a prolonged walk to get to another car. Since we were at the destination, I reached each arm around the front seat, gouging my thumbs into the boy's eye sockets. It was an intriguing sensation when the eyeballs burst. Once the force of his cranium bore down on my hands, I removed my thumbs.

We were finally at Sacred Remains Cemetery. It was a puny cemetery, so we each picked a row to find the precise gravestone. I took quick glances at the words etched in stone until I found the correct grave. I stumbled into it, literally, in the back corner, under a withered lightning-struck tree. The gravestone read "Olaft Gutinstein". It shows how much America neglects their fallen soldiers. They couldn't even get his name right.

Without warning, out from the uppermost section of the tree, tumbled a cadaver that remained still when it thumped onto the hollowed ground. Grandpa pushed Nazm and me aside to get to the body. Nazm was highly insulted as he stomped away, seeking the attention that he would never acquire.

Grandpa flipped the carcass over onto its back so that he could inspect its facial structure while he pulverized it, suspecting that it was Olaf. I was guessing that because the cadaver was in a Vietnam uniform and still hadn't decayed completely. Olaf opened his eyes, pleading for Grandpa not to hurt him. When he was confronted with the inquiry of why not to obliterate him, Olaf was forced to reveal the description of why to both of us.

As it turned out, he faked dying in Vietnam, because he had always been a zombie. The rationality of why he plotted a plan to turn Grandpa into a zombie was simple: Olaf had been in love with Grandpa, since the first day that he met him, knowing fully that Gramps would never go for it. Olaf knew that Grandpa would eventually decipher his curse, but, if Grandpa was a zombie, too, the relationship might work. I interrupted to ask Olaf why he didn't just convert Grandpa into a zombie right away so then they could've been together longer. It was suggested that I shut up by both parties.

Grandpa's expression softened, and a look I'd never seen crossed his face…one of love. Gramps also admitted that the love Olaf felt was inside of his body too. They pressed their lips together in a romantic moment between two defunct retired Vietnam vets of the same sex. Their tongues petted each other as the thick saliva strings intertwined. During the kiss, Grandpa wasn't the only thing trying to get inside of Olaf as a shovel prevailed in piercing Olaf's skull. It missed Grandpa's face by a mere millimeter or less, spilling the contents of Olaf's head onto Grandpa's face. He slurped up as much hemoglobin and gore as he could, not even thoroughly comprehending what had transpired.

Once the shovel twisted, Olaf's head split in half as Grandpa began spitting out whatever he had consumed. Olaf's frame downgraded to the grass and revealed that Nazm was ranked there with the shovel in hand. He delivered Gramps the thumbs up, trusting that he had achieved something respectable. Grandpa approached Nazm and asked if he could see the shovel. When the shovel was firmly placed in his hands, he took a swing, re-chopping Nazm's cranium off of his neck. Nazm's head rolled across the ground with a look of disbelief plastered on it as Grandpa chased it down. He consistently struck it with the shovel, mincing the thought factory into pieces.

I scampered up behind Grandpa and struggled to pry the shovel from his hands, but it was no use. I pounced on his back and put pressure downward with all of my might, driving his forehead into a gravestone. I didn't letup ramming it against the stone until I could feel a juicy texture exiting from the back of the skull. I grouped the five lumps of Nazm's brain and stuffed them into my pocket.

A car pulled up, so I broke off one of Olaf's ribs that were protruding from his chest. When the lady driver came running up and wondered if I needed her service, I stuck the rib against her throat and disclosed that she could assist me by taking me to the airport.

She took me to the car without much hesitation, without any escape attempts, like any cooperative hostage should do. Still, I occupied the rib near her jugular the entire time. I even got in the car on the same side to keep it stable and in place. It was a pain clambering over her lap to get to the passenger seat. Sweat gathered around the sharp edge that was pressing against her skin as I started thinking murderous thoughts that dwelled from the recent events. Repeated violence left my cold frame with no remorse.

I could've used her brawn in my beef stew and not felt any sympathy.

I was lost in thought while pressing the broken bone harder against her throat, which caused her to drive faster. We made it to the airport in no time; it seemed. I had her park in the parking ramp on the level closest to the sky. I hate it when the cars don't just drop off people. They wait there for as long as it takes for their passenger to show up. The violent thoughts that conjured in my brain made me unwillingly inject the bone into her windpipe. My hand was dyed red before I could even conceive what was going to manifest itself. I released my grip from the bone, leaving my hand sticky and uncomfortable. I deserted the body, where it was since there weren't any other vehicles that high up. I rode the elevator down to the first floor so that I could infiltrate the magical sliding doors.

The interior of the airport was jam packed with the masses, holding their luggage tight, like their material possessions were the most important thing in life. It's insanity when all you can think about is something manufactured in China for thirty cents; the globe has a lot to learn. I didn't possess any currency to purchase a ticket home except for the ten dollars in my pocket. I ruled that I might have to do a jig or something to make the rest of the money.

I decided to rummage through the untouched compartments on my pants before subjecting myself to such public humiliation. My brain must've been functioning properly that day, because I found at least a grand in my back pocket that someone must've slipped me when I wasn't paying attention. I drew near to the considerably lengthy line, waiting for approximately an hour before I made it to the counter. Once I got there, I was briefed on how it was for luggage, so, to access a ticket, I had to be delayed in another line, which was equally as outstretched. It was credible that my brain wasn't functioning as well as I anticipated it was.

I waited in that line for another hour before receiving my one-way ticket to home. I swear I was searched at least three times before I was fitted to reach the waiting room for my flight. When I got to the waiting room, all of the seats were taken, primarily from people napping on them. I leaned up against the window for some downtime until the plane was ready to board.

I must've dozed off, because, when I became aware of the boarding call, my eyes burned like bread that had been made into fresh toast. When they obtained my ticket, they put it through a machine that split it in half with no repentance. The hallway to the airplane was so slim that it felt like I would fall through it if I deposited my foot against the floor too roughly. I was crowded by other heavyset pedestrians who made me feel less special. I thought that I was obese for my age, until I came into contact with a fat, zit-covered ten-year-old. He wiped some sweat on me before moving on. The seats in the aircraft were narrower than my ass, so I could only pray for a divine act if I wanted coziness.

My seat, of course, was between two other overweight people that were to the obese stage. I treated one as if he was a pillow and the other as a footrest on the way home. They never conveyed a word to me, but that could've been due to the blood that tarnished my palms. The comfiness factor was much better than my bed at home; I was out in seconds.

After a restful nap in an unrestful plane, I departed into the airport closest to my origins. It was smaller in size, but it held just as many fat people as before; nobody wanted to jog to their destination. I had to catch a taxi on my way home after the plane made it to my destination. I always considered a taxi to be yellow with the black and white checkers, but the one before me was a bronze minivan. It sure defeated the purpose of a taxi being a recognizable vehicle. At least the driver was weird, considering how he kept peeking at me in the rearview mirror. It wouldn't be a taxi ride without that. Every time that he smirked at me, I gave him a wink to throw him off.

I was brought to the driveway of my residence, which appeared to be abandoned. There wasn't yellow tape blocking the doors anymore, but a fresh auction sign was placed in the front yard for a month from the present time. The city was selling my childhood home for dirt-cheap. I would've cared more if I had someone to grow up with inside of it.

I provided the driver with all of the money that I had leftover, since I had no use for it anymore. It was not like I could afford to pay for the house with a couple hundred dollars. The crunching of the pebbles beneath my feet made all of the emotions hit home once again. My key still worked in the lock after being fished out of its hiding place inside of the gutter drain. The place seemed to be the same as it was when I was there last, minus a few dead bodies.

The carpet had been shampooed, and the rotting stench of flesh was gone. I seated myself in my late Grandpa's decrepit rocking chair after popping in a VHS of "Guiding Light". It was the tape with episodes 99, 213, and 14 on it. I assume that I was hoping that if I tried to relive what it was like before, I might've been transported back in time -- as if that had ever come out with satisfactory results for anyone.

I picked up the matchbook that previously belonged to the old fool that lived within the household. I presume that I was notably distraught with him, being that I gave up everything to help him out. Yet, I received no recognition for it, besides putting me through more trouble. In addition, he slaughtered the only friend that I ever had and caused me to forfeit the love of my life. Anger and depression flooded through my veins, making me hallucinate. The butt from Olaf's cigarette, the last cigarette that Grandpa had ever smoked, was still on the floor in front of me. Everything I cared about was gone. So, why should I give a fuck?

ABOUT THE AUTHOR

Born in the decade of permed mullets and anti-disco, Jason Stryker has been writing since learning how to spell his name (which may be a lie --it could've been a couple years afterwards). He's a dedicated horror film aficionado and children's book reader. Don't worry, he reads stuff with bigger words too, and he also hates speaking in third-person. Shaving is also a pet peeve. *Death Runs in the Family* is his first novel of the soon to be trilogy.